THE
DRUM
WARS

A Modern Maya Story

CAROL KARASIK

© Carol Karasik. All Rights Reserved Worldwide.
ISBN-10: 1478147202
ISBN-13: 9781478147206
Library of Congress Control Number: 2012911677
CreateSpace Independent Publishing Platform
North Charleston, South Carolina

Cover: Water Lily Jaguar by (c)Alfonso Huerta

Photo Credits:

Richard Johnson (fractal by Steven Rook), p. 266;
Edwin Barnhart, pp.104, 161;
Miguel Marquez Murguia: frontispiece and p.127;
Alfonso Morales, p. 253;
Sanya Olman, Part 1, "Mexica Drummer";
Susan Prins, p. 283;
all other photos by the author.

Sources:

Ginsburg, Allen, Journals: Early Fifties, Early Sixties, ed. Gordon Ball. New York: Grove Press, 1999.

Greene, Graham, The Lawless Roads. New York: Penguin Classics, 2006.

Hartak, J.J., The Book of Knowledge: The Keys of Enoch. Los Gatos, CA: The Academy for Future Science, 1996.

Pakalian Group of Mexico, "2012 Prophecy Notes on Tortuguero Monument 6," in Lord Pakal Ahau's Maya Diaries. 2007. URL: http://pakalahau.wordpress.com/2007/11/23/2012- prophecy-notes-on-tortuguero-monument-6/

There is another world, but it is a world inside this world.

PAUL ELUARD

It's like a finger pointing at the moon. Don't concentrate on the finger or you'll miss all that heavenly glory.

BRUCE LEE
"ENTER THE DRAGON"

CONTENTS

PART III

PART IV

PROLOGUE

When I received the call from Podwell to come to Palenque, I was living in a small fishing village on the shores of a dying lake. Over the years I learned to pronounce, syllable by tongue-tripping syllable, the illustrious name of my humble town—Erongaricuaro, "Place of Mirrors"—as well as to repeat the euphonious word for the magnificent ruin on the opposite side of the dull, gray water—Tzintzuntzan, "Hummingbird," capital of the Tarascan Empire. No one knows where the hummingbird warriors came from—out of the northern desert or from the coast of Peru—but at one time they beat the Aztecs into submission and dominated all of western Mexico. Great trading canoes pulled up to the stone wharves of the capital, and their rich cargoes of copper bells and gold were ceremoniously stored within seven stout towers, all for the greater glory of the sun king and the gods of wind and water. That was before the Spaniards arrived and the lake began to sink.

Volcanoes now rose from marshland and murk, and when the morning sun struck the smoking peaks, gulls would scatter, cattle bawl, and the earth convulse with a deep shudder that shook my windowpanes and sometimes knocked me to the floor. No one else seemed to notice, although I could set my kitchen clock by the daily tremor, which a marine biologist from the University of Michoacan said was related to the seepage of water through a wide crack under the lakebed. Around and down went the fishes, like month-old bouillabaisse, feeding the immortal sirens that thrived in the vents. He swirled his test tube samples and said the soup was full of scales riddled with errant bacilli, and nothing could be done about it because the forty-million-peso grant from the United Nations had gone down the drain with the speckled mermaids. "The sirens are mutating, they're growing pockets. And it is getting worse, like everything else. Best to keep a sense of humor," he said with a straight face. "Who knows, perhaps the lake will follow its natural cycle and return in a few thousand years. All we can do is wait."

Meanwhile, my neighbor kept filling her milk bucket. The hippies who lived in the wooden *trojes* at the edge of town were getting high on ketamine, which made them drool and stare at their hands, just like the aging fishermen in the park who slowly lifted their battered hats as the boys on bareback drove the cows down to pasture in the silt.

The cobbles echoed day and night, but nothing ever happened. The local inhabitants, born during an earlier Aquarian Age, were living specimens of thirty-thousand-year-old carp. The mud flats and tremulous volcanoes were remnants of that primal landscape from which life originally bubbled and sprang. But somehow the miraculous chemical mix that had brought forth the first amoeba was now creating strange, debilitating symptoms. My memories were stuck in a dry pond. My death was an event I could barely recall. I knew I had to take action, but couldn't, so lulled was I by the negative ions wafting off the polluted waters, enveloping my mind and body in a state resembling grace.

I'd be watching the pijijis feeding at the edge of the marsh or the young bulls stamping in the pasture when the phone would ring. One morning, while I was staring at the bloodshot eyes of a dead fish, Podwell's voice was trembling at the other end of the line: "They threw me into detox. It was against my will! Don't ask me how I escaped. I wasn't even drunk, for Christ's sake!"

Here was a genius whose brain matter swam in a mysterious liquid that nibbled away at his round cells and turned them into rhomboids. The condition was often discernable in his ice-blue eyes, and it scared everyone around him, including himself. One evening, while I was gazing at the moon's reflection in the fractured water, he calmly admitted that he saw the world in six dimensions. Maybe he was seeing beyond the synaptic circuitry inside his head and picking up on light particles extruded from invisible objects hovering on the watery rim of infinity. That was just a guess. He was certain he was born this way for a purpose and that his work on Maya geometry was, like the tiny square at the heart of the pentagon, part of a grander equation. If only I would come down to the jungle and help him put his thoughts on paper. There was no time to waste.

Immediately I examined the moth-eaten contents of my wardrobe, itself a working biology lab, and found nothing at all suitable for death-defying treks through the jungle. A few months, a year at most, I remember thinking. But as I warmed to the idea, my dreams became a continuous loop of a long, winding, tropical river, and in the end I packed up everything—Huichol shaman's chairs, Ocomichu devil masks, Dylan tapes—everything that would mold—and sent it on ahead. The truck never arrived.

I took the bus.

PROLOGUE

There are five mountain ranges between Lake Patzcuaro and the hot plains of Palenque. Riding over the last ridge, I recalled that, in 1840, the artist Frederick Catherwood had traveled this same route while seated in a mahogany chair strapped to the back of a Maya Indian who trotted down the mountain trail without ever taking a breather. Aside from suffering multiple bruises to his jangled bones and aching conscience, Catherwood had to spend his whole feverish trip gaping at the gnarled landscape he was trying to forget. I, on the other hand, was speeding along a treacherous two-lane blacktop, bracing myself at every curve, careening down the mountains and back in time toward the mineral-green, jewel-like splendor of the mysterious city Catherwood would capture so exquisitely with his pen.

In the inert world where I had been living, the Purepecha Indians attributed the slightest change in luck or weather to the sirens' songs. You could hear them in the high-pitched waves or languid tides ringing the islands of reeds. For every story of voluptuous maidens diving into somebody's nets, there were darker tales of sea hags drowning young lovers, of babies bought and sold. The devils were everywhere, crying on street corners, laughing in church. It was a losing battle. At least the jungle promised perpetual sun, which has a way of casting moral laziness in its best light. Heaven glistens, the hell gates glow.

The Panchan Hotel was a conspiracy of cabins equipped with light bulb, bed, and ceiling fan that propelled my room deeper into the trees. Shrouded in elephant leaves, light penetrated at the permanent angle of late afternoon. The Maya had built a city in this twisted, weeping maze. It was exhausting to contemplate, impossible to think. The forest hummed with red-throated resins, snapped with the sudden chop of crows. At dusk, the east wind, the buzzard wind, ripped through the palms, showering black feathers over the brass ponds. Sunset shrank to a shapeless, dusty orange, and through the last crack of light poured flocks of parrots and nightlong swarms of insects. Then the drums began.

The low throb that emanated from the earth soon overwhelmed the croaking frogs, the howler monkeys roaring in the trees. The desperate beat stirred the part of my brain devoted to unlived memories, and out of that ratcheted film reel shuttled the image of Deborah Paget standing on the edge of a flaming volcano. Wrapped in a red sarong, she was walking barefoot through molten lava, and as she neared the glowing mouth, the savage drums beat louder and Jeff Chandler leaned over and kissed her trembling lips before she leaped into the fire. Her sacrifice pleased the gods, for at that moment the rain began to patter.

I opened the door and checked for familiar signs. There weren't any. I set off in search of the owner, Moises Morales, but his house was gone. And where was Podwell?

On my way to inquire at the restaurant, I passed a spike-haired blond who was hurrying up the path with a wet bundle of joy. Thin white streams were running down her midriff, and seeing she was in a state of alarm, I quickly stepped aside. But the path was narrow, and she had to slow down anyway and—what's this? Her baby looked like a plastic gallon of milk leaking big white drops on the trail. "Got to boil it," she shouted back, which didn't make me feel any better. White drops, crimson drops, breadcrumbs, string.

I sat down at a corner table and noticed yoghurt on the menu. My Rumanian grandfather used to put milk out on the windowsill until it turned sour enough to keep anyone from growing old. My grandfather was a gypsy, they say, and used to travel the roads between Bucharest and Rome peddling pots and pans. A lot of the dishes on the menu were pastas in cream sauces, which the Italian cook was stirring over a high flame. A young Mexican with a shaved head was rolling out dough and shoveling it into a brick inferno. Sweat was running down his cheeks and bare chest. The heat was awful. I ordered the pesto and looked around. Same *palapa* thatched with palm, but the size of the restaurant had doubled.

Other things had changed since my last visit. The hotel was once a refuge for vagabonds and fugitives from the law. But now it had become a haven for techno-wizards and spiritual seekers on extended drum-healing holidays. These rootless trekkers had flown in from New Zealand, Tokyo, the Middle East, but looked like they came from the same tribal village. The dress code was stringent: rings in their noses, wooden labials in their lips, hair twisted into yellow Rasta ropes, shoulders winged with Indonesian dragons blue as the tattooed foliage of the jungle. They say they're drawn to Palenque by the mysterious forces of the Maya. The Egyptian pyramids are taller, the Babylonian bas-reliefs grander, the temples of Tibet unspoiled by sacrificial blood. Here there are no snow-capped mountains to scale, no white sand beaches, no surf, only jungle rot and stinging ants and hallucinogenic mushrooms in the cow pastures. They'd heard about the psychedelic mushrooms and the great prophecies of the end of time bouncing off the worldwide web. The mystical waves from the satellite beams buzzed inside their wired heads, the magnetic field radiating along the ley lines of the earth sprang through their bare feet, igniting their chakras, igniting their blood. When the moon began to troll among the clotted cedars, the drums grew louder than the pulse of cicadas. The fire dancers spun their chains. Blue flames whirled beyond the eerie haloes of visible night.

The teahouse where the drummers hung their hammocks stood a good distance from Don Moi's new plywood palace, but the thunderous riffs stamped across the creeks and beat against the timbers. His shining towers were a labyrinth of planks and ladders capped by tin roofs slung to the four directions. For all his sensibilities to art and architecture, the man had lost his sense of structure. Perhaps he'd lost his mind. He descended from his private quarters clinging to a rope. The vast, cross-hatched folly looked like the lurid daydream of a shipwrecked sailor cast away on a tropical island with a bag of three-by-five nails.

Though he greeted me warmly, pleased to engage in the first of many evening chats, he wore a scowl on his thin, weathered face. "Let's walk like the cows," he said as he took my arm, and together we strolled through the woods.

Above the din, we heard the sharp alarms of the *muwaan* bird and knew there would be mercy. The *duendes,* the mischievous spirits of the rainforest, would drive the drummers mad, and then swallow their souls in one gulp. "Let them beat the skin off their city hands, set fire to their hair. I'm not the police," he shrugged, and turned a cold shoulder on the coiled loneliness of his place.

Long ago, long before history, long before myth, long before the current rage for superstition, when nobody cared about alien space ships and galactic tribes, he would hunker like a monkey, jabbing his short fingers into his pressed khaki pants, searching for a stick, a stone, a branch of air to illustrate the magical swing of Venus through the heavens, and if the words would not come, curl his lip and be gone, straight up the temple steps, bone-white in the blinding sun, and survey his kingdom of stones. Cold stars at night, he would wade through rooms of muck, calling to the dead who lurched down the subterranean vaults and through the still unopened shadows in the rock. At daybreak he would lie on his back in the center of the ball court, whistling through a blade of grass as toucans broke through the trees and the howler monkeys roared on Quetzal Mountain. When Venus, morning star, slipped behind the Temple of the Foliated Cross, he licked his hair and headed toward the entrance, a dapper man ready to charm the tourists.

Moises was the best guide in Palenque and at the height of his tricks. To him, the archaeologists and their blue-eyed wives were excited vacationers on an intellectual spree. His pointless stories, mystifying facts, were designed to lead them astray. When American epigraphers deciphered Lord Pakal's name and noble lineage, he spoke of signs in Cassiopeia. When Alberto Ruz discovered Pakal's royal tomb, Moi mentioned that he and a renowned Brazilian psychic, while strolling through the woods with a dowsing rod, found the bones of a prince, buried without fanfare, beneath the roots of a ceiba tree. But after the Germans packed the gods in crates and shipped them to Berlin, he sulked in bitter silence. Every stone, stucco, and bas-relief was a perfumed rose in his private garden. Wasn't it enough to love them and let them be, untainted by theories bound to be proven wrong next week? He had a secret place where he would sit for hours, half-believing the unresurrected heap of stones was his castle in a former creation. There he would take the rough and tumble anthropologists, the Swiss girls with long blond hair who didn't mind an old man whispering in their ear, "The universe is a pink flower," in February when the ceiba trees were in bloom, or "The world is chaos," in May. When summer rains poured down in columns, he sat alone while the pale stuccos crawled slowly back to lime. Then he would do the deed, have a few tequilas with his friend Mingo in the crabbed darkness of the cantina, shoot off his pistol, and go home and slap his wife. He told anyone who would listen that a man with eleven children had a right.

If you nodded, he would disagree, play the prosecuting attorney, judge and jury, his life, like every grain in the cosmos, always on trial. "I was very macho," he confessed before launching into a rambling story of which he was the butt. Once he was dressing for a date with a French psychiatrist, preening too long in front of the mirror, when his wife, Paulina, asked him to feed the chickens in the yard. "No, I have an appointment, I'll be late," he told her. But Paulina was very clever. She followed him down the street, and in front of the Hotel Maya, for the whole world to see, she pushed him into a puddle of mud. Moi was sopping wet, his shirt and pants filthy, his hair uncombed. But he kept on going. He stumbled into the psychiatrist's hotel room, a drooping peacock, completely unfit for love. "The French psychiatrist taught me about manhood," he concluded with a twinkle. But wasn't it his wife?

He came from the Sonoran desert during the worst dry spell in history. It was at the end of World War II, and he had spent the past five years on a naval base in California, flying cargo planes, eating oranges, and drinking rum. Then the Americans dropped the bomb, the Japanese surrendered, and, as Moi put it, the good life was over. When he appeared at the door of his parents' shack, dressed in spanking whites and captain's hat, his mother could barely speak, his father could not lift himself from the bed. The cattle were walking cactuses. Thorns burrowed under people's skins and blinded their eyes. In the merciful dark they staggered to the blown-out schoolhouse, lowered the boards used for wakes, and passed around a glass of rubbing alcohol. Moi's brother stood up to make a speech. It was a brief story of desperation, followed by a salute to Trotsky and a toast to Captain Moi. "You're the pilot. You're the one who goes around the world. We'll send you."

After a year of roaming, Moises found Palenque, a steamy little southern town with the highest level of rainfall in Mexico. He wrote his brother a note saying he had discovered paradise. Three months later, four hundred men and women arrived with bundles, cardboard boxes, and strings of children wearing red bandanas around their throats. They had walked across the Sonoran desert and down the Gulf Coast. It was positively Biblical. But the Palencanos didn't like Communists. They didn't like foreigners, German or Mexican. Gossips, fools, cattle-breeding brawlers, they didn't like themselves. For the first three years the market vendors refused to sell Moi's wife a liter of corn, a liter of beans. Her sons starved. Within five years, half of his countrymen had died from dengue fever. But Moises was in love with Palenque, not the town but the ancient Maya city at the edge of the sky.

Moi immediately fell in with the local intelligentsia: a pretty English teacher who couldn't speak a word of English, a French piano tuner who later lost his head in a train wreck, and an heiress from Montana who had come here to write. "An independent woman," he described her, "sassy and frank and made no bones." The schoolteacher knew a rancher who was friendly with a politician who drank with the governor, and in the mysterious way the world works, the man from the desert, whose family had nothing to eat, landed a job as chief inspector of surplus food for the state department of agriculture. Guardian of the public granaries, he protected against thieves and rats the hills of corn heaped in every government silo along the road. And when the roads gave out he kept driving, over the rugged mountains, across the broad green valleys, past lagoons and swamps, and into the heart of the jungle. Oh, he'd go home periodically to check on the wife and kids. And during those brief visits, he noted that his brothers were steadily climbing the abominable ladder of success. They were buying up real estate, building small hotels, anticipating the tourist boom they were sure would come one day, while the xenophobic Palencanos watched and wrung their hands. Moi sympathized. By then he was living in the rainforest with the last Lacandons, completely cut off from anything resembling civilization.

Moi's friend Kin Bor taught him how to track wild boar and hunt spider monkeys. "If you are stung by a scorpion, the only cure is to catch it and eat its tail. If a jaguar is stalking you, turn around and pull its whiskers." When Moi accidently hit a goat while making a hair-raising landing on the fogged-in runway at Bonampak, Kin Bor straightened his white tunic and told Moi that even though he was an excellent pilot, it would be better if he flew blindfolded. "Each eye tells a different story. You have to learn to see without your eyes. You have to listen, but not with the ear."

Moi was reminded of the day he spent at the ruins with the great British scholar Sir J. Eric Thompson, who was in his late seventies then. Thompson was being interviewed by a BBC film crew, and after sitting for hours under the burning lights later confessed to feeling what he called "a slight twinge of fatalism, a mild case to be sure, but I think it rather odd that I've never discovered a single important artifact during my long, distinguished career." Before Moi had a chance to answer, Thompson changed the subject. "But let's not discuss archaeology," he said, "let's talk about music." They sat on the steps of the Temple of the Sun listening to the toucans. Thompson compared the temple to Respighi's "The Birds." As shadows lengthened in the late afternoon, he compared the Temple of the Inscriptions to Bach's "Goldberg Variations," and as the sun went down he likened the red-tinged pillars, the pale, risen figures, to Mozart's "St. Mathew's Passion." Thompson died two months later.

"My friend," Moi said to Kin Bor, "it's sometimes possible to hear with your eyes."

There is no word in Lacandon Maya for synesthesia. But there are many ways to describe the life of the spirit. When Kin Bor came to Palenque, he told Moi that the seven nobles buried in Temple XV had been murdered.

"How do you know that?" asked Moi.

"Because those poor corpses were left lying in one piece. No one came along to scatter the bones and teeth. Their souls had no way to escape their bodies, to take the white road to their next shape."

Little by little, Moi came to believe that the soul was part of nature. This he discovered soon after his wife Paulina packed him up and he moved to the trees. His twenty glorious acres, acquired for less than a song, came with one proviso: La Condesa made him promise to let the place go wild. It was the only promise to a woman he would keep.

As soon as Moi hung his hammock, his friend Mingo appeared out of nowhere, built a fire, and began cooking the beans. The two of them were as free as birds. "She's tossed me out because of the drink," is all Mingo said. "I know how to fish and hunt. If I have to, I'll haul stones at the ruins."

"Oh, you only think you are a part of the wild, Mingo, but I know you grew up on a cattle ranch near Salto de Agua, probably not too far from where Lord Pakal was born. You're very good at hunting cows. You're even better at wasting time."

"Not as good as the American poet who stayed with us for six long months. He could watch the clouds for hours. He wrote down every dream."

"Ginsburg, you mean, the skinny one from New York." Moi threw his head back and closed his eyes:

> All the jungle: all these rocky ruins. And suddenly
> a vast unfathomable god—
> and writing, the gift of writing
> thought seems like a candle in the wood.

Little by little, Moi planted long lanes of wild ginger, sweeps of bamboo. He plodded through the underbrush in oversized rubber boots, following the course of the river that flowed down from the ruins and through the jungle of his property. He built containing walls, rerouted the streams, dammed the rivulets with rocks. Water poured in chains of falls and bathing pools under the cascading boughs where he hung his bed. The walls of his room were made of screens open to the tumbling hills. Across the treetops a swinging bridge led to a plank floor he called his kitchen, with a sink and stove installed among the branches. It was easy to fall off the kitchen because there were no railings. But Moi was in his element. He danced across the planks, glided over the bridge, all the while cooing to Mono, the pet monkey that never left his shoulder. The sons who visited on Sundays were nervous when the children toddled towards the edge, but not Moi. His monkey soul laughed at everything, even when he cared. He never missed the desert, he said, the empty sky, the pitifully barren life. "Just a bunch of old farts waiting for minnows to swim into their nets." No, he was sixty-five years old and loved his treetop cradle, "like being in the arms of a good woman," he crooned. "A man has many souls and many lives."

Speaking of spiritual matters, Moi once saw a black jaguar prowling the length of his back fence. One night he woke to find his father sitting at the edge of his bed. "Papa!" he called, but his father was dead.

But nothing was as strange as the Argentine woman and her frail teenage daughter who pulled up to the gate in a black limousine, insisting that Moi accompany them to the ruins. As the limo rounded the sharp curve at the base of the ridge, the woman called to the driver, "This is the trail. Stop!" She clamored out, beckoning Moi to follow as she scrambled through the brush, her black silk skirt catching on thorns, her red high heels sinking in mud. "Very strange," Moi thought. The woman claimed she had never been to Palenque and yet she knew this trail better than he did. They reached a clearing among the madrone trees. The Argentine spun on her mud-caked heel and wildly scanned the ground. "There!" she pointed. Wordlessly they scraped at the dirt with their small, nervous hands. A few minutes later her daughter struck a rock. Moi and the woman lifted the stone, and inside the hole, about thirty centimeters square, lay a cache of small brown bones and a baby's deformed skull. The daughter winced and turned away. The woman wept, then hastily clutched her daughter's hand and stumbled back to the waiting limousine.

"But I thought you found the bones with a dowsing rod," I said to Moi.

"No, no, that was the Brazilian psychic. This was an Argentine. She saw the bones in a dream."

Immediately after the Argentinean incident, Mingo returned to the ranch. "Poor man," sighed Moi, shaking his head. "His wife kept the house, he had his cows, and the *dueña*, Mrs. Steel, had her books. It was an odd *ménage*. Of course, it didn't last."

Time passed. A few more clicks of the wheel, another toss of the dice, and a German angel moved into Moi's nest. It's hard to know when exactly, because Moi's stories have no chronology; they lie side by side in a narrow bed, come together like true lovers and never seem to disentangle. Nor are the sentiments ever crystal clear, which is particularly true with this love story.

Gudrun lost her husband in a car wreck, and sometime during her spiritual journey to the sacred shrines of India, she lost touch with her children. Her lonely pilgrimage to the east eventually brought her to Palenque, where Moi became her compass, her lodestone. The moment Gudrun spied the lofty cedars at his gate, she sloughed off her widow's sari and settled for Moi's humble version of paradise. The archetypal waif, dressed in a woman's ripe body, had found her earthly home. Of course, it's impossible to forsake every memory; certain habits dwell in the hands and manifest automatically. Gudrun set for herself the tormented task of cleaning house, of sweeping out chaos and decay. The land had possibilities.

Even in the jungle the wheel of karma rolled. A slave to the wheel rather than Moi's intermittent affections, Gudrun soon built a separate room above the kitchen, a blue meditation cell over the leafy sea and smoking bread oven. Gudrun's passion for the Maya never reached high temperatures. Moi loathed the Vedas. Still, he took delight in the surprise fate handed him on a Meissen platter. Every afternoon he watched her lower her big naked bones into the pool and prayed the water would soften her heart. One day, when the yeast failed to rise, she ran to him across the bamboo bridge, sobbing. She tripped, dropped like a boulder over the edge, and landed, sitting in a full lotus position, by the wood shed. It was a miracle, a moment of enlightenment, a sign from Shiva. Two days later, Moises was measuring out new ground across the stream banks of ginger. The land was flat and clear there. Once again, posts and beams started climbing, this time with cement supports and a façade of hand-painted elephant leaves. With her last bit of money, Gudrun built a white gazebo in the bend of the creek where she recited her Hindu prayers. Finally she changed her name to Rakshita, and that was it.

Things were falling apart. At the same time things were hurtling toward the larger void we live in and cannot comprehend: yin and yang, the endless dualities of the Maya space-time continuum. The Maya never dreamed of satellites, but their hieroglyphic images of jaguars and toads, read as a whole, defined the basic structure of a universe wherein the difference between the word and the world was infinitesimal. The breath barely formed in the mouths of the gods swiftly transmuted into an eroding stone. Footprints were on the road months before there were men to fill them. The constellations took a nanosecond longer: the raising of the sky upon three stone pillars, the placement of the World Tree in the black rift of the Milky Way, and the quick reel of the god's heel that set time and space spinning.

Once again Moi was left to his own perfection. His island was one of the stone pillars that held up the sky, kept the racing clouds from sinking below the water surrounding him. Moi spent the rest of his life searching for designs in the stars and leaves. After Rakshita moved across the stream, he named his place and put up a sign: EL PANCHAN, mystical land above the serpentine sky. Seventh Heaven. Paradise. A man with a monkey's soul knows the sky is a blue snake, trees are lizards, and the earth a ravenous monster. And a man with a monkey's soul can change.

Maybe it was the big-boned foreign woman stubbornly chanting among the limes, or their own stiff uselessness. His eleven sons and daughters started claiming rights to Moi's lush parcel of land. These loveless negotiations began with Sunday picnics up in the old man's crazy tree house. They brought along fried chicken and coolers of beer, their delinquent boyfriends and frowzy wives. Drunken weekends extended to lost weeks drinking tequila until the menfolk broke the animal nights with wild Mexican hallooing, which is something between a peacock's proud shriek and a barely human, throat-catching sob. They were gypsies really, with a home that tossed and buckled around them like a horseless runaway wagon. At three in the morning, when the ranchero ballads and Hindu rites stopped making sense, Alberto whipped out his pistol, aimed at his brother Chato, and fired. The bullet tore through the trunk of Moi's new avocado tree.

Life changed fast after that, like the change from reggae to rap. Moi's sons were after tourist money, and all Moi would say before loping away to the forest was, "They're my sons. They can do as they please." Land was cleared for tents, cabañas roofed with thatch, simple shacks where hammocks hung like slivers of raspberry pie. Bathroom stalls emitted a ripe stench in the rainy season because no one bothered to install proper drains and sewage pipes. Sinks and showers went dry because the river that once watered the royal city of Palenque always gave out at the height of the winter tourist season. People living here year-round complained about the steady invasion of dopeheads on their paradisiacal terrain.

Moi's heirs, on the other hand, preferred their jungle crowded with paying guests. Soon the brothers were sending dollars from the States so that Ariceli could open a launderette. Instead of fighting like bantam roosters over the half-naked women strolling by, Alberto and Chato were battling over parking spaces for campers and RV's. Two nasty divorces entrenched them deeper. And while the brothers scrambled, Rakshita's Mexican-Indian retreat, complete with healing hut, chapatis, and cottages painted in day-glo mandalas, struck spiritual paydirt.

Pasta, pizza, curry, drums, and a cheap place to sleep: the perfect recipe for success.

In the midst of all this haphazard construction, the family zeroed in on Moi's private castle. His woodpiles were an eyesore, they complained, his tree house took up too much air space. But before they threatened to tear it down, Moi beat them to it. Board by board he pulled his house apart and put it back together, a huge, muddled hulk at the farthest reaches of his land. He built the towers three stories high, so he could catch a glimpse of the northern acropolis flashing white on the distant ridge. He called this monstrous labyrinth the Linda Schele Center for Maya Studies.

It was a pie-eyed dream come true. When Mingo came for a tour of inspection, he simply shrugged. "Things could be worse," he prophesied, and he was right. By the time the Center was up and running, Moi had already lost interest. If the archaeologists stopped by to discuss the solar alignments of the temples, Moi accused them of idle speculation and ran them out. After forty years of watching the stars make their rounds above the roof combs, he claimed his knowledge came through blessed intuition. Yet he had spent six months tracing the angle of the sun as it poured through the T-shaped window inside the Palace Tower until, on summer solstice, the light cast a perfect glowing T on the eastern wall of the chamber. At sunset he saw a shaft of light pierce the western window of the Temple of the Inscriptions, shoot across the central corridor, exit the window on the opposite wall, and illuminate the Temple of the Cross, one hundred meters away: a stunning example of architectural alignment, engineered after years of solar measurements made with the aid of two crossed sticks.

Now the man who had a great gift for bringing diverse scholars together, who helped organize the Palenque Round Table conferences year after year, fumes over every new idea. He used to delight in showing me his Golden Guest Book, signed, "To Moi, with love, Jackie Onassis," and "Thanks for the magical tour of the Maya galaxies, Carl Sagan." But lately he's taken to lumping the VIP's with all the other mediocrities. Nevertheless, in his honorary capacity as Historian of Palenque, he's compelled to discuss whatever puzzle is on his mind that day with the Chinese ambassador or queen of Spain, with blissed-out hippies, and anyone out in television land who happens to tune into his weekly cable series. The old man has lived long enough to see temples rise from their graves, bones and stones and works of art destroyed by volcanic ash, layers of bat guano, and human stupidity. Now they were stealing the calendar, stealing time. "No one knows anything," he grumbles. "Palenque is just a toy."

I told him I had come here to learn about the Maya, and since Podwell hadn't appeared, I wasn't making much headway.

"You should forget about the Maya," Don Moi said. "Whatever you write will be wrong in two weeks. That's the way these scholars are. Haven't you noticed? Time is moving faster."

But if the Maya calendar was right and time circled endlessly, then, I reasoned, the joys and disasters that had transpired in the remote past would happen again in the future. All I had to do was wait and knowledge would stream through the hole in my screen door and I would catch a glimpse of something unimaginable in the pattern of the stones or stars or the meandering course of the Motul River.

"As for me," Moi said, "I'm tired of this place, tired even of attention. I should go into hiding, find someplace quiet where I can think. Maybe land in the Tulija Valley or a ranch near Salto de Agua."

"I think you'd miss these trees," I said.

Most evenings he roams the woods, short tail twitching, horns shorn, eyes glowing with a bitter animal fire, an old stag heading for water on another moonlit night.

"Besides," I said, "you're probably hiding many secrets underneath your animal skin."

"Better to be the head of a mouse than the tail of a lion, my father told me. Then again, too much tranquility can be very dangerous."

"Ah, but you just said you were searching for a place to hide."

"All right, let me ask you this: If you go to hell, would you rather have horns drilled into your head, a tail screwed into your ass, wings nailed to your back, or wallow in shit? I'd rather wallow in shit. It's more like life."

I was too stunned to answer.

"Don't you know, the gods have sent you here? This is your destiny."

I did admit that, against my better judgment, I was becoming enmeshed in the daily intrigues of the Panchan Hotel.

"*Eso!*" he said. "You'll be better off writing the story of my life. And this is not mere vanity. Because, you see, I want to be invisible. Write the story as if I'm not there."

PART I

Chapter 1

CHICHONAL 1982

Only the one who owns the earth and thunder knows why Mingo had such good luck. His wife said it of him when he'd been missing for days with that aging *coqueta* whose rosewater perfume clung to his wrinkled shirt when he staggered home, surprised at the fuss. The men drinking in the cantina said the same after they tired of talking about imaginary beauties, the bristling kind that turned into putrid trees when you hugged them, and the conversation got around to real snakes and the time Mingo got lost for a week in the jungle, or Mingo's adventures on the Gulf Coast, or the time he'd escaped from the maw of death after he'd been working at the ruins for a solid month and found himself lying in his hammock, alone in the afternoon, a dull fever in his bones, and wishing this house had a real mirror so that he could see himself and the state of his eyes. For a long while he stared at the brown spider scuttling across the roof thatch, which also seemed to be crawling, the lashings around the wood joints beginning to fray. Then he put one foot on the floor and the earth came up to meet his feet. "Holy Mary, I'll never drink another drop," he muttered, reaching for the house post, and he clung to that shaved tree like a man caught on the offshore oil rigs during a five-day norther. Many times, when he went to pray before the cave on San Juan Mountain, he believed he saw the gray line of the sea creeping over the swamps. And once, when he was looking for construction work in Champoton, he saw a black tanker slide like a steam iron across the rumpled foam. The turbines blasted through his sleep, and now that long ship pressing down on the rolling waves of his dirt floor was about to collide with the heap of ash spilling over the tumbled hearthstones. The cooking fire was dead. His wife was gone.

"A miracle," he thought. "The princess won't say anything." He rummaged through the toppled jars of rancid cooking oil, the gourds lying on their faces, still dizzy but conscious enough to be wary of the scorpions that liked to sleep behind the shelf. "Shh, shh," he whispered to the great silence. There it was, in the can of brown shoe polish, his morning libation, burning liquor, medicine of the gods. One sip, two, and a bit of chile to clear the headache.

A strange tune came into his head, a low cluck like the distant hens, and then a buzz that seemed to come not from his blocked inner ear or the sawdust in his brain, but from somewhere beyond the gaping hole in his mud wall. Mingo took another swallow, screwed the lid on the can, and grabbing his machete, stumbled out into the dirt yard. "Thank God I slept in my pants," he said. The blinding sun had bleached everything white. The hen house lay in a heap, the woodpile scattered like matchsticks, his corn patch a snarl with broken teeth. But there was no sun, only a cold gray cloud hanging over his head. The pitiful arroyo that ran along his agave fence had deepened overnight. A wide rift cut him off at the front gate and the back. He stared into the brown crack, rubbing his eyes in disbelief. It went down forever. He was an island on a riven crust. His neighbor's house was gone. Not even the dogs. What would he eat? Cold beans stuck in the pot. The hens were cackling on the other side. That was a good sign. His roof and wall could be fixed. But why, without María Refugio to nag him? No work today, and the next and the next. Where was the spoon to hold the medicine for his bad eye? Not a single dry tortilla in the sack. The water jar was empty. Where was she? He would walk until he found a place to cross, leap if he had to, despite his swollen knees.

A slow white drizzle, warm and dry, fell like fine powder on his scrawny face. He searched for the new aluminum pot he bought with last month's pay. "I've been good to her, sweated over the broken stones every day, piling white stucco in a wheelbarrow and carrying it away, rooting through the rubble like a pig, scratching like a hen among the clods of ancient filth. For what? Fifty pesos!" Barely enough to feed his little Julio walking north, Luci, his jewel crowned with lilies, wearing a bleached muslin dress over her torn slip and walking barefoot to the well of her wedding day with that worthless, good-for-nothing

Rigoberto. "Well, one less mouth to feed," he shrugged, burying his head in his hands.

"Palestrina," he called, as he always did when he was deep in his cups, her face smooth and taut, dark eyes flashing like Delores del Rio urging the peasant women to stand up and fight, though the last time he went to see her, Palestrina was worn out and cross as she poured him another drink, the loud music and staggered hooting of the crowd muffling the words he wanted to say.

He woke again, lifted his head and watched the rain fall like tiny new centavos into the pot. The blue enamel held a cloud of powder. The ground was white with frozen money. And now that braided, midnight woman had left him, clutching Tito, clutching Melchior, prodding Teresina, who was too absent-minded to watch the pebbles under her feet, the swollen cracks of the Mother. Yes, his old woman waited for a temblor to get up the nerve to do it. Round-hipped woman, waddling away in a panic she started herself, probably showing off the bruise on her rump like a badge. "Damn her! Left me to die!" He shouted so loud he woke himself again. His heart was beating fast. Perhaps it was just a dream. But the hole was still there, the cracks, the senseless hum, the silent dogs. "Forgive me, Holy Mother." Perhaps she tried to wake him, but he was lost in his stupor. Had to save the children, grabbed the last of the *atole* and the beans. Well, he was alive, even though he was dead inside and somewhere on the rim of Hell, which used to be his home. As soon as he could straighten up and walk he would go to the caves, take his candles, take his stones, take the clay figure sitting cross-legged underneath the bed. He had found it the day he and Pepe were working on the mound called Temple XVIIIA. Pepe sold his to a Frenchman. But he, Mingo, had kept the blackened figure with its shattered nose and broken paw, because the face resembled his grandfather, of whom he had no pictures. Put him under the bed and fed him coffee, sweet rolls, cigarettes. Maybe that was it. He held the clay figure in his brown hands and shook it. "Why?"

The head escaped, rolled across the floor and scraped the aluminum pot. The face of his ancestors, far older than his grandfather, stared accusingly from the widening pool of dust. "Thief!" Wasn't being stranded on this spit of land, alone, without his wife to feed him, punishment enough? Nothing had happened to Pepe, his wife was still at home to please him. Nothing evil had visited the looters, who owned chainsaws and pickup trucks and had enough left over to buy sunglasses, packs of cigarettes, and bottles of Jamaican rum. The doctors, who lifted entire statues, were always smiling and growing fatter, though one of them had sprained an ankle falling off the temple and another suffered dysentery so bad he landed in the hospital, which was enough to shorten the life of any man.

Mingo lifted the head gently, wrapped it in his handkerchief, and bolted the leaning door, leaving the rain and hollow light to guard the chairs and bottles. He started walking, crawling really, over the broken yard, the whiteness blinding his good eye. He came to the crevice at the gate just as the sky cast shadows across the white hills, turning the valleys into deepening wounds. Once he had a dream in which his angry wife left him, departing on a cloud. "I'll never drink another drop," he promised then. The sky was the same gray color when he woke. "This time I mean it," he said to the fog.

The moon was in his left hand. On his right, the sun hung motionless, a pale disk on an old clock that had ceased to tick. The moon was an old crone bent over her wash. The land was a lake of soap, and across the mountain a thousand white bed sheets were spread out to dry, pants and skirts and shirts draped over trees and stiff magueys, and the people, wherever they were, were probably naked and caked with dust, their brown skins as white as the Spaniards at last. It took misery to bleach their brown skins, but the ash would also change their souls. The sun had kept a record of their names and crimes.

White sack of a dead dog on the road, stiff white horses, the awful stench of death filling his burning lungs. He saw two ghosts moving through the raining wood, an old woman frozen under the tangled hair of the trees. She must have been there for some time because her eyes were two gray stones. As he crossed the last ridge he heard voices. There were footprints and then three sleeping figures lying with their arms wrapped around each other under a blanket of powder. "María Refugio," he called. "Come home!"

By the time he reached the cave he was a dead man. He expected a multitude, but there were only five or six dreaming creatures, strangers from Salto de Agua, no one from Naranjo, huddled inside the rock. One man was on his knees, praying in a low monotonous drone while a woman waved a white branch over the sleeping form of her son. The man produced an egg from his shirt pocket and ran it along the boy's twisted leg. He reached into his net bag and brought out a dirty bottle, removed the corncob stopper, and took a swig, then spat it out, in a wide spray, to the four directions. He passed around the bottle. "Grant a little pardon," Mingo said. The liquor warmed his belly, gave him the strength to stand. He offered a prayer to Don Juan, lord of rain, lord of thunder. "Where is my wife? Where is my son?" he beseeched. Another swallow and he was on his knees. The creatures were wide-eyed, their faces streaked with tears, and rasping cries welled up from their throats. The *curandero* cracked the egg, threw back his head, and poured streaming yolk and mucus down his dry gullet. Angry shouts went up. Mingo swayed and fell over. When he woke, the creatures were gone. He crawled deeper inside the cave, the black walls pitching around him. He was clutching the headless figure in one hand, running the other hand up and down the rough stones. He could barely see the light seeping through the door of the cave. His fingers found a ledge. There he placed the broken clay figure and the head. He rested his back against the wall. Who knows how long he sat there, staring. He heard the sound of a drum beating somewhere deeper in the tunnel, a drowsy flute, and distant murmurs. Then he slept.

That's how they found him, curled up and empty as a shell.

After that, Mingo was never the same. For two years he lay in his straw bed, occasionally moaning. When his wife returned, he didn't know her. The curers said he had suffered soul loss, and none of them could bring him back. His daughter, Minerva, who sat by his side for hours, sensed that he was traveling through a world that was as white and ashen as this one, though there was no sun, only moonlight spreading through the bare branches. Sometimes he moved his leg or tossed his head abruptly, and she heard him mutter, "skull." He was walking on a trail that wound deep into the forest, crawling underneath the thick liana vines that grew in the woods on the other side of the mountain where the huge limestone boulders stood. She remembered that place and knew her father was not as far away as the shamans said. All the same, those living rocks were a torment. At the end of the trail, he came to a gray mound pitted from centuries of rain. And now he noticed a black hole at the base, and above it, two round, empty eyes. The overhanging leaves looked like green pupils set inside the round sockets, and as he approached, drawn irresistibly toward that thing, he saw that the black hole was large enough for a man to crawl through.

He sat outside the cave mouth for a while, gazing at the white hills and white trail he had spent so many days walking, but he could not see his footprints. Somehow his mind was too confused to consider the reasons for the absence of shade, the amorphous light, the lack of sensation in his body. "If I were dead, wouldn't I know it? And if I am dead, why, then, I'll just curl up and sleep." He slept and dreamt that inside the skull was a box filled with something precious. When he shook himself awake he lifted his left leg and crawled inside. It was blacker than his hen, blacker than a buzzard, and it stank like a buzzard, too. He reached out his hand and felt his way about the narrow space, just as he did on nights when he came home drunk, his hammock a swinging vine, the wooden house post a smooth stone column or maybe the devil's marble spine. But the wooden chest he tripped over, the chest that held his family's possessions, was the box he had just found in his dream. Lord, not a sliver of light penetrated the eyeholes, nose holes, or mouth. He knelt down and prayed, then lifted the lid. It came off without a struggle. He was panting heavily now, and his daughter ran to fetch a cup of water. His hand fumbled inside the box and found something rough and hard and rippled, like a carved stone, and next to it a shape that felt like tree bark. He lifted it out. It was as smooth and as soft as paper. He stared into the empty space trying to imagine what that smooth, soft bundle could be. He felt a cool hand press against his cheek, heard a far-off voice say, "Drink." Then he opened his eyes and saw the brown thatch and brown roof poles of his house.

Chapter 2

DEATH AND MONEY

The story ended where it began, much like a classic Persian tale in which the hero wakes from a deep sleep induced by too much wine and upon gazing at another gray, stone-lipped dawn discovers that the fantastical places he has visited were but a dream, and his humble house streaked with flour, his broken chair, the spider scuttling under the roof thatch weaving its web of ash, were also part of an endless dream from which he would never wake.

The volcano that exploded into life and just as suddenly vanished in its own catastrophic flames was one in a chain of dormant peaks wrapped in timeless cloud forest. Blue morpho butterflies floated among giant ferns, pendulous black orchids spilled from living rock. Along the smoking ledges grew sunless stalks of corn. The Zoque farmers hidden in fog-bound valleys or scattered across the misty hills were called Cloud People, and since ancient times, these last remaining descendants of Olmec civilization—the "mother culture" of Mexico—had worshipped the god of fire. Hundreds perished in streams of molten lava, thousands were forced to flee the wrath of the creator and destroyer. Ashes blackened the sun for twenty days. Clouds of ash drifted across the Pacific and descended over central Asia, dimming the golden domes and blue minarets, the diamond eyes of the Buddha, and coating the brown steppes with a fine powder that clogged the lungs of Tibetan monks and Chinese miners, herds of Kyrjk goats and Urghur ponies. The Zoques and the Maya prayed for rain, and when the rain came, it turned the dust to rivers of white mud that buried the sick in their hovels. Acid rain washed away the murals in the Palace, destroyed the already eroding art and hieroglyphic history of Palenque.

"At least one good thing happened," said Don Moi. "An amazing change occurred in the dreamer's life."

Ever since his miraculous return from the land of burning bones, Mingo sits on a stool all day, writing words in a green lined schoolbook. All day, every day, 365 days a year x 20 years—a full *katun* in Maya time—and still the words pour across the pages like ink-stained shadows left out in the rain. No one is permitted to read them, Mingo says, until the work is finished, and anybody who tries will lose his eyeballs. For this reason, none of the other men drinking at the table was willing to call him a hero. It's not that they were cynics. Heaven forbid! They firmly believed he had brought back a message from the other side. But without knowing the nature of the message, each man harbored strange misgivings, which grew more sinister as time slipped away. Maybe the owner of the cave had whispered something evil in Mingo's ear and then paid him off in gold doubloons. Maybe the bundle he'd found in the chest contained an ancient book of spells whose magic words jumped off the paper and into his feverish mind like sparks from a witch's black candle. Maybe the words fell out of the sky like grains of moonstones or poisonous dust from shooting stars. The words were the noisy crows squawking on his dead avocado tree. And what about that pair of laughing falcons he was always seeing? The feathers worked like a charm, he said, you just had to steal them from Mother Wind. Yes, there was definitely something unnatural going on. Mingo was either a witch or a seer, no two ways about it. For sure he'd become a writer!

There were jovial *saluds* all around and the clinking of shot glasses. Everyone agreed that Mingo was a lucky man, but also completely mad.

"Just look at the way he mixes into things," Virgilio Flores said. He placed his cowboy hat on his fat middle finger and twirled it like a top.

Victor Hugo started fanning himself with his New York Yankees baseball cap. "And his daughter playing with fire. Now there's a story!"

"What's that?" said Marcelino Vega, narrowing his eyes like a movie detective.

"Nothing, nothing. I mean she's almost ripe, that's all."

"Pretty, yes, very pretty." Marcelino leaned back and stroked his long handlebar mustache. "My friend without an ounce of reason, her dancing in the dark, and the world outside the door whiter than a corpse."

All of a sudden the men lapsed into silence, their stubby hands pressed flat on the plastic table. It looked like a cattlemen's séance, but there were no sounds of tapping. Usually the consumption of five or ten tequilas prevents the muscles from moving at will, but this was more than temporary rigor mortis. It was as if a glass bell had dropped from the pitched tin roof, creating an instant vacuum. In such extreme cases, people said, electric particles can become so hopelessly tangled that time stands still. Nothing can be done about it. Those hard-bitten, leather-skinned ranchers sat in a catatonic state for what seemed like hours. Eventually I heard the man beside me breathing through his nose.

The Indian called Pepe stood up abruptly and said he had work to do. The minute he was gone his three mestizo friends started grumbling.

"Thieves, all of them."

"Yes. Don't waste a drop of sympathy. Look what happened to us."

Virgilio lost a son, who choked to death. Others suffered lacerations or concussions when the roofs caved in. The survivors swept the buried rooms and piled the ashes in the streets. Trucks would haul the ash to the edge of town, and the wind would blow it back again. The same thing day and night for three years: ashes sifting down from the eaves, ashes under the beds, ashes under the cooking pots, ashes lodged in the lungs. The dogs and cattle never rose, the birds never returned.

"It was a terrible punishment. But we at least are decent Catholics. We know how to pray."

"The sins of man are never washed away," said Moi. "People never change."

The local church, like any other nineteenth-century public auditorium restored after the war years, drew inspiration from the average human frame: plain, stout, flat-footed, and favoring the left side where the squat bell tower leans against the building's broad shoulder. Along the aisles, the modest plaster saints float on cotton batting clouds and carpets of plastic roses. Smiling wanly, they look like honored speakers at a religious convention for second graders. "It is hard to believe the Holy Spirit resides here," wrote Graham Greene shortly after his 1938 visit, "though in this state the churches still stand, great white shells like the skulls you find bleached beside the forest paths . . . ." During the auto-da-fé, "the statues were carried out of the church while the inhabitants watched, sheepishly, and saw their own children encouraged to chop up the images in return for little presents of candy."

A century earlier, John Lloyd Stephens and Frederick Catherwood reported that certain villagers decorated their houses with fragments looted from the ancient site of Palenque. During Désiré Charnay's expedition of 1881, the French explorer noticed several broken tablets propped on a German settler's front lawn. Sometime before the First World War, two great bas-reliefs, stolen from the Temple of the Cross, were ensconced on either side of the church door: the life-sized portrait of Kan Bahlam in full ceremonial array facing the grinning, cigar-smoking Lord of the Underworld.

Graham Greene's bleak travel account, *The Lawless Roads*, gives no description of them, probably because the disillusioned English author found Maya art as contemptible as the jungle and its people. And so I wondered aloud what the priest and villagers might have thought of the extraordinary carved figures, dressed in pagan feathers and jaguar pelts, quietly looking on while the church was ransacked.

"Who remembers?" said Victor Hugo. "My family never went to church."

By way of an answer, Marcelino told me that the original church and the original town of Santo Domingo de Palenque lay in ruins at the end of the airport runway. After the church crumbled, the villagers moved deeper into the hills, carrying their antique spoils with them. The collapse of the chapel, followed by the arrival of strangers, every thirty years or so, were seen as signs of darker things to come.

The habit of suspicion hadn't died. When I expressed interest in visiting the ruined church, Marcelino, who seemed like a civilized man with his distinguished white mustache, told me flatly that there was no reason to go searching; he knew there was no gold buried on the deconsecrated grounds. Evidently he had gone over it with a spade.

"No, during the Conquest, the Spaniards hid their gold in the caves. That's why the Indians started going up there, supposedly to pray." Later, the pirates who plundered the Spanish galleons sailing from Campeche stored their booty in those same mountains. "It's only sixty kilometers from here to the Gulf. And in the rainy season there's a narrow channel from the lagoon of Catazaja to the port of Frontera.

The buccaneers would keep the ornaments and sell the brazilwood and cochineal. In those days the red and purple dyes were worth a hundred times more than gold." Even the famous pirate Lorenzillo traveled to Palenque with treasure chests full of coins. He came to see the water birds and to buy off the state politicians. They say he also made a deal with the Indians.

"You see, they only pretend they're poor. Once I found a piece of Chinese porcelain, Ming, and a little silver locket from Singapore or Persia. That was all. Those Indians are richer than we are. How do you think they buy the guns to fight their revolutions?"

During the 1930s, when the fanatical Red Shirts under Governor Garrido stopped at nothing, including murder, to force the Catholic Church underground, a local priest, himself a prime target of terror, did an about-face and accused the Chol Indians of practicing pagan rites. Ignited by the rumors of gold circulating throughout the cow-sheds and cantinas, a pack of vigilantes set fire to the sacred cave on Don Juan Mountain. The raiders were just as zealous about stamping out any spark of rebellion, judging from the sentiments being expressed at this table.

"Yes, they're nothing but heathens, communists, and Trotsky's."

"They still pray to the caves, they still pray to their idols. They stash their loot up there. They drink and get riled up. And remember, the cave, the entire mountain, was the property of Señora Steel. She was good to the Indians. But of course she's dead. Anyone can tell you why."

Chapter 3

WINTER SOLSTICE

The mysterious death of Mrs. Steel had to wait in the wings due to the abrupt turn of events caused by Mercury's forward motion conjuncting with the winter solstice sun. I imagined the señora slipping into the back seat of the green station wagon Mingo was driving and slowly cruising the vast gray zone where Frida Kahlo, Trotsky, and Pakal were cooling their heels in one of the many refreshing waterfalls which grace that idyllic land. Actually this image was not so far-fetched because, as I had learned earlier, the señora and Mingo had spent quite a bit of time together on her ranch in Salto de Agua. And there is no reason not to suppose that Frida and Trotsky, had they been in the vicinity, would have been welcome guests. Pakal, as we know, was born there. In any event, it is in the nature of things that the gray zone—limbo, the Mind, the fourth dimension, whatever you may call it—has a revolving door through which the living and the dead may vanish or spring at any moment, and under circumstances beyond our control.

Through that portal Podwell suddenly bounded, toting a heavy leather briefcase stuffed with charts of bisected squares. He said he'd been at the beach. His eyes were as bright as sand berries, his chrome-colored hair standing on end, as if he'd been driving for the last two days in a flying saucer with the silver top down. He was as breathless as a solar wind, talking a mile a minute, on and on, until his newly discovered hypotenuses swelled to cosmic proportions. I listened quietly as he pulled out his computer and started superimposing red lines over the green contour map of Palenque. The lines connected the center of the Temple of the Cross to the northern facade of the Temple of the Sun, the southern platform of Temple XV to the eastern Palace door, then up the hill to Temple XXIII and down again to the base of the Temple of the Foliated Cross. On the screen before me, a nest of forty-five-degree angles embraced the ancient temples, whose beautiful proportions were pure embodiments of the elemental structure of space.

Sacred geometry was only one slice of the pie. The thin red lines on the map also traced the alignments of the temples to the rising and setting sun. Geometry and astronomy were in perfect harmony. And, as Podwell pointed out, because the great meeting of earth and sky occurred within the holy sanctuaries, this spectacle possessed a spiritual dimension whose depth and breadth encompassed the very soul of Maya thought and religion.

The precise angle at which the blinding rays of the sun penetrated the temple interiors—the sacred angle at which the spiritual was made manifest—had been calculated by royal mathematicians for maximum dramatic effect. Now the sun was being tracked with the same passionate intensity by three archaeologists staying at the hotel.

Barnaby, a big-boned, red-faced, square-dealing Texan, could often be seen ambling through the restaurant with the confident, rolling gait of a jungle explorer, eyes permanently fixed on the ground, ever in search of some telltale sign of something buried underfoot, "like a pyramid, maybe, or an entire city with temples and painted palaces and . . . ."

"Right under our noses," said his friend Alux, "a lost city underneath the Panchan!"

"We'll dig it up and put it back together like a Lego set. How great is that?"

"Good old American plastic," said Alux. "Guaranteed to last forever!" Whenever a smile creased his face, you knew that there was deep mischief hiding behind his prolonged, moody silences. He bore all the burdens of a self-absorbed artist, possessed all the wiles of a Maya night spirit. "C'mon," he said, tying his black hair into a ponytail. "Let's check out the coffee plantation." Alux was always hunting shadows in the woods.

Podwell was the most charismatic of the three, good-looking, good-natured, with a steely edge balanced by a bumbling, boyish restlessness and an infectious, manic enthusiasm. When the three of them sat at a table, unwinding after a long, hot day in the field, Podwell had a habit of commandeering the napkins and steering the conversation toward his latest theory, which had just hit him on the head like a piece of flying plaster. Alux would eventually wander off like a slug or slump in his chair, wishing he were home, tinkering, or working clay, or watching Jackie Chan and vegging out with his boy. On the rare occasions when he brought himself to speak, he would put on his glasses and mutter some oblique, contrary opinion.

"It can't be sixty-three degrees."

"Why not?"

"Because it's sixty-six degrees."

When the numbers started shouting at each other, Barnaby would call time, then laugh like a riveter drilling holes through ice.

"Okay, okay, I'll work it out tonight," said Podwell amiably. "It's all for one and one for all, right!" And the three men clicked their beer bottles.

They made an odd trio, these peacocks, these married bachelors living in isolation, bonded together in a solitary search for truths that would add up to scientific and spiritual oneness. It was definitely heady stuff. I could barely add, but since they needed an extra pair of eyes, I immediately joined their momentous enterprise.

The solar observations proceeded with the sun, but despite the air of urgency, not at the sun's daily pace. That would have been impossible given the bureaucratic red tape involved in getting permits to watch the sky during hours when the park was closed. Instead, the researchers had to settle for specific days when the sun reached a key station on the horizon; that is, solstices, equinoxes, and zenith passages.

In between these grand events, life went on as usual. A French photographer lost her room key and ended up sleeping in the hammocks with a bongo player from Budapest who drove a dusty black limousine with a trunk full of peyote buttons. The spiritual healer from Edinburgh overdosed and was saved from drowning in the falls by a Nicaraguan lobster diver. The kids had to swim in the kiddy pool after that. But otherwise, the conch blew at six, the workers started hammering at eight, and time marched to the beat of the midnight drums. And every two months or so, before the crack of dawn, there'd be a sudden flurry, downing a quick cup of coffee, and rushing out to the site in time for sunrise.

At that hour the temples were locked in monumental stillness. Beneath my feet the mown grass rippled as if another earth, just below the surface, was slowly pushing upward. Toward the east, a faint red glow tinged the hills, and as I raced across the plaza I noticed the sun flare above the broken horizon. My heart sank. But I kept on running, over the plank bridge, over the shadow river, and up the twisted path, the rising sun trailing me, looming ahead, now dropping behind the trees. When I reached the doorway of the Temple of the Sun, the stones still lay in darkness.

According to an earlier generation of astronomers, the Temple of the Sun was aligned to winter solstice. The first rays of light, they predicted, would enter the central doorway at a perpendicular angle. In fact, no one had ever witnessed it.

Off in the distance, light crawled across the northern plaza toward the Temple of the Count where Barnaby stood poised with his camera, ready to capture the morning rays. Podwell was waving from the Tower, his starched white shirt glistening through the upper window. Yet the mountain before me lay in shadow, and night still clung to the Temple of the Sun. On the carved panel at the back of the sanctuary, the fierce eyes of the Jaguar God of the Underworld stared through the gloom. As Alux and I waited in the mournful atmosphere, I felt that cold, wintry apprehension the ancients must have felt before the sun's return.

At 9:23 A.M., the sun finally broke over the perfect peak of El Mirador Mountain, sending out a radiant crown of golden light. The first rays slipped through the doorway at ten degrees off center.

Something was wrong. Was it the shift in the earth and sun since A.D. 690, when the temple was built? Or were the thick trees on the once naked mountain terraces now blocking the original trajectory? The sun goes up and the sun comes down in a different place each day, and for us down below, watching its immense, ever-changing arc from a small stone temple hemmed in by wooded mountains, the sun flutters, opens, disappears. With everything in motion, where was the right place to stand?

I mentioned my dilemma to Alux. After a long period of reflection, he suggested the top of Temple XXVI, buried on the tall slope behind us. Podwell, who was now lunging up the steps, sweating and out of breath, was already shaking his head. "El Mirador," he said, the peak directly in front of us.

Both viewing places were now overgrown and involved such arduous climbs that neither man was willing to take the risk. Podwell confessed that he had braved it once and was afraid to try again.

Three years before, he and a colleague had set off in search of the legendary caves on El Mirador. No sooner had they skirted the base when they promptly got lost in the steep ravines that sliced through the mountains. For hours they wandered through darkening forest, reduced to a half-liter of water and a cigarette between them. Just as the sun was beginning to sink, they stumbled upon a grove of lime trees. In the dusty light the ground seemed to waver, and the scattered stones slowly merged into a wall. Laden with moss, the green wall connected to another and another, until Podwell could make out the shape of a rectangular house with three tilted doors. It still had its roof comb, mottled with orange lichen in the last glow of light. There were other structures just beyond, six in all, in various states of decay. The buildings were exact replicas of Palenque's temples, except for one detail: they stood only three feet high.

Romney shook his head and slid to the ground. "Maybe they're some kind of models," he said. In the spreading dusk the two men started guessing, until their guesses took them further and further afield. Podwell finally said, "They're the houses of the *aluxes*, the spirits of the forest." And as soon as he said this, a blue morpho butterfly wafted downward. They followed it through the trees until it disappeared in darkness, and they were standing in the main plaza, dumb with relief.

Podwell stamped the mud off his boots. Alux stared at his sandals. Barnaby glanced at the sky. The universe was changing, and along with everything else, the Temple of the Sun was out of kilter.

Podwell took a swig of Gatorade and said, "There's no use lamenting, Barnaby. Besides, the universe doesn't change that fast, maybe two or three minutes every five hundred years." The electrolytes must have charged him up again because he was talking about 819-day cycles, five-thousand-year cycles, twenty-six-thousand-year cycles and the precession of the equinoxes. Alux peeled a begonia and started chewing on the stalk.

Then Podwell remembered the perfect spot for observing the solstice sunset: a small viewing stand on the upper platform of the Temple of the Cross. He had literally stumbled upon it when he and the team were up there, excavating the narrow ledge. The memory of it set Podwell dancing.

"The stones started slipping and sliding and then the dirt caved in. The next thing I knew I was lying flat on my back between two low walls in the middle of the original terrace. I almost broke my ankle, but it was worth it."

In the late afternoon we sat on the upper terrace, high above the plaza. As the last tourists trickled out, toucans began chattering in the trees and swallows darted across the empty courtyards of the Palace. A lone falcon flew from the Tower and perched on the bare pillar above us. Over the great pyramid that contained the tomb of Lord Pakal loomed the hollow disk of the winter sun.

"Palenque was the gateway to the Underworld," said Podwell. "Human souls that descended with the sun woke again, transformed, at winter solstice."

Then he pointed to a distant notch in the western ridge. "There!" he said. "That notch is the passageway, the portal to the place of transformation. And through the same open gullet— the giant maw of the Earth Monster—305 degrees azimuth—the moon and planets sink below the horizon."

Podwell was sure that Pakal's heir, Kan Bahlam, sat where we were sitting, to view the setting sun. With a grand flourish, he assumed the classic royal stance and reenacted a role he had played a hundred times in his dreams. There he was, stiff as a stone, decked in opulent jewels, his resplendent feathered headdress glinting iridescent green, as the golden sun, of which he was the living incarnation, slowly descended into his father's tomb. Down on the main plaza the crowds—nobles, peasants, merchants, priests—looked up in awe. Huzzah, huzzah! Great Sun-Faced Lord! Podwell flung his arms toward the heavens, and the sun's last rays shone upon his radiant figure.

"Has anyone ever been up to that ridge?" I asked when we got back to the hotel.

Chapter 4

A Trip to the Cave of Don Juan

We took the paved road, then the dirt road, and finally the bone-breaking track up the spine of the cliffs. There was dust and rock everywhere, and the pickup had no traction. "This is what you'd call a forty-five degree angle," is how Podwell put it. "See what I'm saying?"

I did. Every time Podwell shifted gears we ricocheted like June bugs trapped inside a tin can.

"We'd be better off on foot," Alux said. As soon as he found the trail, we were knee-deep in thorns. Soon it started drizzling. This we took as a good sign from the Owner of the Earth, who controlled the rain and thunder. Podwell pointed to the remains of a temple perched on an upper shelf, but as we approached, the walls disappeared and we were standing in a ring of boulders. "It's just the Earth Lord playing tricks," Alux smiled, although he looked a little nervous.

After an hour of unsteady climbing, we reached the cave. A bleached wooden cross, lying on its side, marked the entrance. The splintered cross looked like a dead man reaching out one wasted arm. I was scared, but Podwell and Alux had put on their headlamps and were already crawling through the narrow cleft.

The ceiling was draped with cobwebs, the walls were oily and black. Here Mingo had found refuge after the eruption of Chichonal. Here the pagan Indian rebels met secretly before the priest flushed them out. Potsherds littered the charred floor, but there were no burnt idols.

Alux was fanning the walls with his flashlight, illuminating waves of rock, when his light landed on two stout pillars on either side of a gaping hole so deep it swallowed the halogen beam and left behind traces of smoke. The passage was steep and narrow, stones scraping my shoulders, steps slick with water, and blackness tighter than skin. "Step, now stop, now breathe," Alux was saying. The air smelled like a root cellar. "Step, now stop, now breathe . . . ." And then there was silence.

We entered a great chamber lit by a moon-sized window in the high dome. The huge buttresses arching overhead were the ribs of a ship, and I was standing in the dark hold. The ship rolled like the sea, and when I looked at the moon above the stone sails I saw storm clouds and the churning sky. Then I noticed a fine mist filtering down upon a patch of giant ferns.

"We've found our way back to the beginning of time," I said.

Podwell and Alux saw it differently. They were two small candles flickering on the floor of an ancient shrine.

"The rulers of Palenque came here to pray," Podwell whispered. "And when they built the temples, they called the inner sanctuaries *pib na*, 'underground houses.' The temples were meant to represent caves."

The similarities were purely symbolic. I couldn't see any real resemblance between the temples at Palenque and the spare, cathedral-like beauty of this cave. Nor did I notice any works of art on the cavernous walls.

Podwell and Alux started poking around. By sheer luck they discovered traces of blue paint and faint outlines of the hieroglyph for *ajaw*, "lord." After a while they found fossilized copal incense under a heap of calcified bat guano. They were chirping like geckos, but I was afraid their idle burrowing was disturbing the Earth Lord. I decided to wait in the garden of ferns.

"The kings came here to fast and pray," Podwell continued. "They sat in the pitch black, not eating, not sleeping, sometimes for twenty days. After weeks of sensory deprivation they probably saw all kinds of things."

"The kings did what our shamans do in dreams," said Alux. "They crawled through the underground passageways. They crossed the underworld river. They saw fields of corn and flowers, singing birds, and giant ceiba trees . . . ."

"Demons, monsters, all sorts of weird, stinking beasts," said Podwell, swinging his flashlight into the black corners.

"They wandered among the dead souls, searching for their ancestors."

Podwell and Alux fell silent. The drumbeat we heard was only water dripping on the black rocks. The drone of human voices was just the wind humming through the dead corridors. This immense cavity inside the earth was a skeletal human body: gray ribs, gray bones, bloodless arteries, and hollow nerves.

There were no messages from the other world. There were no treasure chests or stashes of loot. The headless figurine that Mingo placed in the niche by the entrance was gone. Who had removed it? The cave was empty. The spirits had fled, leaving only their amber perfume.

I stepped into the rain and looked back at the tiny white temples of Palenque tucked like gnome houses in the clouded hills. I turned toward the west and noticed a notch in the next ridge, and the next.

Chapter 5

LOOKING FOR TROTSKY

There was another curious thread left dangling from Mingo's story of Don Juan's cave: the inexplicable scorn heaped upon Leon Trotsky, still rumbling like the Earth Lord's thunder after all these years. Naturally I was eager to know more about the Russian exile's secret role in the region's violent intrigues, and so one night I asked Don Moi, *sotto voce*, "Is it true that Leon Trotsky, Frida Kahlo, and Diego Rivera visited Palenque?"

"Oh, that was well before my time," said Moi. "But I will give you the names of some people in town who might help you."

I began by asking Don Tenorio, the flower seller, a literary man who had read Gabriel Garcia Marquez and Mark Twain for the insights those giant authors might shed on a life dedicated to the cultivation of hothouse flowers. While we admired his black gardenias, he confirmed that Diego and Frida had made several trips to Oaxaca, but the journey to Palenque was less certain, because at that time there was no road. "Sugar cane is dangerous for trucks, impossible for a 1930s Ford sedan." Again I assured him that I had heard that Diego, Frida, and Trotsky had visited Palenque, and after weighing all the elements—time, distance, soil factors, degrees of moisture and heat—he shrugged his shoulders and said, "Then it must be true. They probably took the train and then rode to the site on horseback. That was before President Cárdenas nationalized the railroads and decreed that cutting down trees was a crime. The next year Cárdenas threw out Standard Oil, and then came the war. I was just a boy crawling in the dirt. I couldn't pronounce 'bougainvillea,' much less understand why they let the Germans plant rubber trees all over the ruins. It was a miracle that I discovered Mark Twain and the secret of propagating lilies without manure."

Don Tenorio did know a few songs from the Cárdenas era and kindly offered to write down the words. With luck, I might find the sheet music in the nun's shop up the street. Learning that the Sisters of Guadalupe operated the stationery store was a minor revelation, although I should have guessed by the devotion the saleswomen exhibited as they kissed each coin before wrapping my sheaves of blank white paper. Up until now, my purchases had been a pure act of charity. I had no way of knowing I was supporting the convent's benevolent deeds, because ever since the Mexican Revolution, the law has prohibited nuns from wearing habits in public. The edict, designed to erase distinctions between ecclesiastics and the suffering masses, was first proposed by Father Miguel Hidalgo, whose drive to separate church and state surpassed the most radical bounds of social idealism and sanity. Blessed with the sublime innocence characteristic of his vocation, Don Tenorio told me that during the Feast of the Ascension last August, Sister Columbina rose into his private pear tree on the wings of her hat.

"Palenque has moments like Macondo, the little town in Marquez's book. Surreal and unexplainable moments, but time here is much, much slower." Then, lifting his eyes toward the motionless clouds, he asked if the same were true for Twain's Missouri. I explained that Missourians were famous for not believing anything unless they saw it with their own eyes, not at all like Mexicans, who believe in anything hidden from ordinary sight.

"Well, if you don't find the sheet music, then you'll have to make it up," he said, as if everything hinged on a song.

As I walked to my next appointment, I pictured Frida struggling up the Temple of the Inscriptions, embroidered roses trailing from her hem. The carnation pinned to Trotsky's shirt wilted as he guided his delicate mistress up the rough limestone stairs. His taste ran to jasper and rubies, even in exile. Despite Diego's passion for pre-Columbian antiquities, his big feet were more comfortable on a ladder, raising him above this world of skulls toward a heaven of silent peasants where clouds parted and Zapata's white horse, Relámpago, trampled the conquistador's sword. Frida dressed her steel figure in

Spanish-inspired velvets from Juchitán, because Indian women there were tall and plump, their hands coated with corn meal rather than vermillion squeezed from a tube. The Indians of Chiapas wore rags. It was their endless war against the rich plantation owners, against the Spanish oppressors—against the ancient lords who commanded the building of the pyramids—that brought the famous threesome to this state. Graham Greene, who stopped in Palenque while investigating the government's brutal attacks against church and clergy, does not mention having met them. Nor is it known whether Frida acquired her jade necklace on that trip.

"I almost met her, would have met her if I wasn't inside my mother's belly," the dentist said with a forced laugh designed to calm my nerves as we waited for the Novocain to take effect. "My father was a jeweler. Frida drew a picture on a piece of paper and brought it to his shop. He made earrings for her out of solid silver melted down from coins." I wanted to ask if her father had saved the piece of paper, but Dr. Lourdes, anxious to start before the drug wore off, inserted the whirring drill into my mouth.

It made a certain sense that the jeweler's daughter became a dentist, insofar as the tools and metals were identical and both professions required the same innate patience and steady hand. Why she chose to apply her gifts to the repair of strangers' teeth was nonetheless difficult to comprehend. To encrust tiny holes with porcelain, gold, or silver, to wrench rather than adorn yellowed enamel seemed to me a miserable art since the remains go into the trash or grave. After the ordeal was over and my mouth regained its shape, I could not help but admire the woman's dedication to staving off, after a brief hour of torture, human suffering and decay. But the drill that rattles the brain is a piercing reminder of dead nerves and naked bone, as is the mortal blood spilled into the white sink, whereas silver earrings are eternal. Before I turned to leave, I noticed rows of false teeth lined up on the shelf, waiting to serve a regiment of hungry jaws: bicuspids suspended like stalactites; molars round as budding chrysanthemums; bridges of incisors, held on wires, that soon would come together over a crisp apple or broiled steak. The impoverished went about with one or two fangs hanging like withered plums from their mouths. As always, I promised to brush, though I knew my teeth one day would join the richly animated clacking sometimes heard underground.

I held Moi's list in my hand as if it were an answer, but decided to postpone my conversation with the priest, who, I was told, played dominoes every afternoon at the café across from the church. Mainly I was afraid he would know nothing and so subject me to a sermon on the cardinal sins waged by the Zapatista rebels and Maya Indians in general. The dentist's feeble mother might have imparted some delicious piece of information in her younger days, but instead she croaked, "No Germans here."

In fact, the town teemed with sweating armies of Germans, French, and Israelis dutifully touring the ruins before taking off for the breezy Caribbean. Not a single tree shaded the park or the sun-glazed boredom of the streets. Once past the souvenir shops, the pavement petered out into canyons of green swill. The barber played MTV as he scalped men's hair. The cybercafés stayed open all night. Pop music blasted from every market stall. But the soporific stupor caused by the awful heat blinded customers' eyes to the bins of wilted vegetables and rotten fruit trucked in from the north and the cheap sandals, watches, and cell phones shipped from China.

"What did I tell you? Nobody cares about art," Moi said when I returned, bedraggled, to the hotel. "I've lived here for fifty years. Nothing ever changes."

"I should speak to your friends Marcelino Vega, Virgiliano Flores, and Victor Hugo. They are the ones who mentioned the rumor about Trotsky and Frida in the first place. It's incredible that his political influence spread this far."

"Cowboys! What do they know of love and passion? They've only seen it in comic books. And you, you would be wise to forget about those rich and famous. They're too tragic. They'll only corrupt your spirit."

I had obviously touched a nerve, and Moi knew I knew it because he quickly changed his tune. "This is what you need," he said, pulling a well-worn little book from his back pocket. "An old-fashioned romance."

Chapter 6

WHEELS

That evening I read a vivid account of Désiré de Charnay's 1881 expedition to Palenque, written by his traveling companion, the Countess Vadishkova. She had boarded the train to the Gulf of Mexico, and as the cars lurched past crocodile-infested lagoons, the Frenchman described a paradise in ruins, palaces of divine pleasures, pyramids appointed by the gods. The explorer was not a handsome man, the countess tells us, though he possessed a certain rumpled vigor and distinguished cut to his gray mustache. His heroic exuberance apparently captured her interest, for when the train lumbered into Santo Domingo de Palenque she disembarked with him. The town was then a disappointing batch of palm-roofed shacks blistering on the jungle rim. They found hospitality with a jovial German rancher as well as a New Year's celebration, with plentiful food and drink, in full progress. Soon they were dancing with the local peasants round and round the bald lawn. During the festivities, Charnay invited the countess to his hut, and there, among heaps of maps, chemical solutions, and photographic plates, lay proof of the buried paradise: vision after vision of monumental decay. That night, amid the most terrifying roars, a peccary crashed through the door of her cottage and tore her mosquito net to shreds. Convinced that the bristling beast was merely a pig and not a bad omen, the countess set off with Charnay at dawn.

The ruins of Tollan lay through woods inhabited by a mysterious tribe called the Lacanhdong. Loaded down with packs and tripods, the pair tramped for hours through black mud. Pain and heat dissolved her strength. The green fever seeped into her bones. "Don't lag behind, my turtle," he called. "Fine wines await us at the palace."

"Where were the bearers?" she asked herself. Hernán Cortés made his march in the bright company of musicians and jugglers. Her guide was an irritating, boisterous, non-stop talker.

Adding to the dissonant choruses in the trees, Charnay maintained a measured patter concerning the grandeur of the Toltecs—temples of jade, palaces of gold, books adorned with turquoise stones—all of it the creation of a wise flying serpent named Quetzalcoatl, who was also the wind and Venus, Morning Star. When the trail grew steeper, Charnay's voice rose to operatic pitch as he counted out the names of the sacred calendar days: One Wind. Two Jaguars. Three Lizards. Four Snakes, and so on.

At midday they reached the royal cascades that tumbled through the lower gardens of Eden. An otherworldly atmosphere, enchanted and melancholy, hung like vapor in the trees. Charnay floated like a dead man in the pool while the countess sat by the water's edge, soaking her toes. Other women, she sensed, had wrested secret powers from this silver-veiled sanctuary. When her fingers touched something hard and smooth in the sand, she believed she had found forbidden fruit. The apple turned out to be a small clay disk with a perfect hole in the center. No doubt the ancients had a purpose for this instrument, but what was it? As Charnay swam slowly towards her, she smiled and held out her treasure. Out of the pool he lunged like a giant flounder and snatched the disk as if it were a fly. He looked ridiculous, a grown man on hands and knees, scooping up mud and giving no thought to his bare behind. As she observed the fevered spell he labored under, he uncovered three identical spheres. She placed the circles together and supposed that the addition of ten more would make a stunning little choker.

"You are a genius!" he cried as he wrenched from the earth a little clay dog wearing a round knob on each paw. "Wheels! You have discovered the wheel!"

Still searching the ground, Charnay found two thin sticks, pushed them through the holes in the knobs, then inserted the ends of the sticks in the spy holes, bead holes, air holes—*Voila*! To the sound of great cheers, the toy dog rolled into the water and swiftly sank. Then Charnay climbed into his shirt and pants, indicating that it was time to resume their journey. The countess tucked the dog into her bag, alongside her other mementos, not realizing that she had made the greatest discovery of the century.

They reached the sacred city by late afternoon. Gigantic trees enveloped the temples. The Palace Tower tolled for the mosses. Though the stucco figures had lost much of their form, the countess was able to discern a few noble portraits adorning the broad pillars and galleries:

"The ancestors are veiled in leaves and vines, yet the heart of the jaguar and wings of the trogon still beat within. Over numberless lifetimes their souls roared and sang, knowing the bodies of animals from memory, the shaking feathers from proud remembrances of flight. Lords of heaven grasp the tails of dragons and cradle them in their arms. The king, sitting cross-legged on a jaguar's back, his fingers plucking the air like a Balinese dancer, wakes from his long meditation and tells his story. Under the cold stone of the setting sun, his story winds like a serpent down the corridors and across the open courts: the wheel of the dog and the wheel of fate one clay, one blood, one family."

Under the cold stone of the setting sun, they made their way across the plaza and up a stony path to the House of the Count, a claustrophobic den, suspended on a cliff, with the darkness of the firmament for a roof. These austere chambers had provided a temporary home for the French-German pretender, peripatetic painter, and counterfeit scholar Count Jean-Frédéric Waldeck. Full of theories about ancient travelers who sailed the seven seas, he saw the features of wandering Chaldeans in every portrait, the sublime style of Greek and Phoenician artists in every smooth line of muscle, the trunks of Indian elephants on every god of rain.

The countess suggested that, to her untrained eye, the serpentine patterns surrounding the baroque figures had originated in ancient Ireland, an idea quickly met with loud guffaws. After the countess remarked upon the uncanny resemblance between Toltec motifs and Chinese dragon masks, Charnay beamed. He produced from his pocket a jade figurine carved in the likeness of a Cambodian leopard with eagle claws, serpent scales, and gold-tipped phoenix wings. The supernatural beast contained the most precious transformative symbols of the cosmos. Further, the rare feline dragon was a hollow vial holding thirteen drops of a powerful liquid, which the Javanese prince of Soerakarta guaranteed was the elixir of immortality.

"I drank. Flames burned the immense jungle fronds. Red macaws squawked, the fearful roar of howler apes trumpeted across the quaking forest canopy, and out of the jungle strode the regal apparitions of immortal Toltec kings. Behind them strolled three Celtic druids draped in ash leaves; Chinese sages in dragon silks, phoenix feathers flowing from their caps; a row of bald Egyptian priests bearing, on little silk pillows, green vials filled with tiger blood. Atlantean maidens swept into the moonlight, encircling the Vikings. Bearded Hebrew prophets, dressed in starched evening attire, raised their glasses as the women of the court made their entrance: the marquesa under a tiara of green quetzal plumes, the Spanish duchess in a black pearl gown, the Phoenician harem buzzing behind purple parrot fans. The Toltec queen lifted her jade train, revealing dainty bird slippers, the tiny sorceress adjusted her clay hat, and they reeled to the music of flutes and rattles. Grecian athletes leapt to a horned gavotte, the Chinese stepped to the gongs, the full orchestra struck up the Polonaise, and Désiré took me in his arms."

Not everyone imbibes a dram of foul liquor that makes one mad instead of wise. No sooner had the couple set up house than Charnay started chipping at those beautiful stuccoes with a hammer. Building bonfires to dry his paper impressions of the bas-reliefs, he accidentally burned down half the forest. The enormous frailty of his ego was made plain when he carved his name, in huge letters, on a column of the Palace. Next he made the mistake of charting the wrong goal.

Charnay's lifelong dream was to discover the lost city of Yaxchilán. According to legend, a subterranean tunnel ran from the Temple of the Inscriptions all the way to the remote site. Instead, Charnay and the countess followed a trail marked by jaguar skulls. Almost immediately they lost the mules. Then, after a brief but harrowing journey down the Usumacinta River, Charnay's ambitions were dashed in the last great bend of the river. The lost city was in the hands of the British.

Alfred Maudslay was bred of Anglo-Saxon wire, his trim body a vessel of nervous resilience, which he strained to suppress in the company of other mortals. Yet the thrill of being the first Western explorer to lay eyes upon the lost city shone through his bones. Maudslay had arrived by way of the Guatemalan jungle a mere two days before. Charnay was inconsolable.

"Today is March 20, 1882. I have missed my destiny by two days!" he cried. The artistic riches of the kingdom would go to the British Museum and not the Louvre.

As they climbed the main pyramid and gazed upon the river below, Maudslay commented on the whims of fate that had steered him directly to his goal without the slightest mishap. "Come, come, I make the ruins over to you. You can name the town, claim to have discovered it, do what you please. You may even dispense with mentioning my name."

Charnay declined this most generous offer, though he did confess that he had planned to name the site Lorillard City, after his wealthy patron, J.P. Lorillard, the French tobacco mogul. Maudslay had already named the city Menché Tinamit, after the Lacandon tribe that lived nearby. Inside the temple sanctuary, surrounded by pools of myrrh and smoking candles, sat the tranquil image of their god, Hachakyum, Lord of Creation, who has reigned over infinite cycles of death and resurrection.

Lingering at the feet of the huge stone idol, Maudslay imparted one final revelation. "They say dozens of sites lie along the banks of this river. The Usumacinta is the Nile of the New World, the heart of Maya civilization."

"Maya?" bellowed Charnay.

Maudslay took the countess's hand, and on the pretense of showing her a particularly fine stone, led her down the path. "My dear," he said, "Charnay is a rather pleasant chap, but he does not strike me as a scientific traveler of much class."

Chapter 7

SATURDAY NIGHT

Venus was making its first appearance as evening star, and the archae-ologists were throwing a party. Dr. Barnaby calls their pad his "base camp," but the name is misleading, because nobody on the map-ping team actually camps there nor is the place remote, although that depends, of course, on where you're coming from and where you're at. It squats in the middle of the Panchan Hotel, a faceless two-story structure with the rumpled, lived-in look of an all-American fraternity house. There's always a party going on. The five graduate students who crash there, upstairs and down, have plenty of energy to burn. Every morning they're out in the jungle tramping through the mud, follow-ing the course of the streams, charting, measuring, and mapping the unknown remnants of the city. It's tough physical work, and at two in the afternoon, when the sun has fried their brains to Rye Crisp and their chests are sweating like beer bottles just out of the fridge, they go home in a daze and start throwing down a case or four of Victoria's. They've been in the field for thirty months, but the ruins cover a three-mile radius and the work is never done.

Yesterday the crew discovered a new temple, the fifth this week, after the two hundred they've found this year. Eleven hundred new temples in all! They will go down in history, even if they never accom-plish another thing for the rest of their blessed lives.

When I came in, the boys were shouting about a tertiary intrusive they'd uncovered three feet under a jungle mound. Jim had set up his laser transit and was getting ready to shoot a point when he glanced down to check the legs of the tripod and saw two red eyes staring up at him through a chink in the gutted stone.

"I was scared shitless. Maybe it was a rat. Maybe it was a poisonous snake. There are plenty of them around. I'm just a surveyor from Houston. What do I know?" Jim took a quick swig of beer. "So Kirk sees me standing there like a zombie and comes running over. He stuck a long stick down the hole. But the eyes didn't move. It was spooky. The two of us were, like, thunderstruck. So we hollered for Pepe."

"Good thinking!" Barnaby nodded. "Pepe's absolutely the best man with a machete on the whole damn work crew." Barnaby's the boss, and he likes to keep his cool, but occasionally he'll loosen up and reveal his fallibility. "One time when I was walking through the brush, my boot landed two feet away from a nauyaca. They're deadly, man! The snake was about to strike. Pepe was standing fifteen feet away. 'Don't move,' he whispered. He raised his machete, it spun through the air, and the point landed right in the middle of the snake's head. He nailed it to the ground!"

"Hey, man, I was right behind you," said Jim. "Anyway, Pepe just sidled up and peered down the hole. Then he called for a pole and three shovels. They started digging, in that suffocating heat. Who knows what got into them. They must have been digging for hours. Pepe and them were soaked with sweat." Jim shook his head, totally bewildered. "It was a belt buckle, a Texas Longhorn belt buckle, with two red rhinestone eyes! How in the hell did it get in there?"

Everyone looked baffled.

"Must be an omen," said Podwell.

"Just another mystery of the Maya," Barnaby laughed, and poured himself another rum and coke.

"Way too deep for me," said Kirk. He was hunched at the dining table, one hand on his girlfriend's knee, the other scratching furiously on a yellow legal pad. He said he was calculating the hydraulic pressure required to fill the royal baths.

Mandolino, who usually chimed in with some witty repartee, now seemed perturbed with his buddies. Mainly he was trying to have a serious conversation with his mentor, the eminent Dr. Rhodes. In this crowd the genteel doctor stood out as a living artifact, silver-haired, lean, and a little stooped yet remarkably resilient after excavating potsherds for fifty years. It was his precise, painstaking work that established the chronological periods of Palenque, from its earliest days to its sudden demise.

"You know, I never found a plain, ordinary, everyday griddle," Dr. Rhodes was saying, "the kind they use to heat tortillas. I can't honestly prove that the Maya cooked their food."

Mandolino looked genuinely downcast. He had a different sort of problem. "Sir," he said, raking his fingers through his tousled blond mane, "I've found a beautiful polychrome vessel with a picture of a dog painted on the side. A floppy-eared dog! The zoologists say the only mutts in Pre-Columbian America were hairless, short-eared Chihuahuas. This pot proves they're wrong."

Barnaby interrupted. "We're working at the most beautiful site in the Maya world. I thank my lucky stars every day just to be here."

Rhodes was momentarily caught off guard by Barnaby's earnestness. "You know, son," he began, "oddly enough I came here purely by chance. One evening I was having dinner with David Rockefeller, Miguel Covarrubias, and his wife. 'Where in Mexico will you want to work?' Rockefeller asked. I said I didn't know. Covarrubias fetched a map and spread it across the dinner table, then picked up a linen napkin and blindfolded his wife. María turned twice, wagged her finger, and took a stab. Palenque!"

"Wonderful story, sir," said Barnaby. "But what I want to know is just how big, how vast, how old Palenque really is."

Dr. Rhodes frowned. "Patience," he murmured. "We just have to keep digging."

Barnaby kept shifting his feet, hoping for a better answer. Finally he said, "Damon, over there, sir—Sorbonne, second year—is analyzing changes in architectural styles. He thinks he knows the history of the buildings, but he's hiding it under his black beret."

Damon, so suave, so debonair compared to these Texans, was sprawled on the couch, drinking directly from this year's vintage bottle of Sangre de Toro. Now he roused himself from his post-existential doldrums and responded on cue, "Man is the essence of memory."

"Sweet," said Barnaby. "A propos of what?"

"The present is knowledge, the present is pleasure."

"Rousseau," said Dr. Rhodes.

Damon nodded. "*The Art of Enjoyment*. Derrida cites him in his essay on the origins of writing."

"Give me a break," Barnaby said. "We don't really need to hear more deconstructivist mumbo jumbo when we're working in a place that's already totally deconstructed. You're beginning to sound like the space cadets over at Rakshita's."

"There's more to my philosophy than you dare dream," Damon grumbled. "But I will admit, the French philosophers have little to say about Maya hieroglyphics."

Someone put on Lucinda Williams, and the conversation turned to Temple XIX and the delicate hieroglyph of a heron, or a hawk, or a cormorant with half-swallowed tail feathers and bird claws in its beak.

"Amazing image," Matthew piped from the corner of the room. "It resembles the emblem of Palenque. And the cormorant, *mat*, is part of the name for *Matwil*, the mythical birthplace of the gods."

"Did it ever occur to you that *Matwil* is a real place?" said Kirk, hurling his pen across the table. "Why does everything have to be so goddamned mystical? Think about it. Birds. Water. Maybe the gods and kings of Palenque came from some nearby lake. Those bird images look pretty real to me."

Matthew adjusted his glasses and stared at the image in his notebook. "All right, my brother, but how do we read it?"

"Not my territory, man. I'm sticking to aqueducts and water tables."

"A little more reverence, please. We are talking about the mother of the gods, represented by these glyphs: *muwaan*, a hawk, and *mat*, a cormorant with a mouthful of teeth. So, is her name *na-nal-ix* something *Muwaan-Mat*?" he asks, carefully enunciating the Maya syllables in his slow Texas drawl. "I've been wracking my brain all night."

"Beats me," says Jim, "Perhaps you could work it out by yourself and tell us later." It was easy to pick on Matthew because he was so clearly a nerd.

The birds appear on the recently discovered throne in Temple XIX, which shows a portrait of the king, Akhal Mo Nahb III, flanked by his nobles.

"No problem," Matthew says. "But what about those cords twisted around the nobles' necks and the coiled rope in the councilor's arms? It's a real puzzle."

Alux, who has been leafing through the bookshelf, wanders over to the table. "I don't know," he mumbles, "maybe the knot is related to the *pop* design, the woven rug the kings sit on. Anyway, the rope shows up everywhere in Maya art. Just like snakes! Maybe it *is* the skin of a snake, the longest snake on record." Now he's laughing and holding his stomach. "Maybe it's some poor guy's intestines!"

Podwell leaps to his feet. "No, it's 3, 4, 5! It's about root rectangles, Pythagorean rectangles, and the Golden Mean, the divine proportion! At the beginning of creation, the gods used a cord to measure out space. It says so in the opening passage of the *Popol Vuh*."

Kirk's girl gets up to dance, and three of the boys start shuffling to the strains of country rock.

"If only the Maya had left us diaries," Matthew sighs. "Or love letters."

Before the party I had done a little more reading and learned that the Maya originated in the mountains of Guatemala and then, about four thousand years ago, started spreading into Yucatan, Chiapas, Honduras, and El Salvador. Eons before, they may have journeyed across the Bering Strait, in the first or second great wave of Ice-Age hunters. They followed the herds and lived in caves not too far from Palenque. Some say they sailed from Asia on rafts. When they put ashore they settled in small fishing villages, casting nets across the placid waters and feeding on an abundance of clams. The remains of these shell mounds litter the dense mangrove swamps along the Pacific coast of Chiapas. Because their pottery resembles Japanese wares circa 1800 B.C., as well as bowls made in Ecuador around the same time, a handful of scholars assume the Maya continued traveling the seas, trading with Asia and South America. This notion of a prosperous, sea-loving people helps explain the Maya fascination with knots. The same was true of Bronze Age Celts, which may be why some nineteenth-century scholars believed that Irish sailors settled the New World.

The Maya have been living in southern Mexico and Central America since 3114 B.C., the mythical date of the fourth creation. The Great Calendar Round, with its endless cycles of repeating time, defined the course of history and daily life. Around 500 B.C. the Maya began building pyramids. Villages swelled into city-states and clan chiefs rose to the rank of gods who controlled the nine layers of the Underworld and thirteen levels of the sky. By A.D. 600 there were many centers in the Maya realm vying for political and religious power. Palenque stood at the western gateway to the Underworld, path toward death and transformation. A haven for artists and thinkers, the city became the Florence of its day under Pakal the Great and his son Kan Bahlam. Art, science, and religion created a unified vision of the universe. Scribes recorded the acts of the gods and the deeds of divine kings and queens. Mathematicians plotted the sublime proportions of the temples. Astronomers made sure the planets aligned with major royal ceremonies. By their calculations, the physical and spiritual worlds corresponded; plants, stars, and human destiny were intertwined. But the arrow of time flying swiftly forward toward the future also twisted slowly around in circles. Nothing could stave off ceaseless warfare and ecological ruin. The collapse of Classic Maya civilization marked the end of the rule of divine kings and the birth of a more egalitarian society rooted in pantheistic beliefs that survive among the six million Maya of today.

This slim historic outline was unknown a hundred and fifty years ago. When the first Western explorers stumbled upon ancient cities buried in the jungle, the Maya were a complete mystery. And they remained a mystery. Those early adventurers—army captains, priests, nobles, lawyers, and spies—had nothing to rely on but hunches. In time, they themselves became the stuff of legends, forging a history of discovery marked by innumerable, and indelible, false trails. Captain Del Rio, who found Palenque on the basis of glowing accounts provided by the eleven-year-old grandson of the Bishop of Chiapas, reported that the Palace resembled a ruined Roman fortress. Count Jean-Frédéric Waldeck, the notorious artist and rake, depicted the stucco figures as heroic Greeks. Désiré de Charnay believed the Maya came from Indonesia. The wondrous presence of pyramids convinced the Abbé Brasseur de Bourbourg that Maya civilization had its roots in ancient Egypt. After rigorous linguistic research, Augustus Le Plongeon proved to his satisfaction that the Maya, under Great Queen Móo, settled Egypt, Babylon, and China. Lord Kingsborough staked his fortune on the submerged continent of Atlantis. The Maya were simply muddled together with whatever exotic culture and secret philosophy captured the florid imaginations of the day.

While debates raged in esoteric circles, the average upper-class housewife learned of Maya art from the pages of interior decorating magazines. The vogue for drawing rooms furnished in "Maya style" predated Frank Lloyd Wright's house in California by a century. Public taste for the exotic made Stephens and Catherwood's travel accounts instant bestsellers. Essentially, Stephens concluded that the ancestors of the humble Maya Indians who lived near the ruins had built the temples and that the language of the hieroglyphs was their own written tongue. In time, this hypothesis proved to be the case.

It wasn't until the turn of the century that the slow, painstaking work of archaeology began bringing the past to the surface. While excavators were laboring in the jungle, unearthing pots or recklessly causing inestimable damage, linguists and librarians were quietly doing their own detective work. With the decipherment of the calendar dates, the Maya became a race of mystical stargazers with a preternatural knowledge of time. Thanks to recent decipherments of hieroglyphic texts, we can read the chronicles of once great kingdoms and marvel at their metaphysical wit and sensibility. The story is still unfolding as the young scholars at the Panchan bring their knowledge to bear on everything from puppy dogs, belt buckles, and indoor plumbing to hieroglyphics, art, and astronomy.

"You're all full of shit!" said Alfonso Morales, a chubby man in his early fifties who was looking a little bleary tonight. Alfonso was Moi's second son and a prominent archaeologist. "Not one of you shovels, not one of you digs, not one of you scrapes. None of you has lifted an artifact to the surface and pieced it back together."

"What are you talking about?" shouted Podwell. "I was the one who put together the whole damn stucco in Temple XIX!" He lit a cigarette and started pacing.

Dr. Rhodes walked over to Alfonso and placed a pale hand on his shoulder.

"Okay, okay," Alfonso grumbled. "But listen to them talk. They think archaeology is a priestly vocation. They look at a stone or a stela and see the gods. But it's all about spadework. It's just a job for the dumb."

Alfonso's cynical brand of wit is usually accompanied by nervous giggles and a wicked gleam in his eye. English and Spanish rush from his lips with the rapid-fire action of an AK-47. Like all his brothers, he started out as a stone carver, but because his brain raced too fast, he became a reporter chasing crimes and corruption throughout the state. When that career became too dangerous, he fell back on his fondness for limestone, went off to study at the University of Texas, and came home a dirt archaeologist. As Director of the Las Cruces Project, he and his team meticulously uncovered, beneath the jungle thickets where he played as a boy, the great ceremonial complex built by Ahkal Mo Naab III. Now he was waiting for a permit to excavate the tomb he discovered inside the immense Temple XX. Government delays were beginning to try his patience.

Podwell was still pacing. "And I'm the one who spent a year lying on my stomach, breathing in all those mercury fumes, excavating the royal tomb of Yax Kuk Mo at Copan, tunneling in every day, working with a goddamned dental pick." His face was bright red.

"The mercury's gone to your head!" said Alfonso. Podwell spun on his heels and headed for the porch.

Matthew ripped off his glasses and threw up his hands. "It's Venus, man, god of war."

"Uh, oh, here comes one of the high priests," Alfonso giggled as Barnaby handed him a cold beer. "And I'm the king," he beamed, rubbing his belly. "I require sacrifice and daily libations."

"Any news from the government?" asked Barnaby.

"No news is bad news," Alfonso said. "I may have to solve the problem in the traditional Morales manner—with a gun!"

"It's the curse of the tomb!" Barnaby laughed. Alfonso's face turned sober and bitterness crept into his eyes.

"I am your director, man. You'll see, the same will happen to you!"

"The boys are making maps, my friend. They're looking for solar alignments," Dr. Rhodes said softly. "The objects are lines. The artifacts are light, evanescent and fleeting."

"Pretty, pretty, pretty, the science of archaeology. And deep, deep, deep these human questions. But no, my friend," Alfonso smiled, "it's just a high-class form of drudgery."

Alfonso turned to leave when the woman moving her hips to the music caught his eye. "Hah!" he squealed. "What we need is sex, more sex, and more savage rituals."

The mysteries of the Maya grip men's souls like the tango, all fire, passion, and pose. But the dance they do is far more primal. Even men of heroic bent, who never cared for dancing, often find themselves practicing on the muddy jungle floor, alone. They will stomp their feet out of sheer frustration, accompanied by the dull beat of a hollow drum and the heartless drill of locusts rubbing their hind legs together. The footwork is basic: two steps forward, two steps back, whirl three times at some alarm, and always skirt the center. At the center lies an unbearable void, the weight of an unknowable history. Every carved stone is a question mark, a small encounter with mortality.

"There goes a brilliant man," Rhodes said to Barnaby, "having his waltz with death."

That night there was a party at Rakshita's, with the spiritual freaks gathered around a single guitar player who was singing old Beatles' songs. Over at the Jungle Palace the Sicilian reggae band was smoking up a storm. Tourists at Don Mucho's restaurant were dancing to Cuban *son*. No one was talking about the Maya. The drums kicked in at midnight when the fire dancers took the stage. The new one, Minerva, spun like a firebird in a red spangled bra and cutoffs. The drums at Alberto's bar shook the trees as Venus scaled the horizon. The spiritual freaks must have caught the planet's piercing vibe, because next time I passed by, the harem girls were clapping their cymbals and rolling their ecstatic butts. In the farthest reaches of the Panchan, the old sailor was adjusting his fishnet stockings and singing along to an old Judy Garland tape. "Some-where o-ver the rain-booooow . . . ."

And somewhere in the distant night came the sound of a single tom-tom beat, the slow, steady timbre of the Long Count calendar, which begins with the image of a hollow drum and echoes through the mansions of the moon and the celestial quadrants of the Nine Lords of Night: one *tun*, two *katuns*, three *baktuns*. . . thirteen *baktuns*, one million, nine hundred thousand *tuns* to the end of the Great Round—2012—and back to the beginning. Zero Day. Creation.

THE SPIRAL: AN INTERVIEW WITH DR. RHODES

I'll begin by saying there are two possibilities. The first cannot be tested.
The second, by employing neutron activation analysis,
is a greater possibility, and since this is the case,
I prefer to put forth the second
and not discuss
the original,
although
in time it may
prove to be correct.
That is, after a long career
of continuous excavations, I can say,
with only slight reservations stemming from
circumstances at the time—poor working conditions,
hostility on the part of certain parties—no names, of course—
my own youthful inadequacies—my methodology was perfectly sound.
In other words, I began digging close to the center, or rather
what I considered the center, since the site was then
shrouded in forest and only the ruins
we know as the Palace, Tower,
Temple of the Inscriptions,
and the Cross Group
were at all visible.
Later we found
the walls of earlier
structures, terribly decayed
and completely infiltrated by tree
roots thicker than my thigh, which obscured
the very idea of there being a deliberate
pattern to the stone. So, yes,
I began in the plaza,

digging a hole
three meters
by three meters,
down to the lower strata,
not as deep as one could go, of course—
not all the way
to China—
but still the proper
depth to determine that below the Pre-
Classic level there was little sign—scattered
ephemera, really—of human occupation. It was hot out there,
grueling work for me and the men, and at two we'd knock off and drive
back to camp for a beer. My wife, Gaby, would wash the sherds,
which, in hindsight, may have been a bad idea since
with the kind of technology we have now
it's difficult to date ceramic phases
when there's no trace of dirt.
In those days we washed
the pieces to get a good
look at the painted designs—
snakes, frogs, monkeys—and incised lines.
Who wouldn't? We dated by the art, the patterns on the cracked
plates and bowls. We used our eyes, never dreaming
atomic radiation would change all that.
At any rate, Gaby was pretty
miserable living in a tent,
scrubbing dried blood
and caked chocolate
out of everyday cups,
erasing the hard evidence,
as it were. It was our honeymoon,
and in hindsight I shouldn't have dragged her
into what became, for better or worse, a paralyzing obsession.
We could have stayed in New York, but we didn't.
I could have taught at Columbia or Harvard
but I wouldn't. I could have pursued
my deep interest in Olmec art,
particularly the mysterious

images of were-jaguar babies.
But instead I started on the second
hole, ten meters away, then the third and fourth,
slowly moving out from the center in a lazy spiral until I reached the
edge of the plaza and the woods. Heat, mosquitoes, and snarled
branches, the ants doing a better job than I at raising
grains of clay, slivers of obsidian
up to the surface.
You could
drown in mud,
lose an eye in that maze
of twisted roots, get tangled in the streams
—scorpions, centipedes, rats—
mistake a dead branch
for a mighty fer-de-lance.
Damn, those fat snakes can kill!
By then I was surveying the western zone,
getting gray sherds by the hundreds, and I knew
that area of shattered walls was once densely populated and
turning out pots a whole lot different from the pots
in the center. They lay there, flat and colorless
below the crumbling platforms. Or I fished
them out of the river, leaves and muck
clinging to the rims, handfuls of
plain, dull, weathered crockery,
the squat legs of the serving plates
looking like goose eggs, a sliced onion,
and I called that phase after the name of the river,
Picota. That's what I kept doing as I spiraled out and
found the orangeware and then the yellow and the white,
going down in layers like a huge wedding cake to
where there was nothing left but sand and
quartz pebbles. I had the whole
kaboodle—the ceramics of
the western periphery.
I could have stopped there.
Instead I moved slowly around toward
the east, where I came upon the bat designs that decorated

the wares of the nobility. The royal compounds
lay a stone's throw from the cascades,
and believe me, it was a pleasure,
the sound of water rushing
over the falls, the beautiful faces
in the eroding stone—jaguars, snakes, primordial
shapes with gaping teeth. And I could swim in it, the deep
blue pools glistening in the sun, and cool off whenever I
took a break. It occurred to me then that the sherds
were brown bubbles floating inside the earth,
bubbles inscribed with tiny messages
spouting from the nostrils of those
monstrous animals sulking
in the thickest part of
the teeming forest.
One night I was out there
with Gaby and the crew, and they
were truly spooked, the water in the moonlight
flowing like the giant white snake the Maya believe is
the road to the Underworld. When Gaby heard me talking like this,
she'd pack her bags and fly to Atlanta, which is where she was from,
or take the children to the beach for a month or two and come
back with a suitcase full of shells. Gaby tried so hard
to keep my head on straight, but by then, you see,
Palenque wasn't enough. After I found
the remains of imported ceramics—
vessels of widely different clays,
colors, styles, shapes, refinement—
I had to go further, find the sources,
cities that supplied them, whether the city was
part of the Palenque kingdom or not. I was
now circling, making my radius, maybe
thirty miles from the center, doing
just the same, digging a hole,
sifting through the mutable
sediments, which had shifted
to the alluvial beds you find on the plains.
Cattle getting in the way and ranchers who didn't give

a damn about ruins and thought I was completely mad. Ofelia,
who became the best damned field assistant I ever had,
despised those cows, but she had her ways
of convincing those stubborn ranchers
to let us excavate their swamps. I thought
if we could just get a bit further we would reach some
agreeable spot with a few trees where we could hang our hammocks
in the late afternoon, out of the way of the dust and wind. But no,
she married a ranch hand and left me out there with two heifers
and a chestnut mare. The land was full of oil derricks
pumping day and night, and the only good thing
about field conditions was the relative
softness of the bleeding earth.
Those boys were getting filthy rich
drilling the same black dirt. Oh, I've had my share
of passing pleasures, it's just that my desire, my overriding passion,
demanded so much physical effort with only occasional rewards.
Time, you see, was passing, the sun beating down on my head
day after day and lulling me into some blind reverie about
the past, a reverie so powerful I could see the hands
of the women coiling those flanged bowls,
turning the delicate lips outward
as they pouted in the shade,
brushing away long
black wisps of hair
from their bare breasts
as they leaned forward to daub
the exquisite polychrome I held in my hand.
On my fiftieth birthday I was standing in a pit up to my neck,
stiff as a rake and half delirious, hungry and thirsty
for more, sixty kilometers from the center
and searching for the frontier.
At the age of sixty, I was
digging more shallow pits
beside the Usumacinta River,
eighty kilometers from Palenque and
surrounded by jungle. The river had to be the border,
beyond which lay another kingdom wracked by roots and time.

To prove it, I would have to cross over and dig another pit.
Guatemalan rebels occupied the territory, I could hear
rifle shots at night, and several times I dove in
to rescue someone floundering in the water,
trying to escape. Sharks and crocs
infest that great muddy river,
and nobody knew how to swim.
I waited far too long for my opportunity,
what with the civil war and Gaby's illness. 'Too bad,'
she said to me toward the dreadful end. 'You never found
a kitchen full of plain cooking pots, black from the fire.'
It's difficult to admit that I never got down to
the bottom, and I never reached
the other side. And after all is said and done
I could have simply dug in a straight line. But I was
looking for artistic limits, the frontiers of shape, color, and style.
The spiral offers no escape, no frontiers, and no borders.
The spiral, I discovered, leads to infinity,
and if I were able to peer down
from a magisterial height,
the spiral would resemble
the sweeping arms of our galaxy,
the same design we find on the most ancient
Chinese pots, and perhaps if I had dug deeper, as I said
in the beginning, I might have found the pattern here,
but since I was moving out in space
as I was moving down,
I had no time.

Chapter 8

MAYANOIDS FROM OUTER SPACE

The trouble is, people don't care what archaeologists have to say. Certainly the ancient Maya are as fascinating as snowflakes and salmon and other marvels of our universe, but in an age of information over-load, coupled with—and this is no secret—an insatiable lust for enter-tainment, the average person finds he's better off avoiding subjects that require more than ten seconds of concentration. Widespread aversion to intellectual content, and the snooty experts who deliver it, brings on bouts of knee-jiggling impatience and the dread ADDS, defensive by-products of our revved-up sense of time for which modern medi-cine has no cure. The symptoms are especially common among the lunatic fringe, who, according to random tallies taken by the part-time sub-director of the Palenque Office of Tourism, Alberto "El Capitan" Morales, account for ninety-nine percent of the guests at the Panchan as well as a significant and growing majority of visitors to the ruins. Their opinion is not to be sneezed at, says Morales, and their opinion is that one or two interesting facts are sufficient. That leaves archaeolo-gists out of the loop.

In the rarified field of Maya studies, there are no facts, just edu-cated guesses and strong intuitions at the midnight hour of the day. And so, when a buff Israeli woman wearing combat boots and steel studs in her navel demands to hear a grand theory on the order of the Big Bang, Barnaby visibly shrinks; the best he can come up with is an uncertain, two-hour scenario that describes the Pre-Classic hiatus or the Late Classic collapse. When queried about Maya religion, Podwell stammers and stutters, at a total loss to explain the profound, multi-dimensional nature of the gods. The fact is, none of the archaeologists can relate to these supernatural beings, with their long noses, drooping lips, swirling eyes, and mirrored foreheads. Matthew usually ends up saying the gods of Palenque are gods of thunder and fertility. That puts audiences at ease. People with names like River and Luna, vegans on a natural high, are simply seeking confirmation that all cultures, all gods, are one.

Our resident archaeologists also live transcendental lives, contemplating forgotten theorems, forgotten wars, a dead written language, and the impenetrable nature of the gods. The material world they see each working day is completely fragmented: broken bowls, decaying temples, lifeless human remains. Nothing is ever whole. They waltz with Death, stare him in the face, as Dr. Rhodes commented, hoping against all odds for the great resurrection of the bones. And yet, after years of analysis, speculation, and sudden revelation, the local brotherhood of anthropologists still upholds the credo of their vocation: the truth lies in cultural differences.

Differences are a fact of life, for families, species, nations, and even for utopians who wish it weren't so. But the ancient rift between reason and revelation, between lumpers and splitters, sometimes cuts no deeper than appearances. When Podwell, Barnaby, and Alux huddle at a table, arguing about Maya this and Maya that, they attract wary stares. Only the bravest tattoo artists have enough nerve to approach them with a question. Was Pakal a reincarnated Egyptian pharaoh? Are the hieroglyphs Chinese? Is Palenque really ten thousand years old? Only to be put off by some long-winded discourse on the manufacture of stucco. Experts are just too square, too sharp around the edges. But looks are deceiving. At heart, the guys masquerading in cargo pants and Tiva sandals see themselves as spiritual descendants of a noble line of misfits, a line that includes madcap eccentrics like Lord Kingsborough, who manufactured, out of thin air, an article of faith New Agers cherish almost as much as healing crystals: the Atlantean theory.

In a bid for conciliation, Alux offered a free public lecture on Maya art at Don Moises's Center for Maya Studies. His PowerPoint presentation focused on portraits of men, and the question of the evening was not whether these figures were human or divine but why they had straight noses and long beards. Native Americans do not grow beards. Who were these mysterious strangers?

The evening backfired. Critical thinkers in the audience pooh-poohed every possibility Alux put forth. If Celts had journeyed to the New World, they would have carved Irish knots. Wandering Chinese monks would have built wooden pagodas with expansive spaces indoors. Greeks would have insisted on marble temples, Egyptians on pyramids faced with granite. As for the Atlantean theory, well, it was simply old hat. The Maya were never island dwellers. They knew they lived in a large country because they had walked across it, and they knew they lived on a planet, albeit one that floated like a turtle in the cosmic sea.

Apparently a new wave of thought had penetrated the diaphanous spiritual shield surrounding Rakshita's. Almost overnight, it seemed, a dozen blissful meditators adopted the 260-day Maya sacred calendar as the circular path toward salvation. Now the lives of Yellow Galactic Star, Caban, and the others were in step with the colors, tones, and auguries ordained for each blessed day. It didn't matter that this system, with all its intricacies and false hopes, was merely a springboard into the unfathomable pool known as Time.

The bottomless pool ripples in random circles from the incredibly complex mind of Jose Arguelles, an art historian turned mathematician and seer. The Dreamspell Calendar, as he calls his invention, borrows freely from the Maya sacred calendar and adds to it a set of philosophical equations so convoluted, so insubstantial, they would send Pythagoras running for his life through fields of beans. The system requires some rudimentary knowledge of arithmetic, so naturally the Panchan initiates have developed their own spin on the Dreamspell, avoiding all the numbers and concentrating on the dream. This way they can proclaim themselves an independent sect. The Palenque branch of the worldwide Dreamers worships the changing phases of the moon and at the same time believes the ancient Maya were displaced Hindus. Its blissed-out members are the white-robed hippies who sit inside the Temple of the Cross chanting Om.

The hardcore diffusionists—people who are always bumming cigarettes and saving up for bus fare to the next anti-globalization march or the annual Burning Man summer spree—are convinced that the only explanation for the Maya's astounding mastery of arithmetic and planar geometry is that the Maya came from a place further than Asia, further than Egypt, further than the sunken continent of Atlantis.

They came from outer space!

But which planet? Again, there is dissension in the ranks. Podwell may talk about Maya observations of the five visible planets, but those planets are not far out enough. No, the Maya came from a planet at the center of our galaxy, in the constellation of Sagittarius. Wrong, say the channelers who claim the home planet is somewhere in the Pleiades. Alcyone, a blue binary star born one hundred million years ago, is the popular favorite among the most esoteric astro-psychics. Old-school adepts are putting their money on Orion.

For years, Mayanists have searched the vastness of the night sky for the patterns of Maya constellations. After studying ancient texts, poring over painted ceramics, interviewing Quiché timekeepers, and observing the nightly motion of the heavens, art historian Dr. Linda Schele identified three stars in Orion—Rigel, Saiph, and Alnitak—as the mythical "Hearthstones of Creation," the birthplace of the Maya cosmos. Instantly she won a following among book-reading space cadets. But when epigraphers deciphered the ancient Maya name of Palenque as *Lakamha*, or "Great Waters," trekkies with contacts on Klingon were crest-fallen.

In short, alienated sci-fi addicts and old-fashioned racists refuse to believe that Maya Indians created an advanced civilization. As far as they're concerned, the ancient Maya disappeared from the face of the earth.

"Yes, it's a terrible shame," is on the lips of every star-crossed space tripper leaning at the bar. Mainly they're moaning about invisible forces threatening the world, supernatural entities beating them down, or mutating viruses that rot their teeth and make them itch to be on the road to Arcturus or Avebury Plain, to take a gander at the new crop circles. This aching, itching, peripatetic condition is clearly a warning of worse times to come.

"*Dios mío*! If they want to see hard times they ought to take a good look at the world around them," says Alfonso. "If they want to know about fatalism, let them study the real Maya calendar."

Actually it's a degenerative occlusion in the mind's eye. They cannot imagine that the cooks in the kitchen and the men waiting on tables are descendants of the people who built Palenque. It's easier to conceive of alternate universes, wormholes, and seven-foot lizards from Uranus.

And so, in the midst of growing angst over the state of the earth, all eyes turned heavenward. Not that anybody gave up sex and booze while waiting for deliverance. Just the opposite: the banshee screams got louder, the music more methodical in its madness. Bobo, a drummer from Haiti, and Guido, a drummer from Italy, put their shaggy heads together and with long cascading riffs on conga and bass became the pied pipers of the Panchan Space Project. Sure there was dancing, man, until your butt turned blue, and splif and yank and balling. But the main object of these moonlit sessions was to rediscover the mystical rhythms that accompanied the wild rituals that supposedly took place every night at the royal court. If Bobo and Guido could strike that beat, the sound would carry around the world, penetrate the widening ozone layer, soar through the stratosphere, and blast like a manic heartbeat across the light years to the Maya home planet.

What began as an innocent scientific endeavor, a driving need to communicate, led to deafening, non-stop drum practice and, in the end, all-out war.

Chapter 9

THE BOY IN THE CAGE

The distance between cosmic and mundane reality—a speeding comet streaking across the galaxy and the two fried eggs on my plate—sometimes collapses to the size of a bean or swells to encompass the edge of our solar bubble. Random fluctuations in time and space turn out to be more frequent than previously supposed: One minute you're up and the next minute you're down. It's a common experience, seemingly propelled by fate, and simple to explain if your mind races at the speed of light or you're able to leap through the paper-thin membranes that divide our world from the parallel universes spinning alongside us. Simple, that is, until Don Moises told me about Mexican stew.

A week after winter solstice, when the sun had just begun its journey north and dawn broke a minute earlier each day, Moises came up to my breakfast table and started moving the salt and limes. I thought I was in for another lecture on the solar system. But no, over the bare white cloth he unrolled a large white map and then used the napkin holder, ashtray, sugar and salsa bowls to pin the corners down. Throughout this careful operation he didn't say a word. By now I was expecting to see the precise location of a pirate island in the Caribbean, marked with an X. Instead, it was a crude layout of the landscape immediately around me, flat, lifeless, and buried under snow.

"Here's the key to all our troubles," said Moi, "the twenty-acre family vault." His diagram had none of the sophistication of Barnaby's site map or the elegance of Podwell's geometric charts, but I knew it represented layers within layers of emotional turmoil. I could almost see the thighbones and Moi stirring the pot.

The fortunes of eleven children were carved into thick rectangular chunks. The red lines that defined these separate properties slashed through trees, split streams, made neat and bloody cakes out of the chocolate mud. The lines bisected the trails of leaf-cutter ants, severed the roots of giant bamboo. From the dark smudges made with a dirty eraser I could see that fortunes shifted over time, just as dying trees put out new shoots and climbing vines strangle the *castañas*.

Trades had been made, private swaps, indicated by dots and dashes. One section of Doña Paulina's original parcel went to Chato, to support two cabañas and a long-term rental, for which he pays his mother a monthly percentage. In order to build Don Mucho's restaurant, Chato convinced Alfonso to throw in his lot for a share of the business. Enrique also turned his open plot over to Chato, three days after trading it for a piece of his mother's secluded orchard where he built a concrete bunker painted in army camouflage. Ariceli sweet-talked Aida out of a sliver by the stream, large enough to accommodate the two-room cottage she shares with her unfaithful boyfriend and two pet foxes, all within earshot of the late-night racket from Alberto's bar. Alberto's inheritance has doubled since he paid his father fifty thousand pesos for a strip of land running from the main entrance to the old swimming pool. His father spent the money on blue Oxford shirts and a color TV. The swimming pool, once marine, is now a nesting bog for vipers.

Some parents divvy up their assets while they are still alive so they can watch their offspring enjoy it. For Moi, it's brought nothing but sorrow. Worry fills his eyes. His magnanimous gifts have become, in the flash of a knife blade, the wave of a gun, an excuse for endless wrangling, of which Moi is the ultimate victim. "Another argument," he sighs, "Another round of macho threats."

Faced with the deadly competition between Chato and Alberto, Moi's sadness has turned skeletal. He's losing weight, he says, suffering "like an old woman" from curious fainting spells. It is impossible to tell him that at the core of his condition lies an ungodly blindness as his sins come to haunt him toward the end of his life. "I will do something," he pouts. "I will talk to the governor and the judge. I have a plan." His eyes brighten. Yet it is obvious that whatever feverish scheme he has up his sleeve will invariably make matters worse. Like Lear, he cannot help himself, another pawn of destiny cursed with the tragic flaws of pride and vanity.

His rash decisions are usually fueled by a night of drinking at Palestrina's whorehouse. He goes armed, and after a clash with the police or an argument with the whores who occupy the ten-foot, roof-less cubicles, Enrique, the big brawn in the family, has to drive out to the railroad tracks and carry the old man home. Sometimes Moi escapes without a nail scratch. Other times he gets so drunk he wakes up in a ditch with cuts and bruises and a gash at the back of his skull that requires fourteen stitches. The clotted wound or temporary limp takes less time to heal than his bad decisions.

It took a few days for his new plan to fester. With swollen lip, right arm in a sling, and the family gathered around his sickbed, Moi made a hoarse announcement: he would bequeath the last of his own land to Rakshita. She could keep her vegetarian diet, her Hindu prayers in peace and quiet. Who was he to mind? As for her vow of chastity when-ever he came around, all the more proof that she was his soul mate, his ideal love.

Rakshita promptly took a vow of silence, packed her saris, and left for India.

In the nick of time. Like bees smoked out of the hive, the children started swarming. The queen bee, Moi's estranged wife, swiftly retali-ated. Just to spite him, just to remind the old man of his marital bonds, she announced that she was moving to the Panchan.

At daybreak the workers started digging postholes along her prop-erty line, which wove through the brush, followed the stream, and came out alongside the main footpath. The dogs used the holes to bury their bones, but every few days some clumsy guest would fall in and break an ankle. In the wee small hours, their bone-chilling screams echoed like the anguished cries of a great demonic night bird. Besides the hellish effects on people's dreams, this eerie manifestation of Moi's feckless scheme was disrupting business, not to mention the delicate balance of the eco-zone. Guests and monkeys stayed away. Water seeped into the postholes and the streambed went dry. A plague of Indian horn beetles descended upon the native insects and left the cedar trees leafless. All these natural calamities were blamed on the invisible night bird.

Finally, after weeks of accidental spills and repeated threats to the environment, the job was done. The black dots and dashes that cluttered Moi's map materialized as a long row of wooden posts bound together with barbed wire. The mysterious bird disappeared, and in its place the clawed fence stood as a blatant reminder of Doña Paulina's formidable presence. As it turned out, Moi's shrewd lifelong opponent had no intention of moving to the Panchan. In her considered opinion, the hotel was just a breeding ground for mutant forms of life. Nature proved her right, because as soon as she flashed her steel wings and flew back to California the fence was swallowed by hybrid Japanese vines: living testimony to her incontestable half of the property and to her unshakable grip over that blond usurper who stole her husband's land and thoughtless heart.

After the posthole episode, the twists and turns of the family saga lifted off like a rusty propeller, mangling the local airwaves. Last Saturday night, Alfonso appeared on Don Moi's weekly cable show. That evening, on live TV, father and son tossed family issues aside and instead took aim at each other. Clearly outranked as a scholar, Moi rhapsodized about the advantages of independent learning, free from conventional academic constraints. "My knowledge comes through pure intuition," he crowed.

"Well, if you know so much, then write it down!" Alfonso insisted.

To his proud, impatient son, Moi muttered, "There are many things not written in books."

"Bull!" Alfonso shouted.

"Bureaucrat!" answered Moi. "You're just a peccary rooting in the sand."

Cut! The audience loved it.

Immediately following the show, live music resumed. That is, if you call a zombie bass beat competing with thumping Andean drums music. The congas chattering at mega frequencies don't count, of course, because their redundant racket is chiefly intended for non-human ears. Nonetheless, human ears were listening and grooving to the mix. You'd think there was a party going on, what with all the tourists writhing on the dance floor. But it was just one step away from an all-out row.

Something about the jungle brings out the savage beast, the dull, reptilian paranoia lurking at the base of the skull. For anyone unfortunate enough to be loitering in the immediate vicinity, the contests were worse than watching two cavemen bash each other with clubs. The brothers started sparring by steadily turning up the speakers. Soon they'd pull out their guns, stick out their tongues, and spit like iguanas.

Poor Alberto, born with a nameless condition, became the perfect scapegoat by the age of seven. Whenever he failed to play by the rules, his brothers locked him in the chicken cage and poked sticks at him until he went wild, lashing, thrashing, breaking china, striking at anyone within sight. This behavior the local doctor diagnosed as insanity.

The morbid part about these childhood games is that none of the boys outgrew them. Alberto became more perverse and cunning in his desire to blame and be blamed. And beneath their white business shirts and scholar's rags, Chato and Alfonso liked the smell of blood. They nursed their wounds, picked at the scabs, kept them sore and raw.

The father took Alberto's side because he was a crazy loser like his son. After every violent rumble, the exhausted Alberto would cry like a baby for his papa. And when Papa stumbled in, he'd beat the boy with a leather strap or hold Alberto's head under water until his defiant little face turned blue. As soon as he wriggled loose, Alberto would pick up whatever was handy—a lamp, a candlestick, a wooden mallet—and whack his father bloody. In the morning, Moi would forgive him. Now that Alberto was a grown man the two of them would sit at the Mono Blanco downing tequila shots at six A.M., Moi wearing a few stitches, Alberto all smiles. Joking happily, they were the perfect image of father and son. But when Don Moises started leaning over the table and whispering drunken words in Alberto's ear, you knew he was instigating another spineless plot against his eldest son. Chato the workaholic with gallstones and high blood pressure, Chato the rich one, Chato the success. The plot always involved a new and louder band.

The first petition to end the noise went nowhere. The second petition begged for police intervention. Nothing came of that document either. The third, again addressed to Alberto, with a copy to his boss, met with a three-page retaliation, accusing Chato of a host of illegalities: illegal possession of a gun; tax evasion; cutting electric wires; and hiring undocumented workers from the United States. What would the Secretary of Tourism say about that? *Ni modo*, she stated briefly, the problem was beyond the scope of her jurisdiction. Tourism, after all, was her main interest, as tourism was the main interest of the Panchan Hotel.

The long-term guests who were living here, soaking up the heat and mold and trying to bury their heads in the ancient Maya, were inevitably swamped by the brown wash of family rivalries, forced to stand by and listen as the late-night battle of the bands pitted brother against brother. So it must have been in the most ancient of days. Gunshots are intermittent.

Chapter 10

The Palace and the Tomb

Mingo was standing in his corn patch, looking at the sky, when Moi and I came up the path on a little mission of mercy. Mingo had been out of sorts lately, more distant than usual, Moi thought, and perhaps our visit would cheer him up. Moi's sullen expression betrayed his good intentions. His shoulders sagged as we walked across the dusty yard. Mingo had his back turned to us and in a ringing tenor was invoking the names of the three patron gods of Palenque—Hurricane Thunderbolt, Newborn Thunderbolt, and Raw Thunderbolt. He must have heard our footsteps crackling over last year's broken corn stocks because when we reached his side he was muttering about Lord Pakal's three sons, Kan Bahlam, Kan Hoy Chitam, and Batz Chan Mat.

"Pakal was cursed," Mingo was saying, "cursed by the gods. He simply lived too long. And the worst thing that can happen to a man, whether he is a king or a peasant, happened to him just the same. He buried his youngest son. God knows if the boy was murdered or if he died of envy. All we know is that he died."

Mingo turned around slowly and looked Moi in the eye. "The second worst thing that happened to Pakal is that his own sons wished him dead." Moi nodded grimly, wondering why he had come.

"Oh, they paid him homage when his round was done," Mingo continued. "But by the time his two sons got to sit on the throne they were already old men."

"Kan Bahlam finished his father's tomb," Moi said. "He built the Cross Group, with all its intricate hieroglyphic puzzles. He probably spent his years of waiting studying astronomy and mathematics. The years were hardly wasted. Those are subjects that teach a man something about time."

"Yes," said Mingo. "But by the time Kan Hoy Chitam became the king, he was so feeble that he was captured by the ruler of Tonina. That was the end of Palenque!"

"Well, they eventually let him go," said Moi, "after playing cat-and-mouse with him for ten years."

"The point is, my friend, no matter how often they dream about it, none of my sons will be anything more than workers at the site. Digging and piling stones Pakal's sons left behind. But you know what? Even though divine blood flowed through their veins, even though their sap was filled with silver rings and obsidian mirrors and little copper hatchets, invisible to the eye . . ." Mingo clapped Moi's shoulder and flashed a broad, welcoming smile, "they were probably a lot like our own sons—fighting all the time!"

Moi ignored the smile. He was watching the crows squawking in the naked avocado tree. "I see you have some very stubborn visitors," he said. He picked up a black feather and examined it in the light. "Even so, there's a beauty in their awful presence. You wouldn't want them to leave."

"Don't you see, Don Moi, it's all our fault. Even if we can barely walk, we're the ones to blame. You and me, we're like Seven Macaw. No teeth and too much pride!"

Moi was still distracted by the crows, the feather, the dappled light. Finally he said, "I think you spend too much time thinking about the past."

"Yes, I am thinking about the past, Don Moi. But I am also thinking of the present and the future. In my mind, they are mixed up together." He wandered over to the edge of the yard where two discarded children's chairs were lying on their sides. He dusted them off and motioned for us to sit. I folded my knees and dutifully sat on the little chair. There was a long silence while Mingo rocked on his haunches and drew a line in the dirt. "That's it, then," he said with a sigh. "If you won't tell the señora the story, I will." His eyes scanned the sky as if the words were written in the clouds.

"Long before the world was made, long before there were crows in the trees or fields of corn or anything besides water on the surface of the earth, there was a giant bird named Seven Macaw. His feathers were the rainbow, his beak was a golden beam of light, his eyes were made of precious metal, and his wonderful teeth were made of fine turquoise stones the color of the sky. He shone like the sun, long before there was the sun. 'I am great,' he said. But he wasn't the sun. His light didn't reach beyond his perch to every corner of the earth. He just puffed himself up. And his two sons—Zipacna the Crocodile, maker of mountains, and Earthquake, mover of mountains—acted just like him.

"The twin boys, Hunahpu and Xbalanque, didn't like it. 'He's just metal and jewels,' they said. 'What if everybody acted that way?'

"So they hid in the leaves of the nance tree, and when Seven Macaw came to eat the fruit, Hunahpu shot him with his blowgun. The shot hit Seven Macaw right in the mouth. His jaw was broken and his teeth came loose.

"Just then old grandmother and grandfather came along. They were traveling around curing people's eyes and pulling worms from people's teeth. Seven Macaw was lying on the ground screaming his head off. 'We'll just replace them for you,' said the kindly old couple.

"'Please do me the favor,' said Seven Macaw. So grandmother and grandfather pulled out all the bird's turquoise teeth and replaced them with white corn. His face completely sank. And then they trimmed his eyes and all the metal fell out. He lost all his jewels, all his pride and arrogance, and he died. There was evil in his vanity and self-magnification."

"Very good," said Moi, "but I don't see what that story has to do with me. I've never had jewels and riches, or even a good set of teeth."

Mingo was just as irritable the week before when the three of us paid a visit to the ruins. It was a cloudy morning, and the stones seemed to be made of ice. The sweeping staircase of the Palace had a hollow ring, and the great halls were weightless. Centuries of rain and ash had dissolved most of the stucco scenes on the massive white pillars. Moi pointed to a fish stranded in the underworld sea, a sandaled foot, a snake, a seated figure held by the hair still waiting to be sacrificed.

"Pakal was only thirteen when he became king," Moi told me. "And the first thing he did was build this palace."

"Yes!" Mingo interrupted. "But the rooms are too long and too narrow. Who would want to live here? These are rooms made for pacing."

Mingo straightened his cowboy hat and with the confident stride of a Mexican rancher started counting out the length of the hall. "Seventy-two," he called as he turned the corner. Rows of wide-eyed stucco masks scowled from the mansard roofs as we followed him onto the sunless terrace overlooking the great sunken court. Mingo was down on the bare grass, counting.

"Here the king entertained his guests," said Moi, spreading his arms before an invisible throng of women dressed in fine gauze robes.

Mingo paused before the two-ton slab that served as the royal throne. "Who knows, maybe he lived in the dungeons underneath us. He could lie there on his long stone bed and think. Things were in bad shape, you know."

"Not as bad as things should be!" said Moi, taking my hand. "If you mean the war with Calakmul, it happened long ago, in his grandmother's time. Calakmul, it's over in Campeche. As you can see, Pakal brought this magnificent city back to life." His serene hand gestured toward the giant figures leaning against the eastern stairs. "There are his noble captives, with bloody paper strips in their ears, clenching their fists, stilling their pounding hearts."

"Think about it, Don Moi. It didn't happen overnight. It takes a lot of work and sacrifice."

Moi wanted to linger in front of the house he called the coronation room. Its white plaster walls were decorated with floating yellow eyes. Through the doorway I could see the portrait of Pakal seated upon the double-headed jaguar throne as his mother, kneeling beside him, offered her son the crown. But Mingo, disgruntled with the scene, said the queen was just a harpy. Off he strode, across the yard, past the Tower, and down a black hole.

The tunnels were damp and muddy. Many passageways were blocked. A white, unworldly light seeped through two thin gashes in the wall.

"This is where he came to pray. Here is where he lived," Mingo said triumphantly.

"What kind of tour is this, leading people through the dark? This is no way to see the Palace."

Moi was right. Being in the company of two quarrelsome old men aggravated the hostile presences. Despite what Mingo said, the subterranean chamber was haunted by brooding, nagging despair.

When we came into the light, Mingo was contemplating the great pyramid. Moi said, "All right, then. If we want a grand view of the Underworld, we should see the tomb."

"No thanks," said Mingo.

I saw what he meant. The tilt of the stairs was so vertiginous I felt I would plummet, without a sound, into an abyss deeper than the tomb. This was the way to the land of roots, of lost souls laboring under the night sun, and skulls laughing in the dark. The stones were slippery, the windowless air cold. With every step I thought, "I am in the house of death. I will look upon his face and beg for a longer life."

At last we reached the thick triangular door and stood before the immense sarcophagus lid. I had less than a minute to reflect on the figure of Pakal hovering above the skeletal jaws of the Earth Monster.

"What do you think?" asked Moi. "Some people say the king is falling into the Underworld. And some say he is rising up, reborn."

"Up? Down? For sure he died, took the road like anybody else," said Mingo. "And then he came back to life, not right away, of course, but just as soon as he paid off his sins: so many years for beating his wife, so many years for envy, lying, cheating, stealing, setting himself up like a god in his own house."

"But he was a king and a god," said Moi. "He wasn't an ordinary man like you or me."

"Then they should take these bars off the door. You'd think he was in jail."

"He rose like a planet and joined his ancestors in the heavens."

"Hah! So that's the answer, then. The carving is showing us both— life, death, death, life." Mingo knelt in front of the bars and crossed himself hastily. "Thank God my sons can't afford to bury my corpse under huge blocks of stone and leave me to rot here, cold to the bone."

"But maybe you wouldn't be lying here for long," said Moi. "There's the great tree carved in the middle, reaching toward the sky."

"Ah, but you have to be dead to climb it, Moi."

"If you listen to some people—people who know nothing about the Maya, people who know nothing about trees—the picture is showing Pakal driving a rocket ship. Yes! They say the beard of the Earth Monster is the flame of the rocket ship and Pakal is sitting at the controls."

"Shit! Excuse me, señora, but it would be far, far worse to escape that way."

"True. No matter how bad it is down here, you'd never want to leave the earth, especially on a cloudless day."

"Lord, I've seen the sky rain down with ash. And so have you, Don Moi."

"Yes, fire in the desert. Thorns in the cattle."

"Besides, Pakal had the soul of a king vulture. Why would he ride in a rocket ship when he could fly?"

"A vulture? Where do you see a vulture?" Moi bent over, trying to peer through the bars. "Hah! You mean that bird at the top of the tree? If we could get a closer look, you'd see it's partly a bird and partly a snake."

"Too many birds!" said Mingo.

The magic bird lingered in Mingo's mind over the week, because after he finished the story about Seven Macaw, he said to Moi, "That snake bird on Pakal's coffin lid, it's not a vulture and it's not the vain parrot either."

I mentioned the invisible night bird that haunted the Panchan. "One too many birds," I joked.

Moi confirmed that indeed a host of mysterious avian creatures inhabited the Maya forests. "But not too many," he corrected, "simply birds of another dimension."

Mingo looked a little sheepish when he turned to me and said, "Moi is right, señora. He's not at all like Seven Macaw. He's never done anything that would make him feel guilty. The reason he has no money or a single tooth in his head is because he is as innocent as a newborn baby."

With that, Mingo picked himself up off the ground and steered Moi towards the house. "Come on, Moi, I'm going to make you a present."

Mingo's old thatched house was gone. In its place stood a square concrete block with a red tin roof and a wide covered porch. His son Tito, home from his job digging at the site, was stuffing tortillas into his mouth. Mingo's daughter Minerva was standing primly at the *comal*, heating the tortillas as fast as her brother ate them. Without looking up, she placed bowls and spoons on the wooden table. Out of the corner of her eye she glanced at her father as he slowly ruffled through the pages of his green notebook.

"A lot of good that does us when we have nothing to eat," Tito spat. "Remember that idol our father used to keep under his bed? If we had it now, we'd be rich."

Mingo glared at his son. "What sort of talk is that, little father? We have beans, we have plenty of tortillas for our honored guests." Tito removed his old straw hat and shook his damp black hair. His thin face was streaked with dirt.

"Let him, talk," said Moi, rolling a fresh tortilla in his hands. "Some friendships can stand up to money. But you know," he said, turning to Tito, "money is useless in the end. The ranchers would like to buy your land, your cornfields. But then you'd be homeless."

Moi glanced at the tree, the mountains framed by the doorway. "Listen, I will tell you something. When I was a boy I grew up in Buenos Aires. Oh yes," he laughed. "But it wasn't in Argentina. It was the toughest neighborhood in Mexico City. The streets were full of rats, the kind with four legs and two. At the end of my street there were little trees. They were growing in the cemetery. My mother gave me a handful of seeds. 'Here, plant these,' she said. And that's what I did. I climbed the wall and planted them in the graveyard, there among the crosses and the bones. And they grew, ten tall stalks of corn. It was a miracle! I thought to myself, 'We are so lucky, so lucky!'"

Tito was silent for a while, and then he said, "You're right, of course, Don Moises. But just think if the government would pay us for what they've taken away. It's we, the Choles of Naranjo, who own the site of Palenque. The temples and the pyramids still belong to us. We should fight them. We should take it back."

Moi smiled. "And you, Tito, will lead them into battle! You're skinny, tough, and angry. You would have fit right into my old neighborhood."

Mingo looked up from his notebook. "Pakal was a great warrior, too. He was also a great magician. You can see it in his eyes. They look blank because he is hiding something inside, something sweet and cold. He's calm, like a doctor. They say he was also a great ball player, but you can't believe he sweats. No, when they talk about the great magician who was a prince, you know they're talking about him."

"Is Pakal, 'the great magician,' as you call him, going to defend us against the government? Is he going to feed us?" asked Tito. "And where are his gods? The Lacandons say the gods have abandoned Palenque. I believe it's true."

Mingo tore two pages out of his notebook and handed them to Moi. "Patience," Mingo said. "The story isn't over."

Chapter 11

CORN

I woke to the sound of wheels rolling on thunder, and for a moment I believed that the Maya had invented the wheel and the wooden cart, which would spare them from hauling a hundred pounds of corn on their backs, stacks of wood, sacks of jade, or cages stuffed with squawking parrots. Bent under their heavy burdens, occasionally stopping to wipe away the sweat, the men plod along the jungle roads just as the gods carry their burden of days over the hills toward home. When their bags are full of corn, the men say it's a small price to pay for a handful of Our Lord's sunbeams.

Chachalacas were streaking through the trees, scratching black lines in the reddening sky, and the cicadas were ringing electric. The world around me was growing, decaying, sucking up light, excreting fumes, animal and plant life constantly competing, building things up, tearing things down, and despite the incessant clamor, I felt as if I were living in a vacuum.

In fact, I was living in a hotel, and the wheels were on the undersides of giant suitcases rolling in and out of rooms at dawn and down the path of the Ruta Maya: a steady stream of tourists come to see the ruins before flying home to Germany or Peoria. They were on the move, not lingering long enough to catch the green fever or sense the shriveled souls buried beneath the clay.

Or are the dead just idle seeds waiting for the rains to release them, to sprout and burst forth for a season in the heat, put out one solitary cob, and shrink again into the tired soil? Corn does not move, corn does not need a vacation. Mountains, swamps, and deserts are its home. It pervades every ecosystem except the long white beaches of the Mexican Riviera. There the gulls are dependent on fish, not flora, and tend to ignore the hard green husks. Corn relies on human populations if it wants to wander and reproduce. White corn, yellow corn, red corn, blue corn, black corn.

A people who believe they are made of corn have no desire to roam. Their sap thrives on rainwater. Their feet seldom stray beyond the furrows. They use the kernels of their teeth as units of measure. Their graceful arms ward off the gathering crows. Females tie their hair in braided tassels, which they toss flirtatiously as they walk the fields. When moist May breezes sweep the glowing dawn, they brush against the boys as casually as feathers. And so they multiply, in a seasonal rush related to the directional winds and the benign angles of sunlight. Too strong a wind and they will topple, too weak, and they will wither.

The miracle is they created a civilization based on the conviction that they were essentially vegetal, golden yet motionless. Animals may be heartier, but animals wander and die. Corn decays, but after a long, arid winter its seed springs to life. This is the singular advantage so difficult for the rootless to comprehend: people who plant themselves in the soil have a rounder sense of time.

Imagine a culture composed of a million plants spreading across mountain slopes, jungles, and marshes, beating off invading armies like epidemic pests, and then raising shrines where they worshipped corn.

How humble a god whose greenery dusts the blazing dirt, whose silken tassels sweep the sunlit air, guzzling water like no tomorrow and waiting, always waiting, to be plucked from the stalk, boiled, ground, pressed, and tossed on the griddle, then rolled and nibbled—sacrificed—like a common vegetable.

The natural pattern of living and dying, growing and decaying was the first law of being. After each small death, life began again. "Life, death, death, life," said Mingo, and indeed it was hard to know which was the beginning and which the end. Did the promise of a new birth allay his fears, provide genuine comfort, and a reason to go on breathing? He seemed to face this undivided world of dreams with furious resignation.

There had to be another purpose, a greater god behind this grandeur. There had to be more to life than eating.

Chapter 12

MINERVA

Minerva standing over the sink, Minerva down by the stream scrubbing sheets, Minerva sick and tired of her brother. Always angry, always with a chip on his shoulder. "*Bruto*," she wanted to call him, but of course she didn't. He might throw something at her, you never knew. All his big talk against the government, against the ranchers, was just a little boy complaining about his supper. Yes, they were poor, but like her father said, they had enough to eat, not chicken every day but chicken once a week. There were always eggs and sometimes crawfish in the spring. She would fix greens if anybody would eat them. She'd make pork if they had a pig. Complaining just didn't seem right. They should be grateful for what they had, she thought, grateful to be alive. That was the trouble. Tito was never grateful for the smallest thing. You'd think the saints owed him sweet breads every day, instead of the other way around. But he never went to Mass, he never even prayed. He'd just strut around the house Sunday mornings and then go out and chase the girls. Stupid macho. That was what bothered her most of all. He thought he was a gift, even though he couldn't grow a decent mustache, just went around the neighborhood whistling in those baggy jeans Melchior sent him from Texas. And the way he expected her to have comida waiting on the table when he came home from the site, smelling like a monkey. Just because their mother was gone didn't mean she, Minerva, had to do all the chores. Why didn't he bathe before he ate? Why didn't he sit down quietly and ever ask her how she felt? She had watched that movie where María Felix hits that *huapo* ranchero over the head, and she had heard about the fuss over Gloria Trevi, and though she hadn't given herself to any man yet, she would one day, and that man would be rich and kind.

But where would she find him? Not sitting beside her stove. And how could she attract him when she had no clothes? She'd seen pictures in the magazines of long-legged blonds with big breasts and pouting lips. They were lying on the beach in Acapulco or waiting for a taxi on a crowded city street, black silk with little silver stars falling from their shoulders. She could never manage that, no matter how hard she wished. It was bad enough crossing the main avenue in Palenque, and Palenque was just a little town, people said.

Once her father offered to take her to the ruins. It cost thirty pesos for one ticket, and they couldn't afford it. Her brother was right: the ruins should belong to her people. Yes, it would be a good thing if Tito and the others told the government about that. But what if he picked up a rifle? He was crazy enough to do it when he got riled up. And that was the other thing she was afraid of, his temper. It could get him killed, and as mean as he treated her he was still her brother and she certainly didn't want him dead. Look what happened to Gamaliel down the road when he joined the Zapatista rebels. Shot in the back in Ocosingo and buried in some ditch. So handsome, and her friend Maria's older brother. Those raccoons in the army don't care about shooting Indians, and they're Indians themselves.

She, Minerva Maruch Krus Krus, knew her people descended from royalty, because her father had told her about the great queens of Palenque, Lady Yohl Iknal and Lady Sak Kuk. "One day I'll show you, *mi reina*. I promise." He called her "my queen" even though she was short and skinny and had no breasts. "You wait," he said, but nothing had come bursting out yet.

The queens were the daughters of Grandmother Moon, and all their powers bloomed like melons under her light. The queens were moon goddesses in human form, shimmering and dark, luminous and wrinkled with shadows. "A young girl is the crescent moon," he told her. "The new moon is a toothless old woman, the full moon is a woman in her prime."

For many nights she dreamt of the moon stepping down from the sky and turning into a beautiful lady draped in silver. She looked like the Virgin Mary, Queen of Heaven, except that her bridal train was a long lizard tail and she sang with the husky voice of Toña la Negra. Oh, the mystery of the moon's many sides was deeper than moonlight, and the change from moonlight to a living queen was stranger than blood. Her own monthly blood was tied to the phases of the moon and the river tides. And that's why so many women conceived at the new moon and had babies when the moon was full, her mama told her. Their flow was in harmony with Our Mother. And so Minerva started walking in the *campo* late at night, and when the moon began to rise, she'd feel a warm wave rising inside her womb and flooding her entire body. She'd feel like a Maya queen. But she never saw the moon bleed. And she knew she wasn't a queen.

It was then she wondered why no one talked about the princesses dressed in gauze skirts and jade earrings. Her life could be like that, because after all she was Maya. Even Tito, when he was in a good mood, called her *la princesa*. For weeks she saw herself as a dark Maya beauty wrapped in a white sarong, sweeping the palace halls with a good straw broom, rising at dawn to heat the tortillas over a silver *comal* and feeding them to her brother, because that was the kind of princess she was, and after her father and brother left for work she'd entertain the Lord of Tonina and the Lord of Tortuguero on the porch. They always brought wonderful presents—spangled dresses and crystal beads—but when they asked for her hand, she turned her head and whispered, "No."

And when she thought about why she always said No in her dreams, it occurred to her that what she wanted most of all was to escape from this house and be free. Free as the moon, free as her mother.

"You cannot leave," said the king. "You must stay here and take care of me."

And that's when she started thinking about the Panchan Hotel and the girls she heard about who danced with fire.

Minerva forgetting the salsa, Minerva banging the pots, Minerva dancing around the yard at twilight, Minerva stitching sequins by the fire, Minerva gone from the house for hours, Minerva spending the night, two nights, three, at Maria's. Minerva!

Chapter 13

FANDANGO

Alberto acquired a new weapon. His name was Pedish, a sad-eyed minstrel from Veracruz whose voice was a cross between a foghorn and a toad. His guitar sounded like a dull hatchet that chopped anthems by the Beatles, hymns by Bob Marley into leaden calls for hopeless revolutions. Night after night his merciless grunts through the bad mike distorted love into hate. And yet he was no bigger than a cannon. After he belted out "Born to Run," guests who were trying to sleep got down on their knees and prayed he would disappear down some lonesome road to hell. Chato tried to pay him not to sing. Big John threatened to wake him at six with Tchaikovsky's 1812 Overture. That would show him. But when Pedish turned up the amps and his croaks splintered the nervous edges of the forest, setting off the howler monkeys and ragged parrots, why then it seemed certain that his brash caterwauling was some sick provocation. He was a wounded animal with a tin ear just asking for trouble. Throw rotten tomatoes at him. Drown him in the river. Shoot him!

You had to admire the guy for malingering in a place he wasn't wanted. But his steadfastness was not born of courage; he was stubbornly hanging on for dear life. Finally he had a permanent gig, which kept him on stage every night, through sudden storms and insect swarms, a dedicated postman with no letters to deliver. There was never an audience. His awful voice, his stringy white hair, his diminutive stature, made him a target, a desperate sorrow. Karma was at work.

It was hard to believe he was just a pawn in Alberto's demented plan to attract customers. He did his job too well. Pedish pitted his voice against the soaring Andean flute, shouted down the thumping drum pounding out "*El Condor Pasa*" with a gravelly rendition of "I Shot the Sheriff." No one was interested. They were eating garlic bread and pesto and downing margaritas at Don Mucho's. How could he compete with the anguished drums that accompanied the frantic girls dancing inside the flames? "What's Goin' On?" he would sing. Well, the cow with bad milk, the woman with blue eyes, the bitch with a grudge, the man with a gun.

But after the Andean music and fire dancers stopped for the night, a few tourists would straggle over to check out the noise. On weekends the heat-soaked rowdies from Palenque would screech into the parking lot, sit in the back of their pickup trucks, drinking beer, and scream until four A.M. Compared to the local disco dives, the Mono Blanco was free. Here was a live showman who could drink toasts in twenty languages—*salud, l'chaim, skol*, here's looking at you, bottoms up—take a swig of Fandango rum, and launch into a trumpet solo he played with his lower lip. Then he'd croak some colorless song about marijuana and shake his snow-white hair.

One day a bear of a man arrived from Austin with a guitar case and a voice like James Taylor. He sang the blues. He sang the sweetest lullabies. Chato hired him to sing at ten o'clock, just when Pedish began to bellow. The first night, Pedish sat at the edge of the spotlight, croaking to no one, while the bear held the crowd in his paw. Of course the music clashed, but no one would have guessed that Panda's mellow sound would arouse the gnome's ire. A tormented wail split the air, followed by horrific shrieks and howls. The bear answered with a deep growl. Words of pain and loss, of troubles by the score, ricocheted off the hills, the stone halls of the Palace, and filled the sleeping town and forest with plaintive human cries. Croak and roar, moan and shiver, trumpet farts and arching slaps on the guitar echoing as far as the rings of Saturn. "My ba-by left me . . . ."

The dark and dirty muse of American blues was driving Alberto mad. He got out his pistol and threatened to shoot his brother. He cut the speaker wires, beat his wife, threatened to knife the musicians, strangle the bear, and smash the gods. He was on a rampage.

The gunshots sounded like firecrackers—pop, pop, pop—but the cracks were too fast and there was no hissing aftermath. People eating dinner dropped their forks and stared, stone-eyed, at their pasta. Then the squeal of rubber tires and a vehicle crunching gravel.

Enrique was the first to see the bleeding bodies lying prone in the parking lot. They lay like rag dolls, in flattened jeans and empty shirts. The gravel was silent; the river stopped running. Then the sirens blistered in, and ten policemen started searching the pickup trucks. The rest of the force huddled together like a stand of frightened trees. Alberto was wearing an insane smile and playing the perfect host while Don Moises stood in the shadows, drawing a picture of a black sedan.

Was it a drug deal or a case of unrequited love? Alfonso, the cynical ex-reporter, shrugged his shoulders. "This is Mexico," he said with a nervous laugh. "We'll probably never know."

The bodies were still lying in a red pool. The restaurant was hushed and the waiters stiff as pillars until the cashier put on Manu Chou. The guests went back to their cold bolognesa. The fire dancers wiped their tears and wandered off to change for the show. Panda strummed his blues guitar, Pedish downed another rum and swung into his deadly rendition of "Let It Be."

Miraculously we received news, or at least the official version of the news, this morning. Maricela Sandoval of the nearby town of Pakalna asked her fiancé and her new boyfriend to meet her at Don Mucho's restaurant. Her fiancé was a bartender, her boyfriend a waiter, and they both worked at the same seedy joint, known to be a hangout for drug dealers and crooked cops. The girl had been engaged to the bartender for two years when she suddenly broke it off and left town, the little diamond engagement ring still sparkling on her finger. Supposedly she met her young lover at computer school in Sinaloa, a dangerous place by anyone's standards, and the two came back to Palenque together, very much in love but without their diplomas. For some reason, the girl gave the engagement ring to her new beau, who wore it on a gold-plated chain around his neck. Her old flame was still bitter about the breakup but enraged about the ring. And so, the teen femme fatale arranged a meeting at a pleasant outdoor restaurant where the three of them could talk peacefully. She didn't show up, but both rivals arrived with seconds. The four men stood in the parking lot. Two of them were armed. Without a chance for an argument, the bartender shot the waiter and his cousin six times. Bullets entered the knees, the legs, and the head. The bartender and his friend jumped into a black sedan and drove over the bodies on their way to the main road.

The dead lover had a cell phone in his pocket, and the first number listed on his phone belonged to Maricela. The police found her house without any trouble, and when they broke down the door, the girl was drinking tequila with the man who shot her lover. Thanks to the swift hand of justice, the murderer *and* the young woman were already in jail.

Obviously a number of particulars were being swept under the rug. That, along with the abnormal efficiency of the local police, raised suspicions. Of course, a town dependent on tourism had to demonstrate some respect for law and order. But usually the degree of respect was in direct disproportion to the high level of anarchy and unsolved crimes. Enrique thought he had seen the bartender and the victim drinking one night at the Mono Blanco and singing along to one of Pedish's old-time favorites, "Cocaine Blues." There was a girl at the table, and both young men had their arms around her, until the girl stood up and requested the latest hit, "*Cambios.*" It was remarkable that Enrique had remembered these fine details.

We may never know the truth. For now, Alberto has decided to lower the volume on Pedish and cut off his croaking promptly at midnight. The brothers are dining at Chato's restaurant tonight.

Chapter 14

SANTA CLAUS

I had to move. As I explained to Don Moi, I didn't want to leave the Panchan altogether. I liked my characters. I enjoyed my work. The landscape, beautiful and relentless, more than compensated for the slow service and lack of amenities. But the music was taking its toll. The endless drumming, aimed at breaking through the Van Allen Belt, was attracting underworld demons instead.

"The people are all mediocrities," he interrupted. "The archaeologists are arrogant snobs. The mapping is very important, but the astronomy, it's worth less than cat shit."

We were sitting at his kitchen table, surrounded by twenty cats howling for their lunch. "These are my only friends," Moi said as he began opening big cans of sardines and setting them on the floor. Then he wandered off, leaving me alone with the calicos and tigers. The table sat level with the branches, and from my point of view the rest of the half-marbled, half-feral, interbred coven of skunks appeared to be drowsing in the trees. The image didn't last long, because the cats and dogs started scrapping over the sardines and the parrots commenced to squawk. I was about to flee when Moi emerged from his bedroom with the map. Once again he laid it out, this time carelessly, on his fish-stained wooden table. The sardine oil soaking through the paper formed little ponds where none had existed previously, and the ink lines were beginning to blur.

"You've just made a new stream," I said. "And a black fishing hole."

"That stream runs through my uncle's land, but he's too old to care. I built a shed back there to store my worthless piles of rust. I took a look at it last week: broken stoves, machine parts, coils, a headless Buddha from China. So, I'm giving it to Big John—the shed and all its dissolute contents—and he can do with it what he likes."

"You mean that giant with the long white beard?"

"Yes, the one with the roly-poly belly who looks like Santa Claus. But he's a Texas redneck, very rough around the edges, and not at all jolly or polite. I despise Texans, and that one is a perfect specimen, worse than mediocre. He's all banged up and he's lived a hard life, completely deprived of civilization. But on the other hand, things are not so simple, as you can see by my menagerie. Eleven children and fifty cats fighting with each other, and all of them completely dependent on me. You may think it's funny, but Santa Claus loves me. He is like a son to me. What else can I do?"

I turned back to the map and pointed to a tract of land shaped like a megaphone.

"That Spanish fan at the end of my property is another story," said Moi. "It belongs to my cousin Alex. He's queer. He thinks he's an artist. He thinks he's an ecologist. But his land is peaceful and quiet. Maybe you would be happy living back there."

"But the shape, Don Moi. It looks like a horn."

"Then why not think of it as a slice of mango pie? Or an old gramophone playing my Puccini operas."

Or the triangular door to Pakal's tomb. Hmmm.

I set off in search of the funnel.

After the last cabaña, the path vanished under a convulsive array of tire tracks. Directly ahead, tangled in the brush, sat a rusted pickup truck, its wheel hubs bound with green creepers, its crumpled steel bed blooming with orchids. To the right stood an amazing, silver, star-spangled shack that appeared to be modeled after a modest farmhouse somewhere on the Martian prairies. Made completely of corrugated tin, this windowless little space station gleamed like an immense sardine can sealed by the broiling sun. According to the hand-lettered sign taped to the immaculate metal door, mushroom tea was served there every afternoon at five o'clock. No one was home.

Just beyond rose Don Moi's monstrous three-story shed, really a pitched aluminum roof teetering over a mountain of junk. Moi's own dwelling was enough of an eyesore. And whatever Santa Claus was planning to do with this land-locked wreck would inevitably turn into another architectural dead end. The landscape boasted an impressive thicket of elephant ears whose leaves were large enough to serve as umbrellas for the pestilent weeds clogging the stream that divided the two properties, which should have been declared a no-man's land by all rules of decency and good taste.

Sure enough, there stood my potential neighbor ordering his workers around. Too late, he saw me and waved me over. "Santa's little helpers got shit for brains," he roared. "And it looks like you're damn near lost, too."

I started off when he shouted again. "Hey, wait a sec'. I wanna show ya somethin'. Take a gander at this." He handed me a drawing of a long, skinny rectangle with tiny rectangular cells multiplying inside it. It looked like some kind of primitive life form.

"Do you own a microscope?" I asked.

He closed one eye and glared at me. "It's a blueprint. Can't you tell?"

I studied the drawing again while he stroked his raggedy beard.

"Huh, whatcha think? Pretty as a baby's ass, I'd say."

"Well, it's not a Maya temple," I said. "I mean the proportions are off. Podwell . . . ."

"Forget Podwell and his damn square roots! This is *my* temple, my future house. Look here."

With a wave of his massive arm he engulfed the trees, the stream, and Moi's giant shed.

"See, that's where it's going, my house, underneath that three-story roof. The classes will be on the first floor, with the kiln in back. The kitchen's on the second floor, next to the library. Air-conditioned, for all the art books. An' on the top there'll be one, big, wide-open space where I can walk around butt naked and look at the stars."

Block that image. Who'd want to think about that big bruiser wandering around in his bare ass and hanging balls. It was too much. He could have the treetops all to himself, I decided.

"What classes?" I asked.

"Ceramics. I'm gonna teach these kids how to make clay pots. Give them a trade, like their ancestors. They can make bowls. They can make gods. That's why I'm putting in two johns, boys and girls, for the workshops I'm gonna be running. And in front there's the ramp for me when I get too old."

"I had no idea you were a potter," I said.

"Longshoreman, kickin' ass all my life. Been a potter ever since art school. Anyway, over here's the real deal." He pointed to the brown runlet inching through the creepers. "I'm building me a pool, and inside the pool will be an island, and on the island there'll be a ten-foot-tall stepped pyramid with 365 square niches decoratin' all four sides. The whole thing'll be a tiny replica of Tollan, the sacred City of Reeds."

"But why not build something Maya?" I asked.

He scowled again. "Because the gods of Palenque came from Tollan, in central Mexico, that's why! I'm calling the whole damn place Teotihuacan South. It'll go on the wall in brass letters so you can see it when you drive up the back road. Now what do ya think, huh?"

"But this is Mayaland," I said.

"Ya know, girl, I can see you don't know shit from shinola, so I'm jus' gonna ignore that." For a long while he gritted his teeth and then forced a crooked smile. "But if it'll make you happy, I'm gonna carve an Olmec head outta stone and stand it up on my other island. And then I'll make a portrait of Don Moi. It'll be there on a pillar in the pool."

He rubbed his bad leg and hobbled over to the streambed, which was turning a dull copper in the afternoon light. There was a pile of white rocks his workers had dumped there, and he eased himself down. Now he was sitting with one elbow propped on his scarred right knee and his overblown head resting on his thick knuckles. He looked like a Celtic king home from his last battle, breathing hard and trying to shake the weight of the world off his big shoulders. "This is my Tollan, my paradise, and I owe it all to Moi."

"Very ambitious," I said. "I'm sure it will keep you busy for a long time to come."

"Better than bein' worm food. Better than unloadin' containers full of Chinese washing machines and Ecuadorian brooms. Beats gettin' your back broke every goddamn day."

He was staring so hard at the gravel I thought he was about to croak. "I'll just take this opportunity to slip away," I said to myself. But before I could make a move I heard him growl.

"Keep talkin'! I can hear ya. It's just these damn painkillers, that's all."

"Then what made you come here, of all places?" I asked. "I mean, it's a long way from Houston and any sort of decent medical help."

"Ya got that right, sister. And it's a long way from my granddaddy's ranch he settled after the Civil War. Yes, m'am, this is one story for the books."

He pulled back his hair and, with considerable effort, straightened himself up.

"My dad and Moi were friends during the war, the second world war, that is. They were stationed together in Illinois and then out in California. Lucky for them they weren't sent to the Pacific. After the peace, them two flyboys stuck together, went down to Durango and started a cement business. At least that's what my mother told me. My dad never said anything about cement because I never saw him more than twice in my life. 'Strange little guy,' she said, speakin' about Don Moi. I found out later she got almost everything right. The only thing she couldn't remember was Moi's name. 'Moses,' she said. 'Moses Rodriguez' or some damn thing. C'mon, let's grab a coke, huh? I got one here in the cooler."

He drank his down in one long gulp.

"I always thought one day I'd go lookin' for this man, my daddy's best friend, you know, so I started traveling around Mexico searching for Moses. I been all over Veracruz and all over Oaxaca, because I had a hunch this Moses what's his name lived somewhere in the south. Well, ten years of that and I got to likin' this country, and I practically forgot about lookin' for Moses. As it turned out, it's best to forget what you think you're doin' and concentrate on something else, because that's when what you really want comes true. You know what I mean, doncha? I'm sure you got some wishes, too." The light caught his eye and he smiled that crooked smile.

"One day I found myself in Palenque and I was up at the ruins talkin' to a guide who spoke good English. I was full of questions and I could see he didn't have a clue. He knew it and I knew it, and finally he said, 'You know, you should really talk to Moises Morales, he can tell you what you want to know.' 'Naw,' I said, 'maybe tomorrow.' I was tired by then and brushed him off. He asked me my name and I told him, and he said, 'Okay, I see you *mañana*, Jon Galagair.' That night I'm readin' a book on the Maya, and it mentions the name of this expert, Moises Morales. So I say to myself, 'Damn, I shoulda gone to talk to this guy.'

"But the next day when I happen to run into the guide, he says to me, 'Moises wants to see you. He lives at the Panchan.' Well, I was happier than a pig in shit even though I thought it was kinda strange that this great man wanted to see me. Of course I drove right over there and saw this old guy sittin' in a chair, talkin' to somebody. They talked and talked and I waited and waited until the other fella stood up and said goodbye. Eventually the old man motioned me over, and this is what he said: 'I know who you are. I changed your diapers when you were a baby boy.'

"Yes ma'am, you can take that incredulious expression off your face, however you say it. I stumbled right into him, and into this tiny slice of God's green land. It's almost enough to make ya a believer."

Chapter 15

NIGHT HUNTERS

I turned right, climbed the hill, and came to an iron gate. The vine-choked trees fell away, and from the clean, raked soil grew a manicured forest of palms. At the end of the lane the palms parted, and the blue sky came pouring down into a kidney-shaped swimming pool coated with dry leaves. Under the shade trees stood a small cottage with a covered porch and shuttered windows. One whitewashed wall bore these words in bold black letters:

> Love is the finest silence,
> the most earthshaking, the most unbearable.
> Lovers search,
> lovers abandon,
> lovers change and divide.
>
> Lovers walk like madmen,
> because they are alone, alone, alone.
>
> Lovers are the hydra in the story,
> they have serpents instead of arms.
> The veins in their necks are knotted
> like serpents, ready to strangle.
> Lovers are unable to sleep
> because if they sleep
> worms will eat them.

The poem, by Chiapas poet Jaime Sabinas, seemed a grim choice for such a tidy place. The owner was apparently a man of extremes. He had added another bizarre touch that lifted this otherwise predictable retreat into the realm of the surreal. On the other side of the swimming pool, a narrow walking bridge, painted red, spanned a deep and waterless runnel. The bridge led nowhere. I was captivated by its peeling mystery and decided to move in.

Cousin Alex's eco-experiment served as a kind of buffer zone against the pastoral and the wild. To the south, the rainforest melted into sunlit pastures stretching toward the hazy blue mountains. To the east, the jungle was overtaking the neighbor's vast coffee plantation. Toward the sunset, an untamed wall of vegetation spiraled across the bridge to nowhere. Giant ferns muffled the rumble of the drums, the clickety-clack of rolling suitcases, and the steady hammer blows of Santa's little elves. Only the voices of nature sullied my poor, sensitive ears: the bawling cows, the monkeys' roar, the dark wind rushing through the trees.

Then one night I was awakened by a strange noise. It sounded like a dog or cat lapping water. In my groggy state I couldn't be sure whether the sound came from the bridge or the pool or my dream. When I closed my eyes I saw a black jaguar pacing on the other side of the barbed wire fence. In later dreams, two of them stole across the bridge and padded silently underneath my bedroom window. The images of those black beasts were so vivid I couldn't sleep. A curious musky smell hung in the air.

One evening I was walking home from the bar, eyes alert, knees shaky, brain a little bleary from too much wine, when I saw a white horse grazing in the moonlight by my door. I slipped into my cottage and could still hear him snorting and chomping on the other side of the wall. When I mentioned the white horse to Don Moi, he said, "There is no white horse back there. But there is a black jaguar."

Before I moved to Palenque an old friend warned me to beware of the jaguar spirits that haunted the ruins. "They'll eat your soul," he said. At the time I shrugged it off as idle superstition, but now I wasn't so sure. After all, he was an anthropologist who had studied the Maya for years, and if there were any truth to their beliefs, he would know. On the other hand, maybe he was just projecting his own fears on me.

Nevertheless, I had to ask myself why he had planted the idea in my head. Was he trying to scare me or prepare me?

All of these mental gymnastics seemed irrelevant after Moi told me that my dream was real. Then again, whether imagined or real, I still had to protect myself, didn't I, against the fearful symmetry stalking me in the night. Podwell knew how to knap obsidian blades and spear points. But I lacked the ability and the will to use them, even in my dreams.

I read somewhere that lack of will was an early symptom of soul loss. Obviously I had to get a grip and strengthen my spirit. Surely then my stalkers would recognize me as a brave warrior, one of their own, and leave me "alone, alone, alone." But it was difficult to strengthen my soul when I was so terrified.

I began with a simple exercise. During the day I'd test my nerve by standing beside the barbed wire fence, watching the cows graze in the pasture. At night, when the cows turned into black jaguars crawling through the tall grass, I figured they'd ignore me. But cows are cows and jaguars are another species entirely, and instead of fooling them I was fooling myself. In other words, my exercise in wishful thinking was muddling, rather than sharpening, my mental faculties. Perhaps the jaguar spirits were already nibbling at me, because I noticed that, along with my stamina, I was losing weight. It would be a slow death, and one morning I'd wake to discover that I was an empty, listless, staring zombie. If I woke at all.

I decided to ask Don Moi for further details.

"Oh, that black jaguar was here years ago," Moi said with a dismissive wave of the hand. "But now that I think of it, the lady who saw him reminds me of you. I think she was Norwegian. No, Swedish. She fell in love with Palenque. She fell in love with the light. And she fell in love with the beautiful jaguar in her dream.

"Night after night she dreamt. The jaguar was pacing the ridge, or crossing the Murcielagos River, or up on El Mirador Mountain, sleeping in the caves. One morning she told me he was prowling behind the Temple of the Foliated Cross. 'He's getting closer,' she said. She was in a panic. It was driving her mad.

"'He's in danger,' she said, and it was true. The guards saw him. He was over by the Foliated Cross. And for no reason they shot him as he was coming down into the plaza. I heard about it right away. The woman already knew. 'My jaguar!' she cried. He was lying nobly in the sun, his black fur shining, maybe a phantom, maybe the spirit of Kan Bahlam, 'Serpent Jaguar,' the last great king of Palenque. Certainly the last great jaguar anyone has ever seen at the ruins."

"There may be others," I said, and I told Don Moi about my dreams.

"Be careful," he said. "Love is very powerful."

I thought about the story, thought about the king, Serpent Jaguar, thought about the lovers with serpentine arms, and everything came together all at once: spotted snakes and dream jaguars existed in this world as sure as fear was love and love was fearless and I was the madwoman walking irresistibly up the trail toward the abandoned coffee plantation. It rippled under cold cedars, under the frozen eyes of two giant iguanas, a sprawling orchard scattering blossoms white as pearls across the untamed jungle. Further on, the shadows grew steeper, and as I climbed I realized that the broad stones beneath my feet were manmade steps leading toward a ruined temple. When I reached the top I noticed several smaller mounds overgrown with berry trees. It was some sort of architectural complex right on the fringe of the Panchan Hotel. Perhaps jaguars were sacrificed here and their spirits continued to roam the forest. Perhaps the foreign captives offered to the gods possessed the brave animal souls of jaguars. Perhaps local captives met their fates here, chiefs of prominent clans and heads of families.

It dawned on me then that Moi's troubles, all the blind acts of greed and jealousy among the brothers, were caused by something ancient and sinister eating away at their souls. It was a curse, as Barnaby said, a little too jovially, at the Saturday night party a few months ago—the curse of the Temple of Doom.

My head was on fire, my blood turned cold, and although I told myself that my imagination was working overtime, it seemed the trees were deliberately weaving a thick web of shadows around me and the best thing for me to do was to back away slowly from that place and as soon as I was free of the hanging branches—run.

When I was safe inside my room I noticed two sheets of ragged paper lying on the floor. Immediately I recognized them as the pages Mingo had torn from his notebook and given to Moi. There was a third page, a page of stained parchment that got stuck in the hinge when Moi, or someone else, tried to slip it under the door. The page was covered with hieroglyphic writing and came with a note written in Spanish: "This is the prophesy of Yax Chuen, Balam of Lakamja."

PART II

Pakal the Great

—from *The Book of Mingo*

Pakal came from the town of Salto de Agua, just down the road. He had a wife, three sons, and who knows how many daughters. He had a mother who spoiled him terribly. The queen, Lady Resplendent Quetzal, ruled the roost. No one did a thing without her say so. But she loved her boy, and by hook or by crook, she saw to it that he became king. He was only twelve years old. There's a picture of it in the Palace, and it shows his mother handing him the crown. This was one of his big problems: How to wrestle the power away from his mother, because she was always trying to rule the kingdom for him. He had to do it in a nice way, of course, since he owed his mother everything. Besides, she was the Goddess of the Moon.

92

Things were in bad shape. First he built a little temple in the old part of the city. But he was not the one doing the building. No. He was the one who was thinking and planning and praying. He did a lot of praying.

Then he built the Palace, but you wouldn't want to live there. When you look up you see tall arches reaching for the sky, but the air up there is not for living. And the empty rooms below are too long and too narrow. You can walk the width in three steps. Those rooms are made for pacing. Yes, there are open courtyards, but the sun is so strong it drives you back under the long porticos. There were indoor baths, a row of them, one right next to the other. The children splashed in them and then ran into the grassy courtyards where they played their games. The king sat on his throne above the grand courtyard where he entertained his noble guests. They ate tamales stuffed with opossum, tamales stuffed with grubs. People danced under the sun and stars. Meanwhile, his captives crowded together in a little room, their hands tied with ropes and their hearts trembling. Just before the party was over, they dragged out the captives to show them off before their heads were split. Then the king went down to the dungeons where it's cool. He could lie there on his cold stone bed and think and plan and meditate in the gloom. Things were in bad shape.

The former palace, which lies to the west, was no better. It sits upon a high terrace, and the view from there is really wonderful. Salt lagoons and fog that floats like a seagull over the water. But we didn't see the enemy marching in the distance, we didn't see them crawling through the brush. The soldiers set fire to everything. They burned that palace down. They destroyed the idols of the gods, crushed them, stamped them, tossed them down from the heights. And that is why things were in terrible shape and that is why Pakal was always pacing. Should he go to war against his enemies or should he try to win back the gods? Before he even finished his new house he had to fix things, pray, open the portal between this world and the next.

Chapter 16

THE WEB

I took the parchment over to the base camp and knocked on the door. After a few minutes I heard groans and heavy footsteps.

"Who?" shouted Barnaby. The door swung open and there he was, standing in a sartorial pair of boxer shorts decorated with pink pigs. The place was a mess: wine bottles, beer bottles, ashtrays overflowing, the dining table piled with books, papers, and three open laptops. Matthew was sprawled in the easy chair, dead to the world. I showed Barnaby the parchment. He rocked on his heels and sank into the moth-eaten sofa.

"Where'd you find this?" he blinked. I told him I found it under my door, with a scrawled note in Spanish that read, "This is the prophesy of Yax Chuen, the Balam of Lakamha."

"Hmm. Give me some time," he said. "I'm not sure I can decipher all of it, but I'll try."

Down below we could hear Podwell mumbling and pacing. The more he paced the louder he cursed until it seemed he was working himself into a full-scale panic. Finally we heard the thump of heavy boots pounding up the stairs, and Podwell charged into the room, shouting. "Man, I had a bad dream, a nightmare."

Barnaby was sitting at the table, pouring over the columns of glyphs. "You're always having bad dreams," he said, without looking up.

"No, this one was really bad. Worse than the one with the dwarf."

That dream occurred when Podwell was living in an attic, studying

Spanish, in Antigua, Guatemala, and he came home one night to find a small creature, something like a little man, sitting in the corner. The midget jumped on Podwell, punched him in the ribs, and then sprinted down the stairs. That dream was more like a supernatural encounter.

"In this one it was supposed to be equinox or solstice. I was just standing there, looking at the sun, when these black thunderheads swept over the Temple of the Cross. Then the clouds turned red, the whole sky opened, and a burning ball, bigger than the sun, started hurtling down. It hit the roof comb and then the trees. The whole world was burning. There was no place to run. I was scared. I'm still scared. Something's going to happen. I can feel it."

"Maybe you've been watching too many movies," said Barnaby.

"That dream was an omen. I know it. We've got to do something. Prepare."

"You could begin by ignoring those conspiracy theories. Those web sites are getting to you," said Barnaby.

"No, this dream is not about 9-11. This dream is the future. Maybe 2012. But it could happen sooner."

"Well, tomorrow's equinox," Barnaby announced, "and I, for one, will be going to the ruins." Podwell glanced nervously out the window.

"How about some coffee?" Barnaby asked.

"Sure," said Podwell. "I'll grind the beans."

"No, you just relax and I'll do the grinding. This is probably the only electric grinder in all of Mexico and I don't want it to melt."

"I'll make some toast," Podwell offered. "Where's the bread?"

"Toaster's been broke since you used it last Wednesday."

Podwell stomped over to the stove. "I'll just heat the bread over the burner," he said, striking a match. Nothing.

"We're out of gas," Barnaby grumbled.

"You ever make toast in the microwave?" Podwell asked.

Barnaby and Podwell were best friends. They didn't look alike, their personalities were completely different, and yet they were bonded like psychic twins. It started when they applied to grad school at the same time. When Barnaby showed up at the department of anthropology, the registrar just smiled and said, "Congratulations, you're in." Barnaby went off to celebrate, and ten minutes later Podwell appeared at the registrar's desk, exhausted after a red-eye flight from California. "I'm

Podwell," he said, "I wrote the paper on Maya math." The registrar looked confused. "But weren't you just here?" he said.

"No, sir," Podwell said. "I had a dream. I flew here on the spur of the moment." The registrar picked up the phone, whispered into the receiver, and then told Podwell to go over and talk to the chairwoman of the Latin American Studies program. That's what Podwell did, and before he knew it he was doing preliminary fieldwork in Guatemala, without even taking a course.

"Great paper on the mathematical origins of the calendar," the professor told Barnaby. Or "Very interesting interpretation of the Dresden Codex, Podwell. Needs some work." Barnaby had spent months examining the Dresden Codex and knew his case was watertight. But what was even more annoying was that his professors kept getting his name wrong. The mystery of mistaken identity wasn't resolved until the two archaeologists began working at Palenque. One day Barnaby was making his way down from the Temple of the Inscriptions and Podwell was racing towards the top. They met in the middle, on step thirty-three, to be exact. They recognized each other instantly, and when they shook hands, it seemed as if they were crossing an invisible barrier, as Podwell put it, passing through to the opposite side of the mirror. They'd been brothers ever since.

"There are a lot of things besides dreams that are difficult to explain," said Podwell. "Maybe it's possible to be in two places at once. Maybe it's possible to vanish and then show up somewhere else. Maybe our atoms can truly rearrange themselves. Or we can enter other bodies."

The handyman named Terrence dropped his wrench. He was under the sink, fixing the leaking water pipe. He was a wiry little guy who hardly ever spoke and mainly stayed in his tent at the Jungle Palace.

"That's right," said Podwell. "My grandfather was a physicist. He used to tell me about lots of incredible things. He worked on the Philadelphia Experiment."

Terrence crawled out from under the sink and pulled himself up to his full, five-foot-five height. "You know, I may be as crazy as a shithouse rat," he said, "but I'd put a lid on it if I was you." His bony face looked grim and threatening. "This leak'll have to wait till tomorrow!" Then he grabbed his wrench and stormed out the door.

"Drip!" Barnaby whispered. "What's his problem?"

"Well, it's sort of top secret," Podwell whispered back.

"It can't be so secret if it's on the web."

"All the same, my father's site is being tapped by the CIA. Every time I send him an email, it gets lost and my computer crashes."

"It's your famous electric touch," said Barnaby. "What's the Philadelphia Experiment, anyway?"

Teleportation, man!"

Matthew muttered something and went back to sleep.

"Okay, listen to what I'm saying," Podwell whispered in his best stage voice. "This isn't your beloved Captain Kirk and the Starship Enterprise. No, this was the USS Eldridge, an American destroyer escort back in World War II. It was lying at anchor in the Philadelphia Harbor. There was a lot of green fog—and poof! The boat vanished, and two minutes later it reappeared in Newport News!" Podwell gave Barnaby a few seconds to swallow his coffee, and after weighing the depths of his friend's incredulity, decided to backtrack. "No, seriously. It was part of the Navy's efforts to evade radar detection. They worked on it for years, built an electromagnetic generator that supposedly would prove Einstein's unified field theory. Anyway, when they tried it out, surprise, they discovered invisibility!"

"Are you telling me that the military knows how to do that shit? Then why are we fighting wars the same old way? And why is the space program so slow? Why haven't we entered the world of tomorrow?"

Podwell hung his head. "Risks, man. Very big risks."

Barnaby had run the emotional gambit from disbelief to anger and back to his initial, grumbling skepticism. "Name one," he barked.

"Well, I hate to tell you this, judging by your current mood, but the entire crew went stark raving mad. And not only that. Some sailors got plastered to the ship metal and had to be pried loose. And the second mate got stuck in that other dimension and vanished for good."

"Jeez," said Barnaby, "do you really expect me to believe this horseshit? I mean you're beginning to sound like the Twilight Zone."

"Okay, okay. But just to answer your first question, there is an element of outer space to the whole episode." Barnaby's ears perked up. "Yes! According to a guy working in the lab, the researchers had helpers. They were little fellows, elflike really, and their skin was gray, and they said they were here to assist mankind, not like the ones who are here to do us harm, the long-tailed, reptilian . . . ."

"Dragons?" said Matthew, coming to.

"Large lizards," Podwell corrected. "Chameleons, specifically. They can change shape."

Barnaby threw up his hands and knocked over his coffee. "This is just great!" he shouted, grabbing a sponge. "But you know what? I think I've had enough fantasyland for one day."

Later that evening Barnaby came to my room, carrying his notepad.

"Did you notice anything strange on the way?" I asked.

"Yes, the lights on the path went off, and for the first time in months I was able to see the stars. Jupiter's very bright tonight, and so is Mars. In fact, they're close to conjunction. It would be a hell of a coincidence if they were in conjunction when this hieroglyphic passage was originally written." Barnaby's sunburned face turned pale. "Oops, sorry about that," he said. "You probably think we're all out to lunch."

He paced for a minute, then finally sat down and lit a cigarette. "Okay, I didn't show it to Matthew, so this translation is pretty rough. He's still freaked out about the aliens, and I didn't want to push him over the edge. You don't have any rum, do you?"

"Rum and coke," I said.

"It's part of the job, you know. I mean, being down here without the wife and kids is hard. She can't take the heat, worries about the snakes."

I handed him a drink.

"Well, here goes, then. I'll just read the critical part:

After 13 baktuns the cycle will end on 4 Ahau 3 Kankin.
B'olon Yokte' K'uh will descend into Ek'-u-Tan.

"There. What this is saying is that after 13 *baktuns*—that's thirteen periods of four hundred years, or 5,125 years, roughly—the Great Round will come to an end on December 21, 2012, or thereabouts. On that day, *B'olon Yokte' K'uh*—either the nine gods who hold up the world or some god of the Underworld—will fall back into darkness, the black place at the center where this creation began."

"That must mean that the dark lords will lose their power," I said.

"Or the world will begin again in darkness."

"Darkness followed by light."

"It doesn't say. The inscription breaks off here," said Barnaby. "Another double-edged prophecy. Beautiful, but definitely weird."

Chapter 17

THE GRAYS

The next day Terence completed his drain duties in shrouded, monk-like silence, and now he was hustling back to the workshop, a collection of makeshift huts surrounding an open bog, off-limits to all but the Sons of Vulcan: nuts and bolt men who vowed to screw up everyone and everything as long as the gods gave them breath. Their grungy, monastic lair spread like fungus on the bleak frontier of the Panchan, past the broken toilet tanks and disemboweled washing machines. The air smelled of soap and bleach as Terence parted the laundered sheets. The other side of hell reeked of diesel oil and solder, and he had to cut a wide circle to avoid the sparks or risk getting his nose burned off, which is what happened to Loco, the welder, last time he went on a toot. So Terence crossed the sawdust flats, rubber gulch, and scrap metal mountain before dropping his monkey wrench in the lean-to shack that doubled as a sleeping rack for the retired navy captain. And since the slimy bastard was gone to meet his new connection and Terence wasn't talking to him anyway, he knocked off early and took his scrawny self up the bow-legged path toward his favorite meditation place. Alone on the rock, high above the tree line, he could scan the open pasturelands and brood.

He was a feisty sort of loner, stubborn in his solitude, and when I later learned that he had participated in top secret projects while serving in the army I wasn't at all surprised. When I tried to probe, he simply said, "The world is a dangerous place, more dangerous than you think." Usually he left it at that, an ominous fold in the black cloud hanging over his head. It was odd that someone living in this tropical splendor was so withdrawn, but then, he was a man in his fifties with a long past to scour.

He spent his childhood roaming the desert outside Roswell, New Mexico, searching for arrowheads among the bones. And when he became a grown man, trading used cars and laying parquet floors in the suburbs, he'd comb the canyons every weekend or follow the volcanic dikes—"dragon spines," he called them—always in search of signs. All the other buzzards were out there with Geiger counters, sweeping the badlands for extraterrestrial spoils: crash sites, cosmic wreckage, radioactive residues, the toeless pod prints of the skinny, sloe-eyed, alien dwarfs whose pictures appeared in the FBI reports. Terence came home with bags of stones that had been altered by prehistoric human hands, stones used for pounding, chiseling, cutting, and splitting bigger stones. During one of his hunting forays, his wife emptied their bank account and hopped the Greyhound for Denver. Last he heard, the Paleolithic tool kits were sitting in a suitcase under his mother's hospital bed. Maybe his son would take an interest, but his son was into girls and sports cars.

One evening I found him muttering over his beer, pressing his right hand against his ear as if he were receiving an urgent message. The line must have got cut off or the drums were causing interference, because out of the blue he started talking about his Harley. After a few more beers he told me that he once had the honor of meeting Sonny Barger, leader of the Hell's Angels. That private conversation changed his life. He left behind his sanders and floorboards and became a knight of the road, chasing the wind and saving damsels in distress from impending doom. All he would say about the coming cataclysm was that he had seen it clearly during one of the army experiments. It made him shake just to think about it.

Now the sun was sinking and he was scanning the upper strata, his mind racing from the Stone Age to the Arthurian Age to the grim future, looking for a slit in the vapor that he could squeeze through and possibly, just possibly, emerge full-blown into the present.

If he overheard the talk about a ship evaporating in green fog, then chances were he caught the drift of Podwell's dream. Christ, the guy's grandfather was in on the project since day one; no wonder the kid was having nightmares about fireballs and midgets going ballistic in his attic! And chances were, Terence was still paying attention when Barnaby mentioned that today was the first day of spring, though who knows if Terence cared since he came out here every afternoon, rain or shine, to stand vigil, and those dumb college boys only when the spirit moved them.

As a matter of fact, Barnaby, Podwell, and Alux were totally on the case—transit, cameras, tapes at the ready—inside Temple V. A few scenic frames of the pink sky, the sun gliding through the Palace . . . . And then this blinding ray of light shot through the door and raced toward the corner of the god house! Podwell braced himself against the wall, speechless, but Barnaby had the presence of mind to say, "Holy cow! This temple's in perfect sync with time!"

The diagonal split the room just as the sun, beating down on the equator, divided the hemispheres into spring and fall. At that moment, light and dark were equal. The cosmic diagram was etched into the floor with a luminous blade, and they, men of average height, neither gods nor superhuman giants, could cross the line instantaneously, magically, from winter shadow to wild springtime fever.

Terence couldn't see them. From where he was standing he couldn't even see the Palace. His eyes were riveted to a spot on the eastern horizon where the big shiny spheres zoomed in after sunset. Sometimes they appeared in clusters, glittering like newborn constellations. In the last week alone he counted thirteen of them, pulsating—*signaling*—above the purple hills.

Terence was not the only one who had noticed the UFO's. The Lacandons had reported strange lights circling Lake Naja at midnight. A group of teenagers partying in the Palenque graveyard swore they saw a saucer hovering above the white mausoleum where Doña Berta Rosado is said to sing during the new moon. One evening, six archaeologists watched a glowing ball streak across the eastern sky, then change direction sharply and blaze toward the south. Of the existence of flying saucers there was little doubt. It was the identity of the aliens, and the meaning and purpose of their mission, that were the subjects of heated speculation.

Followers of Jose Arguelles and the Dreamspell Calendar believed the visitors were Maya kings returning to Palenque from their home planet in the center of the Milky Way. This, hands down, was the most popular notion among Panchanecos, who could always claim the hefty support of thousands more around the world.

The drummers took exception to this theory, largely because they were bent on communicating with the home planet and not the other way around. According to Bobo, the Maya planet was an ethereal shrine of primal sound set in the center of the galaxy for the sheer delight and musical pleasure of the gods. Composed of pure vibrations, this sonar planet of rhapsodic tints was the source of the music of the spheres, which wafted on rainbow waves throughout this universe and beyond. Bobo was an Afro-Cuban voodoo prince who believed his magic Xango rhythms kept the universe spinning. The fire dancers, he said, played a pivotal role in the cosmic revolutions.

But none of the fire dancers agreed with Bobo's advanced theories, even though they were devoted to spinning nightly under the stars. Fire was their element, and fire was an earth thing, no? When he sat them down and explained the metaphorical link between the circling balls of fire and the uncongealed gases whirling through space, Bliss told him that dancing inside the flames was pure escape, "and that goes for Minerva, too!" Aliens? Minerva was wide-eyed. Lilo and Margarita just laughed. For them, aliens were the tall, blond Germans passing through the Panchan.

The archaeologists were even less willing to engage in talk about aliens, per se. But whenever the question came up, which was at least three times a day, Podwell was adamant about one point: the existence of the Black Transformer Place, the *Ek'-u-Tan,* the door to spiritual transformation. "It says so in the hieroglyphic inscriptions, so there's no doubt about it!"

"It's probably a black hole," Alux interjected.

Podwell nodded. "Of course, we can't come right out and say the Maya knew about black holes, but they definitely had the concept. And the one they write about in the myths and in the inscriptions is probably located in the vast dark space below the North Star."

"But a black hole is the complete opposite of a planet that sends out sound waves in rainbow colors," said Bobo. "And the North Star is a long way from the center of the galaxy."

"Who said anything about cosmic drums? Who said anything about the center of the galaxy?" Podwell shouted. "We're talking about what the Maya say, and the Maya say the place of creation is in the con-stellation of Orion. But if—big if—the Maya came from outer space, I want to go on record as stating that they either came from the North Star or the M42 nebula." Just then the lights went off, Podwell stopped waving his arms, and Bobo left the table, completely unconvinced.

As for the myriad speculations concerning the reasons for return, large or small, fat or thin, they all boiled down to a single conclu-sion—the time was ripe. Confirmations of this perfectly vague observation poured from the mouths of the major seers of our apocalyptic age. Jose Arguelles was not the only doomsayer. His predictions of disaster were outmatched by none other than Edgar Cayce, "the Sleeping Prophet," who learned of the bleak tidings from books he saw in a dream. As far as we know, the self-professed incarnation of ancient Egypt's greatest clairvoyant had never touched alcohol, cigarettes, or methamphetamine nor had he foreseen space ships landing on Palenque's main plaza. He did predict imminent chaos, however, and in a rare, unguarded moment, reluctantly disclosed to his most intimate acolytes that the global cataclysms about to be unleashed had been foretold by Maya priests in 10,000 B.C. He knew nothing about the Maya, but lying in his bed, looking out on the shipping harbor of Newport News, Edgar Cayce had a vision of a lost civilization in the Americas, populated by shipwrecked survivors from Atlantis. They had committed their knowledge to paper, and these encrypted codices, which he had skimmed in his sleep, lay sealed in a wooden box buried at Piedras Negras, a remote Maya site marked by three black boulders jutting above the turbulent waters of the Usumacinta River. Piedras Negras, Cayce said, was the sacred home of the hallowed Atlantean Hall of Records.

Another kind of box exists, this one an elaborate coffer, dipped in gold and set with rubies, that hovers, despite its gargantuan Byzantine weight, overhead in the seventh heaven. The Merkabah glows like the Ark of the Covenant and rattles like thunder. At the end of days, which is coming very soon, it will descend out of the mists, and winging from its golden bosom the 144,000 Ascended Masters, including Jesus Christ, will drift down upon Palenque, the first of the crystal cities of light. So it is written in the holy Book of Enoch, the peripatetic Hebrew prophet who visited the New World.

All this yackety-yack set Terence's teeth on edge. There was nothing spiritual about alien creatures. The Grays weren't all that nice, and the Lizards were positively evil. But not as evil as the US shadow government and its plans to rule the world. Of this Terence was certain: the worst devils were the faceless agents in the Department of Mind Control. He knew because they used his mind, and the minds of hundreds of volunteers like him, to transmit catastrophic thoughts into the subliminal wave generators circling the earth. He saw the accumulated pictures. They scared him shitless. And all he could do was tell no one and try to keep his mind a blank.

Chapter 18

A SIMPLE SOLUTION

Were the Rainbow People the Grays or the Lizards? It was hard to know. They called themselves "children of light" and appeared in robes of white for the annual spring equinox celebration, so one would assume they were on the side of goodness. The trouble was, so many half-lit little cherubs were overrunning the campgrounds that the hotel ran out of water. And not just this hotel but all the hotels along the road to the ruins and all the hotels in town. Local wits started calling the Rainbow People the *Drainbows*.

Home from the ruins after making his solar sightings, Alux was planning a ritual sweatbath in honor of the joyful day. He would decorate his *temascal* with flowers, his son would blow the conch shell trumpet, and as the nubile Rainbows sat sweating in a circle, he would speak of the universal balance and harmony that equinox represented. But when he turned on the faucet to fill his little pool, there was not a drop of water.

After two days without water for bathing, water for flushing, water for washing clothes, a few souls began to consider the matter.

"Fucking idiots! I'll blow them outta the water," Santa Claus huffed. "I mean, outta that there mud, huh. Drier than Pakal's peter!"

But the reason for the water shortage was deeper than the sudden invasion of the Drainbows. The sacred springs flowing over and under the ancient city had tapped the last stone, the last liquid shimmer, and had left nothing for the snakes. Here it was, late March, and the rains would not begin for another month.

Palenque, pearl of the forest waters, had lost its luster. Its teeming aqueducts, bottomless aquifers, and abundant streams were sinking into anonymity. "Hopeless, nameless, prosaic," Podwell said as he contemplated the ruined kingdom finally succumbing to the most fundamental global issue of our time.

"It sucks," Alfonso agreed. Not one to waste precious words, he organized a public march against the water department, which had not even bothered to investigate the main tube, as he had done the previous day, climbing the convoluted limestone cliffs, losing a boot in the mud, as he traced the rusty, forty-year-old pipe to the mountaintop high above the Temple of the Inscriptions. The spring had dwindled to a trickle, and that meant insufficient water for the crops and the people. Sadly he went home and checked Kirk's computer data. Alfonso couldn't see a long-term pattern in the figures supplied by the four steel flow meters that Kirk had anchored in the streambeds, certainly not the kind of long-term pattern indicated by the deep core samples taken off the coast of Venezuela, which indicated four cycles of drought that came in fifty-year periods, sometime between A.D. 700 and 900, and eventually wiped out Classic Maya civilization.

Earlier theories blamed the collapse on intensive warfare among the rival city-states and the ultimate powerlessness of petty kings to forge a unified empire. Some scholars imagined a widespread revolt against priests, nobles, and the entire institution of divine kingship. Others attributed the fall to a rare pathological trait, which compelled the Maya people to fulfill the prophecies of their sacred calendar—as if there were a gene for fatalism. But the paradigm of the moment, in keeping with our current conundrum, is wholesale environmental destruction.

Forget about hurricanes. Thunder, wind, and lightning are the elemental forces driving this divinely inspired creation. No one thinks much of earthquakes either, or the tremors that rumble through the cavernous underground as regular as rain. Despite the indelible streaks of smoke and ash on the horizon, there have been only two recorded cases of violent eruptions in ancient times: one, in A.D. 100, which destroyed the great city of Cuicuilco and made the fire god the major deity of the central Mexican plateau; the other, in A.D. 630, which turned the town of Cerén, El Salvador, into a New World Pompeii. The most astounding explosion of modern times occurred in 1936, when a live volcano burst from a farmer's corn field in Michoacan, pummeling the nearby Tarascan village of San Juan until all that remained was the church steeple poking through the lava beds. That disaster overshadows the eruption of Chichonal by its sheer, awesome strangeness, and though it could happen again at any time, such shocking upheavals do not occupy the top tier of popular prediction lists.

On the other hand, the tidal waves that recently struck Southeast Asia have provoked abnormal forecasts of tsunamis in the Gulf of Mexico, the occurrence of which largely depends on shifts in the magnetic field and a sudden flip of the north and south poles. Geophysicists cannot say for certain when—perhaps they are hiding the truth—but sooner or later giant waves could sweep across the swamps and up the Usumacinta River, destroying the last remains of a great civilization, not to mention all human and animal life.

Alfonso ordered a truckload of water for the house and then called the acting chairperson of the local water committee. The next morning two hundred Maya women showed up in front of city hall, waving placards. "*Ha! Ha! Ha!*" they cried in Chol: "Water is life." The protest was mildly reminiscent of the dramatic demonstration that occurred last January when Subcomandante Marcos, the charismatic leader of the Zapatista Army of National Liberation, followed by five thousand barefoot men and women wearing black ski masks—"the faceless ones, the hidden ones"— marched into Palenque's main plaza to demand justice, equality, and subsidized electricity for the poor.

Light was a nefarious issue at the Panchan, but light could wait. The people needed water—now! And so Terence and the other workmen set up electric pumps that would hopefully draw sufficient water from the rocky streambeds to supply the public bathrooms and private cabañas. "This is the beginning of the end," he said, as he uncoiled the hoses.

Just then a gaggle of Drainbow sylphs wandered up the path, chanting and waving branches of red ginger. When they reached the clearing by the pool they squatted in a tight circle. Arms raised, they continued chanting until one in their midst waddled into the middle and let out the most god-awful croak. The rest of the women leaned forward, stretched their arms on the ground before them, and produced an agonized medley of swollen groans. As night fell, they built a raging bonfire, hot enough to melt a witch's cauldron and singe the whiskers off the rabbit in the moon. By two in the morning the crackling blaze and frog-like croaking had summoned thunder. Then it rained a rain of silver bells dipped in drops of morning glory wine. The women were soaking wet but nevertheless kept singing: *ricket-ricket, creak-creak,* mixed with the sound of smacking lips and long, throaty screams. It was a hideous sound, a hideous sight.

Chapter 19

LIBERTY

For some people, freedom is like stuffing a goose or punching a young heifer down the shoot. There's always a lot of kicking and hollering that comes painfully close to prayerful begging when ladies aren't present. But tonight, at Moi's table, ladies were present. They were jiggling in their seats, primed and ready for the slightest embrace even though it came whipped with scorn and burning frustration. The floozy opposite me had breasts the size of pumpkins that burst through her bra lace and buttons like newborn twins trying to wriggle out of their adorable frills and deliver. The blown hair, the breasts, the olive she held on the tip of her fork were all for Romero. And all Romero had on his drunken mind was cattle, Swiss cattle shipped from Switzerland and now chomping miserably on the dry swamp he called his ranch.

"Imagine, cows from the Swiss Alps, beautiful mountains covered with snow, here, now, in La Libertad." I tried to imagine a herd of Guernsey cattle ambling across the flat plains toward the splintered shade of the coconut palms and lying down quietly beside the humped white Brahmins gazing pacifically through huge, compassionate, almond-shaped eyes.

"I've got cattle from Stokesville, Oklahoma, two bulls from Waco, Texas," he continued. But milk cows from Lausanne, accustomed to Alpine grass, getting a bellyache on plantains—it seemed like a cruel transition, even for a cow.

"How do they know what to eat?" I asked.

"They know, and what they don't know they learn." I appreciated his positive attitude, although I was stunned by his blind faith in what I considered the dumbest beasts on the planet. "They learn very fast not to eat cactus," he said flatly. The image of a lolling tongue stuck with thorns almost aroused my sympathy. "Trial and error."

He stared at me so fixedly I wasn't sure whether he was engaging me in a contest or waiting for a response to his last stock phrase, excuse the pun. Had I not turned away to sip my drink I believe he would have turned to stone. Finally a question welled up from deep inside his stupefied heart. "And where are you from?" he asked of me, not a cow certainly, but some kind of unidentifiable creature.

"Canada," I said.

"Alberta!" he shouted, referring to that great western reserve for beef on the hoof.

"Nova Scotia?" Antonia asked. "I have a cousin with a husband in Halifax. She says it's an island. The people speak English. She writes to me: 'Please send a big bag of *chiles pasillas*.' She says it is very beautiful, but they don't eat chiles."

"They eat potatoes," I told her, struggling for the Spanish words for herring and kippers. "The people are very poor."

"Is Nova Scotia the city or the name of the state?"

"State!" Luci broke in. "Look at a map!"

"Province," I corrected. "We have provinces."

Luci stared at the menu. "Is that so?" she said.

Antonia's eyes came back to life as Romero brought up the cattle from Cuba. "Cuba!" she wiggled. "The music. The beans." Yes, they had just returned from Cuba on a three-week, cattle-buying spree, a weird glut of suet and lard, gulls and sand, maracas shaking on the deck of the hotel, and warm stars pulsing to the rhythm of *son*, not the cool *son* of Veracruz but the wilder, blacker stirrings of crashing waves and rum.

Another round of Cuba libres and Romero was banging on the table. "Ecology. I love this ecology! Fresh. The leaves, the scent. I gave her the choice, La Libertad or the Panchan."

"Panchan!" Antonia smiled. The waiter brought another plate of garlic bread.

"I take a taxi here and back, sometimes late at night," Luci confided. "I love this garlic bread." She leaned across the table and said to

Antonia, "It's margarine and garlic. You mix them together in a bowl. But this whole wheat bread, you can't find it. This bread, they bake it here."

"I'm on a diet," Antonia sighed, patting her round belly.

"One order of garlic bread costs six pesos. The taxi costs eighty," Luci shrugged. "Maybe I'm crazy. I like to come to the Panchan, eat the garlic bread, look at the trees."

Everyone clicked glasses and beer bottles. "To the Panchan!" we toasted.

Antonia was originally from Tuxtla, her baby was in Tuxtla, but she'd been living in Tamaulipas for the past ten years and now Ciudad Victoria, waiting for the divorce to come through. She popped another olive into Romero's open mouth and said, "I'm glad to be home in Chiapas." Then her face sagged. "But there is so much poverty. Barefoot children on the street, barefoot children in the Indian villages. So much poverty." Her face twisted in despair. Her breasts heaved like two fat frontal wings.

"It's the cold. They have no blankets. They have nothing to eat. Just beans and a small fire," said Luci, her voice taking on a chiseled gravity.

"The government has money," Antonia pouted.

"But the money doesn't get to the children. It's the corruption."

"I can't stand thinking about it. When I think about it I cry," Antonia murmured.

"Corruption!" Luci repeated. She stopped jiggling in her chair and turned her inflated body to me. "I know about the corruption. I am a social worker." The table fell silent.

"Ecology!" Romero shouted and ordered another round. "We just got back from Yaxchilan. Tell us about the Maya, Don Moi. Don Moi knows everything about the Maya."

Moi, who had been gazing absently at a hole in the trees, simply smiled and said thank you.

"The Maya, the Maya," Romero intoned.

"But I've never been to Tikal. I've never been to Copan. They wouldn't let me across the border," Antonia sighed.

"They let you in for one day, to see the ruins. You don't need papers," Luci said emphatically.

The pasta arrived. Antonia was still picking at the cucumbers on her large salad special. "Too fat," she said, clutching her stomach.

Romero, who had been leaning on his elbow, staring at the ground, suddenly leapt out of his chair and considered the stars. "That moon is huge. Look how much bigger the moon is over the Panchan." But the moon was merely the large floodlight on Rakshita's third-floor terrace.

The dentist, slumped in his chair, said he was too tired to move. He turned to Don Moi and rasped, "Three accidents on the road. Yesterday I had to fly to Mexico City and back. Two cars and a pickup truck on its side. Awful."

The women excused themselves and headed for the toilet. Their mini skirts were so tight, their high heels so spindly, it was a wonder they could set one long tree trunk of a leg in front of the other. Their men didn't seem to notice the ritual of the reined-in, tight-assed stroll. But Marcelino Vega and Victor Hugo, who were standing at the bar, certainly did. They were slapping each other on the back as they pulled up two chairs, gathered their paunches, and leaned across our table, mumbling about land prices in a smarmy, conspiratorial tone.

"Fifty hectares off the main road, big enough for two hotels. There's only one problem," Marcelino winked. "The neighbor is a narco dealer from Villahermosa. He's putting in a landing strip."

The dentist said he'd seen an ad in the paper for two hectares, view of the ruins, no water, no well: one million pesos.

"The only solution—may God forgive me—" said Victor Hugo, crossing himself, "is to buy out the Indian *ejidos*. All we need to do is sell off some cattle, somebody's cattle, and pool our money."

"Crazy," the dentist said. "We're better off in La Libertad. There's still water. Nothing to do, but the land is green."

"We protect our trees. We protect our land," said Romero, the enlightened cattleman.

The drums started up as Antonia and Luci elbowed the crowd. The fire dancers, one, two, three, four, were wrapped around one another, entwined in flaming circles. The waiters were hooting and whistling and swatting the lampshades over the bar. It was a spectacular show.

"That girl there," whispered Marcelino. "The one in the red sequins. Isn't that . . .?"

Victor Hugo swiveled in his chair and blinked. "Little Minerva? Our *compadre's* daughter?"

"Calm yourselves," said Don Moi. "It's just her long-lost twin."

Calm unto sleep, the dentist roused himself and stretched his arms. Lightning flashed in the distance. The night promised rain.

"Hmm, an early rain for this season. Just what we need," said the dentist. "All in all, a perfect evening. Come out to the ranch sometime, Don Moi. Bring your Canadian friend with you."

Romero yawned. "Here it's fresh. Not the lowlands, not the mountains. Just right."

"Yes," Antonia trilled. "The children in the mountains are dying of the cold."

Just then the soporific air was split by blood-curdling screams.

"Jaguars on the prowl," Moi said matter-of-factly. "Eating the babies, eating the cows."

Chapter 20

SERAFINE

The screamer's name was Serafine, after the character in the book I am reading about blood feuds in Corsica. There the dead, sometimes two or three at a time, are laid out in the parlor, and the women proceed to weep, gnash their teeth, and tear out their hair, whipping themselves into a cold, calculated frenzy designed to appease the mourners; and like the character's antics in the book, Serafine's healing séances, sudden communiqués with the dead, high-flown operatic bouts of incoherent chanting were performed for a handsome fee. As a child, Serafine had once summered in Corsica, but she remembered nothing of the island except the drab sky that hovered over the salt lagoons like a listless seagull. Had she known about the Maenads, her flights of madness might have taken on the color and depth of true possession, but as it was, Serafine never left her tall, bony body long enough to praise the great Mediterranean god of toadstools, Dionysius. Dressed in her white gown, she floated along the paths, and when she lifted her eyes, there was always something startling and new about the world before her: an immense *castaña* leaf or a long-tailed green iguana. Her little cries opened a door through the trees, for often I would see her standing in a grove of bamboo or lying in a patch of weeds, staring at the magnificent shadows cast by the moth-like wings of a dry bromeliad. With more concentration, she might have become a naturalist, but for her, nature was a shimmering mirror of the unseen. This life, human life, she said, was a tool.

Because Serafine was from the Swiss Alps, I immediately thought of the ten-thousand-year-old man found frozen on a tor, his head crushed, apparently, by thieves on the path, his body and clothes intact, including, to the delight of Paleolithic anthropologists, the small leather pouch in which he carried his awl. Even now, forensic specialists are examining the body for other tell-tale signs: the food he ate, the water he drank, the state of his yellow teeth, the diseases he suffered before the sudden attack ended his brief and wretched life. We can only wonder what daily tools or treasures those ancient robbers coveted enough to want to bash him over the head with a hardwood club, the species probably oak, which grew prolifically on the lower slopes during that epoch. Of course, this begs the larger moral issue of the crime, if there was a crime at all, and not a fallen rock that hit him because of something he did wrong, or merely a flawed interpretation due to the social conditioning of the scientific researchers, who, though they claim to be objective, cannot always override the movies they've seen or the news they've read. This is precisely why Serafine did not read the newspapers—they were full of senseless crimes. And so I concluded that she knew nothing of the ten-thousand-year-old man with the ten-thousand-year-old awl and assumed that the tool of life she had in mind was a Swiss army knife, complete with screwdrivers, scissors, magnifying glass, blades, nail file, tweezers, toothpick, cork-screw, and saw.

She applied none of these to her trade. For her line of work, she used her God-given hands, which she placed on the hats of generals and heads of state and gently shook for one minute. This skill she had acquired from a renowned sage in southern India. After weeks of practice, she set off on her private mission armed with profound psychic abilities and enough cash to fly first class. No matter where she traveled—presidential palaces, sheiks' tents, rebel hideouts, winter bunkers—she made it a point to arrive promptly in her black, chauffeur-driven Cadillac. While her chauffeur paced, she showed me a thick portfolio of photos and newspaper clippings bound in plastic: Serafine's right hand on the receding hairline of President Fox of Mexico; Serafine's left hand on the balding pate of Prime Minister Jean Chrétien of Canada; Serafine's fingers coiled in the bristling hair of President Clinton of the United States of America; Serafine blessing the bowed heads of bemedaled generals from North Korea. None of them looked particularly reptilian in the photos, but you never know.

"My hands will shake the world loose from the malevolent grasp of demonic forces that hold it by the neck. And by the privater parts," she said, lowering her eyes demurely.

"You don't go around touching them there, do you?" I asked.

"No, no, I don't shake their dicks," she blushed. "Just their, uh, puny heads."

I told her that my Aunt Marian, in one of her fits, had tried to shake some sense into my head, but the method never worked for me. Nor has it had any discernable effect on the world's great leaders, as far as I could see.

Nevertheless, without statistical evidence or verification from newspapers and television that the world has improved or the war has ceased or that humanity has in any way evolved since the Neolithic, Serafine continues her independent campaign.

Since her arrival at the Panchan, she has shaken the heads of a dozen children and has organized their mothers for morning meditation. Aside from the first impromptu croaking session and regular midnight rain chants, there are "daily shake" workshops in which class members practice deep breathing to the strains of Serafine's silken voice. Then, turning slowly towards the person on the right, each participant demonstrates the pure love she has been rattling on about by vigorously shaking his or her neighbor's tender scalp.

Serafine's current subjects are not soldiers and politicians, of course. They are cooks and waiters, the entire maintenance crew, four fire dancers, three *charanga* players, two members of the family Morales (Don Moises and Alberto), one pizza maker, one welder, a solitary student of Maya iconography, plus an already converted army of sworn pacifists: the nomadic, unwashed, freaked-out, mushroom-eating, water-guzzling, drum-thumping Drainbows and moonstruck Dreamspell drifters for peace. The results have been amazing, to say the least.

Chapter 21

FIRE

When the moon hits your eye
like a big pizza pie,
that's amore.

They were just friends, we were told, but it looked like the real thing: bite-sized pecks over the chopped tomatoes, juicy kisses in front of the blazing pizza oven before Minerva took the stage at eleven. The courtship between the fire dancer and the pizza man was a sumptuous feast prepared and served in the hot Sicilian shrine of love where, amid the pungent smells of basil and oregano, the two gazed into each other's olive-dark eyes until the waiter shouted, "Okay, you lovebirds, one prosciutto, one blue cheese!" The pizza man would rush to the counter and begin pressing the dough with his nimble fingers until it was as thin as a milk-white mirror, then toss it into the air, once, twice, turn and catch it, race down the counter sprinkling spices, herbs, and cheeses, and with a grand, final flourish, shovel it into the flames until the pie was bubbly and crisp. A bravura performance in less than two minutes!

In between the bustle and clatter were heightened moments of poetry. During one of her head-shaking sessions, Minerva had overheard the Dreamers discussing the lunar phases, and when she compared her wayward moods with the rhythmic cycles of the moon, the pizza man nodded sagely. "Pizza is like the moon," said the pizza man, "white as the moon, round as the moon. And like the moon, pizza is made of cheese." This made Minerva smile. Then the red-faced cooks would grin and whisper, "They go together like garlic and oil."

Pizza was the Italian pizza man's life, and the pizza arena at the rear of the kitchen his private sanctuary. There he dreamed his dream of winning this girl away from Don Chato, who, in the short time she'd been dancing at the Panchan, had taken a shine to her himself.

If Chato didn't know of the pizza man's affections, it would have been a rare oversight, because Chato had eyes in the back of his head. He also had a gift for fixing things before they broke, of intuiting someone's feelings long before that person was even aware of them. So he probably knew but didn't let on, because he would never admit to having romantic sentiments, much less an attachment to a girl young enough to be his daughter, and although, in a moment of pride, he once acknowledged that she would benefit from the worldliness and financial security of an older man who could buy her an education and a better way of life, he was wise and self-effacing enough to know the arrangement would isolate her from the normal experiences of grow-ing up and also keep him reined in and shackled. After all, he was a macho with two ex-wives, a daughter, and a tangle of other women, a busy man with a web of responsibilities, the *patrón*, wound up and ambivalent as a cuckoo clock.

Being an innocent and head-over-heels, Minerva followed the strings of her heart, blindly it seemed, for if she did foresee the conse-quences, which would have been unusually prescient at her age, then she was, as they say, playing with fire.

Fire was in her blood, that much was clear. Fresh and new and fearless, she ran the flames like feathers over her thin arms as she spun around the dance floor, igniting the hearts of the crowd. She was the spark and the conflagration, the blue incandescence of joy and pain. From the first morning she snuck out of the house, racing from her cooking fire to the metal chains, she was a light, whirling as if she had no mind at all, until the day she set the Kevlar balls on fire and became a living flame. She stopped going home at night because, as she explained to her father, she got off work too late and couldn't afford a taxi at that hour, and besides, Don Moi always looked out for her. Never mind that the old man put his hand up her leg as he professed his eternal loyalty to Mingo. The all-seeing Chato finally stepped in and took Minerva under his protective wing, gave her a room at the Jungle Palace, two free meals a day, and promised to intercede with her father. It never came to that because Minerva went home twice a week to cook the food, clean the house, and do the laundry, without so much as a hello or thank you from Tito or her father, who buried his head in his notebook the moment she stepped through the door.

"I could be a perfect stranger, a hired drudge, he thinks so little of me. Not even worth beating," she told Don Chato.

"Ay, *chiquita*," he said, and gave her a hug. In no time the paternal hugs became intimate caresses, and without her being aware of how it happened, they began sleeping together in the same bed.

What Minerva didn't learn from him she learned from her closest friend. Bliss was an older woman of thirty-two who had been on the road since she was fifteen. She had danced on 42nd Street, danced in Vegas, danced at every roadhouse, honky-tonk, and shit-kicker bar between Boston and California.

"Ten times across the U S of A, down through Mexico and back up north, just by sticking out my thumb. You wanna do the same, spread your legs and keep your wrists together. That's right!" Her classes were filled with lots of advice.

"Clam chowder, artichoke hearts, *pollo con mole*. My grandma made the best schnitzel, but I had to leave Milwaukee. *Auf Wiedersehen*, that's 'adios' in German. Schnitzel, it's German, too. I know I look as if I haven't eaten since. Vampire Lady. Just hyper, I guess. Now slow down and bend. Lower, lower! Who wants babies and a belly anyway? Not in my tiny dancing togs! I'd rather be independent. Wait, I'll show you," and Bliss broke into the wild jungle stomp she saw in a tropical nightclub in Kansas.

One night she came out wearing nothing but a veil, a pole-dancing snake charmer writhing for the men. She was barred for a week after that.

"Lucky for me the veil didn't catch fire," Bliss laughed.

"But why do you go around looking like that?" the other girls asked, referring to her black stringy hair, black nail polish, black lips. They called her "the owl" because her blue eyes were big circles of runny black mascara whenever she came home. They called her "the witch" because she wore black in the stifling heat of May.

"Show biz," Bliss shrugged. "It's part of the act. Even my name."

Minerva was fascinated. "Maybe I should change my name, too. But what?"

"How about Ruby Red Ruby? Or Opal. Opals have fire. I like it!"

Whenever they went into town together, people stared as Bliss paraded down the street in a long, black, velvet dress and high, black, platform boots, a New York Goth carrying a bottomless black bag in one gloved hand and a polished obsidian ball in the other. Bliss said she could read everyone's fortune but her own.

She never said that something genuinely dark followed her like a starving street dog. After she started shooting ketamine, she and the shadow fused. The world went from dark to light, light to dark, day and night. The drug made her drool and ponder her hands, as if she were peering through a glazed windowpane in winter before her grandmother wiped away the frost. Then she was the queen of heaven, laughing and euphoric. "Rub-a-dub-dub," she'd sing for Moi's kittens. It wasn't clear whether the animal tranquilizer or her deep sorrow drove her into love affairs with wounded strays. For a few days she gave in to their whimpering demands. But soon the Gulf winds shifted, bringing clouds, like witches' hats, down from the north. She rose and spun in the morning air, the palm trees flailing before the coming storm. "I'm going through the door, Opal. I'm never coming back." And she was gone.

FIRE

Fire burns, but it also kindles its opposite. Fire chills, freezes, cauterizes the heart. And here lies the true danger for those who dance with the great, all-consuming lord. People who play with fire do not dissolve like the glazed puddles of gasoline left on the floor after the night's performance. They become as hard as tempered steel.

Now that Minerva was on her own the other girls behaved like Cinderella's stepsisters. While Chato was in Villahermosa doing the weekly shopping, a chore that often took several days—Walmart, Sam's Club, Toyota dealer, lunch at Vip's, cinema, hardware, Chinese or Thai, night with Leti, back to Sam's—the girls would make her clean the bathrooms at Don Mucho's. Or they'd refuse to share the gas she needed to light her chains, and she'd have to go out to the parking lot, with a rubber tube and a coke bottle, and siphon off somebody's tank. Or they'd hide her sequined tops or "lose" her chits for free meals at the restaurant. That's how she became friends with the pizza man. If nothing else, she could always eat pizza topped with cheese, tomatoes, mushrooms, chard, pepperoni, pineapple, and salmon. Not such a bad diet after all, especially after a regimen of beans, beans, and more beans her whole life long.

When Chato came home bearing gifts—a new dress or a dozen CD's—she wouldn't say a word about the other dancers. And she'd barely say thank you to him because she knew he was running around with other women. He didn't even bother keeping it a secret. But more to the point, she couldn't hide her passion for the pizza man from Chato, the man she loved. Her eyes sparkled when she talked about pizza, her body swayed when the pizza man delivered a pie to her table. Her dancing became more sensual, and as Chato rushed back and forth, shirttails flying, behind the bar, he noticed that when she swiveled her hips, her eyes fixed on the pizza man, not him. There was no sense talking to her about the infinite varieties of love. He downed a quick tequila and went off to see what his first ex-wife was cooking for supper.

It was while he was visiting his second ex-wife, reminiscing about happier days over a bowl of tortellini, her Umbrian grandmother's private recipe, that the young lovers slipped away. As soon as Chato returned to the Panchan that night, he noticed that the pizza man hadn't wiped the counters. His house was dark, and Minerva wasn't waiting for him upstairs. He flew out the door and discovered that the safe was empty. He ran to the parking lot and discovered that his car was gone. The next morning he called the police, issued a statewide alarm, and posted fliers all over town.

WANTED

Tender, fifteen-year-old, almond-eyed beauty abducted by long-haired, skinny, Italian runt both without brains in their heads

That's what he wanted to write. Instead, the handwritten posters contained a brief description of the fugitives—names, ages, physical characteristics—below two blurred black and white photographs arranged side by side. "Large reward for any knowledge of their whereabouts, and my brand new, air-conditioned Toyota van."

"They'll be back when the money runs out," the police assured him, by way of excusing themselves for actively doing nothing in the search. "Just sit tight and wait."

And that is what Chato did, dart and duck and pace around while the poles tilted and the world was shaken off its hinges. He was jiggling the keys to his new SUV, big enough to seat sixteen, when he slipped behind the bar for a quick refill, and the first thing he noticed was that the coffee tasted bitter and the pesto reeked of cloves. When he stormed into the kitchen he found three of the waiters slaving over the burners so that three of the cooks could stay home and nurse their sick babies. The rest of the cooks were wearing new baseball caps and flip-flops, small gifts of gratitude from the waiting staff. There were larger acts of unprecedented kindness. On their own, the waiters decided to share their tips with the kitchen, counting out the change in even piles and handing it to the women before escorting them to their paid taxis home.

"Good deeds don't make up for slow service, bad food, and lousy coffee," Chato told them.

"We'll try harder," the waiters said. Indeed, the next day when I sat down at a table, two waiters rushed over to take my order and then served me the finest *Sopa Azteca* I've ever had.

Still to deal with was the grave absence of pizza on the menu. "Where am I going to find an Italian pizza maker in Mexico?" Chato cried.

The unemployed pizza assistant, sitting dejectedly on his barstool, not knowing where to go and not having any money to get there, lifted his poor, pitiful head. "Me?" he said. "I'm *norteño*, but I have been watching the kneading of the dough."

"Put your apron back on," Chato barked. "What are you waiting for, a call from Hollywood?"

As for the rooms, the doors of three cabañas had been varnished shut. The maintenance crew, a lazy, drunken, incompetent gang of thieves, had turned over a new leaf and without orders from above were painting the rooms flamingo pink. Terence was teaching them how to lay floorboards, and on their own brisk initiative, they were replacing the rotten, termite-ridden porches and stairs. That meant only two rooms were available for guests.

"Monkeys!" Chato shouted. "Who told you to do all the work at once?"

"We thought of it by ourselves," the foreman answered proudly. "And we're not stealing the toilets and sinks. No, no. We're fixing the plumbing and the water lines."

"And who's going to pay for it if we haven't any guests?" The men shuffled back to their brushes and hammers.

"I'm not minding the store," Chato said to himself.

He blamed his distraction on the fact that he wasn't sleeping. When he stumbled in at four in the morning he noticed the unusual quiet. The drums were silent. He could hear the insects, the howler monkeys in the distance, the waking birds. "This is why I came back from the States. I was going to do my sculptures and paint. Now it's all business, business, business. There's no time for my art or anything else."

When he finally dragged himself out of bed at noon he overheard the artisans feuding over gemstones. The Drainbows and yoga adepts were quarreling about the moon. Everything was upside down everywhere he looked. He thought of talking to Rakshita, who had just returned from India, but after their last confrontation over the land, he decided to save face. Instead, he marched past the Mono Blanco, seemingly on a mission, only to see his father and Alberto merrily drinking tequila.

"Plotting against me again," he laughed.

"Alberto just told me a very funny joke," said Don Moi. "Sit down with us and I'll tell you."

"I'll bet the joke is on me!" Chato griped.

"Calm down, calm down," said Alberto. "You are making me nervous."

"How can I calm down when everything is falling apart?"

"Why not get a massage or have your head shaken by that Swiss Serafine?" Alberto suggested.

Chato went to the beach with a blond he picked up at the bar, but he was back in two days. The more he drank the less intoxicated he became, the more he smoked, the straighter he got until he was hang-dog sober and growling orders while draped in a bathroom towel. That's when he realized he must be in love.

Chapter 22

WIND

There is a wind called the spindle wind that rises out of the northern deltas, and as it spirals across the swamps, bearing black humors and blue miasmas, it infects people's brains. The wind is stronger than a hurricane, though silent, leaving its dispirited victims hopelessly unraveled and their loved ones sick with the worm. "It may be a superstition," Moi added, "but far more intriguing than medical explanations or religion."

Turning, turning in the invisible wind, along with so many other desperate species, the Drainbows and Dreamers, once fun-loving hedonists, morphed into moralistic creatures frightened for their souls. "Spiritual dilettantes. Holier-than-thou-ers," Moi pronounced. "There's nothing worse, except having to look at the foggy face of my lovesick son."

No one could have predicted this sudden twist, though if you gave it more than a passing thought, the headlong plunge from decadence to sobriety seemed inevitable. After all, the Dreamers were already living by the lunar calendar, as Christ did, and were counting the days to the apocalypse when the Maya gods would obliterate the world. They had never shown signs of contrition before, merely a dumb smugness about the terrible purge to come. Something must have clicked. Now they were getting ready for the end by punishing themselves and browbeating our neighbors.

"You'll see, they'll soon renounce this foolishness and go back to their former ways," said Moi. But they didn't.

In other words, we couldn't just blame the Evangelicals operating in the vicinity for what was becoming a mass conversion. Other than passing out leaflets, the two waiters and one accountant who had joined the First Pentecostal Church of Pakalna seldom spoke to the guests. As far as we knew, no one had been born again on this property.

It's possible that some people staying at Hotel Margarita's, adjacent to the Panchan, may have been imbued with the proprietor's deep Christian piety. I have not mentioned Margarita before, out of deference for her privacy, but since we are talking about faith, it should be said that this woman is a sturdy example. To avoid using harmful, foul-smelling insecticides, Margarita hunts for giant, predatory wolf spiders, picks them up in her bare hands, and plunks them in the cabañas so they can prey on indoor bugs to their heart's content. For her, cleanliness is next to Godliness, and her rooms are shining proofs of this adage. Margarita may speak of God in conversation, spend several hours of her day kneeling in prayer, but she is far too discreet and far too busy managing her maids, the laundry, and the well-diggers to interfere in the private consciences of her guests. Although she takes a dim view of smoking, drinking, and partying in her rooms, as any proprietor would, Margarita would never bother to change people's behavior. She just gives them a good scolding and asks them to leave the premises. As her late husband always said, "Live and let live."

Whether caused by the winds or internal pressures, the moral climate of the Panchan shifted to the right. The drums ceased. The wild became sedate. The alien threat took a back seat to matters of proper etiquette. Some of the results were most welcome, such as, "Excuse me, señora, may I help you carry that heavy bag?" or "I'm sorry, señora, for stepping on your foot." Sometimes the guilty apologetics could get out of hand, as in, "I'm such a clumsy, stupid twit I don't deserve to go on living," or downright hostile: "I'm sorry for breathing," "I'm sorry I ever met you," "If you don't say I'm sorry, I'll kill you."

The one person to benefit most from this viral rash of kindliness was Santa Claus, who, because of his resemblance to jolly Saint Nick, attracted scores of young lovelies to his castle-in-the-rough. The lord himself did the barbecuing—slabs of pork, bushels of corn, sacks of Idaho potatoes—in case a heavy crowd showed up. Every night he'd draw them in with succulent aromas, and every night he'd dish it out, dinner among the sandbags, until he became the most popular old gent at the Panchan.

But for the most part, the glaring conformity, the mind-numbing passivity that had characterized the Drainbow drifters soon devolved into cantankerous rivalries and ultimately, the total collapse of spiritual unanimity. Bobo, the voodoo prince, still tapped out his celestial rhythms, the odd pair of lovers still coupled in the bushes, unredeemable dopeheads still wandered naked through the bamboo thickets. Nothing could be done about these stubborn miscreants. The theological splits became genuine dangers when, for example, Kan and Cimi, two long-haired hippies dressed in bed sheets tied with red string, were ambushed by a gang of shirted young men who shaved, because it is written in the Bible that hair is an abomination against God.

Incidents of a similar nature erupted over tattoos. Since it was impossible to erase either the butterflies and rainbows or the jailhouse babes and biker skulls, judgment was heaped upon tattooists. Chuck Norris, famed for his faithful reproductions of Maya art, had to pack his bags after an angry encounter with a sword-waving aikido expert. It did no good to explain that he was not the real Chuck Norris, he only slightly resembled Chuck Norris, because the point was, Chuck Norris, or whatever his name, irreparably marred the flesh. Even Manik, an artist who employed only traditional instruments—natural inks and an old-fashioned, non-electric needle—was forced to close shop. People voluntarily removed their earplugs and piercings. Any form or notion of self-inflicted pain received harsh censure. Unfortunately, the use of branches, thorns, and lighters could not be enforced.

Ironically, this eccentric Puritan revival evolved in the shadows of a great Maya city thick with the ghosts of heathen souls who, on feast days, consumed their enemies' roasted thighs washed down with blood from their own pierced ears and sliced fingers. In those days, as in the Holy Land centuries earlier, self-sacrifice was an essential part of life.

The Maya also celebrated a period of time, or rather a period *outside* time, called the *Wayeb*, which fell at the end of the solar year. During this perilous five-day interlude, the social fabric was turned upside down, inside out, and backwards. (To this day a Maya man who meets a devil on the road will turn his pants inside out, stick his arms through the legs, and his legs through the arms of his shirt, and in this manner completely confound the devil.) In our epoch, the

Wayeb coincides with spring Carnival, a time of raucous merriment when mockery and mayhem are given free rein. In the Dreamspell Calendar, the *Wayeb* is celebrated for one day only, July 25, though not with the same ritualized abandon or spiritual stamina witnessed in Maya communities, where boys throw horseshit, bulls run rampant, men behave like monkeys, and, after five days and nights of drunken bingeing, purify themselves by running through fire.

Why the Dreamspell Calendar is out of sync with the Maya calendar is a complicated matter, which Podwell sums up by saying that the chosen beginning date is in error and the mathematics wrong. This means that people's names and signs and colors are out of whack, and they are really someone else. That is their problem, though less so since the ban on all forms of fortunetelling went into effect. The Dreamers were surrendering their identities and their futures! And besides, the five-day spell of prescribed catharsis had gone way beyond its outer limits.

But let's get on with the story.

Dismayed by the religious divisiveness growing in his backyard, Alux attempted to restore equilibrium by holding a sweat in his beautiful *temascal.* Imagine his surprise when ten svelt Drainbows—leading figures in the morality campaign—showed up in navy blue sweatsuits. Blake, Ginger, Daisy, and the others sat in a tight circle, dripping and clutching their zippers. When Alux's son blew the conch shell, the once hirsute Noah, now shorn of dreads and beard, let it be known that his ears could not bear any sort of native excuses for music. Instead of chanting songs to earth and sky, the sweating chorus broke into a cheerless rendition of "By the Rivers of Babylon." After inhaling eucalyptus for ten minutes, the entire group filed out, expressing their disgust with incomprehensible and lewd Maya rites. Thereafter, the former Drainbows and Dreamers began calling the resident scholars pagans. Matthew went back to Texas. Podwell and Barnaby took refuge in Alfonso's air-conditioned library, where they could continue their independent research and drink beer in peace.

On the land where Drainbows formerly stomped all night, out of control to the techno beat, the new building blocks of charity were laid. A person who dared to bum a cigarette was forbidden to smoke it alone. A bowl of leftover carrot soup had to be shared by at least three itinerant beggars, a combination plate by five. A woman walking alone through the woods could no longer be considered fair game by dim-witted, sex-starved louts lying in wait. Though loosely followed, these rules seemed just.

Prohibitions against hoarding private possessions, such as cameras, computers, and cell phones, rankled the few who owned them. They called a general meeting, held on the neutral grass in front of Rakshita's cabañas, a safe distance from her Hindu meditation temple, Don Mucho's restaurant, Alberto's bar, and Margarita's lint-free Christian emporium. Of the fifty attendees shouting at once, not one possessed the logical mind of a Donald Trump or Oral Roberts. Those who were listening were treated to a scrambled rehash of political theories dating back to 1960. At least the Europeans knew their history, speaking at length on the rise of the merchant class during the Middle Ages and quoting a few lines from Karl Marx. They were quickly told to shut up.

"Who cares if the workers own the factories! Who wants to work in a factory? Just look at what the factories produce!" Anti-globalization activists insisted that traditional tribes and Third World nations should forsake all twenty-first-century products.

"But *we* are a tribe!"

"Yes, but not in the sense of the Maya living around us. They are traditional people, even if they buy watches and cars."

"Didn't we agree that Maya civilization makes no sense?"

"Let's talk about other cultures, like China, India . . . ."

"Talk about exploitation!"

"We should go back to the barter system."

"What do you have to trade? Do you own anything? Do you grow anything? Do you fish? Do you hunt? Face it, we're useless."

There was a long, abject silence.

"Slavery begins in the kitchen and bedroom," Ginger announced, "the hearth of the wigwam, the sleeping bag and tent. Every couple, straight or queer, has to fight it out on the private battleground of whatever they call home."

"What are you saying?" Blake pleaded. "I've always been faithful."

"We're not even married," Ginger sobbed.

From then on we heard romantic paeans to communal living, beginning with the caveman, leaping forward to the short-lived Shakers, who didn't believe in marriage or sex, and ending with the Essene Jews, among whom Christ dwelled. Politics and religion got all mixed up. In the effort to reach a consensus, the Luddites received ten votes, divine kingship two. Capitalism and communism tied for zero. By the time the congregation disbanded, no one had come up with an alternative and no one was willing to share his or her cell phone.

The half-baked public debates spilled over into feuds among the laidback brotherhood of semi-skilled artisans. It began when a Mexican bead stringer lost six jade beads, which he insisted were Pre-Columbian and worth a great deal. "Pre-Columbian jade is worthless," he was told. "If you want to sell that dark green crap you deserve to lose them." To which the Mexican retorted, "Same for your turquoise paste from Arizona. Who needs it when you can buy these beautiful, rutilated, Chinese stones for a song."

One Parisian vendor went so far as to slash his prices on Austrian crystals. Rumor had it that, contrary to popular belief, quartz crystals had no healing properties whatsoever. Who started this rumor, nobody knows, but it spread like a possum's tail on fire.

That really miffed the Argentines, who were trying to get rid of rare amber nuggets dating back to the Jurassic. The vendors from Chiapas got into a huff because the best amber, they said, came from ancient Maya mines in the nearby mountains. That's when a Rasta pulled out his superb cache of Jamaican blue. A big mistake, because the vendors selling Baltic amber were so filled with envy they hatched a plot to filch his stash. Meanwhile, one of them pocketed the Rasta's needle-nosed pliers.

A month ago nobody would have been upset if an artisan stole an earring design. In fact, copying designs was standard practice. Everyone made the same things, to lessen the stress on indecisive customers. Now, following the herd was tantamount to highway robbery. Overnight the ban on originality was lifted, and artisans who were once afraid to stand out in the crowd were challenged to prove their metal, as it were. The results were a cavalcade of tortured wire adornments bent into shapes nature had rejected. One jeweler outdid nature by creating necklaces of woven twigs festooned with hummingbird nests, beetle horns, and dragonfly wings. And he wasn't even stoned! I wasn't the only one befuddled by the sterling examples of imagination run amuck. The artisans themselves were the cruelest judges. "What's that creature with the chandelier for a nose?" "Who's going to wear a three-pronged goose on her ear?"

The judgments served a purpose. Many artisans were forced to leave, freeing up space for the winning jury, the least gifted craftsmen, as it turned out, but the most competitive. Now they began jockeying for prime retail space. Setting up earlier was not the whole answer. Like barnyard roosters, they compensated for their limitations with colorful displays and a lot of crowing. When that failed, they circled like sharks, using lines that dated back to the Stone Age: "The eagle speaks to me. I will show you the secret waterfall of Queen Mo." But try as they might to woo starry-eyed buyers, the women weren't biting. You expected someone to shout, "You guys are nothing but a bunch of penniless, money-grubbing capitalists and gigolos living off women in your spare time." But no one did, except the old drum carver, John, who muttered words to this effect as he retreated to his wooded hermitage on the other side of the bridge to nowhere.

Restless and bitter over dwindling sales, the artisans began poking at the Dreamers. "Chicchan sounds like a crow," they jeered. "Akbal looks like an unpeeled beet." And before you knew it, there'd be real fisticuffs that ended with bloody noses and loose teeth. By then the air had grown so stale the Dreamers had lost the calendar count, didn't know whether the day was 11 Dragon or 12 World Bridger, and forgot the solar seals and tones.

It finally got to the point of mass decampment, with the artisans, Drainbows, and Dreamers wandering off in opposite directions, leaving the Panchan a becalmed ship in a waterless ocean. The few stragglers started thinking that maybe all the head shaking was a bad thing for the mind's harmony, the body's equilibrium, and the balance of nature and human society. They turned on Serafine.

Serafine, growing grayer every day, began to complain that mold was eating away at her skin. She was constantly scratching. The growth that began as a pimple on her upper lip blossomed larger every day until it covered her lower cheek. She walked around with a bandage, until she couldn't walk or sit. Her nose was growing longer, at least that's what people said, and she couldn't sit in a full lotus position for more than five minutes before her tailbone started aching with a vengeance.

"What's that poking out in back of your skirt, White Dragon?" "What's that bandage for, Lizard Face?" "Whoo-hoo, Witch Fingers!" "Cat got you tongue, Pussy Claws?"

She lay on the grass, scratching her head, scratching her flaking arms, and decided to cancel the daily head-shaking sessions and the nightly rain chants. Yesterday evening the five toads who showed up started a brawl when one of them said, "It's already raining," and someone else said, "This isn't rain, it's liquid acid, bozo."

When Serafine decided to call her driver to come pick her up, she discovered that someone had stolen her cell phone. She rolled over and wailed, but according to unreliable witnesses, nothing came out but a tiny, lizard-like chirp. They say her driver appeared out of nowhere, a phantom dressed in a powder blue suit and cap, helped her into the backseat of the Cadillac, and slowly drove her away, into the gray zone.

The next day, or the day after that—it's hard to keep track when one day melts into another and time revolves like the wheels of a silver Toyota van—Minerva and the pizza man came home.

"We've been to the beach. I learned how to swim," she told Chato, who immediately reinstalled her in his house and in his heart.

"As for you," he said to the pizza man, "we've found a replacement. If you want to stay, you can work as his assistant. If you're not happy with that, you can leave. You're lucky I'm not throwing you in jail for stealing my money, stealing my car, and stealing my girl. You'd never see the light of day." For the meanwhile, the pizza man accepted Chato's offer.

The following morning the artisans banded together and braided a simple cross out of bamboo reeds, at the foot of which they offered their finest jade, amber, turquoise, and crystal stones. Once more the Dreamers residing at Rakshita's sang to Mother Moon. Everyone breathed a sigh of relief, which gathered into a gust of wind blowing toward the Pacific coast. And life went on as if nothing had changed.

Chapter 23

KILL THE PIZZA MAN

"Time can be cut down and sliced," Roque said as he punched the dough for a second rise. "Fifteen minutes. That's all it takes to make the perfect pizza." He let out a mad cackle, as if he had just made an even greater discovery somewhere in the depths of the red-hot bricks, something extraordinary that defied the laws of physics. His wiseacre grin resembled the delirious snicker on one of Breughel's peasants, merrily sliding pies into the oven as Icarus dropped into the sea. It made you want to slap him. In fact, that's what the Italian assistant did before storming off the job in a Sicilian flurry of curses.

"I have a new idea," Roque beamed, tapping his middle finger to his shaved and sweating head. No wonder he liked the French. During the five years he spent in Montreal, he had picked up their flair for deep thoughts. "It's revolution!" he sputtered, glancing at the framed photo of Leon Trotsky, his hero, buckling above the pizza oven. "I must keep up, you see." Then he leaned over conspiratorially. "Tell me the truth. Hamburger?"

"So-so," I said.

"Chicken in the cream sauce?"

"Too creamy," I said. "And the iceberg salad. Awful."

"Hmm," he nodded thoughtfully. "I trust you. You are my friend." And then he whispered, "Corn, the stuff of life. Corn pizza! I will serve you some tomorrow."

But when I returned to the kitchen the next afternoon at five, Roque was sitting morbid and dejected on the barstool. "Everything changes," he shrugged, his dark eyes filled with dark tears. "My pizza is the best in Chiapas, maybe in all of Mexico. And you know what? There's no wood for my fire. Soon there will be no wood in the world."

That's how I found out that Roque was the new manager of Don Mucho's restaurant. And little by little I discovered that my succinct epicurean reviews on the tang of the hamburger, the texture of the fries, the overpowering whiteness of the sauce, the limpness of the lettuce and the uninspired dressing had been reported to the boss and used as arrows to target the belated kitchen manager freshly plucked from her post.

Every day the woman arrived in the late afternoon, two round babies in tow, and in between changing diapers at the bar and spooning gruel into the toddler's hungry mouth, the harried mother still had the strength to snap commands at the overheated cooks slapping from burner to burner in their flip-flops and cut-offs and thigh-high skirts. "Don't forget to mop the floors!" They didn't have a minute to catch their breaths after feeding a hundred people an hour, dicing the onions, dishing the pesto, slice and dip and fry. Mopping the floor, scrubbing the counters, keeping the walls greaseless and white were basic to sound kitchen operations, more vital than the food, according to the new manager, who happened to be an ex-army sergeant and Chato's kid sister. "No one's gotten sick eating here," said the cooks. "She could at least try to be nice." Maybe she thought that being a relative gave her the right to boss the staff, but unlike her brother, she was just as cold toward customers. Friendliness, it seemed, was outside her realm of responsibility.

So was quality. It was no secret that the food had gone downhill, and by the blameless looks on the cooks' worn faces it was the new tyrant's fault. Since she had no time for shopping, the produce now came from the market in taxis, the sprouting carrots, ragged lettuce, bearded potatoes, and sleeping squash handpicked by the sleazy vendors. That was life in the army, life in the Commonwealth of Virginia where the rednecks ate gravy and grits.

No one eating at this restaurant knew what a redneck was. It's just that Aida carried a chip on her shoulder, and her husband had a bigger shoulder. The bruiser was six foot two, wore a crewcut and a mean lip. He scowled at her as if sizing up how long she had to live. Theirs was an arrangement made in the boudoir of hell.

Aida hadn't counted on the bond between the boss and the new pizza maker. Years ago her big brother had rescued her from the night-club bouncer, found her a job and a place to live, given her a chance to meet someone new. And what did she do? Get pregnant with this lummox. The guy was in the used car business, which was some sort of euphemism, and since he was on the road again, her brother called her into his cluttered kitchen, which served as his private office. As usual, he was dressed sartorially in a bright orange towel.

"The buns are stale," Chato began. "There's no garlic in the garlic dressing, no bacon in the bolognese."

Since she was an ex-sergeant and the one who usually put people in their place, Aida pushed away the kitchen stool and said, "Why don't you get out of bed and stop fucking that bozo cokehead?"

"Who's fucking dopeheads here?" said her brother.

"You're calling me a dope. You're the dope!"

"Fucking that jerk and making babies. Is that what I'm paying you for?"

"Fuck you!" screamed the sister. "And fuck the whole damn place."

Standing in his orange towel, staring at the piles of crusted dishes in the sink, Chato thought of firing every one of the monkeys who worked for him and then he'd be free to retire. Instead he swallowed hard and fired his sister. Aida was already in tears and heaving one leg after the other out the door. Too late, the deed was done. But what dumb monkey could take her place? Who was the best choice of possible victims?

Roque with the black, sunken eyes, Roque with the black rafts under his drowned sockets, Roque the scalped eraserhead who looked more like a reverse telescope than a man.

From the moment he took charge of his ambiguous position, he began to mope like a monarch, sagging under his invisible crown even as he ordered the waiters around with newfound authority, yelping like a pup at the cooks, sighing and gazing heavenward for guidance from a God he never believed in until now. Raised to a position of great responsibility, he was figuratively lowered to his knees, begging for divine assistance. He knew where to buy boneless fish, stringless chickens, fresh buns, eyeless plum tomatoes, and real spinach for his calzone. His past life at the prep counter was long and hot yet filled with accomplishment and simple satisfaction. Now he had enemies, one by one. They were all armed and ready to shoot him.

First among them was Don Moises with his old .22, rabid at the dishonor done to his beloved daughter, beautiful and capable in all ways, and now let go—fired—for that idiot, that pusher, that pimp. Everyone knew Roque was stealing money from the cash register, stealing from his gullible son. He was also ruining his son's health, that swindling, furtive link in the chain of Chato's high blood pressure and mindless, macho womanizing.

Alfonso agreed. Roque had caused a split between him and his own brother. A wedge had been driven between them, and he who drove the wedge had to be killed.

Chapter 24

GURU KARL

Over at the spiritual zone, Rakshita was stirring her yin yang soup. Normally at this hour she would set forth the daily rule on the yoga way toward higher consciousness. Today, as the red beets bled into the white potato puree, she proclaimed she'd had enough. Life wasn't frozen in the eternal present; it was spinning like a broken tape, repeating the kind of intolerable noise that instigated violent behavior. The evil forces besieging the Panchan were blocking her serenity and driving her business downward. But, Rakshita announced to all within earshot, and to friends and soul mates in cyberspace, she had one more card to play. The wonderful guru she had met during her last trip to India had accepted her invitation. Yes, he was the real thing, and he was coming to Mexico, and anyone willing to pay six hundred dollars could attend Karl's lectures and receive full room and board. For residents on the grounds, the fee was a mere two hundred dollars for a week of enlightenment.

Although Guru Karl lived in a cave at the bottom of a sacred mountain in southern India, he was not exactly a Hindu. His first life-altering vision came to him several months after reading Carlos Castaneda when he saw in a dream his own outstretched hand. That flash of recognition showed him the meaning of life and death.

When I suggested to Rakshita that we make a flower garland for her guru, she smiled mysteriously. "Guru Karl is not that kind of guru. He is honest, very direct."

Rakshita had a history of infatuations with spiritual teachers who invariably came up short. "She is obsessed with gurus," Moi said, and he would know, for she hung on his every word until his Napoleonic nature outweighed the wisdom he had to impart.

Rakshita's deep admiration for the young and beautiful Gurumayi, "the hugging saint," took her to India three times and to the ashram in Vermont where she spent several months meditating and cleaning house. When it was disclosed that Gurumayi was wanted for tax evasion in thirty countries, Rakshita flew home to Germany, where the guru had found safe haven, and there, sitting at the master's feet, no more than two blocks from the lingering signs of the war's destruction, the traffic horns and wailing sirens brought back memories of collapsing walls and flying glass and fires burning everywhere, and Rakshita's faith in the power of love waivered.

Upon returning home, Rakshita was drawn to a Maya healer who was performing miracles throughout the mountains of Chiapas. Don Lauro had an amazing past. Born to humble Chamula parents, he carried firewood, fetched water, hoed and weeded the stony fields until he reached the age of twelve, when his father suggested it was time for him to look for a wife. A few days later, while tending the sheep and gazing tearfully at the hills and streams of his childhood home, the boy noticed three strangers dressed in flowing robes and peaked felt hats ascending the steep path to his family's thatched hut. Accustomed to walking mountain trails, the men climbed steadily, pausing only to plant little colored flags at every craggy bend. There was something magical and familiar about them, especially the gifts they brought: brass cymbals, turquoise beads, and a pair of soft red boots, which fit the boy's feet perfectly. Who knows how the visitors explained their mission, but after a half hour of gestures and nods, the boy's parents agreed that the monks could take their son with them to Tibet. The unworldly couple had no idea where Tibet was, but when the men pointed toward the east, the family assumed Tibet was the name of a Maya village in Guatemala. For seven years Don Lauro lived in a monastery high in the Himalayas, where he learned Buddhist prayers, the secrets of Tibetan healing, and the art of walking on snow. In his dreams he wandered across mountains hidden in mist, and when he awoke he remembered how the clouds clung to the invisible slopes above his family house until the sun broke through in late morning and illuminated the lush green peaks. It was time for him to go home.

When I met Don Lauro, he had been back in the highlands for less than a year and had already acquired a huge following. During the workshop he held at the Panchan, he asked us to sit in a circle and breathe deeply. Swirling his long, white, dragon cape, he lifted each of us to our feet, and with an enormous smile, wrapped us, one by one, in a loving embrace.

Three extraordinary things happened during that visit. First, his effervescent spirit sent sparkling bubbles into the tremulous atmosphere. Second, while Don Lauro was having supper—a heaping plate of French fries instead of the healthy vegetarian curry Rakshita had lovingly prepared—a traveler strolling along the night path suddenly lost consciousness, reportedly because of a bee sting. Don Lauro leapt from the table, cradled the poisoned man in his arms, and brought him back to life.

The third incident occurred the next day—the healing of Rakshita. Nervous and distraught, she confessed to Don Lauro that although her work was far from done and her land was in dispute, she was ready to leave the Panchan. She had posted signs throughout the grounds, "No drumming permitted," yet the drumming never ceased. She had made overtures toward every family member, but her conciliatory efforts were brushed aside. She had implored Don Moi to love her more, or love her less, and conceding to both her wishes, he professed his love and then ignored her. It was driving her mad. Out of the blue, the Tibetan *curandero* suggested they talk to Lord Pakal. Off they sped, the White Flower of the Jungle bound in a silk sari and the Chamulan gnome enveloped in his dragon cape, down to the tomb to ask the great king's advice on the practical matter of real estate. Waiting anxiously at the bridge were five of Rakshita's handmaidens swathed in belly-dancing scarves and weeping silver bells. An hour later Rakshita stepped out of her car, a pale smile flickering across her damp cheek. "I'm not leaving," she whispered. "Pull up the 'no drumming' signs!" As Don Lauro gaped in astonishment, the women fell to the ground and kissed Rakshita's feet.

"Not that kind of guru," Rakshita had said. The website presented a blond lifeguard who communicated with dolphins at John Lily's research center in Florida. Later he became an artist, photographer, and poet. After that, he studied yoga in Goa and Thai bodywork on the beaches of Phuket. "Divine, blissful," sang the blurbs. The cheesecake photo of Karl's butt in a bikini bathing suit said so much more, about him and about Rakshita. Even if he turned out to be vain and shallow, with less upstairs than down, that all-American teddy bear sort of guy would have been a great improvement over the Karl who arrived. This was the odd thing about Guru Karl: he was a walking, talking, cosmic alternate who happened to land in the salvation business. The boy who swam with dolphins was the light Karl. The man who appeared before us was the dark Karl.

Karl's face was flat and wide, topped by receding mouse-brown hair raked straight back with a thick plastic comb. His body was white and flaccid, the skin on his face stretched tight, and when he smiled his teeth protruded like the poplar toothpicks stuck in the mouths of Eskimo scare masks. He smiled often: an artificial devil's smirk. You could easily imagine him living in a cave or padded cell, so gray and washed out was his appearance. He was not at all the master we anticipated.

Now why did the universe bring us the dark Karl, the bitter reaper? The man ate nothing and survived on black coffee, no sugar, no cream, thank you. The wild ginger and coconut palms left him speechless. Certainly the grounds needed pruning, but he absorbed the scene so quickly with his non-gardener's eye that I knew the landscaping was not the source of his open displeasure. Could this modest-looking man in rumpled brown slacks be so enlightened, so disciplined, so remote from this world that the overpowering force of nature failed to flutter an eyelid or penetrate his nose?

"Pretty, isn't it?" someone prodded.

"The picture before me is an illusion," he frowned, "no different than a Tarzan movie."

Was he dissatisfied, then, with his lodgings? His room was appropriately bare of amenities, furnished with a cot, cold shower, and wooden deck beginning to warp in the rain. Karl had lived for years under worse conditions, after all, without a bed or sink or walls. Was it the food? He had his choice of banana pancakes, tofu fritters, *bibimbab*, sauerkraut, *sambar dal, spetzel,* and apple dumplings better than his German mother made. Why did he refuse to eat? No fish bones to choke him, no jellied calves' brains to turn his stomach, no wine to plunge him headlong into gaiety.

At last he commented on the rain, which thankfully falls at this time of year. "It rains a lot," Karl said dryly, his thin smile displaying abundant pride in his subtle powers of observation.

Curiously enough, it hadn't rained since Serafine's desertion. But the night Karl landed at the airport a heavy storm prevented the driver from picking him up on time, and Karl had to wait for two long hours in the hot, half-lit, flooded lobby. For the next three days we experienced monsoon rains of a force common to India, bone-soaking downpours that carved Rakshita's land into floating islets bisected by foaming streams. Karl didn't like rain. Wasn't rainwater the most transparent, mirror-like element on the planet and the most vivid metaphor for the flow of existence? "Water is an illusion," we were told. Yet the illusory substance most like the Reality he was trying to describe made Karl grumpy. The rains poured down upon the temple. The rains poured down on our sandals left at the door of the temple. The rains roared so loudly it was difficult to hear Karl speak. It roared so vehemently Karl could barely hear himself think. Wasn't that another good thing, not thinking, not using the illusory mind and achieving the state of No Mind, attainable thanks to the hurricane's roar? The sound that muffled Karl's voice made him grumpy. It was somewhat of a surprise, nevertheless, that when Gretchen, one of the women sitting in our circle, boldly asked, "What is Karl like?" Karl responded, "At night I say bye-bye and fall into that deep sleep that is most like pure Self, pure Conscience. In the morning Karl always wakes up angry."

That was the first clue, inexplicable as the mystery of Selfdom, which may be another non-existent layer to be peeled off in the empty search for the illusory heart of existence.

"Karl," said John, a young man of twenty-two, "I am, uh, thinking maybe of going to India possibly. Maybe studying at Osho." I knew how difficult it was for John to make this momentous decision, because the woman who raised him was the founder of the San Cristóbal chapter of I Am the Presence, Liberation of the Sacred Fire as well as a loyal disciple of Elizabeth Clare Prophet, the spiritual leader of the Church of Universal and Triumphant (CUT), a cult devoted to the coming paradigm shift in consciousness and among the staunchest survivalist groups headquartered in Montana. While CUT members waited for the dawning of a New Age, they stockpiled weapons and maintained intimate communication with thirty-five spiritual advisors, all Ascended Masters, including Morya, Afra, Hercules, and Jesus. John's mother regularly channeled the undead alchemist St. Germain, along with hundreds of the angelic host, first and foremost her own mother. Keeper of the Violet Flame, the "Angel Lady," as we called her, wore amethyst beads and lavender dresses, drove a purple car, lived in a grape-arbored purple house, and ran a purple-appointed sushi bar where her son served as *sou* chef and waiter. For John to break away took great courage.

"You will learn nothing," Karl said.

"But I . . ." John stammered.

"There is no trail to enlightenment. Buddhism, Hinduism, Sufism, Shintoism, all the isms, plus meditation, Hathayoga, hanging by your heels, or running hundred-mile marathons. Love is illusion, detachment is illusion, the Tao void is illusion. All these honored paths and byways are pure and pointless dead ends. Next." The boy broke down and wept.

"Karl, I have a personal question. My daughter is very sick. She is studying at university in Bruges and yesterday they called to tell me she is in the hospital. Should I fly there or wait?"

"It doesn't matter if you go or stay here listening to me. She is not your daughter! You are not her mother! Your relationship with this girl is an illusion."

"Easy for you to say," the woman blurted. "You're a bachelor, a bachelor who lives in a cave!"

"A caveman, yes, that's me," Karl laughed, "staring at the shadows on the hollow walls, like Plato, and knowing they're not real."

Rosalie bolted from her meditation pillow. "Wait a minute, Karl. Are you saying that nothing means anything? Is that what we're supposed to think? I'm a New Yorker. I don't have children. I work day and night for an environmental organization. Most of my friends work for non-profits, too, on behalf of hunger, poverty, Third World peoples. If everything is an illusion, what's the point?"

"All your efforts to help are self-serving. They make you feel better. But what is feeling better? Feeling good or feeling bad is meaningless."

"But the world is full of pain and suffering. Isn't it possible to improve things a little, create a better world?"

"There is no escape. The earth and all who live upon it are figments. All we have done or not done in our brief and miserable lives are tricks of the mind, idyllic fantasies, phantasmagoric nightmares. Hunger and poverty are illusions. Violence and war are illusions."

"What of the devastation of World War II?" Rakshita asked. "I saw it with my own eyes. I remember."

Karl rolled his eyes, exasperated. "Doesn't anybody have a good question to ask Karl?" He looked around the room, breathed deeply, and said, "The war never happened. The Holocaust never happened!"

A strange vapor, smelling of decay, hovered in the sudden silence. It had stopped raining. The moon was rising like a puff of steam from a ghostly liner lost beneath the sea of trees.

Hesitantly, Rakshita asked whether it was worth maintaining her religious retreat, and Karl told her that the retreat, as she called it, was a reflection of her ego, and her spiritual path another vaunted expression of her ego.

"Thank you," Rakshita whispered, bowing her head.

Later she told us that after everyone left, Karl berated her for not recruiting more participants, complained that the fees were not worth his time and that the questions were idiotic. Rakshita ran back to her house tower in tears.

The next morning, as the sun was glaring in a cloudless blue sky, Guru Karl was pacing in and out of the dappled light, visibly shrinking and growing more irritable. Finally he hurried to his room, coffee cup in hand, leaving the group to their silent breakfasts. The moment he disappeared Rakshita announced that she had spent the night crying, and in the midst of her despair, she had a revelation. She would renounce her passive demeanor. She would take a stand. She would ask Karl to leave. And she did! Bathed in dewlapped sunlight, she was positively glowing.

In a little while the taxicab came. Karl threw his duffle bag on the back seat, climbed in, and rolled down the window. "Here is one more illusion, the greatest of them all," he beamed, waving a wad of bills. As he shook hands with each of his short-lived students, Karl counted out the pesos and returned everyone's tuition. Crystal told him to keep it. After all, she explained, Karl had played the devil's advocate. Nihilism was his method for waking people from their reveries, their spiritual dreams. His unbearable coldness ignited a spark, a fury, a fire.

Rakshita, for one, had been renewed. Quietly she went upstairs and packed, and the next day, without formal farewells, she left the Panchan forever.

Chapter 25

KILL THE PIZZA MAN II

Moi waited until Rakshita left before sneaking up on Roque and placing the gun barrel at the back of his head. He didn't fire. He simply said, "I will kill you when you least expect it."

Roque's eyes sank deeper into his skull. In the ash heap of his brain smoldered a feral memory of being backed against a wall, tear gas burning his lungs, and shadows slowly lifting his aching arms and flinging him into a metal cage where he lay, senseless, for who knows how many days. He was terrified then and terrified now. Still, he said, "This is revolution. I am not going to run."

Later that night, Moi sat complaining over at Alberto's bar, his furious heart pumping with the bass drum, thud-thump, thud-thump, thud-thumping for no one at the empty tables as the weekend crowd started lining up on the bridge to Don Mucho's, and cold jealousy steeped in the rain coming down. Moi had so many gripes it was hard to know whether he was drunk or sober or which side of the fence he was on. Definitely wobbly by the time Aida and company invaded camp, swelling the embittered ranks and bolstering the old man's misery. While the men got drunker, Aida soothed the babies and her father in the same soft voice. "*Si, mi amor, mi vida.* Yes, Papa, you are right. A thief, an addict, a spy."

Her soldier staggered to attention, cracked his beer bottle, and lunged into the clammy, waterlogged night. When he emerged from the storm he was looming above the prep counter, waving the jagged glass in Roque's face. Roque stepped back. Six waiters were there in a flash, surrounding the bull as he bellowed and snorted and sliced at the hanging lights. The waiters had him corralled, slowly edging him toward the dark, rain-soaked patio. The downpour didn't dampen his rage. He was lurching blindly, swinging the broken bottle crazily. The waiters backed off. He was still roaring and brandishing the bottle when the police arrived. The waiters strode back into the restaurant, clapping one another on the shoulders, their shirts soaked, their faces pale. During the skirmish, Roque ducked out the kitchen door and fled to his leaky room. The next morning he left for the beach.

After Roque was out of the way, Moi vented his spleen on Chato, this time for showing extreme stupidity by summoning the Italian back to Don Mucho's authentic brick oven. The day the pizza man arrived, ready for work, Moi was stirring the pot at the Mono Blanco.

"Here comes another thief," Moi said to Alberto. "Supposedly that son of mine offered a big percentage to lure him away from the Chinaman's. But if you ask me, there's something fishy about an Italian cooking chow mein in a little Mexican town."

"A percentage of the meals or the girls?" Alberto chuckled.

"The man should be locked up," said Moi.

"Which one?" laughed Alberto.

"Your brother!" Moi snapped. "You are as dumb as he is!" Alberto's face turned gray, and while Moi railed about this latest development, Alberto began to seethe.

"I could serve pizza, too," he muttered.

"You are stupid! I am a father cursed with four sons, one stupider than the other!"

Alberto left us sitting at the table and went to stand by the laundromat. A few minutes later Chato came splashing through the wet gravel, shirttails flying, head bent to the ground. Alberto fell in behind him, wrapped his arm around Chato's neck, and stuck two fingers in the middle of his back. "What are you doing on my property?" he shouted.

"Hey, motherfucker, this is my right-of-way. Get your hands off me!"

"No more right-of-ways, you bastard. You've taken advantage for the last time!"

Chato bit his brother's arm, turned, and socked him in the belly. "Try that again and you're dead, brother! You're lucky I don't have my gun."

"You're the one who's lucky. Consider this your last warning."

Moi sat stone-faced at the table, eyes focused on a ruby-throated hummingbird darting among the tulip flowers. "So beautiful," he said, "and such fierce warriors."

When I saw Chato next, he was high on adrenaline and running from one end of the bar to the other. "My crazy brother wants to shoot me. Let him try!" He stopped in his tracks and patted the bulge in his back pocket. "It's a terrible thing, brothers shooting brothers. And all because of that crazy old fart. Don't think I don't know what he's up to, scheming against me all the time. It's been like this since day one."

Thunder rumbled in the distance. Chato grabbed a bottle off the shelf and poured two tequilas. "He never sat down and listened to us. He never cared what we did all day. I made friends with his *compadre,* the doctor. I'd go and talk to him. He was the one who gave me good advice. And you know what? My father forbade me to see him, the Doctor Savilla. It made him jealous. Instead of trying to be a better father, he smacked me across the head! After so many years, that slap still burns."

Rakshita was right: Time was moving in cruel circles.

"It made me tough," he shrugged, "but not so tough that I don't think about other people, don't spend time with my daughter. I'm taking her to the beach next week. I'm taking her to Paris next summer."

He poured another round. "Believe me, I have other worries, the cabañas, the restaurant, the pizza." He nodded toward the oven and rolled his eyes. He didn't put it into words, but apparently the Italian pizza man was flirting with Minerva again. "Yes," he sighed, "I'm responsible for a lot of people. There are fifty-seven workers whose families depend on me. I have to watch them every minute. I have better things to do than fight with my crazy brother."

Chato had a bad case of the jitters. His nervous bravura and peculiar brand of melancholy were bouncing around inside him like atomic ping-pong balls. He was a human collider filled with enough raw energy to spark a grand display of fireworks or set off an ugly chain reaction that nobody wanted to see.

"Too much pressure," he said, and at that moment lightning flashed, wind whipped the trees, and the electric wires shuddered. Chato glanced at the roiling sky and stopped to check his pulse. "Don't worry, don't worry," he laughed. "I need a vacation, that's all."

Inexplicably, the storm passed without shedding a drop, leaving the atmosphere leaden. "Don't worry, don't worry, nothing's going to happen," he repeated. But the rusted color of the sun sinking like a worn machine gave me a shiver.

A local band playing hits from the sixties was performing at the Mono Blanco, and the joint was packed. Alberto should have been in his glory. Instead, he sat brooding like a mad Elvis, sallow and rigid, as his father told two drunken strangers the story of how he, Alberto, got fired from the department of tourism. The story was old, humiliating, and only half true.

Alberto was working in Asunción, helping the poor farmers who were the cursed descendants of the families Moises had led out of the Senora desert. Alberto had just bought a piece of real estate from the cooperative, and now he was telling them how they could turn their one asset, a scenic waterfall, into a major tourist attraction. The men were cutting a path down to the river, following "El Capitan." But "El Capitan" decided to blaze a shortcut through the bush. He took a terrible tumble and couldn't get up. "A real man would not have tripped, a real man would not have gotten lost in the first place," his father said. When Alberto limped into the office three days later, he discovered someone else sitting at his desk.

"It was the end of my term, Papa. The new governor came into power."

"All the same," said Moi. "You ruined your chances in the political sphere and you ruined your reputation with the peasants."

Alberto's face contorted. He kicked over the table and went for Moi's throat. The old man reeled, caught his son by the hair, and the two of them rolled on the ground. Moi punched Alberto in the ribs. Alberto ripped off his belt and swung the buckle in Moi's face. It took three bystanders to pull him off. One of them was Aida's hulking husband, who succeeded in wrestling Alberto away and locking him in his house. You could hear Alberto shouting "Bastard!" over the crashing cymbals of the rock and roll band.

Moi sat in the dirt, holding his throat. "I forgive you, son. You don't know what you're doing," he gasped. But his voice was so hoarse, and the twanging guitars so loud, Alberto couldn't hear him.

When Moi joined Alberto for coffee the next morning, El Capitan's eyes were red from crying all night. "I think I need a dog," Alberto said.

Moi, whose five mangy dogs followed him around wherever he went, agreed. "My dogs are my only friends," he said, although he pitifully neglected the shaggy beasts, feeding them scraps from Don Mucho's kitchen and refusing to bathe them. "Market dogs can fend for themselves. They don't need washing," he insisted. These particular Pomeranian terriers were dull and slow and stank to high heaven.

"Yes, it's good to have a pet," Alberto said.

That's when he went out and purchased the pit bull.

Chapter 26

DREAMSPELL

The week before summer solstice, flocks of full-breasted couch potatoes and hippies feathered in cockatoo white descended upon the Kin Ha Hotel to hear Jose Arguelles play the flute. His skin was as thin as rice paper, his cobalt eyes lifeless, but none of the Dreamers seemed to notice. As the ethereal notes bled inside the sealed room, the spellbound congregation swayed in unison. From the industrial cities of eastern Poland and Uzbekistan, the isles of Osaka and rifts of South Africa, the sands of Belgium and the barrens of Alaska, they followed a whisper, which came at dawn, on the beach, on the train, in the shower, while walking the dog during rush hour, and they all felt the same thing—the voice made their hair stand on end—and the next time they looked around they were on the floor of a pink hotel under permanent construction, surrounded by smoked glass, bleached palms, scaffolding, and plaster; the date was June 15, White Planetary Mirror, and they were celebrating the fifty-second anniversary of the opening of Pakal's tomb. You could hear the Maya workmen with their pick axes and shovels pounding out the magic number fifty-two on the floors above us. "I am guided by the power of death," read the augury for that day, "I am a galactic activation portal—enter me."

Mexican archaeologist Alberto Ruz found the stone plugs to the shaft in 1949 and, after spending four seasons clearing the steep, rubble-filled stairway, reached the great triangular door, pried it open, and gazed into the frozen mouth of the Earth Monster. Between its needle teeth rested a massive stone sarcophagus blanketed with a crystalline substance that sparkled in the sudden light. To hoist the huge lid, the excavators used car jacks, raising the intricately carved block inch by inch until they came upon the sealed inner coffin—a stone capsule shaped like a man. Inside lay the mortal remains of the king, a death mask of jade mosaic over his faceless skull, beads of jade and coral scattered across his sunken ribs, and rings of jade on the bones of every finger. In his collapsed right hand he held a solid cube of jade and in his invisible left palm a perfect jade sphere, placed there perhaps as an indelible sign of his mastery over space and time.

Through the serpentine "psychoduct" leading from the burial chamber to the upper sanctuary, Pakal sends Arguelles timely utterances concerning latter-day events, the echoes of which we should hear today as soon as the music and the hammering cease. Since Arguelles claims to be an incarnation of the king, then, theoretically, Pakal is talking to himself. Yet it is a matter of some concern whether the words are clear enough to penetrate the layers of odd notions seesawing in Arguelles's head. For example, along with usurping Pakal's name, Arguelles calls himself Votan, an underworld god whose legendary namesake was a great warrior who marched across Chiapas beating his drum and causing bloodshed wherever he paused for the night. Coincidently, after Subcomandante Marcos, the charismatic spokesman for the EZLN, suggested that the Maya insurgents return to traditional culture, he adopted the name Votan, Lord of the Hollow Drum. Arguelles's multiple personalities partially explain the soulless stare of a public relations man who casually admits he is really a galactic being come to deliver a message of universal magnitude.

We, the self-selected, the message began, were living at the magnetic, prophetic end of the chaos of history, awaiting the extinction of the Gregorian calendar, whose irrational system of uneven months and years has kept us in this muddled state, out of sync with the natural flow of time, best represented by the Maya Long Count, which may come to an end in 2012 and cast us into deeper chaos. But, Arguelles promised, only temporarily. Although he didn't say for how long, some time following the death of the Fourth Sun and total world destruction, life would take a turn for the better.

Brushing aside his snowy hair, the Closer of the Cycle presented his glad tidings in a smooth American twang deftly interpreted by White Wizard, a healthy Mexican specimen with whom Arguelles enjoyed a telepathic relationship conducted on the 13:20 frequency. Having grown up in Minnesota, Jose does not speak Spanish, although he was sired by a Mexico City cop. Officer Arguelles was dealing with routine criminal matters the afternoon of August 20, 1940 when, in plain view of undercover police, a lone gunman gained entrance to Calle Viena 45 and shot Leon Trotsky in the head. Sometime during the investigations, the Arguelles family left Mexico City and settled in the frigid Midwest. Unlike his twin brother, Joe grew up to be a brilliant student, popular and apparently well adjusted. After high school he went on to study art history at the University of Chicago and later taught at Princeton. None of his high school classmates suspected he would become a fractious lunatic chasing the wayward patterns of the moon, a melancholic exile from the human race so far out there he believed he was an ancient Maya spirit from another galaxy. Mountains were wearing down, the seas sinking, the air poisoned with contaminants and evil thoughts, and the only eternal truth Arguelles could find throughout the realms of mutable existence and in his own dissolute life was a fundamental equation that transcended the cycle of light and dark, the creative and the cataclysmic:

$$T(ime) + E(nergy) = Art$$

On the road to 2012, "the eye of the needle," we will face a series of wars and natural disasters, Arguelles warned. "But if we follow the thirteen-moon lunar calendar and live our lives in the mold of nature, there's a chance we can escape the traps of evil, injustice, globalization, and terror and stand naked before the great and inevitable transformation. The Earth herself is calling for us to live in peace and harmony. By growing organic gardens and eating raw carrots, the next few years of devastation will seem like a summer shower. Through the irresistible forces of Flowers and Song we will survive."

By "we" he meant the elect whose good intentions filled the room with the blended odors of an Indian bazaar and Persian caravansary, those who had surrendered their material possessions or were permanently out of work and trying to survive on organic produce raised by the sweat of their brows. By training their telepathic powers, they, and thousands like them, were creating a perfumed rainbow that would encircle the world and serve as a protective shield against the ominous

rays about to pummel our planet. As for the millions devoted to getting and spending, running giant corporations, or working the night
shift for ten bucks an hour, paying the mortgage, and living on credit,
punishment would be meted out in the form of fire, ice, wind, and
flood. Unhappily, they would perish.

Though the message was painfully familiar and took three interminable hours to tell, the audience applauded the man they call Blue
Spectral Monkey, muttered a word of thanks to Lord Pakal for his latest
communiqué, and without further ado, headed for the buffet.

The line was long. Haggard from his interstellar travels, Arguelles
fingered his turquoise beads and started shaking hands. His staggered
delivery lacked the holy punch of the Old Testament prophets though
his righteous condemnations encompassed the omnipotent rulers royally raked over the coals in Scripture, not to mention the petty tyrants
we regularly see on the evening news. Surely one who had witnessed
unspeakable destruction would bear the scars and horror still burn his
eyes, as when Pakal, just a boy, saw the moonlit temples engulfed in
flames, his loved ones murdered, the gods cast down from the heights,
and turning away, journeyed into the abyss, the Black Hole, to offer his
blood, not once but many times, until the gods stood up and walked
again in their splendid jeweled ornaments. And because of these deeds,
as it is written, his name would resound unto the year A.D. 4772, and
he would rise, a comet, a planet, the seed of new life. The calendar
wheel would continue to revolve through untold victories and defeats,
in accord with the endless flux of history and the decrees of fate.

Arguelles was speaking for himself, not Pakal, when he said the
rainbow of unified consciousness would sweep away the carnage and
the tears, memories of lilacs and snow, and we shall dwell forever in the
peaceful fourth dimension as galactic beings of light.

Standing at the end of the line, it all seemed hopeless. Among the
Maya, rainbows are bad omens, venomous serpents that suck your
spirit and drive you mad. The psychedelic posters of butterflies and
lotus flowers merely hinted at the tastelessness to come. It will take
time to adjust to a disembodied life in paradise. Reading the shadows
of other people's thoughts may make us cry, but we won't have tears or
eyes. Yet people were smiling as they filled their plates, somehow reas-
sured by Blue Spectral Monkey's anxiety-ridden fantasy of the future.

They were moving in slow motion, and I remember thinking that perhaps the sea-green squash soup contained the waters of forgetfulness or the *chiles rellenos* congealing under the clanging steel servers disguised a euphoric that induced amnesia. The melody rose, the violins played, and as people tiptoed from the steam table, around the piles of concrete debris, and over towards the dusty swimming pool it seemed they were waltzing on the ashen ruins of a forgotten civilization.

Blue Spectral Monkey failed to mention the final darkness that inevitably snuffs out a fly, a star, and a man. He circled the sunlit water like a moth drawn to the flame and pressed his turquoise beads to his shattered heart.

Chapter 27

THE RUSSIANS

Lightning streaked across the sky as Saskia lifted her fork and stabbed at her pesto. The lightning and the aluminum fork were interconnected, like the coiled spaghetti on her plate and the spaghetti and her weary brain. This was Saskia's third visit to Palenque, and already she was sick and tired of translating the menu from Spanish into Russian and repeating the names of the Maya days. Odd that she had to do so much talking since the fifteen members of her tour group were professional psychics and Saskia was a well-known medium in Kiev. Whether she wore her pink pantsuit or violet cocktail dress, the woman always wrapped a white turban around her sensitive head because, as she said, being a tour guide and being a medium, they are the same.

"You come to Palenque and right away the soul wakes up. It flies any minute to places you can't imagine. I don't have to tell you it's a wonderful feeling. But they keep me on pins and needles. Not the spirits, the government men. May it happen today. May it happen in the tomb." She spat three times over her left shoulder. "For four days I'm waiting for the permit to go down. The red tape is—how do you say?—a hangman's rope, the Gordian knot, a noose around my heart. For twenty years I'm the minister of culture in my country. No worries, no complaints. The whole time I'm dreaming of being a big archaeologist, in Egypt, in India, in America. I see the cities underground with my own eyes. Now I will tell them nothing. Let them stumble around like bats. No thanks!"

Saskia's group was rigorously scientific. All fifteen clairvoyants were chemists or physicists, as well as long-standing members of the Institute for Scientific Research in Cosmic Anthropoecology (ISICA), before being recruited into the ranks of the Law of Time, the non-profit organization founded by Dr. Jose Arguelles, author of the Dreamspell and other works. They had brought the Kosyrev remote-sensing mirror, along with special instruments capable of weakening the magnetic field in Pakal's burial chamber. Once they got inside the crypt, the Russians were going to train their famous telepathic gifts on the matter of time, tweak it, alter it, and if all went well, change it into something that Einstein predicted it already was—a material force. Similar groups of psychic practitioners would be stationed at strategic power spots around the globe—Machu Picchu, Cairo, Glastonbury, Ayre's Rock, Pilao—flexing their frontal lobes at the exact same time. And as their minds were making enormous quantum leaps, the meters on their black Cosmobiotron would detect the slightest alteration in the temporal flow. The box looked like World War I surplus, but forget about looks. The combined concentration of two hundred and sixty psychics had the mind-blowing capacity to stop the passage of time! There was another incredible possibility: Distant Information Transfer. That is, the mental images beamed out at the infinite speed of time would intercept the Maya 13:20 frequency emanating from the center of the galaxy and beam back the thoughts of ancient sages transmitted thousands of years ago. Needless to say, the change in human consciousness would be earthshaking.

Already I was beginning to detect a hazardous rift among Arguelles's followers. These adherents of the Law of Time viewed the impending end date not as a catastrophe but as a giant breakthrough for humanity. In fact, they vigorously denied the disaster scenario altogether.

"Better not to think about it," Rikvek insisted. "If you think about it, it happens. Antarctica melts, Yellowstone blows its top. Stop!" He clapped his hands over his ears and winced. "Forgive me, I should not even say it. We must not even allow the idea into our heads." Rikvek was a physicist with the Russian space program. He wore a Russian goatee, trimmed to a point where a tiny tuft of white betrayed his otherwise youthful face and demeanor. "Nothing is objective, you see. Nothing is pure chance."

"Our minds are connected, like little lights on the Christmas tree," said Rikvek's pretty blond wife as she took her husband's hand.

"Lula is neurochemist. Looks at brains every day."

"Yes, brain is like the universe, same pattern, same stuff. It runs in all directions at once."

"We try to reach our neighbors with our rocket ships, with our radio telescopes, our probes, but these clever mechanisms are not necessary. Big waste of money," he laughed.

"Yes, we send our thoughts much faster," she said. "We make the quantum leap." Lula kissed her husband on the cheek. It was a good thing Terence wasn't here, because this pleasant talk about Russia's mind control experiments would have made his teeth throb.

"Cheaper to come to Mexico," Rikvek grinned. "More fun."

"Why Palenque?" I asked.

"The Maya are famous for their knowledge of time, no? This everyone knows. But Palenque is home of the greatest astronomers and timekeepers. Right now I am sensing their vibrations."

"You feel it here," Lula said, tapping her heart.

"Yes, the energy is very strong," Rikvek agreed. "We are scientists. We are on the same wave." He paused to ruminate over a new thought that just flew in from the Palace basement and caught him by surprise. "Oh, I will say it anyway," he shrugged. "It's true they make the same mistakes as we do, cut down too many trees, fight too many wars, keep the people under thumbs. They were modern, like us, hiding top secrets in their drawers. Hah! You think we Russians are very hush-hush. We Russians are not half as cagey as the Maya."

Where did these sinister ideas about the Maya come from, I wondered, the gray matter of bureaucratic scientists, the paranoid projections of New Age profiteers, or the coterie of social philosophers who make the rounds of late-night talk shows?

If Maya mathematicians were so secretive, why did they carve their calculations in stone? The fullness of the November moon in 2360 B.C., the total eclipse ten thousand years from now—the formulas are there for those who can read them. Kings and queens ascended to the throne when the sun reached the center of the sky; summoned the gods when Mars, Jupiter, and Saturn conjoined; presented their young heirs when the glorious solstice sun cast its radiance inside the holy of holies. These astonishing spectacles celebrated all fathers, mothers, and sons who stood under the open sky and watched the light grow and fade. Knowledge glittered like stardust, dazzling and ephemeral. The rain ceased, the corn dried on the stalk, the cities fell, and the people followed the gods as they carried their burden of days toward the house of the setting sun.

After lying dormant for a thousand years, the civilization has been nobly resurrected and, like other Third World cultures, raided, robbed, reinterpreted, and beaten into another form. For better or worse, this current wave of supplicants was going about its business bloodlessly. "We only want information," they said, the kind of wisdom that will change the world.

In other words, the Russians were not alone. Last month, three delegates from NASA held a one-day workshop for local schoolchildren. They offered a fine PowerPoint presentation on the ancient astronomy of the Maya. They handed out educational packets, DVD's, and free box lunches. They spoke about the virtues of the Maya cosmos. The curious thing is that they've showed up again, this time to make summer solstice observations from the Temple of the Inscriptions. And at dawn this morning, ten astronomers with the National Science Foundation were monitoring a sliver of light moving diagonally across the floor of the Temple of the Sun. Evidently Palenque was still a lively scientific harbor.

Why had ISICA chosen the royal tomb for their dramatic experiment in synchronicity? Rikvek's notion that Maya mathematicians manipulated time for Machiavellian ends raised my suspicions. Whatever they were plotting, the Russian psychics had something larger in mind than Maya politics, because they showed no interest in Pakal's life and times. No, they were completely focused on the amazing crypt, the huge door cut in the shape of a triangle, and the sarcophagus lid carved out of a fifty-ton stone slab. As far as the Russians were concerned, Pakal's sepulcher was a relay station broadcasting cosmic news.

Moises took the experiment in stride. He obtained government permits for the Russian delegation, and the following afternoon, Moises, Mingo, and I led the fifteen-member team step by slippery step down the long vertiginous staircase to the tomb. Some went down backwards, some on their rumps, others feet first, clinging to chinks in the dripping walls. No one stumbled, screamed, or

panicked, as sometimes happens in the chilling excitement. All in all, the psychic and scientific kept perfect balance until we stood before the carved image of Pakal hovering above the yawning skeletal jaws of the Earth Monster. Several team members, sympathetic to the corpse, complained of the weight of the stone pressing down upon their bare heads. Others wept openly.

Ever the guide, Moi explained that some experts thought the king was falling into the Underworld while others believed he was rising toward eternal life. Up? Down? The question seemed meaningless.

"For sure he died, didn't he?" they said.

"And when his soul was ready, he ascended to the center of the galaxy," Saskia reasoned.

"Some people think the picture shows Pakal driving a rocket ship," Moi told the group. "They say the beard of the Earth Monster is the flame of the rocket ship and that Pakal is sitting at the controls." The psychics smiled knowingly as they checked their watches.

"We're running out of time, please," said Saskia. Two of the men started fiddling with the knobs of the Cosmobiotron. "Please, we ask you now to turn around. No looking."

Moi began to mount the steps, but Mingo, clearly distressed by the black box, refused to budge. "The temples, the pyramids belong to the Maya people," he said. "I will leave when the government pays us for what they've taken away. Pakal was a great magician. Be careful what you try to steal from his grave!" Mingo placed himself solidly in front of the great triangular door, folded his arms across his chest, and closed his eyes. There was nothing to be done.

Moi bent over and shook Mingo's hand. "I will bring food for you tomorrow," he said cheerfully.

"Thanks, my friend. I told you, the story isn't over."

"Yes, we're at the beginning again."

"The beginning takes a long time to find, Don Moi. I think we're somewhere in the middle."

"Enough talking!" cried Saskia. "Please, it's late."

Mingo shook his head. "Such a hurry to stop time! These friends of yours, Don Moi, they must be crazy."

Moi bowed politely, and as we turned to leave, the Russians were hurriedly forming a circle.

When we reached the top of the temple, the sanctuary swam in golden light surrounded by a sea of jade mountains. On afternoons like this it was hard to imagine why anybody would want to huddle inside a damp tomb hoping to escape the earth. And with Mingo guarding the burial chamber, it was unlikely that the Russians would get sucked into a time warp unless they were magicians like Pakal who could break through iron bars and tons of holographic stone.

Moi pointed to the glowing stones. A ray of sunlight pouring through the western window of the gallery was crossing the center of the floor and advancing slowly towards us. As Moi stood motionless, the light ran up his leg and bathed his chest in gold. It lasted only a moment, but in that moment time stood still.

"The solstice sun," Moi smiled. "For one day out of the year I am king!"

"It's a miracle," I said, as the light retreated in a straight line towards the eastern window.

"Yes, it looks like a miracle, this perfect alignment of the temple with the last rays of the setting sun. But it's a human feat, a grand intellectual show, part of the astronomers' amazing bag of tricks."

"Designed to make the kings shine like the sun," I said. "It's a natural spotlight. Pure theater!"

"Magnificent drama! The people down there must have been thrilled."

Moi's eyes welled with tears. "Year after year I come to stand in this place, and I am thrilled also. I've come here with presidents of the Republic, ambassadors from France, the queen of Belgium, who was a very fine lady. Me, a nobody from Buenos Aires." He walked out to the edge of the platform and addressed the invisible crowds below. "I applaud you," he said, and then turning his eyes toward the heavens, clapped his hands, once, twice, three times, and the sound carried across the empty plaza.

"Just to be safe, in case the gods are watching, you know. The real miracle is that my shirt didn't catch fire."

"The tomb, Don Moi. The tomb must be the black hole, the black center, the place of transformation . . . ."

"We will bring tortillas tomorrow," said Moi, "and the next day, if he isn't dead."

PART III

I Dream I Am Dead

—from *The Book of Mingo*

I dreamt I was lying inside a stone coffin. I couldn't move my hands and I couldn't move my feet. When I looked down I could see I was nothing but bones and my bones were painted red, red from head to toe. "This is no good," I said to myself. Even in my dream I knew that the red paint was cinnabar and cinnabar is made from mercury, which is a poison. That's how they covered Pakal's bones. "I could die from this," I thought. But I was already dead. It wasn't like the time I was dead and crawling around inside an empty skull. No, this time I was stretched out in the tomb, absolutely frozen. I started to cry.

"It serves you right," said a voice. "You've done nothing with your life." And then my wife was standing there with her hands on her hips. "It would be better if you stopped thinking."

"I'm very cold," I said.

A woman appeared who looked like Palestrina, except she was much, much younger, and I could see she had a little L tattooed on her left cheek. "You look awful," she said. "I'll bring you some chicken soup."

"I won't be able to eat it," I said. "You see, I'm dead."

"If you still know how to talk, you'll still know how to eat," she said. "Wait a minute. I'll be right back."

Then my son Tito was sitting there beside me. "You look awful," he said. "Look at me, I'm doing very well." Indeed, he was wearing a new cowboy hat and a fine leather jacket.

"I'm happy for you, son," I said. "But where did you get the money?"

"I've been working in Cancun, Papa. I have a good job. I met a girl."

Oh, she was very beautiful. She had long, golden hair. She looked like an angel in her white silk dress. Her white silk dress was covered with pearls.

"Now you can build your house," I said to Tito. "There's room down by the arroyo."

"Not anymore," he said. "You see, Papa, I sold our land."

Just then my Minerva arrived with a silver bowl in her hand. I looked inside the bowl, but it wasn't soup, it was plain water. I could see my reflection in the water. My face was just an ugly skull.

"Don't be afraid, Papa," my Minerva said. "You won't be dead for long. Angelina and I will help you."

The girl with the golden hair put a pillow under my head. Then she took off her white dress and spread it across the bones of my arms and chest. Now she was naked and I thought my heart would burst. But where was my heart? It was probably shriveled now, the size of a plum or a prune.

"That's right," said the woman who looked like Palestrina. "We'll keep you company. The time will pass very quickly."

"Why are you women lying to him?" asked my wife. "I loved him for forty-five years, but it didn't matter. Who knows where he'll go or if he'll ever come back, even with all his promises?"

Just then my head rolled off and landed at my feet. I could see it looking back at me through its horrible, hollow eyes. That's when I woke up.

Chapter 28

The Goddess

As Moi and I set off across the plaza, we encountered a remarkable scene: a group of African women, costumed in brilliant scarlet and ochre, were dancing in front of the Red Queen's tomb. Under the streaming light they swayed and bent, rose and knelt like burnished willows, their prayers to the Red Queen wafting on winds born an ocean away. I forgot where I was, which continent, which time. But when the last glint of the setting sun brushed the gold-wired frames of one of the dancers, I instantly recognized her as Grandmother, the proprietor of the new Rastarant at the Panchan.

The Rastafaris rode into the spiritual zone the day Guru Karl slipped into the sea of dreams and Rakshita fled in his wake. With all the heavy soul traffic, the brothers and sisters barely had time to unpack, because before you could say King Tut they agreed to take over Rakshita's holistic enterprise. Needless to say, these apparitions from the seventies made quite a splash parading around in bright dashikis and brass ornaments. They could have been Egyptian ambassadors on the lam the way they kept to themselves, always traveling in three's and royally crowned in whispers. What were they hiding under those pillbox hats? In a place where gossip was worth more than King Solomon's songs and all the treasures of Nineveh and Tyre, their secrecy only served to keep the rumor mill greased and grinding twenty-four hours a day. Try as they might, it was hard to maintain a low profile in a town that rarely saw blacks, much less American blacks proudly dressed in authentic African garb. Under standard rules of propriety, anyone out of the ordinary could be subjected to no end of razzing and pinned with nicknames that stuck like flypaper for life: Fatty, Skinny, Shorty, Baldy, Pinto, Whitey, and so on. As for skin color, Mexicans were connoisseurs; one hundred years after the Conquest, the official color charts listed nine distinct castes—*criollo, zambo, cholo*, etc.— along with the various combinations of interracial couplings that produced such mixtures, willingly or unwillingly, under cover of darkness. After centuries of intermingling, every Mexican became an expert, able to discern the finest gradations in shading and match them fairly accurately with racial ancestry. *Negritos*, shipped from the islands to work as slaves and foremen for light-skinned Spaniards, continue to occupy the lowest rung of the social ladder, just above the *Indios*, that is, who still tell tales of lusty runaway devils haunting the midnight landscape. Surely the Rastas had some inkling of what they were up against when they decided to display their flamboyant colors and yet remain aloof. Alas, their steady cool drove customers away.

And then one day they woke from the terrible drag of time travel, and the Rastarant started doing a brisk business in soyburgers. At the same time, the men began hauling truckloads of palm fronds, reading how-to books, buying hammers and saws, and otherwise preparing to get ready to build Namibian-style huts that would house followers from the United States.

"Grandmother has given the call!" said Resonant Moon. And they were surely coming, Rasta women by the dozens, flying down from Detroit and Atlanta to conduct a fire ritual that would replace the oppressive male vibes of the Panchan with warm, female grace.

The change in energy had already begun. Sweeping across the grounds in exotic African plumage, darting among the avocado trees and dusky cabañas, the dancers I saw at the ruins were taking stock of all the tropical wonders before them. Clipboards in hand, they were an efficient parliament of birds hovering about a Baltimore oriole whose skin was the color of gold dust. For midsummer's eve, the yellow bird hosted a special concert of African music played by musicians flown in from Bagdad, Ohio. Bells and gongs and tinkling thumb pianos transported the audience to moonlit oases where silk tents swelled with chests of ivory, brass, and mint. A pair of veiled women padded in on jeweled tiptoes painted indigo blue. As the music spun out, the women pounded their heels, whirled, and leaped, and the musicians were jumping, too. The cheering crowds were on their feet, shaking and stomping across the floor. The dancing and drumming went on until dawn.

The foods and fragrances of Africa poured from the fluttering hands of Empress, the Rastarant's beautiful chef, who bore a striking resemblance to Haile Selassie's loving and tortured queen. Portraits of the divine couple—the young Queen Menen seated beside his Imperial Majesty, King of Kings, Lord of Lords, Conquering Lion of the Tribe of Judah, and incarnation of Christ the Messiah—peered down from the kitchen wall as Empress leaned over her wooden bowl and stirred honey into the *fatira* batter. Like most Ethiopians, Empress had cheekbones as high as the Nile, eyes the color of chocolate lilies that flashed along the riverbanks. She danced like a marimba player in front of the burners, intent on every aromatic note, coriander, capsicum, and fenugreek floating on the vapors from her simmering pots. When she spoke, the words bubbled up from some faraway place, not Detroit where she was born, but from vast desert plains rolling with luxuriant memories of an epoch when sand dunes were cedared hills. Her pancakes were as thin as *chapatis*, her soups and stews and soyburgers were full of light.

Grandmother did the worrying. She was not Empress's real grandmother, but she possessed the same regal bearing, although her spectacles made her look like a kindly schoolteacher who happened to wear dreadlocks down her long, narrow back. She was silent most of the time and spoke to the Empress in whispers. Everything between them was silence and whispers and the easy movements of a tribal dance.

"The Goddess will provide," said Grandmother, and Empress nodded, "Amen." Whenever he was in earshot, Empress's twelve-year-old son would shout a quick "Amen," pull his wool cap over his face, and stumble around like a clown. "For cryin' out loud, Mickey," Empress would say. "You're a handful, boy."

Never far from sight stretched a dude so tall and skinny he could have been a basketball player instead of an amateur-league slacker who hung around the kitchen getting in Empress's hair or accompanying Grandmother on her daily trips to the market and cybercafé. This long, tall drink of a shadow did a lot of whispering, too, as he loped behind Grandmother's skirts or pressed the Empress's delicate hand.

"Skate got big plans," says Empress. "Soon as the money comes on the money train, we're buying land and building a spa."

"Skate!" says Grandmother. "No way that man adds up."

"Skate!" says Chato. "He's a dealer for sure."

The strangeness of it all is that they chose Mexico to build their Eden. But then, human patterns of migration are as wondrous as those of whales and butterflies and the popular travel routes older and more elaborate than we know.

Grandmother claimed direct descent from the Queen of Sheba. Her people reached the Motor City by way of northern Canada. She alone continued south, and somewhere along God's glory road she became a Maya shaman who went by the name of Cauac, "Thunder." She looked so frail and wasted because she was still recuperating from an overdose of papaya seeds, which she took to cure something else. When she fully regained her equilibrium—Jump back! The energy would flow to the edge of the universe, good juju would charge the air, and all the distractions disappear. By distractions she meant the constant family feuds. And, she added with a wink, the "spiritual hullabaloo." Although I noticed her at the Arguelles lecture, she had nothing to say on that score. It was Guru Karl who changed her life forever. She just caught him out of the corner of her eye as the taxi was pulling away, but as far as she could tell, he was the reason behind her split-second decision to take over Rakshita's restaurant and resume her medicinal practice.

Yes, thanks to Guru Karl, Grandmother was beginning to hit her stride. Some of the women who had come to sit at Karl's feet were still nesting in Rakshita's temple, too wounded to budge, and just so their journeys wouldn't be a total loss, as they put it in plain English, they decided to dip into Grandmother's wisdom. In less than a day, Gretchen, Remy, and Monika jumped from one theological extreme to the other, from the nature of illusion to full-on immersion in Mother Nature's supreme reality. They were gathering herbs, mixing ointments, imbibing infusions, elixirs, and teas. All this information was imparted freely, although there was a small fee. Perhaps it was a coincidence, but just when the Rastas were wondering how they were going to pay the rent and discovering the hidden costs of running a vegetarian restaurant in a place where fresh produce was scarce and tofu and tempei nonexistent, Grandmother decided to attach a monetary value to her age-old craft. Actually it was simpler than that: she charged a flat rate per hour.

Her wisdom was fairly random. She advised Gretchen, her most promising student, to go on a spiritual retreat, find some isolated place free of distractions, ideally a small hotel room in the center of town, and while sitting inside that simple cell, without a rickety old fan to swirl the heat and only a bare light bulb to focus your attention, eat nothing for three days. Or maybe not. Maybe just a plain broth or a cup of mugwort tea. Lie there in the rank humidity with the sweat pouring down your young loins and the racket from the late-night discos soaking into the lumpy pillow and wait for some other sound to come murmuring on the infrequent breezes, a voice besides the voices of the loudspeakers and whores in the street below, or perhaps, yes, the voices of the people telling it like it is, uttering the truth in unintelligible Spanish and Tzeltal. That would be the ticket. Her most promising student said, "Where would I find mugwort tea in the tropics? Thank you, but no."

She had a point there concerning the mugwort tea, Grandmother agreed. And while she was mulling it over, Gretchen was thinking to herself that something was so wrong about her apprenticeship it was not worth discussing with the master. Besides, she was withholding a larger secret, which normally would have swelled inside her like a helium balloon until her stomach bulged and she blurted it out to the wrong person at the wrong time. But if she had learned one thing in the past few weeks it was how to keep a secret so far back in the recesses of her mind it was barely a thought, barely a smudge on her alpha waves. She had learned from Karl that thought was not thought, mind was not mind. But her new technique—how to blur thought until it became a cloudy veil—she learned from Grandmother.

Gretchen had a vision. Well, not a vision exactly, and not an epiphany either. It happened in the healing hut while she was giving the runaway boy who camped there a genuine Swedish massage. Gretchen was born in Stockholm. Raul, a delicate blond with pink cheeks, grew up in the slums of Mexico City and knew all about the Toltecs. When Gretchen was working on his lower back, he began dreaming of *castaña* leaves plummeting like falcons through the downdrafts and calling to him in the piercing voice of his mother. "Raul, Raul, come home, it's late." He woke just as Gretchen was kneading vertebra 22.

"Do you hear that?" he said.

"Relax," said Gretchen. "There's nothing to worry about. I'm just working on the spot where your mother hit you, maybe with a board."

Raul gasped. Gretchen saw his breath curl like a blood-red serpent, felt the knot in his back disappear. She could hear the trees playing violins; the notes were blue, the birdcalls yellow, and the falcons' wings a violet rush all around her. She could read Raul's mind and body. Her skin prickled. Electricity ran up and down her arms and through her healing hands. She had the power. And she didn't need anyone else to tell her.

If Grandmother wasn't a true healer, then who was she? In one breath she talked about the Goddess, the Dreamspell Calendar, and the Black Panthers. In the next breath she described her plans to build a women's moon lodge and black room where people could meditate in pitch dark for days or months on end. "It's good for the peepers," she said. I heard about her organic restaurant in Atlanta, which was a gathering place for the inner city counterculture, and how she would like to replicate it here at the Panchan. The best I could figure out is that she was a professional daydreamer.

One day I went over to ask her advice about a teenage girl going catatonic. "She refuses to eat, she refuses to speak, she hides behind trees and stares at the bark for hours. I think she's nuts," I said. We were sitting in Rakshita's tumbledown temple at the time, just after the roof had collapsed.

"You know, sometimes I lose faith myself," Grandmother confessed. "Take 2012, for example. I just don't think it will happen. I mean, I've had a chance to visit the ruins for myself. I've seen things— ghosts, spirits, what have you—and I've listened. And something tells me the world just ain't gonna blow. Things will change first, I'll bet my bottom dollar. And you know what? Some things need to be left alone. Well, I got plenty of patience. Six children, five husbands, and that bum, Skate. Plenty of patience, alright!" She took a deep breath and let the air out in a long, slow whistle.

"Did time, too. Yes, ma'am! Ten years in stir. That's when I joined the Nation of Islam and saw the light." She pressed her delicate fingers together and bowed to the east. "Used to drive around in a Cadillac with a pistol in my Gucci purse. I had furs, designer clothes, nothing but the best. Hot damn, you should have seen me, sister! And then I took the name Orisha, goddess of healing waters, and bam, life went from fast to slow!"

We chuckled over that one a while, and then she put on her glasses. "But I want to tell you this, child, because I know you'll understand. I'm really somebody else."

She told me how she got an eerie feeling every time she walked among the temples of Group C or crossed the bridge over the Otolum River where the queen is said to have taken her evening bath.

"Not an English queen, not a Biblical queen, not Holy Mary, Queen of Heaven. And not the ghost of any Maya queen either. I mean the Red Queen, the one who is buried in the tomb."

"You're not alone," I assured her. "There are other women who feel the same way."

For some reason, I started telling her the story of Petra who opened a restaurant down the road called *La Reina Roja*. The restaurant sat on a steep hill, surrounded by huge mango trees, with a beautiful view of the Temple of the Inscriptions. You could even see the shrouded entrance to the tomb of the Red Queen if you knew it was there. Anyway, the restaurant served Swiss fondue on Saturdays, because Petra's lover at the time was German-Swiss. The few guests drawn to the somber hilltop mainly came for drinks. Petra would sidle up to the table in her high heels and tight mini skirt, toss her thick blond hair, and make some suggestive remark kindled by the tequila she'd been swilling since noon, or whenever she woke to a day that was always bright and always sad.

One of her former lovers was a famous revolutionary leader of the Zapatistas, and although she professed undying loyalty to the cause of Indian justice and equality, she wasn't an Indian after all, and the relationship went from stormy to on the rocks after a few months. You could picture *bandoleras* across her ample breasts and grenades swinging from her hip belt. The way her eyes fixed on a man you could imagine her taking aim with a high-powered rifle. But it was hard to believe she could kill anything and impossible to visualize her trudging through the jungle in those red spiked heels. Maybe she had boots then, but how did she hide her massive curls and made-up face under a black wool ski mask? The mask she wore was in plain view, a forty-year-old doll with full red lips and blue eye shadow, left-leaning, tipsy, and committed to the perfect man. "Where do you find one?" she would sigh, eyes damp with tiny doll tears.

"No place I know, sister, and I've been around the block five times!" Grandmother was tickled by my story, occasionally interjecting "my, my," or "dear me," or "you said it," and so I continued.

Business was slow, she and the German had one too many drinking bouts and one too many fights until they were both teetering around with sad, glazed eyes. One night she made a play for the old man, but when she stretched out on the bed, the German pulled out a gun, the two men wrestled, and Petra passed out before the victor was declared. The next morning the German packed his bags and left for Cholula. That was fine with her.

The next thing you knew, the old man was hurling insults at her, and she, ever true to the cause, began keeping company with a longhaired Lacandon Maya. Well, he was not exactly a traditional Lacandon, although he dressed the part. Kayum was a merchant who sold hand-carved bows and arrows from his souvenir stall at the ruins. But he still had it in him, a devotion to the old ways. At the height of their romance, he held a *balché* ceremony to which everyone at the Panchan was invited. Kayum spent four days brewing *balché* bark and honey in a long dugout canoe. He laid out the sacred space with red ginger flowers. Copal incense was burning. The clay "god pots" sat in a row, their toothless mouths waiting to be fed more liquor. The male guests kneeled beside Kayum while the women looked on, fuming and fussing with indignation. Women were not allowed to enter the sacred space, women were not permitted to pray to the gods. So it has been from the day of creation when Hachakyum, lord of lords, ordered his wife out of the first heavenly god house and into the kitchen. On this occasion, Kayum made an exception: we women, being foreigners, did not have to cook the tamales for the gods. And so we simply chatted matter-of-factly, the way women do, as Kayum waved a handful of leaves through the incense smoke and offered prayers on our behalf. After every prayer he gave each of us a well-smoked leaf. The *balché*, which we drank from small gourds, tasted like turpentine. I drank two gourdfuls and left. Petra hung on for as long as she could.

"Variety is the spice of life," Grandmother said. "Where is she now? I'd like to meet her. I'd like to see one of those ceremonies."

"Oh, she's taken up with a paunchy little judge and has moved to Tuxtla. The restaurant has closed, the mango trees are dreary. According to rumors, the judge's wife has threatened to kill *La Reina Roja*."

Grandmother threw her head back, and the bells on her long dreads tinkled. "Well, let's don't worry," she laughed. "The Goddess is a goddess of love, among other things, and she will surely protect her.

But I have to tell you this: The Red Queen is really an African queen according to our books."

She pulled herself up and stretched her arms toward the open sky, bracelets jangling, skirts billowing in the ether. "I am the Red Queen," she crooned, "the African queen of Palenque."

Chapter 29

˙ THE RED QUEEN

Grandmother and Petra are only two shining examples of greathearted women who, in their wayward search for kindred spirits, share a mystical affinity with an anonymous woman who traced her lineage back to the moon.

Even less is known about the original Red Queen than the women I've just described. Was her life anything like theirs? Clearly her material circumstances freed her from most common toils. But did the same passions roil within her female breast? In our terrible aloneness and despair, we long to believe that love unites us, yet during the painful midnight hours when we examine our daily hurts, we often ask ourselves if we can ever truly know another person or, for that matter, know anything at all. Over the widening gulf of time, the burdensome doubts double and quadruple like a Maya equation in which so many days and lives and dying orbits are factored in that our heads reel before the enormity of human ignorance. Not a word was written about the Red Queen's character and history. The only vivid records of her brief existence are her red bones and startling death mask.

Without understanding how certain solemn chords ring out after centuries of silence, Fanny López, a young and inexperienced field student, followed an "archaeological hunch." She had been testing the upper platform of Temple XIII, convinced that the structure below her contained a burial. "Impossible," the head archaeologist told her. "You'll find nothing." Before he finished his sentence, the platform collapsed, and one of the Indian workers noticed the gaping hole. Immediately

Fanny and her female ally began to dig. They dug with an urgency seldom seen in a field renowned for painstaking slowness. There was a compelling fever to this excavation, an out-of-control yearning, a blind race against time. The Zapatista rebels were threatening to invade Palenque. The governor was on his way. Amid impending political turmoil, the royal tomb was cleaned out in a single, backbreaking, twenty-four-hour day.

Perhaps circumstances were similar when the body was laid to rest, with the priests' vain hopes that the Radiant One would abide in her black chamber for eternity. But there was no time for irony now. The skeletal remains of a maidservant and her boy, found at the door of the tomb, were laid aside discreetly, the stone sarcophagus lid hoisted, and the sealed coffin bared. The breathless workers took a moment to stare at the royal bones painted in red cinnabar, the jade beads, and the fantastic malachite mask. The jewels went to the museum, the bones sent to the laboratory in Merida. The bones of a royal woman, it was said: *La Reina Roja.*

Not surprisingly, the head archaeologist claimed the discovery, consigning Fanny López to public obscurity. For years thereafter, learned men argued over the corpse's mysterious identity. Was she Pakal's mother, grandmother, daughter, granddaughter, or wife? There were no hieroglyphic texts carved on the sarcophagus lid or on the walls of the tomb. No name, no dates. Only the resurrected mask made of malachite mosaics, with its white shell eyes gazing with astonished horror on the twentieth century.

The rest of her—ulna, tibia, tell-tale pubis—sulked ingloriously in a cardboard box stored on a steel shelf three hundred miles from her magnificent, cold crypt. For ten years the bones brooded there—an interminable length of time for the living, a teardrop for the dead—while scientists measured every millimeter of her corpse and subjected the teeth and marrow to DNA testing. Normally a lab can arrive at results within a week of analyzing a stray hair or molar. What exactly were they doing with the queen's remains, and why was it taking so long?

A lot can happen in ten years. Winnowing events mildly pertinent to our story: The governor retired with a comfortable fortune, and the nation elected a conservative president. Despite repeated threats, the Zapatistas failed to take over the ruined city of Palenque and instead established a number of autonomous communities devoted to raising lackluster crops like corn and organic coffee. Meanwhile, the ancient Maya invaded public television, word of the end of time spread from Indiana to Moscow, and tourism multiplied one hundredfold.

The local economy was booming, which was good for hotel owners, bad for the rest, who wanted nothing to do with foreigners. Competition for euros and dollars was compromising the moral poverty of the town. Worse, the scuffling beast with a million feet and uncontrollable fingers scraping and poking, nostrils expelling clouds of toxins into the humid atmosphere, was destroying the ancient stones. In the midst of soaring attendance rates, the National Institute of Art and History closed its number-one tourist attraction, the tomb of Pakal. As a consolation, the multitudes who had traveled halfway around the world were permitted to peer into the empty crypt of the Red Queen and to view her stern malachite mask in the museum. They would experience a momentary fascination and leave with a baffled shrug. It seemed the identity of the Red Queen would linger in the realm of minor mysteries forever.

Finally, on the tenth anniversary of her discovery, at the Mesa Redonda held at the Misión Hotel in Palenque, geneticists described precisely what they had been doing with the bones. And the INAH staff archaeologist conceded that young Fanny, not as young as before, was the rightful discoverer of the tomb. A woman had found the Red Queen! When Fanny rose to receive the accolades long due her, she announced that she had narrowed the queen's identity to three possibilities:

1. Lady Yol Iknal ("Heart of the Wind Place"), Pakal's grandmother;
2. Lady Sak Kuk ("Resplendent Quetzal"), Pakal's mother; and
3. Lady Kinuw Mat Cho'k, Pakal's daughter-in-law and the mother of Pakal's grandson, Ahkal Mo Naab III.

The first two women were interesting choices. Lady Yol Iknal came from a place called Toktan, "Cloud Center." After the death of her brother, the king, she seized power and steered the kingdom through twenty years of turmoil and intrigue. It was she who occupied the throne when the rogue state of Calakmul sacked the city. Then, on November 4, 604, when the sun was passing through the Underworld at nadir, Lady Yol Iknal, first divine queen of Palenque, entered the white road. After her death the Snake Lords of Calakmul attacked a second time. Twice they looted and burned the city and cast the deities into the sea. When all was lost, the goddess, Lady Cormorant, rose from the ashes, set her sandals squarely on the path from Toktan to Palenque, and ruled the desolate city for three long years. She may have assumed the form of Lady Sak Kuk or the body of a man, but no matter. The divine blood of the dynasty flowed through her/his veins, for she was the sacred mother-father of the gods.

Nothing is known of Pakal's daughter-in-law. Nothing is known of the legendary Toktan. And for several years after the Mesa Redonda, nothing was known of the Red Queen.

At last the laboratory published its delinquent DNA results and put an end to more than a decade of squabbling and wild guesses. The body expired, they reported, in A.D. 672. A quick search through the records and the mystery was resolved. The woman buried in the tomb was Lady Tzak Ajaw ("Conjurer"), wife of Pakal the Great and the mother of two future kings, Kan Bahlam II and Kan Hoy Chitam III.

Still, we have only the barest outline of the queen's life. Born in 610, the princess traced her noble ancestry to an obscure brother of Lady Yol Iknal, the grandmother of Pakal. In effect, Lady Tzak Ajaw and Pakal were cousins, and like all cousins who play together when they are young, they developed a fondness for each other that would bear up over time. Perhaps she had her pick of other princes but chose him for his serene character. The boy was attracted to her delicate face, wide hips, and thick ankles, which Maya men find so irresistible. Besides, she was a wonderful weaver, potter, poet, and musician and knew the names of the constellations. Let us say their hearts were perfumed. Her parents, seeing it was an excellent political match, gave their consent. Married at sixteen, the princess became a queen with all attendant titles and privileges.

If ancient rulers performed their royal duties as Maya officials fulfill their burdens today, then she shared a hefty portion of Pakal's responsibilities. Lady Tzak Ajaw stood by him through chaos and war, transforming the kingdom from a vanquished state to a conquering realm. She walked beside him in peace as the city grew in splendor, a renowned center for the arts and sciences. They held court for the greatest minds in America. The Palace was a crossroads for the sun, moon, and planets; the temples were homes inviting to the gods. Pakal sacrificed his blood so many times his member looked like a sliced mango. The queen slit a hole in her tongue through which she drew a rope of sharp acacia thorns. Blood smeared her face and robe. Blood ran down his legs, like a woman's. At the height of his reign, Pakal captured Death and cut out his heart. He offered many captives to the gods, ate their flesh, and came home stinking. She, as her name suggests, was a woman of vision; after forty-seven years, one glance from her and he shriveled.

She bore three sons, spaced seven years apart, her first "sprout" born nine years after her marriage. Who knows of the private troubles that transpired during their early years together. The proud day her eldest son, Kan Bahlam, was named heir to the throne, she cradled him in her arms, a homely boy with the deformed foot of Kawil, god of mirrors. She rose at three and walked the Palace corridors, and when she encountered my lord's general, also sleepless, also walking the halls, she issued this command: "My son requires captives. You, my lord of fire, must do the fighting." She taught her boys the arts of writing, painting, and obfuscation. She could handle an ax as well as any man but never had to use it. To this day her aging profile survives in stone, commemorating the day she presented her second son, Kan Hoy Chitam, with the flint and shield emblem of war. She did not live to see him captured and disgraced. She did not live to see Batz Chan Mat, her youngest son, die alone.

In the hour of her death, when white wings are beating and white smoke drifts from the mouth, she heard the voice of her jaguar spirit and went down into that dark place with him as her companion, leaving behind my lord and shield to follow the sun for nine more years.

Three patron gods of Palenque, three sons, three chambers in the royal tomb, and only one was filled. Three temples on the hillside built by Kan Bahlam, each a hearthstone of creation and each a replica of mother's mausoleum.

On either side of the long platform, two staircases lead down to the crypt. The family could pay their respects as often as they liked. And when the time came for the last ritual, the brothers entered the sepulcher and the sarcophagus stone was lifted. The flesh was scraped from the bones and the bones were painted red.

And this is how her eldest son paid final homage: he aligned his greatest temple with hers. And this is how he celebrated her name—in evanescent moonlight. Every nineteen years, at dusk in December, the full moon rises over the Temple of the Cross and illuminates the shrine where the Red Queen was buried, at the foot of the sacred mountain, at the entrance to the sacred cave, where the moon sinks and her spirit now is dwelling.

Chapter 30

THE LAUGHING FALCON AND THE LYING DOG

When Moi went down to Pakal's tomb the next day, carrying a Styrofoam plate of chicken enchiladas, all that was left of Mingo was his shadow. At the African concert the night before, the Russians assured Moi that when they exited the chamber, Mingo was crouched like an animal against the bars. "Stiff as a billy goat and no goodbyes," Saskia noted. "It was eighteen hundred on our clocks." So, by the best possible eyewitness reports, Mingo was frozen at that hour and time was still ticking away.

As Moi lowered himself into the darkness he called Mingo's name, but the only sound he heard was his own hoarse voice rising from a black pool deep below the earth. "I've come to wake you, Mingo," he called to steady himself. "Look, I've brought you a little lunch." But now, standing alone at the bottom of the well, weak and dizzy from the descent, Moi felt the overpowering emptiness of the tomb. Then he thought, "Why should I fall into the silliness that has gotten hold of everyone these days. He probably waited until dark and crawled home."

When Moi told me about it, he was still feeling tired and hollow and frankly disappointed that Mingo had abandoned his vigil. And so we went to Mingo's house that afternoon. Sure enough, Mingo was sitting at the table, writing in his notebook.

"I'm still alive," Mingo said, "but barely. Being in the tomb was awful. They turn the lights out. It's black as death down there. The heartless bones inside that cold stone box, you hear them whining, not like the Red Queen who is living quietly on a shelf. It was terrifying!"

"How do I know you're alive and not a ghost having fun with me?" Moi teased.

"I can still pee!" Mingo wailed. "Ghosts can't pee."

"Let's see," said Moi.

"I'll need something to drink first, my friend. Let me show you and the señora how I can still drink."

After gulping down two tequilas, Mingo confessed that he left soon after the Russians. "I didn't have the nerve to sleep there, you see. Who would? It was bad enough feeling my way up the stairs in that terrible darkness. I felt like a dead man climbing back from the grave."

His shoulders trembled, but then he straightened up and tucked his hands between his thighs, which is how he liked to sit, rocking back and forth as he spoke. "You know, now that I think about it, I'm feeling like a new man, happy to be alive. What's upsetting me is that no one cares about my protest. I came home and my son, Tito, wasn't interested. 'It's the Mexican government you have to convince,' he said, 'not a group of Russian tourists.' My son, the revolutionary, was not impressed with his father's act of bravery."

"Alright, Mingo," said Moi, looking him straight in the eye, "tell me honestly, as honestly as a man like you can be—and we both know you've been a liar since the day you were born—no, a teller of tales, a man blessed with an overripe imagination—tell me what the Russians did after we left."

Mingo glanced through the window at the dead tree in his yard. "I think they've done it, Don Moi. I think they've stopped time. They stood in a circle and closed their eyes and kept repeating the same thing over and over. I didn't understand a word they were saying, but it sounded like a prayer. Everything slowed down. I lost track. This morning I woke up and thought I was still in the tomb. But that was days ago, maybe last week, maybe last month."

"It's summer, Mingo. The days are swelling in the rain. But for me, they're shrinking. The days are shorter and moving faster."

"Give me an example, Don Moi. Maybe it will help me out."

"Okay, a month ago Alberto bought a dog. He built a house for it. He kept it on a chain. Naturally the dog barked all the time and tried to get loose. Me, I let my dogs run free. They follow me everywhere, except when I go to town. Then they lie out in the parking lot, waiting for me to come home. If they lie down inside the restaurant, where there's shade, the waiters come and spray them with water to make them go away. It's not healthy to have dogs in a restaurant, the customers don't like it, they say. Never mind that it's my land and the restaurant is named after me. Chato says the dogs stink. He hates the dogs. The dogs hate water. If they wait for me at my house and I happen to stay out late, the dogs cry. Sometimes they bark, but mostly they howl and cry. Alberto's dog barked. And one day it got upset, pulled out the post it was chained to, and ran to the Mono Blanco. Alberto wasn't there. The dog nipped a little girl."

"That's why Minerva is afraid of that dog. She told me there is a dog at the Panchan that bites people."

"Hmmm. But Minerva has nothing to be afraid of. Dogs have a sixth sense about people."

"But how can a little girl be so bad, Don Moi?"

"You'd be surprised, Mingo, you'd be surprised. I have six daughters, remember?"

"And I have three. It's not their fault if they end up with men who say they love them and then treat them like property, treat them like slaves. But what can I say? You know the kind, Don Moi."

"We're not talking about rats. I am telling you about a dog with four legs. Two days ago, Alberto's dog bit a little puppy. The owner, an American woman, was furious. She let Alberto have it. But Alberto just sat there like a dummy and said it was a lie."

"So far you've been speaking to me about a mad dog. Does this dog know how to talk? Does this dog tell the truth? Does this dog tell time?"

"Just wait and let me finish the story. Someone came to tell me that, purely out of anger and spite, Alberto was about to call the *migra* and have every foreigner thrown out of the Panchan. The young man who was working for me, helping me with the rooms and the guests, hears this, packs his bags, and leaves right away. He seemed like a nice fellow, a yoga teacher, very tranquil, but I suppose he had done something wrong in a previous life to be so afraid. I went over to talk to

Alberto about it, but he wasn't on the phone with the *migra*. He was on his way to Asunción, the waiter told me, and he was taking the dog with him. Alberto is always going to Asunción, and he leaves a waiter to manage his business. The one good thing you can say about Chato is that at least he works.

"The same thing happened to the restaurant Aida and Chato started in town. Beautiful place. They painted my picture on the wall, me shaking hands with Yuri Knorozov, the Russian epigrapher. He was a friend of Saskia's. Who knows what kind of friend! He was a strange man and a little psychic himself. You know, at the end of the war, after the Russians invaded Germany and he was a soldier stationed in Berlin, he was rummaging through the library—he was the studious type even then—and he came upon a plain cardboard box. And what was in this box? A copy of Bishop Diego de Landa's *Relaciónes de las Cosas de Yucatán*. Basically the Landa book was all he needed to figure out that Maya writing is phonetic. It was strange that he would find that book in that place and then become a great epigrapher."

"Saskia, the little Russian woman with the white turban?"

"Yes, she met him when she was the minister of culture. Or the mistress of culture, however you say it. She must have been a beautiful woman then."

"In Berlin?"

"No, Moscow. If she had come here a few years earlier she could have met Yuri Knorozov in Palenque."

"Or he could have come here later."

"He's dead, poor man. And officially, the Russians don't believe in the soul or reincarnation or any type of spiritual flights."

"So, he was very much alive when he came here."

"Yes, although he was half dead after going through all the red tape. Imagine, he spent his whole life studying Maya hieroglyphs and had never seen a Maya ruin. True, he was a devoted Communist, loyal to Russia, but what did that have to do with it? A few scholars criticized his work on the basis of his politics. That's like saying you have to be a monarchist to understand the way the Maya think. I myself was thrilled to meet him at the airport in Palenque. And that is the picture in the restaurant, me shaking hands with Yuri Knorozov at the Palenque airport, me in a blue shirt and smiling, him in a black suit and narrow tie and a cigarette dangling out of the corner of his mouth.

He always had a cigarette dangling out of the corner of his mouth. They say I look good in powder blue."

"And that's when the Italian came back again, to make the pizza and drive my Minerva crazy."

"But it didn't last long because Aida loves to give orders and the Italian is a temperamental artist. For him, pizza is an edible sculpture made of cheese, red tomatoes, and green peppers. I respect that. When he left, the business went flat. The Italian comes and goes, goes and comes, and that Roque is the one who stays and stays. He's worse than a mother-in-law, worse than the plague!

"Anyway, no one was greeting the customers, and no one was keeping the books. This was the second time Aida and Chato went into business together—Chato putting up the money, her acting like the manager—and the same thing happened all over again. They started fighting over missing spoons. There was a big battle over who owned the espresso machine. Chato hired a night watchman just to guard the coffeemaker. Aida's husband hired a gang of thieves to steal it. Chato threatened to bring in *pistoleros* from Zapata. It's a good thing my daughter used her head, because otherwise somebody was going to suffer. Aida and that macho she married piled all their belongings in an open truck—chairs, mattresses, cardboard cartons full of forks and spoons—and stole away in the middle of the night. That was months ago. Now they're back and living in one of Chato's cabañas. They say they're here to help me. We'll see."

"This is very kind of them, Don Moi. And kind of Chato, too. He's very generous to my daughter, even though . . . ."

"Chato is just trying to shame them. And those two are like you, here one minute, gone the next. Yesterday I was crossing the bridge and ran into Aida, who was carrying a suitcase and rushing over to Alberto's. 'Where are you going?' I asked. 'I'm going to the border. Pito is in trouble. I have to bail him out,' she said. 'What sort of trouble?' I asked. 'It's not important,' she said. 'It must be important if you're going all the way to the US border,' I said. 'No, no, I'm just going to the Guatemalan border. Alberto is going to drive me.' And there was Alberto, standing by the car. And there was his pit bull, barking in the back seat. They didn't go to Asunción after all. That dog was here. And then I find out Aida isn't going to Guatemala. She is traveling all the way to Brownsville, on the bus, to bail out that bum! That was yesterday. So you see, time is speeding up."

"Don Moi, I must tell you I am very confused. And I have to pee."

"You don't have to pee, Mingo, you have all the time in the world. And don't be confused either. Some of this story happened before and some of it is going to happen. A good ghost would know that!"

Mingo took a deep breath. "You know the laughing falcons that fly back and forth from the Temple of the Sun to the Palace and from the Palace to the big tree in front of the Temple of the Inscriptions? Well, they brought me a message."

"And what was the message they brought you, Mingo? Tell me before time slips away."

"I can't tell you the whole message, Don Moi, but it has something to do with a woman who changes bones to fire, wind to water, and the land of paradise to . . . ."

"Mad dogs and talking birds! What a magical world we live in, my friend. I hope she is very beautiful. And I hope she will change my life completely!"

"I just thought I should tell you about it, Moi. Maybe it means the Panchan, the land above the sky." Mingo's voice grew faint, and he held his head in his hands. "But to tell you the truth, right now, this minute, I feel like I'm still sleeping in the tomb."

"But Mingo, you never slept in the tomb. If you fell asleep down there, it was only for five minutes. It was just a short nap. That's why I am telling you that time is speeding up."

Chapter 31

1 8

Post by post and plank by plank, Alberto was building a new late-night bar. The sewage system at the old Mono Blanco had reached intolerable levels, and since you can't run an eatery without a kitchen, a watering hole without a hole, the time had come to move the odor elsewhere. And where was Alberto raising his tin-roofed, unvarnished eyesore? In the dirt lot right next to Chato's restaurant. Naturally he hoped to profit from the spillover crowds, and toward that end, he developed a business strategy that was a model of transparency and wishful thinking: guests who had already lost their sense of smell and taste would wander casually into his establishment and gladly lose their money. The real trick was to attract the blind and deaf.

First he ran electric wires to Chato's meter. The extra juice was enough to feed the vapor lights that turned his former sand pit into a UFO landing strip. Then he hired the worst rock band west of the Usumacinta River. That meant that if you tuned into the Andean music at Don Mucho's, you'd get hammered by Palenque's own wannabe Mick Jagger strutting across the monkey stage in his Converse knock-offs, yowling in broken English to his whiskey-blond Marianne Faithful gyrating in the front row. The whole scene was a blast from the past, the pre-Stone-Age past when humankind was in its infancy. The electric guitars tripped and cried, the bass drum thunked at a pace so deadly it split the bicameral mind.

The cross rhythms were especially brutal for the musicians trying to sing *"El Condor Pasa"* to the beat of "I Can't Get No Satisfaction."

After a week of unhinged melodies and flightless chords, the flautist and keyboard man called a meeting with the rockers. "Let's take turns going on stage," Hugo suggested, a sensible proposal that might assuage most members of the listening audience, which encompassed every rancher, farmer, hotel guest, and asylum inmate trapped within a five-mile radius, light years if we take into account disgruntled music lovers in nearby galaxies. But being of different persuasions, the rockers played whenever they pleased and wailed into the wee small hours.

It did no good to complain to Alberto because Alberto took off for Asunción, leaving a red-haired witch to manage his latest experiment in barnyard entertainment for budget-conscious rubes. The woman came out of the hellholes of Argentina with a tin ear, an iron hand, and a flare for attracting the worst scum. They'd sneak up the back road and become part of the great unwashed flow of hangers-on before Terence could pick them up on his radar and name them for the Lizards they were.

"It's only a matter of time before they take over," he warned. "And that poor girl is the one who will suffer."

He was referring to Esmeralda, the witch's pretty fifteen-year-old daughter, who was left to run wild with the tattered, lice-ridden refugees from the barrios of Tampico. They smoked weed and ate fire and took up half the tables. Esmeralda knew how to smile and sneak food out of the kitchen.

Meanwhile, her mother painted her toenails and sipped tequila from a silver-rimmed *maté* gourd. When she wasn't getting stoned, she'd mope over her Tarot cards, shake her little fist at Esmeralda, or chew out her old man, Fernando, a mouse if there ever was one. But he was not the only victim of her spells. All the waiters had bouts of jangling nerves, a serious drawback in the restaurant profession. Whoops, there goes another plate of flying guacamole, another bowl of bean soup in someone's lap. The bartender crossed himself every time he spilled a drink, the cook wore garlic around her throat. As soon as the spotlights burned out and the Lizards lit their pipes, the band tossed their instruments into their beat-up van, swearing they'd never come back. The witch would let out a piercing scream, and in the ensuing squabble, Esmeralda would run hell-bent for the woods. Slumped in the flickering shadows of a solitary candle, Fernando would begin sobbing. The

18

other drunks and cokeheads would start throwing punches, and the dawn would break to blood and tears. By the look of things, the witch was headed for destruction.

Was this red-haired Medusa the woman fated to change the Panchan? There was another female candidate under suspicion, one with an equally brittle disguise.

Every Monday, Wednesday, and Friday, Gloria comes waddling over the bridge with a big basketful of whole wheat bread. "Knock, knock," she titters, "I have garlic bread today." Her eyes are bullet black and her bread tastes like nails. If you refuse to buy her loaves, she curses you with a five-minute diatribe on *The Keys of Enoch*, copies of which she carries in her basket. Fortunately, there is not enough time in this world for even a light discussion of the 144,000 Ascended Masters, who will punish the guilty when they descend upon Palenque in 2012. In the event the Ascended Masters do come down from the clouds and announce a brand new reign of peace on earth, Gloria would make a questionable witness anyway, not only because of her poor eyesight, but also because of her sinus troubles and tics. Her complex kit of ailments is tucked into the tarts she bakes, which are full of salt and sugar and some unknown ingredient with the poisonous tang of sulfur-eating bacteria. These rare life forms, found on the mossy carpets growing in Don Juan Cave, play a critical role in the transformation of organic matter yet emit dangerous toxins when ingested into the human body, as her stunted brain and cockeyed smile make clear. The vision of thousands of winged beings landing on the temples would probably drive her over the cliff. Right then and there she'd go haywire and show her true color—puce. Nothing would save her, because nowhere is it written that Christ and Buddha will save Lizards.

Solomon was her prized pupil. The man once owned a Dodge pickup and a two-acre hippie campground, which he pissed away on cheap booze. He was lying on the bridge, singing to the birds, when Gloria came along with her sulfur bread and tarts and kicked him in the shins.

"Read this!" she said, flipping to her favorite passage in the *Keys*.

Solomon opened his bloodshot eyes and slammed his hand on the page. "Ants! Get 'em off!" he screamed. That's how gone he was.

"Don't be a fool all your life!" Gloria snapped. "These are sacred words running across the paper." And she proceeded to read them aloud:

> *Do not dwell in faint-heartedness, but manifest in the public places all of the spiritual gifts, so that the power in the Father's Throne may be glorified in you, for this is the Age of the Holy Spirit.*

"Manifest in the public places . . . ." Solomon rolled over and got to his knees, swearing he would never touch another drop. He was frozen in that position, tears streaking his grimy red cheeks, when Chato caught sight of him on the bridge, raised the poor tanked-up bastard to his feet, and gave him a room.

Solomon the Wiser started sauntering through the bar, glass of vodka in his trembling hand, telling everyone it was water from the springs of Eden. He preached about the coming of Uriel, Hagan, Fendrin, and Armozelu. He confessed his sins to all who would listen. His voice took on the timbre of the mad prophets of old. "Take heart, the wings of angels are flapping in the branches, the newborn kings are whispering in the storm. Metatron, master of slaves, will fold you in his arms."

The deeper Solomon drank of the waters of life the more fervent Solomon grew, until you truly believed he was intent on his own salvation. Surely the sight of The Illuminated floating down the temple steps would sober him up for good. The Merkabah would trumpet its holy sound, the Ark of the Covenant shake the stones, and the song of Enoch would reverberate in every dewdrop of light.

In the meantime, two unrepentant glue sniffers jumped him for a peso, and in revenge, Solomon started punching out any petty dealer more battered and blistered than a fallen angel like himself. He lost his front teeth and the use of his right arm. As contrite as he was the morning after, he lost Chato's confidence and his rent-free room. From that day forward he wandered the earth, drinking Dago red from a wax carton.

It was Alberto who told him about a cure that involved a complete transfusion of blood. With new plasma flowing through his veins, blood that was free of alcohol, Solomon would supposedly lose the craving. The trouble was, a complete blood transfusion cost money. With the last drop of ambition left in his wine-soaked heart, Solomon set about securing the necessary funds. He began by panhandling on the bridge to Don Mucho's. Then he and the Medusa started eating tarts together, and there was something for sale in her breadbasket besides salt and sulfur. Now that Solomon was in cahoots with the witch, his downhill slide went faster.

Chuck Norris, the tattoo artist, knew Solomon in his better days. After the Drainbows dissed him and his godless calling, Chuck joined the local tourist industry as an information specialist and goodwill ambassador, drilling Maya designs on firm white bodies and brewing mushroom tea for the happy campers at Solomon's pleasure ground. But then the business went belly up, and Chuck had to pack up his needles and inks and take to the road again. He didn't go far. As soon as he stuck out his thumb, Chato came speeding along in his new red Jeep and gave him a ride to the Panchan. Always a sympathetic listener and broad-minded patron of the arts, Don Chato offered him one of his rundown cabañas, and before you could say "fucking lucky," Chuck pinned a sign to a tree and opened a twenty-four-hour tattoo parlor. Every night a line of clients waited at the door, willing to pay good money for a portrait of Pakal tattooed on their biceps or the Lord of Death grinning on their backs. Whenever there was a rave, Chuck was besieged by trance dancers. But the ecstatic, all-night groove made him irritable and restless. The girls got so carried away by the pulsing psychedelic beat they couldn't hold still. And then the beautiful Esmeralda took to visiting him in his room. She was only fifteen, for Chrissakes! Life was just treating him too good. One morning he jumped out of his skin and simply disappeared. The drummers said he was still drinking with Solomon at the Mono Blanco, but maybe their eyes were playing tricks on them, maybe the skinny figure shrinking in his chair was just Chuck's lingering phantom. One of the Indian workers said he met Chuck Norris in the mountains, and Chuck was speaking perfect Tzeltal, although it could have been a blond-haired *duende* out for a midnight stroll. He was definitely seen staggering up the path of the Panchan at four A.M., bruised and bloody after a motorcycle wreck. Two days later he was gone again.

The next time I ran into Chuck Norris he was drinking coffee with Solomon at an upscale café in downtown Palenque. His bruises were barely visible and he had trimmed his scraggly hair. Solomon was teaching English at the university and testifying every Sunday at the Church of the Ascended Lords of Light. He was red-faced but sober. The two of them were sharing a fancy apartment with a large bay window overlooking the main street, and since neither of them owned a stick of furniture, they had turned the living room into a parlor, a tattoo parlor, that is. High on ambition, Chuck was determined to become the first tattoo artist in Palenque, performing a much-needed service for the poor, deprived locals who had been decorating their naked hides with blue dots and numbers made with a crude pen.

And that is how Chuck Norris hooked up with the 18's, an international group of gangbangers known from L.A. to Honduras as the meanest bad-assed dudes to cross the border. Boys of eleven were getting their first tattoo—a bold 18—emblazoned on their foreheads or sallow baby cheeks. As they committed more crimes of theft and slaughter, their tattooed mugs showed the score. But the thin blue 1 and swirling 8 added up to zero, because when gang members turned 18, their brothers snuffed them out. That was the real meaning of the number 18.

Alfonso Morales was among the first good citizens to hear rumors of the gang's ominous presence. He turned the number 18 over in his head. "Drinking age, driving age, the number of months in the Maya year, a multiple of 2, 3, 6, and 9 (Podwell would know the progression), certainly not an irrational number . . . ."

And then he remembered that when he was excavating at Copan, in northern Honduras, he encountered something very sinister. One evening, on the outskirts of town, where the dirt of the streets met the dirt of the pastures, he came upon a bunch of local hoodlums. He knew the kind: stupid, sleazy bastards stealing nickels, trading dimes. He'd grown up with them, except these guys shaved their heads and wore safety pins in their lips. There must have been twenty of them gathered in a circle, waving their arms and shouting obscenities. Must be some kind of boxing match, he thought. But when he pressed forward to see what was happening, he saw a little runt, bare-assed and kneeling, giving it to a girl whose screams were muffled by a rag. The spectators were shoving and humping and urging him on. The boy standing next to Alfonso looked up at him and winked. "She is my baby sister, señor. You will have to wait your turn."

"Fair is fair," Solomon said when I bumped into him one day. "We cannot know what God has in store." He was standing outside his apartment house, studying the sky, and looking more banged up than usual.

"They're thugs," I said, keeping my voice down in case any of the hoods on the street spoke English.

"The 1 is the All One, the 8 is the sign of infinity," said Solomon, still checking out the weather.

"They are thugs!" I repeated. "Killers and dope fiends."

"Don't worry," he crooned. "They will pay for their sins in 2012."

"That adds up to 5," I said.

The cloud disappeared, the white car pulled out, and he finally looked at me and said in his whiskey tenor, "The exact date is December 21, 2012; 12 plus 21 plus 2012 comes to 2045, which is 11, the mystical portal to the higher world."

"But 11 is reducible to 2."

"Think of it this way: 18 is 9, 9 plus 2 is 11. And 18 plus 11 is 29—the 2 and the 9 again—which also adds up to 11. You see! Any way you look at it, you reach 11. So, don't worry. Everything is in perfect harmony."

Gangsta' rap was blasting from the second floor. Punks were lolling on the sidewalk or jiving in the street, and Chuck Norris was upstairs, bent over the needle, doing the tattooing in his drugged-out sleep.

The witch got along without them. During the daytime, she stomped around, red hair flaming, mouth fixed in a permanent scowl, berating the cook and the part-time waiter, scolding her daughter or raving at the wimp. As soon as it grew dark, she wrapped herself in a black wool sweater, curled up in a plastic chair, and sat, shivering, in the empty lot. One night the Medusa told her single regular customer that the ghost of a woman was haunting the bar and she was too afraid to sleep.

The customer was a former FBI agent stationed on the Texas border who liked to brag about popping Mexicans whenever he got the chance. "Another wetback for Bush," he said. We called him Big Mac. This overweight, alcoholic, gun-happy meth head was insane enough to lay his heavy mitt on Medusa's shoulder.

"Mmm, my old lady was a redhead. Weak for redheads, I guess."

He invited her back to his room. But after a few sloppy kisses she broke away. "The ghost won't let me!" she said.

Big Mac jumped up and started fanning the air. His eyes were wild. "Now settle down there, honey. I hope ya don't mean that pale simp of a man you're married to."

"Ghost! *Fantasma!* She enters my dreams. She appears everywhere, the woman I loved for my life. She won't let go!"

Like all killers, Big Mac was a firm believer in the supernatural. One moonless night he was lying low in the desert when three giant lizards crawled out of the dunes and came roaring after him like Godzilla's triple-threat clones. They were ten feet tall, with slashing claws and spinning eyeballs and twin tongues that coiled like eels around his rubber legs. He fought them off until he ran out of ammo. So he picked up a board and started whacking them. It did no good. They tumbled down and played dead, then reared up and came at him again. Only now they were multiplying. There must have been thirty of them lunging and flicking their electric tongues from every direction. He was on his knees and praying to his divine maker when he felt the ground tremble. He turned around and saw this giant tarantula lumbering towards him. The tarantula grabbed those lizards in its hairy arms and crushed them one by one, until all fifty of them dissolved like hot mint jelly in the sand. Big Mac was awestruck but still had the presence of mind to speak:

"What's your name?" he asked the tarantula.

"My name is Carol," said the tarantula, before disappearing over the hill.

"Same name as mine," I said. "What a coincidence."

"Yea, and that's how I know you're my savior," Big Mac said.

It was the worst come-on I'd ever heard. Since Medusa's ghost story was the weirdest putdown Big Mac had ever received, I decided that in a roundabout way this pathetic stooge and I were even.

But instead of keeping it to himself, Big Mac opened his big mouth and told all the barflies that the red-haired bitch was a dyke. Not that anyone cared, but on his way back to his lonesome cabaña, he tripped and broke his leg. With a plaster cast up to his thigh and just enough money to buy a five-hour ride to anywhere, he boarded the night bus for one of those stinking oil towns on the Gulf.

The witch still had the power!

18

The Saturday night outlaws were getting so loaded they didn't notice the dueling rhythms clashing in their heads. Those tattooed boys would just snap their fingers and the rock band would play three decibels higher.

Someone call the police! But why bother? The police were too scared to come out here. Nothing, not even the blood-sucking, mind-numbing, rock n' roll shrieks could satisfy the cold, dark presences stalking Alberto's underworld bar.

Chapter 32

MINERVA TAKES A VACATION

Wind to water, bones to fire: all things change into their opposite. It was one thing for Esmeralda to search the city streets for Chuck Norris, who reportedly was hiding out in a Maya village in the mountains. It was another matter for Empress to abandon Skate and start keeping company with Blue Thunder, a Mexican hippie who never even heard of falafel.

"Lordy me, the Goddess sure pulled a fast one," is all Grandmother would say. "Daytime ghosts, nighttime gangs. We're up against some heavy vibes!"

Her devoted students kept their eyes fixed on the golden pentagon painted in the center of the dining table.

"Come on, girls, we have got to pray harder for the witch who's running that devil's playground. And let's begin by calling the Mono Blanco the Mono Negro!"

No one laughed. The girls who weren't pretending to be concentrating were busy taking long sips from their papaya smoothies.

"Hmm, looks like you're all in cahoots about somethin'. Anybody going to tell me what it is?" After another prolonged silence, Grandmother turned to Gretchen and said, "What's the matter with you, child? Cat got your tongue?"

Gretchen brushed the hair from her eyes, and we could see the angry tears welling. "I-we-have been reading some books, books about your beautiful goddess. And it seems you forgot to mention that your beautiful goddess, full of love and light, she has a mean and ugly side also."

"Yes, ma'am. Dark, light, and all the colors in between. It's about time you figured that out," said Grandmother. "The Goddess has to have many sides because she lives in every one of us. And that means she's not that different from you and me."

"There are portents," Gretchen whispered.

Grandmother straightened her gold-rimmed glasses. "Portents is why we're here today, and I'm hopin' we can clear this up and get down to business. So if that's all that's bothering you girls, you've got no cause for the least little worry."

Gretchen tapped her foot impatiently. "It is not all black and white and rosy, Grandmother. She loves people. She eats people. She is goodness. She is evil, with long nails and burning eyes and flaming hair."

"Well, she sure ain't lazy about showing her emotions," Grandmother chuckled. "Didn't I just say she's not that different from you and me?"

"I don't see why we have to pray for that red-haired bitch!" Gretchen blurted.

"So it's back to square one, is it? Well, listen up, sisters! Black, white, or sixteen shades of purple, two-headed, snake-eyed, with twelve arms waving swords, shells, flutes, and whatnot. Don't you see, ladies? The Goddess is perfect. And the witch . . . well, the witch is a woman, same as you."

Flushed with shame, the women composed a prayer so garbled I wondered whether it would ever reach the right ears. And the subsequent spells, distorted by the sluggish atmosphere, would they miss their mark—always a danger—and strike the wrong person? Time would tell.

Tie her, bind her, scatter the red stone

Throughout the chanting, Gretchen remained silent, her ice-blue eyes lost in a distant blizzard. Little did we know that another secret was swelling underneath her tight, cold-wired skin.

You see, we never expected Chato to take up with Gretchen, tall, blond, and twenty-five and able to handle her own bobsled, so to speak. And who would have dreamed that Minerva, out of raw spite, would have the gumption to escape to Sabancuy, Roque's favorite beach. But she didn't travel to the sun-baked shore to visit Roque on his much needed break from the Panchan's infernal oven. No, she ran off with a longhaired backpacker from Quebec, leaving Chato and the Italian pizza man scorned and bereft.

"Not even a real beach, like Tulum, for Chrissakes!" Chato ranted.

"Not even a real Frenchman," the pizza man whined.

"The guy's a bum," they agreed.

For an entire week the two of them paddled the wine-dark waters of forgetfulness, consoling each other and drinking Valpolicella from the same bottle. The pizza man was too drunk to toss the dough. Chato plowed his red Jeep into a pond of reeds and had to buy a used Nissan sedan, which reared and bucked and otherwise refused to be ridden by its new owner.

"You are a walking accident," Gretchen told him. "It's making my insides shiver and sweat." At the end of the week, she hopped a plane for the Arctic Circle, vowing never to return to the Seventeenth Parallel. Two days later, Minerva came back to the Panchan, boiling.

"Enough dogs. Enough rock and roll. Enough of that gang of bastards hitting on the women. *Ya, basta*! I'm going home." And Minerva packed her sequins and went back to live with her father.

Chato called her cell phone at least ten times a day, but Minerva didn't answer. The pizza man went to the ruins to tell Tito that the Mexican pepperoni had no taste, his crust was soggy on the bottom, and that he couldn't live without Minerva's inspiration.

"For that you are a big fool," Tito shouted. "Go back to Italy and live with the cows!" Then he swung his shovel and hit the pizza man in the knee.

Chato had no better luck talking to Mingo. In fact, when Mingo saw him lurching toward the house in a battered green pickup, Mingo locked the front door. Chato knocked and knocked while Minerva sat quietly at the table and Mingo continued writing page after page in his notebook. As soon as she heard the motor scrape into first gear, Minerva went back to the stove.

"This hen is still very tough, Papa. It needs more water."

"The hen is an abomination," said Mingo, without looking up.

Minerva had tears in her eyes when she grabbed the tin bucket and ran out the door. She still had tears in her eyes when Chato snuck up behind her on the path to the well. All along he'd been hiding behind the house, just waiting and hoping for her to come out.

"I promise," he said over and over. "I promise I'll get rid of everything that bothers you. I'll shoot them if I have to."

Minerva kept walking.

"No more girls, I promise."

Minerva kept her eyes to the ground.

"We'll go to the beach in Campeche. You'll like it, I promise."

Minerva spoke. "I've just been to the beach. I'm sick of sand. I'm sick of waves."

"What should I do? Kill my brother? End the fighting once and for all?"

"Kill, kill, kill!" Minerva wailed. She turned on her heel, ready to swing the pail, when she heard her papa's voice.

"*Buenas tardes*, Don Chato. Good to have you here again," Mingo said, although he couldn't remember the last time he'd seen Chato, here at the house or at the Panchan. Mingo's face was taut, his eyes colder than dew on a hawk as he scrutinized his angry daughter and this wild man, this rich man she had taken for a lover. Mingo was surprised to see that Chato's hair was turning gray, but now was hardly the time to mention the matter of age.

"My son," Mingo said. "You are the invisible man."

Minerva lowered the pail. Chato began waving his arms.

"Forgive me, Don Mingo. I should have come sooner. We should have talked. I should have asked, I should have explained." Chato was racing in tight circles, kicking up dust, as Mingo stood stiffly at the door, waiting for the man to calm down.

"I-I," Chato stopped in his tracks and held out his hands. "Don't you see, I love her!"

"Then why are you fighting? Why have you made my daughter so unhappy?" Mingo asked in a cool, reasonable voice.

Chato looked around helplessly and threw up his arms. "I can't do everything she wants. My brother is crazy. My father plays tricks. It's too complicated. I just don't know how."

Minerva came up and placed her hand on his arm. "I'll go to the beach with you," she said.

"No, no, you are right. There are better places in the world. Paris, India, Peru . . . ."

Minerva looked startled. Chato thought some more.

Suddenly he turned to Mingo and said, "Alright, I will take her to China!"

Chapter 33

THE WALL

Moments after Chato and Minerva left on their Asian holiday, the maintenance crew began a massive building project destined to equal the grand follies of old. It started at the river, and like the rushing river during November's torrential floods, the trench ran directly toward Don Mucho's main stage. Out of the trench, before our astonished eyes, rose a mighty dragon whose armored plates were made of undulating rows of sparkling cinder blocks. In a matter of days, the monstrous worm stood eight feet high, strong enough to fend off earthquakes, tsunamis, phantom marauders, diabolical desperados, random astral projections, and one mean drum machine. It was some kind of miracle, like the Deactivation of the Ninth Gate, and you had to conclude that the masons despised the witch and the rockers as much as everybody else. Yes, the apes had gone beyond Chato's orders and put their hearts into their work. But the big featherless serpent was ugly just the same.

"So, it's come to this," Don Moi said in disgust. "Dividing the jungle, erasing the view." Never mind that the former vista was a treeless, soulless tract of jimmy-rigged tin and lumber. Moi's eyes were on fire, his voice a metal rasp. "I told you everything that Mingo told me about my lovesick son. But this grotesquerie is not about love. It is about human greed and malice."

How to beautify this monotonous concrete hulk? There was talk of planting heliconias and wild ginger, but those opposed to invasives started hunting for indigenous ferns and ayahuasca vines. One of the artisans began painting Maya hieroglyphs on the bald cement. At the same time, a rusty Italian sculptor, inspired by Moi's scrap heap and Chato's graveyard of dead cars, decided to punctuate the immense blank slab with gaping television sets and mangled yellow fenders. But instead of an artistic statement, the monumental barricade became a political symbol, a Berlin Wall painted pistachio green. No two ways about it, you had to take a stand: freedom or anarchy, folk or rock, Mary Jane or crack.

Like the Great Wall of China, the Panchan Palisade failed to stop the barbarians. But it did succeed in slowing traffic and muffling the god-awful rock and roll.

On the other side, the story was different. It was only one wall, but the gray blocks squeezed the high spirits out of the lowlifes and transformed their alien parking lot into a dirt-floored prison cell. The ghost of the witch's lover was confounded. The witch complained of feeling hemmed in, and no wonder. Hunched in her torn black sweater, arms wrapped tightly around her knees, she rocked back and forth like a wounded spider trapped in her own ragged web.

When profits plummeted and there was no money for sugar, Alberto figured something was wrong. Even in Asunción he got wind of the drug deals going down. He grabbed the dog and jumped into his car and arrived in time for the band's slurred rendition of "Knock, Knock, Knocking on Heaven's Door."

Who were those kids with the tattoos on their faces, he wanted to know. He could see the place was attracting a bad element, although the bad element could pay for plenty of beers, which kept them running to the *baño*.

"At least they're not snorting at the tables," Alberto told the witch.

She wiped her tears and said, "It's the ghost."

All the same, when Alberto came the following weekend, he was wearing army boots and camouflage. And of course, he had his pit bull with him, in case things got out of hand.

But the situation was grimmer than any threat a pit bull could handle. One night Esmeralda returned from the woods in a strange, somnambulant stupor, her eyes glassy, her body cold. "It's worse than a ghost," she whispered.

"Have a little spoonful of soup," said her mother. "I bought you some buns today."

Esmeralda just stared at the peeling bark on the madron tree. "It's worse than a ghost," she repeated.

"I'll bring you mint tea in my gourd. I'll buy you a bottle of Coca Cola. It was just a demon, just a night creature you saw. Pay no attention."

"You pay attention, Mama. We have to leave right away!"

The witch looked her daughter straight in the eye. "My Anna says that one day you will go to school. You will comb your hair and wear a dress."

"For God's sake, Mama. There's a body out there. A body without a head!"

RE: Animals
Sent: Saturday July 3 2:35:20 am.
From: podwell@hotmail.com.mx

Hi Carol, Just to let you know that Barnaby's snakebite
wasn't as bad as we thought. The swelling has gone down
and they won't have to amputate. He's pretty woozy
though and as soon as he can walk his wife wants him to
fly home and rest for a while. I told the doctors that with
all the craziness in the world, and the Panchan in particular, I was thinking that nauyaca was more than your
ordinary five-foot long, world's most venomous snake. It
was probably someone out to get Barnaby. Who that somebody could be is a big question since Barnaby has never
done anything to hurt anybody. But as you know, there
are malevolent spirits everywhere and they don't always
show their true faces. The Maya called them "*way*" and
I think there is something to it, these animal spirits that
live inside us and come out at night and haunt the woods
and haunt our dreams. The first thing out of Barnaby's
mouth was, "It's the curse of the Temple of Doom." I was
glad to see he still has a sense of humor, but of course,
I don't believe it for a minute. I believe it's some kind of
supernatural animal, like the jaguars that prowl around
your house at night and give you nightmares. It could be
the pit bull that's always biting people, and even the falcons that bring Mingo false messages. The Lizards could
be supernatural too, supernatural Maya creatures rather
than alien beings which are taking over people's bodies.
The *naguales* explain a lot about the constant turmoil in
Maya history, pitting noble against noble and city against
city, because cities had their *naguales*, or *way*, too, like the
giant serpent centipede with skeletal jaws that you see
on Pakal's sarcophagus lid. They emerge from the uncon-
scious, but they are very real—hyper-real—if you are living
near the ruins and absorbing all the positive and negative
energies. Just look at the art! Those monsters can come
out of nowhere and rip off an arm or a leg or tear off your

head. They can disguise themselves as beautiful women and lure you to their house and then change into putrid, ant-ridden logs full of spiders and scorpions, which is what happened to me once in northern Guatemala. The doctors don't understand this. All I'm saying is that we need to be very, very careful where we step.

Best wishes,
Podwell

Chapter 34

REVELATIONS

I was drinking my morning coffee and watching the howler monkeys swing over my house when the Empress appeared at my door, fresh as a Zimbabwe daisy. Her son had dropped by earlier in search of soda pop and chips, but since I had none in stock, he cheerfully settled for pineapple juice and plums, which he ate with exaggerated pleasure. "Don't worry, I got money for snacks later," he assured me. He was accomplished at hiding his disappointments, great and small, under broad, considerate smiles, and I often wondered where this baby-faced boy acquired his adult polish. As a special favor to me this morning, he let me know that my house was not as secure as it should be. I said nothing about the jaguars that haunted the nearby mounds because Mickey was one of those down-to-earth teenagers with the hard world on his mind. He asked for a credit card and then showed me how easy it was to pick my lock. "And don't leave your keys hanging like that in the bolt," he said on his way out. "Someone could just slip their hand through the screen and open the door easy as pie."

The Empress wasn't looking for Mickey. She came by to borrow a book. I showed her the novels, but she said she didn't read novels because they were made-up stories. There was no point in discussing the limitations of factual knowledge or the power of the creative imagination to clarify human existence, and so I left her to peruse the shelves. To my surprise, she started leafing through my copy of *The Nag Hammadi Library*, a collection of early Gnostic texts that attribute the presence of evil in the world to God the Creator, a fallible being in eternal conflict with the supreme, invisible God, who, with his divine consort, Sophia, rules an alternate universe populated by angelic hosts at constant war with his enemies, both good and evil. The fantastic worlds, the visionary scope contained in these extraordinary heretical works surpass most human experience. Yet the moral anxieties—the evil that stalks, the amorphous light of the great unknown—trouble every waking and sleeping soul and aptly describe the opposing forces splitting the Panchan asunder.

"Sit down," I suggested, and without looking up, Empress folded herself into the rattan chair and became totally engrossed in the revelatory book on her lap. After a while, she asked for paper and a pencil.

"This says the same thing as our books," is all she said.

I had no idea what books she meant, and with little else to go on, I jumped to the conclusion that Empress was a dualist, which was the real reason she and Grandmother made regular jibes at Guru Karl, the Onist, and were drifting away from the Dreamspell in favor of a deeper understanding of Maya thought and culture, especially the figure of the Red Queen, whom they probably identified as a Maya parallel to Sophia, goddess of wisdom. It occurred to me then that the Gnostics and the ancient Maya had much in common philosophically; they shared a dualistic view of the universe in which good and evil beings did battle through successive creations and destructions of the world. The tension between warring gods kept the universe spinning. Whether there was ever a period of sublime harmony we will never know since the four Maya books that have survived the Spanish Conquest deal with astronomy, from which experts must glean the barest notions of the Maya cosmos, whereas the forty buried tractates that comprise the secret Nag Hammadi Library mention the planets only in passing. And whereas the Gnostics despised the natural everyday world and withdrew to the deserts of Upper Egypt, the Maya, in their worried fashion, embraced the profane joys of life.

A good hour went by in silence, me sitting here at the computer, Empress poring intently over each line and then jotting down quotations on the paper. I was about to suggest she take the book home when Skate poked his head inside the door. As soon as he discovered he had interrupted our reading hour, he began browsing. Immediately he picked up the *I Ching*.

"Far out!" he said. "I caught on to it when I was in jail. Helped me see that things are always changing even though my life was standing still. It'll even be a bigger help now that we got a plan."

Skate proceeded to spell out the plan, which involved two wealthy Americans from Wisconsin who wanted to invest in a health resort and spa. "Met them here in Palenque, and they are gung-ho. All I have to do is write it up. Put something big together. It's sweet, man. And if that don't work out, there's always Mother T."

Mother T, I learned then, was the name of the Baltimore oriole everyone was always making a fuss over. I mentioned that I hadn't seen her in the last few days.

"Gone to California. Big fights between the street gangs in East LA. Gone to New Orleans to take a look at the lasting damage. Worst floods in history, man, and no one's done nothing about it. Brothers and sisters still homeless or stuck in trailers in Houston. At least they're out of the projects is one good thing. Mother T is flying everywhere, trying to calm things down. She'll be back when things cool off, you can be sure of that. She likes it here, says this is the Promised Land."

"Maybe she be the one who deliver us from toil," Empress murmured. "The High Priestess of Zion, the Red Queen of Nubia."

"Amen, sister!" said Skate. "We gave up on the Panthers, gave up on Malcolm X, gave up on revolution and shooting ourselves in the foot. Her and me, we don't even listen to rap, and that's for damn sure and good. 'Let the women run things,' that's what I say."

Slowly, wearily, Empress closed the book. "Ah, the music ain't so bad," she sighed. "It's the words I can't stand."

"C'mon, tell the truth, babe," Skate said, placing his giant basketball hand on Empress's narrow shoulder. "Tell her how you was married to that fat gangsta' producer. Left him way back in Detroit and got together with me."

He stopped smiling when Empress pulled his hand off her shoulder. "The man is still Mickey's father," she said, and then turned to me. "But you know how it is, money don't buy happiness. Of course, neither does being broke all the time."

"We're searching for a better way," said Skate, trying to lift the spirit of the conversation. "And the queen, Mother T, is with us now. Come into this life as the wife of our prophet, wife and widow of Elijah Mohammed."

Now that was a revelation!

My earliest encounter with Mother T took place during Saskia's first trip to the ruins. Under the thick trees on the east side of the Palace, a full Baptist choir dressed in white church robes was circling a young tenor who held in his outstretched hands a poorly chiseled crystal skull. The choir looked as nervous as Sunday school truants, too perplexed to speak, especially the tenor in the center whose hands were wrapped around the skull's mouth as if trying to silence any words it might care to utter. Saskia's silver Keds and white turban were drawing attention, too, and as we strolled toward the shade, an older woman rose from the stone bench and rushed forward. The two women embraced. They had met each other years before at a Dreamspell conference in Siberia!

Now that I remembered this accidental meeting, and the amazing fact that Saskia was acquainted with both Yuri Knorozov and Mother T, I began to wonder whether Saskia was a Russian Norn or a living thread connecting seemingly disparate people for some mysterious higher purpose. More to the point, I was completely baffled by the evident link between the Maya and the Black Muslims.

"And since this is the Promised Land," Skate continued, "Mother T's got her heart set on buying Rakshita's property."

"What will Mother T do with the land?" I asked matter-of-factly.

"Oh, probably build a small retreat," he answered vaguely.

"You mean a spa, a healing center?" I prodded.

"More like a camp, you know, with a big kitchen and dormitories. Nothing fancy."

"But I thought you were planning a spa."

"Oh, that's just me and this blessed woman here." This time Skate placed his palm ever so gently on Empress's bowed head. "Our blessed Grandmother, too. For sure we'll be helping each other out. But Mother T, she wants a place where kids from the inner city can come and escape."

"How many kids?"

"Oh, maybe a hundred or so."

"For the summer?"

"Well, maybe longer. When I say 'escape' I mean we need a nice, safe place where the youth can ride out the catastrophes that are coming. I mean 2012 and the end of the world."

Chapter 35

THE GOSPEL OF MUD

The women who heeded Grandmother's call were teenage mothers from Atlanta's inner city, delivered to the Panchan by wishes so strong and swift they were jumping out of their skins, as if they'd been teleported or something. One minute they're wheeling strollers down to the corner Stop n' Rob and the next they're picking bananas off the trees, shaking the city dust off their high tops and strutting around like Sheena of the Jungle.

"Mama, you ain't never gonna believe your eyes! Everything you see on TV is real. They got a waterfall clear as plastic bubbles. They got lizards the size of Gamboa's cat. We get to dance every night, moon shining, stars shining, just singing and clapping and praising everything in God's creation. Next time I got to bring the babies."

Power of sweet joy, reign on forever. Wash away the po' face sadness and shine that heavenly light!

Life was euphoric for a few precious days. And then the angelic hosts on high started napping. The girls fell into a funk no birdsong could stir. Velma fainted dead away at the sight of all God's crawling creatures. Cassandra cried for no reason. Melanie stayed in her room because of the creepy vegetation, Kayla because she was plain tired, tired, tired. None showed deadly signs of melancholic wrangling with the great mysteries of life. Stars still shone whenever they opened their eyes, ever so briefly, before they crashed. "See you in my dreams, sisters," and they were out like a light. This was the main symptom: the young mothers were making up for lost sleep, their own, their children's, and practically every insomniac in the world.

Contagious, yes, fatal, no. As Grandmother needed to remind everybody, "I know you feel as if time is standing still, but this trip ain't no holiday and no free ride. No sir, it was bought by a lot of grant money and private donations from well-meaning folk, and you sisters are here to work." Never mind that the project sounded like a half-baked idea, even to her.

The mission was to build cob houses for the poor, under the guidance of a dedicated Australian by the unfortunate name of Dingo.

"People don't build mud houses in the jungle," he was told right off the bat. "Even poor people. They want concrete."

The Aussie snapped right back, "But organic brought us here, didn't it, mate? And organic is what we're here to do." The bloke had attitude, which he needed plenty of for the uphill climb since he had no map or compass and Grandmother was already nipping at his scrawny tail.

First he led his lazy crew over to the Ark, an island of grass and mango trees where Woofers from across the seas were building a sustainable community off the grid. None of the Atlanteans had a drop of enthusiasm for plain old ordinary farm labor, and after two days of sitting on their rumps, admiring the waves of lettuce and chard, the wilted mermaids went under.

Before they floated away, one of the Brits suggested that the project would be more viable in a cooler clime, perhaps the Sierra Madres along the Pacific coast where thousands of Maya people had lost their homes in the recent hurricane. It was a great opportunity to be of genuine help, and they could probably join the volunteer brigade sent down by Jimmy Carter's Habitat. Dingo wasn't interested in conventional house construction using wood or cement. He was committed to mud.

Back they drifted to Grandmother's cozy haven. Now they were sleeping in hammocks and rising at the crack of noon, then dragging themselves over to the Rastarant where they slumped at the outdoor tables, listening to Dingo rail against stones and bricks. Weeks went by at the conference table, and they still hadn't come up with a plan. Dingo refused to change his mind about adobe, and he refused to change his plaid shirt.

Grandmother was losing patience. "Ten bags of oranges a day, fifty eggs, twenty kilos of soybeans, and there's nothing but talk. You're not the same boy I knew in Atlanta, nosiree."

Dingo cracked a smile. "I've said it before and I'll say it again, Gran, you are the queen!"

"And these teenage girls flopping around like Lucy Goosy. If I didn't know better, I'd say they were under some spell. Right now Empress is mixing my high-octane special into the pancake batter. They won't know what hit 'em. If that don't work, I'll try some stronger juju."

"You are the queen of magic, queen of tasty grub, alright! We both know local involvement is the key, and you've bloody well exceeded all my expectations." Dingo paused to see if his words were having any effect, but so far, no. "And now that my troops are flagging—God bless each and every one of them—community outreach seems more imperative than ever. Just as soon as we shift gears . . . ."

Grandmother looked him in the eye. The bells on her dreads started jangling like a three-alarm fire. "For starters, there's no time like the present. And for seconds, don't be talking that bullshit around my kitchen."

"I walk my talk, Gran," and he turned on his heels and left.

Dingo had enough nervous energy for ten people. "I look like a steak knife," he said of himself. But as far as I could see, his bite was as big as a saw blade and his trajectory was circular.

Pull his chain, as Grandmother did, and he began reaching out to the hippies he heard about who were planting organic gardens in the mountains. By the general look of things, the courtship with Mother Earth had died a quick death, as had all other short- and long-term romances. Most of the squatters trying to live off the land were squabbling down-and-outers, seriously clumsy, and not a green thumb among them. Some hadn't gotten any further than digging a compost hole, a wasted effort, really, because they had nothing to scrape into the hole. They were starving and bedding down in the open. One commune was supporting itself by picking cacao beans off neighbors' trees and preparing organic chocolate balls flavored with the neighbors' chiles. Thirty chocolatiers were sleeping under one thatched roof, shitting in the woods, and going without baths, a form of rebellion Dingo approved of from a great distance. Another group, with a beautiful parcel of land overlooking the ruins of Palenque, had corn in the fields, bamboo houses, composting toilets, and bathing pools spilling with orchids. Medicine rites were open to Arcturian Masters of the Red Road, empaths, telepaths, and druids welcome.

The history of the 1960s was repeating itself in a place far, far older. "How did the ancient Maya survive and prosper in the jungle?" Dingo asked himself.

After three unsuccessful forays, Dingo returned to his favorite barstool at Don Mucho's where he could count on a receptive audience. Central to his project goals, he explained, was a cultural exchange program between young black ghetto women from the States and traditional Maya Indians, descendants of the ancients, who were living like their ancestors in rural communities nearby.

"*No problema*," said the fellow next to him. "I'll give you directions."

The next morning Dingo could not read the chicken scratches on the napkin. So he asked around town, and pretty soon his dogged determination paid off. A combi driver dropped him in the middle of nowhere and pointed him down an unmarked trail leading through jungle scrub to the little village of Nueva Palestina. After hanging out at the tienda for a week, kicking stones, tossing sticks, and buying liters of orange Fanta, the suspicious storeowner got up the nerve to ask his best customer if he knew Chuck Norris.

"Whoa, I've only seen him in the movies," Dingo said, "never in the flesh."

The storeowner smiled and shook Dingo's hand. One friend led to another, and now Dingo was spending most of his time in the village, drinking with his pals. Once in a while he'd come home whistling a few words of Chol before falling into his hammock.

"So," Velma says, "when he come home, I go, 'Where you been, Dingo? We been pining for ya. And he mumbles, 'Community liaison. Don't think it's fucking easy.' But we're not exactly pining like dumb ditzes with a habit. We are positively over that lame, lazybones routine."

"Back from never-never land," Kayla laughs. "Got high-octane running in our blood, and we're sewing and cooking and helping Grandma with her ointments and brews, professional skills she says will give us a leg up when we go on home. Not that any of us want to get back to the street, but hey, we all got responsibilities, and that's a fact. I don't know how the mud houses fit into the picture."

"*Quién sabe?*" Melanie shrugs. "See, I'm learning some Spanish while I'm waiting on tables and meeting women from Italy and Poland. Networking till my jaw is sore. Over and over I got to say, 'We're from Atlan-ta, not Atlan-tis. Home of the godfather of soul, James Brown.'

So Grandmother starts calling us the Atlanta Amazons, and that's what we are telling everybody."

"Feelin' our oats, don't you know," says Cherokee. "So one night Ding stumbles in and tells us the Palestinians are ready to sign on the dotted line, meanin' they have given their word of honor to support us to the nth degree, lend a helping hand building whatever needs building. And they are offering to do all this for free. Not a single dime for their aid and advice.

"'Excuse me,' I say, 'But what we building in two days, Dingo? We been here almost a month now. It's time to go home.' He thinks a minute and goes, 'Sisters, I'm afraid you don't understand the pressures I've been under.' Oh mama, that was a good one! So he swings outta his hammock and chugs a quart o' water, just to give the mud a chance to roll around upside his head. 'We're all ears,' we utter in unison, good as the Baptist choir on Easter Sunday, though the words we're saying is profane. And the brother hollers for the whole world to hear at two in the morning—'A bench! We'll build a wall with a bench. We'll worry about the rest of the house later.'"

It was the dog days of summer when leaves folded their ragged wings, corn in the fields went limp and yellow, and cutter ants strolled listlessly along the paths. With the extraordinary aridity this year, crops were dying and people were afraid the snakes would come out of their dens in search of water. But for Dingo, the dry spell was a plus. In the grips of a major countdown, he set a date for the community-wide, mud bench bee: July 25, the "day out of time" in the Dreamspell Calendar.

"Okay," say the Amazons. "We really got to hustle now."

Friends brought bowls of black beans, pinto beans, guacamole, chips, cases of beer, and *refrescos*. Balloons and crepe paper laced the trees. There must have been fifty adults and children from the Panchan, along with two Indian boys from Nueva Palestina, splashing in the creek. Everybody was having a good time digging up the clay bed and tossing the lumps from one to another in a kind of free-style relay, lobbing the dripping cannonballs to the people on the bank who were mixing straw with the mud and piling it all into a shapeless mud mound. Little by little, the women and children in the water were wading deeper and deeper and the mound was growing higher and higher. Finally Dingo started forming the mud into a curved banquette.

Smoothed and incised with serpent designs, the bench measured four feet in height and ten feet in length when he left it to age in the sun: a private nook beside the stream, with a bucolic view of meadows and green mountains.

That night we had the first heavy storm in weeks. The rains knocked down trees, swept away the footbridges, flooded the rivers. The rains leveled the mud bench.

The next morning, as the Atlanteans stood gaping at the remains of their labors, Grandmother was looking more irritable than usual. "Shit happens," she put it bluntly. "Ashes to ashes, and all that."

Dingo was still grimy from the day before, and his eyes were smarting under a layer of fine grit. He placed his hands on the drowned heap of earth and straw and said something about us being humble lumps of clay before the almighty power of Mother Nature. "But we ain't completely jiggered, are we, mates? No, not on your fancy. This is art. Earth Art. A monument to time out of time!"

That last bit of profundity was too much for the girls.

"Why doncha hum us a few bars?" said Velma.

Cherokee clapped her hands. "If you got the time, I got the rhyme." And the sisters sang out:

> *Yeah, yeah, yeah,*
> *You got yours and I got mine.*
> *Do the Monkeyshine.*

And they did the Monkey, just like their mamas taught them, and the Mashed Potatoes, too. Amen.

Chapter 36

A SHORT FAMILY MEETING

While Dingo and the others were whiling away their time on the mud project, negotiations over Rakshita's property and modest wooden structures were proceeding at a snail's pace. During their initial phone conversations, the former White Flower of the Jungle was impressed by Mother T's soft-spoken manner and could sense the woman's charismatic power through the bad connection. Turning over her establishment to a figure of high spiritual integrity was very important to Rakshita. By all reports, she was also pleased with Mother T's generous financial offer. And why not? It was not her land to begin with.

Don Moi, who owned the land, had no idea who the Black Muslims were and didn't care. He, along with the rest of the family, thought little of blacks in general and considered Mother T and her followers innocent dupes who were willing to purchase a piece of land for which, Moi stipulated, they would not gain title for thirty years.

"It's insane," Chato said as soon as he got wind of the scheme. "The old man's gone crazy again." Enrique and Alfonso, who were sitting in on the impromptu pow-wow, agreed. Chato grabbed a bottle of red wine from the bar and poured them each a full glass.

"Usually he's crazy as a fox. This time he's crazy as a loon," Alfonso giggled. "He thinks he can take the money and run. But he doesn't know what he's dealing with. There could be repercussions."

"It's, it's unethical. It's a f-f-fraud," Enrique stammered. "H-He could land in jail."

"No one is going to put a crazy old man in jail," Alfonso said. "Those people must be crazy, too, or desperate. They could buy land on the Gulf Coast for less. Someone should do us a favor and tell them. Maybe it should be me."

"I'm way ahead of you, brother," Chato said. "I've already talked to the Grandmother and I know plenty. The fact is, business or no business, we can't have hundreds of kids from the ghetto running around, breaking into hotel rooms."

Chato's voice dropped to a whisper. "I've been keeping an eye on that boy, Mickey, and I can tell you he is spending too much money. He buys the others kids cokes, *licuados*, and hamburgers. The Rastas are supposed to be vegetarians. My daughter thinks he's a millionaire." Chato pulled a torn piece of paper from his back pocket. "I have it written down here: 220 pesos one day, 439 the next. Where does a boy his age get so much money? Yesterday I saw him in town buying a cell phone. The boy's in trouble. And I am going to have to do something about it before it gets worse."

"He's fronting for the dealer," Alfonso said. "And who knows who that thin stick is mixed up with. Maybe he's supplying the 18's."

"The 18's are bad news. They kill perfect strangers. But those little bastards are Alberto's problem."

"That kid who was murdered and dumped in the woods, they say it was the work of the Zeta cartel. And he wasn't so innocent," said Alfonso. "They cut off the boy's head. Pretty gristly stuff."

"The 18's, the Z's, that's none of our business," Chato shrugged. "You're ruining the memories of my wonderful vacation."

"It will be our business when the military starts questioning foreign tourists and scaring them away. The soldiers are already doing house-to-house searches in town, looking for the ringleaders. Yesterday they kicked in Rosalia's front door, and they didn't have a warrant."

"Rosalia, cousin David's cook?"

"The same. And all because someone tipped them off that she was running a voodoo parlor."

"Poor Rosi. Everyone knows that David's the one who is practicing *Santeria*."

"Oooh, voodoo, the police thought. That rhymes with booze and hard drugs as far as they're concerned. But all they found in her house was a little statue of Maximon, the saint of cigarettes and rum."

"But the Mafioso usually pray to El Niño de Atocha and Santa Muerta, the Saint of Death."

"They are branching out, brother. They are going in for witchcraft now, and the military intelligence—if there is such a thing—knows it."

"What h-h-happened to ordinary C-Catholics?" Enrique stuttered. "N-Not in our family, of c-c-course, but I remember when everyone believed the same."

"I know this much," said Chato, "the Rastas have nothing to do with the Muslim group."

Alfonso had that mean squint in his eye. "Says who? You're getting awfully trusting lately, brother. First Roque, now this."

"Leave Roque out of it. He's back to making pizzas fulltime, and he's not managing the restaurant anymore. The Grandmother and I are dealing with the boy as quietly as we can. If it doesn't work, they'll have to leave, that's all."

"Two birds with one stone," laughed Alfonso. "Whatever they're up to, there's no way anybody, black or white, is going to move in on our land. You know what our mother said when I told her what was happening? She said, 'I'll burn the place down first!' Those were the exact words out of our sweet mother's lips."

"We'll block the back road," said Chato.

"The only way they'll get in is by helicopter."

And we'll be waiting. Don't forget, we're Mexicans, and we have the right to bear arms."

"Now you're talking," said Alfonso. "2012 is going to start tomorrow."

Chapter 37

PETUNIA

In the twilight days of summer, tomorrow never came.

"Time's just zigzaggin'," said Empress, "like those monkeys creeping along the branches. Mornings they head west, evenings they head east. And in between nothing's happening but a lot of chatter." All this was Empress's way of saying that she was tired of being pestered by the Morales family and was getting ready to leave.

"We think Mickey will be better off going to school in the States," Grandmother said diplomatically. "That boy is just bored, bored, bored all day, with too much time on his hands."

"The coffee's good," Moi said, trying to make up for the fact that he and I were the only customers at the Rastarant. He remained silent on the subject of his neighbors' imminent departure, mainly because he was busy preparing a place for his new neighbor.

"Not Mother T. No, no, I'm letting the grass grow over there until she makes her payments. And not the doctor from Villahermosa or the dentist from La Libertad. And not that crazy woman who sells whole wheat bread and copies of *The Keys of Enoch*." He went through the list of candidates who had expressed interest in purchasing a slice of the Panchan.

"Who then?" I asked.

"It's not a who exactly. It's a what."

"You mean an animal?" I said.

"Warm."

"A monkey, a guacamaya, a coatimundi?" Empress guessed.

"A wild, white-collared peccary named Petunia!" Moi laughed.

"Well, excuse me, Don Moises, but I'm afraid you be laughing alone," said Empress.

"I'm tired of the dogs and the cats. I love them. They are my best friends. But I have to admit it, they are very dumb. Pigs, on the other hand, are the smartest animals in the world. Did you know there are pigs that can count to twenty? Did you know there are pigs that have rescued little children from burning barns?"

Grandmother rolled her eyes. She told him she had heard stories about pigs eating farmers, about wild herds of razorbacks invading the suburbs of Atlanta and Houston and attacking babies.

"Oh yes, some people will tell you they are dangerous, but it's a lie. My Petunia is very shy, and much quieter than Alberto's dog. Yes, if Alberto can have a pit bull, I can have a wild pig." Naturally the three of us were completely stymied by Moi's logic.

"Oh, there's no need for you to look so concerned," he said. "I've had peccaries in the past, five of them to be exact, and I know how to take care of them very well. They used to run around my place and eat at the table. They are really very friendly."

I remembered Petunia Una, the wild peccary that entertained archaeologists and other hardened travelers at Moi's old restaurant. In those days, Palenque was a godforsaken village with little to offer except the family's modest hotel drowsing under the shade trees at the edge of a dry *barranca*. Once you were out of the sun's glare and beneath the dark, thatched roof, you could savor the spirit of jungle living in relative comfort. Moi and his pet monkey provided the local color. And when the bristly boar rubbed her snout against your table, you could truthfully say you had a close encounter with a wild beast. In fact, she was fairly tame by then and accustomed to all sorts of people. Whereas the spider monkey never left Moi's shoulder, Petunia Una was downright fickle. She fell in love with one of the archaeology students, and every morning at the crack of dawn she'd slam against his screen door and rouse him from his tousled bed. As soon as he opened the latch, she'd roll over, and he'd rub her white belly until the sun flared and she was satisfied. To this day, he's never lived it down.

"Unfortunately, times have changed. Too bad, but this is not my place anymore. It belongs to those greedy children of mine, and they're running it into the ground. If it were up to me, the deer would come back. There would be monkeys everywhere, ocelots and macaws."

"And jaguars," I said.

"If only! But we need to be realistic. This is a hotel now, and I'm building a beautiful corral for her. I know she'll be pleased. Come, I'll show you. It's just beyond my House of Illusions, by the Plaza of the Mother Tree."

Moi was dressed in his workpants and carrying a giant pair of pliers, and as we walked along the path he called *Los Frijolillos*, he pointed out various plants of interest: purple maguey for toothaches, *momo* for stomach aches, ramon nuts for times of famine.

"She's a beautiful lady, this ramon tree, the Maya goddess of the forest. And here is my pitaya. You know the stucco portrait of Pakal that was found in the tomb? In his hair he is wearing a pitaya, because it is a night-blooming flower, and when it blossoms in the Underworld, its sweet perfume masks the terrible stench."

When we reached Moi's House of Illusions, he stopped again. "And this is my little papaya tree. I planted it here, in the northern part of the south Panchan, a few weeks ago. I sent you a note, remember?" Of course I remembered.

Mi querida Carola:
John fell! We all know that roughneck with the Santa Claus beard. He's a real Corpus Texan who, with his weight of one hundred kilos—210 pounds for those who like to inflate numbers—conquered the stairs that led to Barnaby's house. Barnaby did not answer the door, because Barnaby was in the mash unit at the general hospital, about to have his leg sawn off by those imbeciles. John's impatient knock created pressure on the landing, and Barnaby's steps, due to temperature and termites, were not obliged to save the life of any bastard, even if he were an American named John. The stairs gave way, and the hospital received another victim. The rumor spread faster than pink eye, though when it reached me it was on crutches and in no real hurry to arrive. To make a long story short, John is walking again, and the rumors that have been stewing for days have become a savory dish at Don Mucho's restaurant.

And so, with my old crazy ways, I thought that a monument should commemorate the event. To celebrate the fact that John is alive, I raised this miserable and wounded papaya tree from the dead. This little tree had already produced a tiny Third World papaya—truly underdeveloped—and seemed determined to pass on into another world. I planted it alongside my house, in a place where I could watch it from my bedroom window. If the tree grew, I thought to myself, I would take it as a sign that John would recover completely, and if one day it produces a large, healthy fruit, I would have a Papa John, who through some miracle is living and now telling the tale.

Your colleague, as Eric Thompson (Sir!) used to say,

—Moises

Midway between Moi's house and Rakshita's cabañas lay a muddy depression encircled by barbed wire. Terence, who was just putting the finishing touches on a flimsy wooden gate, stepped back to admire his handiwork.

"It's fine for the meantime," Moi said.

"It could be uglier," Terence agreed. "But why go on trying? She'll be as happy as a pig in shit."

"We'll put down a ring of cement, to make it easier to clean. We'll paint the ring in rainbow colors. I have many ideas. She'll have to be patient, that's all."

I suggested a sign reading, "Beware."

"No, the tourists are going to love seeing my peccary. They will learn about the natural environment and its wonderful creatures. And this is just the beginning." Moi pointed to several bald spots, shaved of greenery, dotting the edge of his property. "Old Don Eliju did that. He's very good at cutting down trees. That's all he's done his whole life long. One day I will plant a tree for him, too. But first I am going to build a little zoo."

His house was already a zoo filled with fifty multi-colored cats, five inbred dogs, and four speechless, squawking parrots. Moi's last attempt at taming a wild creature was his nasty pet raccoon, which he walked on a leash or carried by the tail. At night the raccoon had a habit of sleeping in my porch chair before it ran away for good. The thought of the peccary escaping its corral filled me with dread.

Keeping family and friends in a state of loathsome trepidation was only one of Moi's perverse motives. More sinister than the corral's future occupant was its rank, symbolic purpose. Sitting directly on the property line between Rakshita's and Chato's, it sent a clear territorial signal to Chato and a rude farewell to Rakshita, who would never have allowed a pig anywhere near her cabins or vegetarian restaurant. If the Rastas had any say in the matter, which they didn't, they would never stand for it either. Worse than that, the corral was right in the middle of the hotel. The old man was thumbing his nose at everybody. In no time it became obvious that he didn't really care about the poor pig.

It took all day to move Petunia from her temporary pen in Moi's rusted backyard to her new quarters in his bald front yard, all day and five beaters, armed with poles and quaking in the bushes, while Moi screamed and cajoled and cooed to the female spirit inside the beast, promising her everything, his heart and his soul, if she would just settle down and trot through the gate. Finally one of Moi's terrified assistants tossed corncobs into the corral, and Petunia went after them in blind hunger.

Alas, that was the last corn she would ever taste. From then on, her diet consisted of stale bread, broccoli, pancakes, and watermelon served up on a dented garbage can lid. But the slop from Don Mucho's kitchen was not all for her. The cats started coming around, and the ravens swooped down. Within days, her corral became a mini-eco-zone populated by clamorous blackbirds, feral kittens, and one displaced peccary—all natural enemies—miraculously nibbling off the same platter.

Petunia's tolerance was remarkable, or perhaps she was just lonely. Moi would stop by in the morning, scratch her neck, and coo, "Yes, my sweetheart, yes my beauty." But the rest of the day she was on her own. If a tourist tried to take a photo, she'd raise her hackles, snap her jaws, and squeal blue murder. When the wheelbarrow full of kitchen scraps arrived, the cackling birds flew back and forth, carrying crumbs to the high branches, while the cats pawed and mewed around the mush pile until they ate their fill. Then Petunia would nuzzle one cat after another with her flat nose and rough tongue.

It was all quite endearing, except for the smell. Her main suitor, a gentleman to the end, insisted that Petunia didn't stink and blamed the offensive odor on the rancid mounds of leftovers rotting in the sun. Alux, who lived behind Moi's house, reminded the old man that peccaries possess three glands, two below the eyes, one on the back, which secrete an indelible, foul scent.

"Petunia has no need for natural defenses," Moi argued. "She's as happy as a clam."

The hideous truth was that the noxious aroma was disgusting on a good day. After a heavy rain a pernicious mist of putrefaction hung over the Panchan and seeped into the ground. One whiff was enough to blow the guests away.

Ordinary complaints had no effect nor did the sudden drop in tourist traffic at the height of the summer season. One of the more dedicated residents put in lengthy hours of research on the Internet and discovered these alarming facts: a mere one millionth of methane released into the atmosphere could cause flu symptoms, pleurisy, and severe respiratory damage.

Petunia, the skunk pig, was a walking plague, a potential killer.

If anyone came down with a slight cough or minor stomach upset or felt a little woozy and slightly out of sorts, Petunia bore the blame. If people smoked or drank too much or went out of their gourds on mushrooms, Petunia was at fault. Grandmother attributed the latest outbreak of all-night sex orgies in the hammock area to Petunia's poisonous proximity. "It's hopeless," she said. "But let's face it, even the Goddess kept a pig."

On the other hand, uncommon symptoms of compassion embraced Moi's sons. When informed of the peccary's toxic effects, the brothers duly expressed concern.

"I'll open the gate and let her run back to the mountains," Chato promised. "We'll shoot her and have a barbecue."

Anticipating such a deed, Moi laid his life on the line and threatened to shoot himself if anything happened to Petunia. According to Alfonso, he was getting old and tired enough to mean it. None of the brothers wanted to take the chance and do away with Moi's beloved pet.

But one day someone did unlatch the gate. Petunia stampeded through the shrubs, ripped through the hammocks, knocked down the clothesline, and shredded the sheets. Now she was in the clearing, clicking her tusks. Now she was rooting behind Don Moi's house, but before he could reach her, Petunia bristled and ran. Next she tore through Don Mucho's restaurant, snapping the legs off two chairs in her wild search for bananas. The terrorized guests went scrambling for the bathrooms, the waiters were standing on top of the bar, and the pig going every which way until the pizza man started pitching avocadoes toward the opposite side of the bridge. That did the trick, because Petunia left behind the puddles of beer and green spaghetti and raced up the path, where she encountered two lovebirds by the fountain. One of the musicians grabbed his flute and began to play a soothing Andean lullaby. Moi clutched his bamboo pole. "Calm down, calm down," he repeated.

But Petunia didn't calm down. She charged. Fortunately, the woman swerved in time, although the animal tore her skirt as it ran past and headed for Alberto's bar, which was just a dismal dirt lot at this hour of the day, except for the single plastic table where the red-haired witch was hunched in conversation with a guy in camouflage. But wait, the guy in camouflage was Alberto, and the white lump under the chair was his snoozing pet. Petunia sprinted across the gravel, and despite Alberto's efforts to maintain order, the witch made a mad dash for the kitchen door, knocking over the chair and waking the sleeping dog. The pit bull wasted no time, but Petunia dodged and aimed for the boy with the tattooed face who was plastered to the bathroom wall. The jaws clicked once, followed by a bone-crunching sound and an agonized howl as 18 collapsed in the dirt. That was when the pit bull lunged. Petunia caught him halfway across the lot, leaving it yelping and covered in blood.

From there, Petunia went crashing through the bushes and made a beeline for the Rastarant. Grandmother and Empress heard the gnashing and made it up the stairs before the pig came rampaging through the kitchen, smashing pots and pans and turning the plates into chunks of white confetti.

"This is worse than judgment day," Grandmother wailed as the potatoes rolled across the floor.

"She's no ordinary swine," Empress gasped. "Earth Goddess or not, I'm taking this as a bad sign."

When Moi appeared at the tail end of the wreckage, Petunia was battering the fridge. "Do something!" the women shouted.

But Moi just stood there in his rubber boots, looking drawn, disheveled, and weary to the bone. "Petunia, my sweet!" he murmured.

Petunia sniffed and shook, made that horrible clacking sound with her jaws, and bolted out of the kitchen.

Right then and there, Grandmother called Moi a fool and a devil, because "only a fool or a devil couldn't tell the difference between evil and good."

"Let's not have words," Moi said, blinking back the tears. "I'm just a man with a wild pig on his hands." Then he quietly shuffled off in search of helpers.

He could always count on Alux, who was hiding out until summoned, and when summoned came forth with a manly swagger and a strong pole. He and Moi found Petunia in front of the former hammock area, rooting in the grass. Swinging their poles, they slowly steered her toward the pen. "I've got bananas for you, my sweetheart," Moi cooed, and it seemed to work, because Petunia trotted along contentedly toward home. But just as they reached the gate, she swung around, chomped on Alux's boot, and darted for the clearing. Alux limped off, leaving Moi alone with the beast.

Moi now changed his strategy. "You good for nothing!" he screamed. "Who feeds you? Who gives you a nice place to stay? Go on, run! Then you'll see the difference," and he wacked her with his stick. She sniffed the air and headed for the gate. He hit her again for good measure.

Now that the peccary was safely in the corral, Moi's young workers, Abram and Umberto, came up to congratulate him.

"We were afraid for you, Don Moi," Abram beamed. "But you have a gift with animals."

"Gave her a good licking. That was smart," said Umberto.

"You were afraid for yourselves, not me. An animal senses fear, and that is why you boys are useless. And besides, I didn't hit her!" Abram and Umberto couldn't think of anything to do but stare at their worn sandals. "Go home now, I've had enough excitement for one day. Besides, that peccary understands everything we say. You go home. I will stay here and keep her company."

"We can't go home, Don Moi. The soldiers are blocking the road."

"They will see at a glance you're too dumb to be thieves or drug dealers. You don't have mustaches, you don't have scars. Now stop looking at your feet and bring me some water." The boys ran off and a few minutes later returned with a bottle of water and a plastic chair.

"That's more work than you've done all day," Moi gasped. "Now please go away."

As soon as Moi sat down, he closed his aching eyes. "Petunia, my sweetheart, Petunia my beauty," he murmured in his sleep.

Chapter 38

THE PIRATE LAGOON

We were in a boat riding across open water. There were other people in the boat besides Moi and me and the fisherman handling the motor. I didn't know who they were. The men were joking amongst themselves while the woman stiffened her back against the wind and scowled. Moi fixed his gaze on the eastern horizon where the sky was streaked with vowels—an upside down A, a crooked I, a serpentine U—and an L leaning on its hip and pointing toward a rosy halo in the clouds. The other signs were unreadable.

The man in the cowboy hat turned around and spoke to me. "We're taking you to the pirate's cove. I promised you, remember?" It was Marcelino, or someone who looked like Marcelino, twisting the tips of his long mustache and smiling. His red eyes narrowed and he said, "I see you still haven't found the answer."

Moi looked perturbed. "Who on this earth has found the answer, my friend? Even if we live a hundred lifetimes."

"I mean she still doesn't know who murdered Señora Steel. Why haven't you told her?"

"It never came up," said Moi, still gazing at the lines chalked on the horizon. "And besides, I don't know myself."

"Now you're telling stories again, like Mingo."

"It's the absolute truth," Moi exclaimed. "If I knew, I'd let her know. But not today. Today we are going to visit the cove."

The voices rose and fell in waves, muted in cruel whispers or stinging my ears as if the wind were harboring a malicious echo.

"Well, señora," Marcelino smiled, "have you figured out the true alignment of the Temple of the Foliated Cross? Have you discovered the Black Transformer Place? Have you at least found out if Frida Kahlo ever visited Palenque?" Marcelino's silver teeth were gleaming. I noticed he was missing a lower tooth.

"Who are you?" I asked. "How do you know?"

"A little bird told me," he chuckled and turned to face the prow.

"Pay no attention to him," Moi said. "He's only guessing."

Just then a winged shadow brushed the water and lifted Marcelino's hat. Up he jumped and started flailing, his big hands grabbing empty air.

"Sit down, you're rocking the boat!" his friends shouted. "Don't you know Imelda can't swim?" Imelda was looking rather seasick under her tightly knotted green scarf. With the first broad strokes of light, Marcelino's volcanic figure began to dissolve into little grains of sulfur.

"Let's see if the devil evaporates," said Moi.

Soon he lost himself in the last trace of stars, which reminded him of rocket flares exploding over the California desert. The flashing waves dimmed to a uniform beige, "the color of my old Air Force drabs," Moi said. He complained that flying sand was making his eyes water.

The boat was weaving through a maze of petrified trees, drowned relics of the great brazilwood forests that once grew in thick profusion on the flood plain a few meters below us. During the eighteenth century, Moi told me, the French established huge plantations here, harvesting the precious hardwood and sending it back to France. Following the old routes of the Chontal Maya, who were the great navigators of ancient times, the French hauled the wood in dugout canoes through the narrow estuaries leading to the Gulf and from there to the port of Campeche, where the logs were loaded on sailing ships bound for Marseille. If the merchant vessels outran the pirate caravels that marauded the coast, the wood would reach the great dye works of Provence. There the pulp was pounded into a rich crimson, used for tinting French velvets and silks. Pirates sold the stolen cargoes to traders from China, competitors in England, Holland, and Spain, and to Portuguese entrepreneurs who had already destroyed the bountiful resources of Brazil. The Amazon jungle smoked while noble lords and ladies whirled about the ballroom in vivid hues of cherry red or filled the gilded opera houses with rapturous tones of deepest burgundy. The storms of love, the wicked twists of fate, the lilting arabesques were played with violin bows made of brazilwood. Musicians and violin-makers whose delicate ears were tuned to the liquid vibrations of a leaf lauded brazilwood as the tree of music. "The wood sings," said the greatest string composers.

For the Indians of the remote lagoon, who had never worn velvet or heard the fiddle, brazilwood was the tree of toil and blighted prosperity, ephemeral as the strains of Brahms and Rossini, although to this day the local inhabitants bear surnames like La Turneuil and Marquesay, being direct descendants of French plantation owners and their overseers. Why the local people did not process the timber themselves and then ship the powdered dye in barrels is a matter that Moi blamed on the shortsightedness of the French and the inherent lack of ingenuity on the part of the Mexicans, failures that inevitably led to the collapse of the industry, the disappearance of the magnificent trees, and the advance of the waters up the slopes.

Swaying above the waterline, the skeletal trunks and branches made a ghostly, creaking sound as we approached a bleak strip of sand that looked like the rippled spine of an extinct sea monster. The members of our party climbed ashore to stretch their legs amid the tangled life forms that thrived on desiccated bones. As gray clouds swept down from the north, blocking the sun, the landscape grew more piteous, and the beached water creature, now cloaked in mist, slipped into an age when its back was once a hill looming above long avenues of trees unfolding in the morning vapor, the red roof of the plantation house, with its French windows shining like mother-of-pearl, the master's children skipping down the wide margin of grass to the pale lagoon where tiny sailboats fluttered in the wind and canoes loaded with logs slid toward the remote horizon, all underwater now. The injured trees would glaze the shadows a deep oxblood, the lakebed a luminous grenadine glinting as if the rising sun were held within it, and the whitewashed walls and lawns and sailing ponds, vermilion.

"Manatee!" the boatman cried, and in my mind's eye the island wallowed like a sea cow over the tile roofs and wheels of old machines rusting on the bottom, saw blades, saddles, wine corks, snifters, a faded purple mourning band worn the day the French emperor Maximilian was shot before the firing squad in Queretero.

I must have fallen into a deep sleep, for when I woke from my dream we were meandering under a patch of brilliant blue sky and Marcelino had disappeared. Evaporated, perhaps, behind the sheer curtains of light descending on the water.

Don Moi tapped me on the shoulder as the patch of blue emptied into black, and we entered a blind passage, no wider than the entrance to Don Juan's Cave. Waves of snowy egrets moved fitfully down the channel. Birds were dropping through the sky, whipping the branches and flying off like bits of foam. Cranes, blue herons, and long-legged storks waded in the shallows while overhead their empty nests splashed in the treetops. The palms grew feathers. The breadnut trees grew scales. Stretched on an overhanging branch, two golden iguanas, brighter than the sun, winked and dove into the water. The boatman poled through a whirlpool of black birds.

"Cormorants," Moi whispered. "The ancient emblem of Palenque."

Imagine the long-necked, hook-billed waders as syllables inscribed on hieroglyphic panels, alongside winged iguanas, claw-footed monkeys, and razor-toothed hawks. An artist with inkpots and rolls of bark paper drifted silently down the channel, and with a few bold strokes transformed everything he saw into marvelous talking creatures. So it was when the waters were rippling at the beginning of time: the Plumed Serpent ruffled his blue feathers and his words became birds of every kind and color. Their wing beats became couplets, their cries became human voices carved in stone, and the stones, painted a deep, disquieting red, became trees where cormorants trumpeted their names—*mat, mat, mat.*

Now the birds were flying in long formations, reeling and dipping over the waves, and we were skimming along beside them. In the midst of their dizzying flight, I looked up, trying to get my bearings, and saw the sun directly overhead. The birds cast no shadow.

When I lowered my eyes, the wharf came into sight and I heard the tinkling of marimbas. Two long banquet tables were set for dinner. The mayor shook our hands and sat us down at the head of the table. Moi said a few words and introduced me to the crowd. A row of chefs, wearing tall white hats, presented platters of fish for our approval. Moi nodded, everyone applauded, and plates overflowing with shrimp, squid, and breaded fillets were laid before us. Marimbas played, waiters brought beer and rum. At the banquet table opposite me, Marcelino raised his glass in a toast.

No one looked the least bit French. The mayor, with his spectacles and thin mustache, might have been mistaken for a Russian bureaucrat. In fact, he bore a striking resemblance to Leon Trotsky. "You must write about our town," the mayor insisted. "It is the finest on the delta."

I had no idea where I was or why, but I had enough sense not to eat anything in case I was in a dream, and tempting though it was to gaze on the blue lagoon and teeming birds, I was afraid of getting stranded on the shores of the Otherworld forever.

PART IV

The History of Water

—FROM *THE BOOK OF MINGO*

The canoes come down the river loaded with goods, and if they have to travel past the falls, the men plant their feet on solid ground and walk the trail that cuts around the canyon. If they are headed west they use the old canal that runs between Monkey River and Pomona. Any time they reach a place where water is boiling they just scramble along the bank dragging the boats through the rapids. The canoes scraping against the rocks sound like dolphins. A hollow ring means granite, a low growl means bottom. Why risk it? If there's a roar on the water and a roar on land you're in trouble. Hunger is always the question when you're traveling the river. Jaguars can swim. Hunger is shaped like a fin. Fear sounds like thrashing. It whips its tail and before you know it that row of pebbles in the muck is beating the

244

sides of your boat. The Milky Way is a crocodile that slides across the stars, blackness above and blackness below us. The stars are butterflies fluttering around the crocodile's nose. The Milky Way is also a canoe loaded down with constellations. The sky is the sea. The river is a huge bird hunting for its prey. There is nothing to do but paddle faster. The man in the bow is all spine. The man in the stern is toothless from drinking too much honey. His blind eye sees trouble after it is gone. The one in the middle is young and lazy. His hands are soft, like corn silk. We hardly talk to him, but he is the one who reads the signs in the ripples, which could be a thing under the water or a war breaking out in the north. Our battle is with the river, which no one sings or writes about. We are just the messengers, just the deliverers between one place and another. Jade, tobacco, cotton, chili peppers, and him in the middle sitting like a prince. We look like stones and stink like fish, but we are made of water, water in our bellies and water in our brains. Paddle faster, dip and fall and rise until the sun stops and stars shower down on the bundles we sleep on. One more peep and we'll dump him where Orion starts to cross the sky. Life is water shrinking to a puddle. Rain is the rattle. Under us there is nothing but water silent as a shell, down where the dead go and we will go deeper, tomorrow or the next day, down to the depths where some say there is fire and some say smoke from the burning sun, and we say water, water, water.

Chapter 39

SUN DOGS

"Very pretty," Moi said to Mingo, nodding as he reread a few lines. He needed more sleep or needed more coffee, but as always he was at his patient best an hour after dawn. "This could be a description of the world before creation when there was only water and the heavens were still lying upon the earth."

"Well, it could be then or it could be now," Mingo said, drawing lazy circles in the air to describe the roundness of time. But long after the circles evaporated into the eternal ebb and flow, his index finger kept spinning like the whirlpool at the center of the primordial sea, the wind god at the center of the whirlpool, the finger of the wind god at the center of the whirlpool—maybe all these things—plus trying to signal the waiter for another cup of coffee.

"It's a little like the dream I had last night," said Moi. "I was in a boat crossing the Laguna de Catazaja. I was sitting next to La Carola and we were watching the cormorants soar and dive."

"A fine coincidence," said Mingo. "But my chapter is about the Usumacinta River, which that river rat, Waldo Hermosillo, was telling me about. You know the one. He smuggles cigarettes."

Moi shot him a look that could paralyze a hawk in mid-flight. "Waldo is a guide, Mingo, one of the best in our unsung profession, the last of a breed, still capable of running the rapids in his miserable, demon-riddled sleep. For sure he's ugly enough to sink an alligator—I've seen him do it—and mean enough to tackle a shark. Nevertheless, he's rich enough to maintain three wives, two boats, and a thirty-horsepower outboard motor. I assure you he has better ways of earning a living than smuggling cigarettes. Now finish your coffee, it's time to go. The bees are about to storm the sugar bowl."

To me Moi said, "I spent all day yesterday chasing Petunia. And then I rode across the lagoon all night. I'm tired."

"But it wasn't a dream, Don Moi. We went to the lagoon yesterday morning. Petunia got loose the day before. I'm sorry to correct you," I said, "but I think you've lost track."

"And I'm sorry you are so sure of everything. Isn't it wonderful that we have had the same dream?"

"I know it seemed like a dream, Don Moi, but I was with you."

"Didn't I just say so? I was very happy you were with me. Not so much that troublemaker, Marcelino."

"Sometimes you are very naïve about people," said Mingo. "I mean he's smuggling *mojo*, Mary Jane, marijuana. I mean men and women, too, Guatemaltecos, Honduranians, packed like sardines into launches and willing to pay any price to get on the train to the US border."

"Who cares about America!" said Moi. He opened his arms to embrace the world. "It's good to be naïve on a day like this. Today is the day the sun will stand in the center of the sky. Let's go to the ruins, old man."

"America is here, Don Moi. Perhaps you haven't heard about yesterday. It was a beautiful Sunday morning. Women and children are out shopping for school bags and colored pencils. Bang! There is a shootout in the parking lot of the brand new Walmart."

"Yesterday *was* an odd day. My Petunia went crashing through Don Mucho's, the Mono Blanco, and the Rasta place. It was a nightmare. The woman they call Grandmother told me my Petunia was fulfilling the wishes of the Earth Goddess. Someone else—I think it was Podwell—tried to tell me Petunia was a witch who turned into Petunia to do everybody harm. But she didn't do any real damage, no. She may have scared a few people, that's all."

" A man was left lying there, in a pool of blood, right where the metal shopping carts are lined up."

"I've never had occasion to visit the supermarket. I've never stepped foot inside the glass doors. Do we know the poor bastard? Is he someone we should be happy to see go?"

"They say he was wearing an expensive blue shirt, so he was probably a gangster from Villahermosa. You can't buy shirts like that here in Palenque, not even at Don Joaquin's haberdashery. Silk, they said, soaked in red. But that's not all, Don Moi."

"If you're going to tell me about that gunfight between the police and some hoodlums, I already know. Marcelino called me on the telephone."

"It happened just as Mass was letting out, in plain view of the priest and the entire congregation."

"I'm sure they were surprised. But it's appropriate for such things to happen in front of the church."

"And not ordinary hoodlums, Moi. The Z's were dressed like federal soldiers."

"Z's?" asked Moi, feigning interest.

"That's what they call the Mafia, the Zeta's. They have nothing to do with the Zapatista Z's. Everyone knows the Zapatistas have no guns, and besides, they are very much against the drug trade."

"If they had been more lenient, the old routes would still be in place. Now the traffickers have to bypass what's left of the jungle. They're out in the open now, fighting for control of the river. No more pussyfooting. The Zapatistas only increased the competition and the violence, all in the name of proper morals and more space to grow their holy corn. But the Zapatistas are terrible farmers. Not one of them can plant a straight row."

"Moi, one of the cops took a bullet in the neck. He left a wife and five children. Now the *federales* are searching from house to house, looking for drugs and suspects. The whole town is terrified. You can't tell who is who."

"What a shame that people are so frightened," said Moi. "The police know exactly who the criminals are. All the same, I am very thankful the murder didn't happen here, in the parking lot of the Panchan."

"You know, your friends might be right about the pig. Petunia could be a *nagual*, the animal spirit of a witch who wants to plague you and the family and cause trouble. I've seen it happen."

"But I got my Petunia back in her corral. And it's as good a reason as any for a holiday. The people of Palenque will have to learn to stand on their own, against the police and against the army."

"The violence could be witchcraft, too, Don Moi. Witches and demons sent to make us suffer."

"You see, I was right about time speeding up and you slowing down. Don't you know today is special? It's zenith passage, the anniversary of the day of creation, and all you can do is fuss over mundanities. For heaven's sake, old man, let's go!"

Moi was anxious because he had placed a wager on the rising sun. "It's not a simple question of when or how or if," he explained. "I'm not a superstitious Aztec cringing in the corner. I'm not a frightened widow from Detroit either. No, it is a question of where on Palenque's glorious horizon the sun will send forth its first green shoots."

Directly over the Temple of the Cross, Alux predicted.

For reasons known only to himself, Moi told Alux he was wrong, and in a rare display of familial harmony, Alfonso Morales agreed with his father. "Absolutely. No doubt about it. One hundred percent negative." Why? They never said. Perhaps it was a genetic trait that had endured despite years of stubborn disputes, but when the subject came up in conversation, father and son pursed their lips and rolled their eyes, dismissing this upstart, this rank amateur, as the unhinged victim of a notion so far-fetched it wasn't worthy of discussion. And just to prove how hair-brained Alux's idea was, they bet a bottle of tequila.

But life is like a bottle of aging wine, unpredictable; one minute a luscious ruby red, the next, murky and sour as vinegar.

When we arrived at the ruins—surprise—there was Tito pacing in front of the main gate. His straggly hair was tucked neatly under his cowboy hat, and though it was a workday, he was wearing his good pants and a clean shirt. He was shouting something I couldn't hear over the idling tour buses, the insistent hawkers and guides. The parking lot was a flattened Babel, the scattered races swarming toward stalls selling bottled water, sun block, and cheap straw hats. We elbowed our way past the browned and burning bodies, the alien eyes, hidden under black plastic, oblivious to the hand-lettered sign Tito was waving:

PALENQUE Belongs To The MAYA

Mingo embraced him. Moi shook his hand. "You've picked a fine day for the beginning of your revolution," he said. "But you shouldn't stand alone. I am in solidarity."

Just then Alux raced by, on a mad dash for the Temple of the Sun. Moi and Mingo were locked arm in arm, too busy savoring Tito's moment of glory to acknowledge Alux's hasty wave and puzzled smile. I assumed that Moi hadn't noticed him. But after Alux was out of sight, Moi said to me, "I think I saw an Alux out of the corner of my eye. Or maybe it was his sullen shadow intent on spoiling my day. On the other hand, if that was the real Alux, he's running very late. All the better for me!"

But the situation was getting worse. The crowds were lining up at the gate when two hefty guards came to warn Tito that the police were on their way.

"Leave the man alone," Moi said. "He has a right." But the guards were on their walkie-talkies and the police were already jumping off the back of the black pickup truck, swinging their billies.

Tito swung his sign, hit three policemen in the face, ducked, whacked two others in the shins, then turned and struck another across the chest. He whirled until he was empty. The police had no choice. They carried him, kicking, into the truck.

"I am in solidarity," Moi said as the cops pulled away. Slowly he bent over and picked up the battered placard. He smoothed it out and asked Mingo if he had a pen. He added these words:

BRING PAKAL'S BONES
BACK to PALENQUE

Then he took Tito's position at the gate. No one had the nerve to say a thing.

Alux was still running. He was late, late, and instead of following the visitor's trail, he took a shortcut, straight up the steep terrace behind the Temple of the Sun. Who knows why the gods laid a trap for him there, but somehow he got tangled in the yellow flagging tape stretched across the unmown weeds to keep tourists from climbing the precipitous slope. He fell, rolled, and threw his back out. It was 7:55, and Alfonso Morales was waiting in the temple doorway, cameras ready, when Alux reached the top step. Breathless and limping badly, he turned to face the east.

And it came to pass that the zenith sun rose directly over the roof comb of the Temple of the Cross in a dazzling burst of light.

"I don't believe it!" Alfonso squealed as he clocked his first shot.

A single solar ray was streaming into the Temple of the Sun; it cut across the floor at a forty-five degree angle and slowly advanced toward the southwestern corner of the sanctuary. There it lingered, a golden spear of light as radiant as the first day of creation.

Alux was glowing. "This is more than a hierophany," he crowed. "It's an epiphany!" There were tears in his eyes as he hobbled down the steps, across the plaza, and out the main gate.

"I'll believe it when I see it," Moi said. He was still holding the protest sign.

"Don't be a sore loser," Alfonso chided. "Alux made a great discovery today and I have the pictures to prove it. Makes the Maya look like high-tech engineers. Very spacey." He said this knowing his father had no appreciation for anything more sophisticated than his old slide projector and satellite phone. "Come home with us and we'll share that bottle of tequila."

"Tito's in jail and Pakal's bones are missing," Moi muttered. "Besides, how can I trust your pictures? I'm sure the two of you are conspiring against me."

Alfonso put his arm around Alux's shoulder and in a voice loud enough for Moi to hear, said, "Never mind that old fart. He's just dishing up the usual fatherly treatment. This makes you part of the family now!" Then he gave Alux a good-natured slap on the back and—oof—Alux doubled over.

When I stopped by Alux's house to congratulate him, he was curled in his hammock, facing the wall. "The gods are punishing me," he groaned. "For delving into their secrets."

"Perhaps it's a devil," I said. "That seems to be the favorite explanation these days."

"You mean bad things come in threes. First Barnaby. Then Big John. Now me."

"But the solar alignments are not the work of gods or devils. The orientations were calculated by architects, astronomers, and mathematicians."

"They were plotting, too. Mystical events. Lucky for some, a torment for others. But never mind, man, just wait until nadir!" With great effort, Alux pulled himself up and limped to the table.

"Let me show you what I've figured out. The sun was at the center of the sky on August 13, 3114 B.C., the day of creation. Nadir passage is the opposite, the night when the sun reaches the center of the Underworld. That's when the gods raised the Tree of Life." Alux grabbed a sheet of paper and drew a picture of the sun above, the sun below, and the great tree that connects the sky, earth, and Underworld. "I know where the nadir sun will rise. I measured it on our map. But I'd rather not say right now. The gods may punish me again."

He checked his watch. "Damn, it's still nine o'clock. What happened?"

"Almost noon," I said.

Alux hobbled out to the yard where he had planted his clay sculpture of K'inich Ajaw, Resplendent Lord of the Sun. "This is my gnomon," he said. "We're just in time." He spread his arms in the fullness of the day and smiled. "Look, no shadow. I'm invisible now, I could disappear."

It was true. There was no sign of him on the ground, and for a split second, standing in the glaring light, he faded into the unbearable flatness of the first dimension. Perhaps he vanished into the fifth, sixth, or newly gauged eleventh dimension, but who was counting? I was dissolving, too, though at the time I was so concerned with buoying Alux's spirits that I wasn't paying much attention. It was only later that the consequences of this momentary loss took hold of my psyche, causing no end of confusion and strife. But I'm getting ahead of myself.

As soon as Alux's cramped shadow returned, with all its brittle burdens and illusions, I said, "Have you thought about the effigy you're going to make for New Year's Eve? The Day Sun, the Night Sun, and the Tree of Life—that would be so awesome."

Every New Year's, Alux manufactures a giant figure out of bamboo, reeds, and dried corn stocks, stuffs it full of firecrackers, and blows it up at midnight. He's created the beautiful Corn God paddling a canoe down the Milky Way and the giant turtle from which the Corn God is born. Before he entered his penultimate Maya phase, he put together a host of flaming parodies: the hunchbacked Father Gloom; a Mexican *charro* with a clay head and big sombrero; a blazing, gun-toting cowboy; nobody's woman in a peasant skirt, blowsy hair, and red-hot lips—all caricatures out of the wild, wild west ready for a lynching. He swings them on a rope tied to the dead limb of a thousand-year-old cedar, and when they are rocking above the stunned crowd, he lights a torch and sets them on fire. Every giant burns differently, popping and exploding in every crazy direction or sizzling slowly toward a mad, ear-splitting crescendo. Golden pinwheels, yellow rockets whizzing from crumbling toes, the legs crackling, the chest bleeding red coals, the arms falling away in long, sparkling streams, flames shooting from the eyes, and the head bursting and dying in a solitary flutter.

Normally he starts working on it the day before, but I thought I'd ask to get his mind off the pain in his back.

"New Year's is months away," he winced. "But there's a party tonight. Same old madness, mayhem, and dissolution. I don't think I can make it."

Chapter 40

OPPOSITES

Alux was flat on his back when the drums started sending signals to the Pleiades. Beyond the crystalline river of the Milky Way, the seven star seeds were trembling, Macaw and Feathered Serpent taking flight, while down below we struggling mortals clustered together, tapping our toes to the *Cumbia* beat. Fans of Lou Reed, Los Tigres, or Noncarrow: what did it matter? It was another spontaneous free-for-all at the Panchan, gateway to paradise, anteroom to hell.

"It's a mystery we've survived this long when it's in our nature to destroy," Don Moi was saying, magnanimously sharing his cynicism with the bow-legged cowboys and varnished NGO types swilling beer at his table. "What else is there to do in this tropical backwater besides chasing heifers, bulldozing trees, and getting thoroughly drunk?"

No one needed a lecture on this combustible August night. Clearly in the right, the ecologists flashed the bold green letters stamped on their sweaty T-shirts: Center for the Preservation of Endangered Tropical Species, CERPENTS, for short. The local cowpokes, stiff from a day in the saddle, continued sucking on their beers.

"Fortunately," Moi went on, "our Mexican schools are so poor that people can't read the signs dotting the fields and pastures, the river-banks and washboard roads—everywhere there used to be forest."

"What's to read?" asked Romero, the rancher from La Libertad. "Those blonds on the billboards are ten feet tall and their boobies are as big as the sun and moon!"

The American beauties at the next table fidgeted uncomfortably in their seats, and then, one, two, three—Ta-da! They stripped off their blouses and sat there, beaming, in matching hot-pink bikini bras. A common sight at the Panchan but a glaring eyeful out on the range.

"What natural wonders," Moi pronounced, though only temporarily distracted. "If they build the dam on the Usumacinta River, you can kiss their enormous air-brushed asses goodbye."

Now the four graces were showing some serious muscle. If this was grandpa's idea of a joke, the jerk had another thing coming.

"Ay-yay-yay!" howled Romero, tipping his hat at the brash young women. "Wouldn't that be a sight, seeing those *chicas* floating naked downriver. It'd be worth losing a couple of hectares of swamp."

"Fucking wimp!" the redhead blurted. To clarify her point, she cut the air with a quick karate chop punctuated by a firm Italian slap on the elbow, the universal one-two combination executed flawlessly for the macho's future benefit.

"The rest of our compatriots will get nothing out of it," one of the ecologists chimed in. "Maybe a job washing dishes at a tourist resort overlooking the new dam."

"They're sure as hell not going to be scuba diving in the reservoir," Romero cracked. "Nobody knows how to swim."

Javier, the ecologist, frowned. "I suppose some of them can handle a boat with an outboard motor."

"But I guarantee they won't be towing water skiers for a living. That is because the boatmen are too busy transporting goods from one side to the other." Romero leaned forward. "Look, my fine, college-educated friend, I've been here long enough to see and smell the whole enchilada and still have a good laugh now and then. All I can tell you is that even with the little extra they make smuggling chocolates for the big cartels, my neighbors can't afford light bulbs to screw into their household sockets. That is the plain reality."

"We are on the same wave length, then," the scientist said, wiping his steamy glasses on his damp jersey. His long ponytail was wringing wet.

"The reality is, they've got better things to screw," roared one of Romero's sidekicks, "though nothing as juicy as those *gringas*." He took out a wrinkled handkerchief and wiped the sweat from his blotchy face. "Let's order a round, professor, before I melt. Then maybe you can teach us something about global warming."

Javier was on the verge of raising the heat when another cattleman, Fecundo Soto by name, tapped his shot glass with his ruby ring, and everyone piped down.

"Forgive me for interjecting a note of sobriety into these joyous proceedings," he began, "but if you were to ask me what is the big-gest—hiccup—impediment to cultural advancement, the greatest deterrent to environmental stability, I would have to confess . . . ." Clinging to the edge of the table, he pulled himself up to his full six-foot-four, two-hundred-pound frame. "I know you will be startled to hear these words from a livestock buyer who spent his crazy youth in the north, as I myself am astonished—hiccup—to find myself preach-ing to you, humbly and a little drunk tonight, though I speak from years of experience and from the purest depths of my heart when I say the foulest, most destructive force on this or any other planet—hic-cup—consumed by methane gas and circling round and round, round and round, is the—hiccup—diabolical cow."

With a loud cheer, the ecologists sprang to their feet, and the beer bottles went rolling. Before the ranch hands could say goddamn, the CERPENTS, whose job it was to study and to scour, got down on all fours and started crawling under the tables. Like the mysterious jag-uar snakes that occasionally terrify jungle travelers, the single-minded reseachers unwittingly set off a chain reaction.

"Pig!" screamed the redhead, kicking one of the CERPENTS in the tail. The blond wadded her wine-soaked napkins into a soggy ball and pitched it at Romero's head. The ball landed on the pizza counter, instantly deflating a mound of dough. Roque's assistant mistakenly tossed the wad into the boiling ravioli. The pink pasta was dished out and served to the local chief of police, who happily shared it with the mayor. The notebook containing their creative scribblings—descriptions of people to finger, outlines for their next plot—accidently fell to the ground. Moi's poodle promptly pissed on it.

A familiar voice cried, "phi!" All this time, Podwell had been hiding at a table in the corner, engulfed in a sea of butcher paper ornamented with hand-drawn spirals, seashells, and five-petaled flowers. He glanced up quickly, smiled, and returned to his listeners. "Okay," he said, "let's get on to the solar alignments."

"We could begin simply, honorably, and in due course," Fecundo intoned. "First, if I may be so bold, we must rid the national park of those filthy cattle. And if you gentlemen agree, I will volunteer to drive them up to Monterrey and over the US border."

"My friend, I think I smell a profit motive here," Romero countered. "Not to mention politics, a subject that environmentalists know nothing about."

Javier, the professor, slammed the table.

"Who does?" Moi interrupted, narrowly averting another scene. "Why not get rid of the farmers, too, those pathetic sons of Cain."

"Cain? You mean the one in the Bible or my second cousin who lives in Zapata?"

"I mean the zenith sun right over the roof comb!" Podwell jumped up and began flailing his arms.

"Hell, we'll rope them, tie them, and lift them out by helicopter."

"Hot-air balloons."

"Douche bags!" said the blond and sidled over to Podwell's table. "Excuse me," she said, leaning seductively over the magic pile of pentacles. "I couldn't help overhearing your conversation. Me and my friends, we're really into the Maya and 2012 and everything. Mind if we join you?"

"Well, uh . . ." Podwell stammered. The four graces were already arranging chairs. Oddly flustered, Podwell ran his fingers through his close-cropped hair. "Allow me to, uh, introduce Dr. Philip Sands. He's, um, a theoretical mathematician, from Guyana, north of Brazil. Teaching at Cambridge. That's in England. Norman here, he's a nuclear physicist from Oslo. Norman from Norway. We were just discussing the uh, zenith sun."

"Sherry," said the tall brunette. "This is my twin sister, Syd. She's shy. That's Morgan the Red, and Margo, whom you already met."

"We go to Brown," Margo grinned, "majoring in women's studies. We were, like, hoping you could tell us about the center of the galaxy."

"Neutron accelerators! Ion colliders!" The cowboys had lost the thread. They were just having fun now, spitting out stuff they'd learned on cable. The CERPENTS were unimpressed. Moi, growing deafer with each drum riff, folded his hands and waited patiently for the big, blistered lips to clamp shut.

"Caballeros!" he finally croaked. "There is no need to waste good time and money, because nature in her infinite wisdom will provide."

"*Salud!*" his audience whooped.

"Yes. Come November and the dumb brown creatures will be washed away in the floods." None of the ranchers thought that was funny.

Tito laughed so hard he almost fell off the barstool. He was in the middle of telling Terence about his morning brush with the cops when he overheard Moi's brutal remark. Terence didn't know what Tito was laughing about because Terence was picking up some very strange static from the mercury filling in his right bicuspid.

"Listen, you can laugh all you want," he said. "You're damned lucky the local police weren't trained in Panama. I don't give a rat's ass about your little revolt. Compared to what's about to happen it don't amount to a hill of bat dung. You better get ready, buddy, because all hell is going to break loose." Terence waved a finger in the direction of the artisans' stalls. "See that guy over there? Well, he's not a guy at all."

"Fairy?" said Tito, choking on his beer.

"Hell, no. Under those Peruvian duds the guy's wearing mean green lizard scales." Terence glanced over his shoulder to see if anyone was listening. "Uh-oh, here comes the expert." Tito quietly picked up his beer and sauntered off without saying goodbye.

Pushing his way through the dense foreign bodies, the former intelligence officer we called the Hermit came marching over the bridge with the deliberate gait of a drill sergeant who had seen heavy action in the watering holes of Saigon. By the time he reached the bar there was a frosty one waiting for him, compliments of Don Chato.

"Must be old geezer night," Chato quipped before darting off to serve another customer.

"Hung myself out to dry, but I got thirsty," the Hermit smiled. For this rare reconnaissance mission, he had worked himself into something resembling sociability, though you could tell that underneath his jaunty exterior beat a heart yearning to desert. His steel-blue eyes penetrated the crowd, and when they fixed on the Peruvian jeweler, the alarm went off.

"Hell's bells!" he said to Terence, cocking his head at the Peruvian guy. Not that he believed in aliens or even suffered from mild paranoia. It was just that after years of intense military training, he, like Terence, had developed a remarkable sixth sense.

"Let's get those mothers," drawled Santa Claus, another flinty old geezer dedicated to the common good.

"When did they let you out of the funny farm?" Terence snapped.

The Hermit scratched his gray head. "Never even heard him sneak up. Just shows to go you can't keep a rotten devil down."

He and Terence bantered amiably but said nothing about the suspect. Big John had a heart of gold, along with an erratic, fast-boiling temper, and that could spell trouble. So Santa Claus was left to lean on his crutch, vacantly scanning the raucous mob.

"Who're them strangers talkin' to Podwell? One dude's black as the ace of spades and the other's completely bald. What they got to attract those gorgeous women?"

Terence shrugged. "Must be math nuts if they're talking to Podwell. Or just plain bananas."

Santa Claus's curious eye came to settle on the dance floor. "Well, in that case, who's the little weasel prancing with the pretty chick?"

"Which one?" asked Terence. "The wrangler in the pointy-toed ostrich boots or Dapper Dan in the silk shirt?"

"No, he means the shark with the dreads and tattooed chest. There ought to be a law," the Hermit complained. "No shirts, no service."

"According to the Square Law, there is a certain inevitability to arithmetic calculations," said Philip Sands. "Once you've observed the precise orbit of Venus, as the Maya had, then, inexorably, you should be able to determine the distance between Earth and Venus, Venus and Mars, Mars and Jupiter. It's spontaneous, unwitting, like rolling over in your sleep. You would know the size of the Moon. And you would know, almost instinctively, that the Earth is round."

Podwell sat back and reflected. "I'm not sure I'm willing to go that far. Not yet, at any rate."

"The ancients were highly advanced," said Dr. Sands, tossing his tightly braided dreads. "They knew far more than we think."

"But, and this is a big but," Syd broke in, "wouldn't they have left behind clues to that effect? As I understand it, the Maya and the Chinese depicted the Earth as a square."

"Oh, Syd, don't spoil things," Margo whined. "They prophesied the end of time, didn't they? It's so profound it gives me goose bumps."

"But I want to know how," Morgan said emphatically. "It's stupid to believe they acquired their knowledge through alien contact."

"Basic arithmetical calculations. It will take a few hours to explain. But first I need to clarify one thing, for the thousandth time." Podwell turned to Margo. "We are coming to the end of 13 *baktuns*, not the end of time and not the end of the world. I'm sorry, ladies, but the Maya made no prophecies about 2012. And while we're on the subject, the galactic alignment happens every year, and the fact that it will occur at the end of the Great Round is just a beautiful coincidence."

"There are no accidents in my philosophy," Norman said, folding his arms across his thick chest. "Everything is connected. If we stop right now and consider chaos theory, we will see it mainly applies to the weather, which no human can predict."

"I must say," said Philip, "this conversation is getting somewhat off the mark."

Podwell smiled. "Okay, just let me say one more thing. The Maya, with all their intricate calendars, were intent on ordering history and time because they recognized the chaotic forces of life. Chaos and order, order and chaos, playing out through endless cycles of creation and destruction. They saw the dualities all around them, in nature and in the stars."

"And they could express the idea mathematically," added Philip. "Like all native peoples, they don't receive enough credit. Man, I come from a Third World country. I know what that's about."

"They made the quantum leap long ago, and we are the ones who need to catch up. We need a bridge, a bridge between dualities. And balance, balance, balance before it is too late!" The Norwegian made a poor attempt at a smile. "Yes, we are running out of time. But if a few of us create a little harmony and project our positive thoughts into the universe, there is a possibility . . . ."

"This is so far out!" said Sherry.

"It's so totally passé," said her twin sister, Syd. "All that boring New Age stuff. It's part of the neo-capitalist agenda."

Norman's dour face turned as red as the beets he used to hoe on his father's farm. "Say what you will, here is where science and metaphysics meet. We have proved this in many experiments. The mind affects the tiniest particles of subatomic matter: neurons, ions, quarks, etc. Everyone now accepts this basic tenet."

"Next I suppose you're going to tell me that Mother Earth is alive. Romanticizing the Goddess only serves to undermine women's daily struggle for sexual equality. And remember, the Goddess has three faces."

"Unquestionably," said Philip. "But let's get back to the capitalist agenda for a moment, shall we? If you are implying that science is a tool of the dominant society, as some of my students argue, I would have to agree, though rather reluctantly. I much prefer to think that science and mathematics are pure pursuits."

"But that eighteenth-century notion has robbed us of our place in the cosmos," Norman argued. "We see the psychological damage all around us. Not to mention the fact that the average person has no idea how the universe works. Relativity? String theory? Everybody is in the dark."

"The Maya understood that everything was interrelated: science, art, religion, and politics. Whatever you think of their practices and beliefs—much of it incomprehensible, at least to me . . ." Podwell paused and took a deep breath. "Well, all I'm saying is you have to appreciate their holistic vision of the world."

"On the other hand, relatively speaking, we modern blokes are isolated and alone. Little specks adrift in the universe."

The table fell silent.

"At times, my life seems futile," Norman murmured. "But I do have some hope. As a physicist, as a human being temporarily stranded on this planet."

The four women moved quietly around the table, embracing Podwell, Norman, and Dr. Sands in turn.

"Holy shit, will you get a gander at those broads!" Santa Claus was referring to Grandmother and Empress, who were doing an African shimmy to the Latin beat.

"Better get in line to say your goodbyes," Terence suggested. "Those gals are leaving tomorrow, and you never know what's going to turn up next."

"Then I better get me a ringside table," Santa Claus bellowed and slowly hobbled away.

"That was a close call," said Terence. "With this kind of crowd— cowboys, good ol' boys, lizards, tribals, queers—the night could easily turn sour, and the next thing you know, all hell'll break loose."

Just then a troupe of Dreamers filed in, and Terence poked the Hermit in the ribs. "Grays dressed in white," he whispered. "But don't worry, they're robots. Haven't got a clue."

"You want clues?" said Chato, back with two beers for the "odd couple," as he called his loyal pals. "Well, listen to this." While he popped the bottle tops with his right hand, he pressed his iPhone to his left ear and gave this running report:

"Alberto is pacing. The tables are empty. The witch is threatening to leave. Wait a sec. This is a good one. Aida, her faggot husband, and my three little nieces just showed up. Hah! Can you believe it? Wait till my father hears. I'd tell him right now, but he's busy pontificating. 'Good news, Papa. Another disaster is on the way!'"

"Who you talking to?" Terence asked. "I mean, if you don't mind."

"That's for me to know," Chato cackled. "Remember, I have my spies."

A second later the lights went out. The music stopped and the dancers froze. Did the speakers blow a fuse? Had Alberto cut the wires? When the clock started ticking again, couples were milling about like deflated shadows. Soon the disappointed sighs ballooned to a collective buzz as scraping sounds started coming from the blacked-out stage. Something was cooking, but what could it be?

After fifteen minutes of polite murmurs on the 4.3 frequency, the cowboys let out good old Mexican yelps that broke the eight-decibel barrier. The crowd exploded, clapping, whistling, and stomping their feet. The place was on the verge of an uproar, when . . .

"Ladies and gentlemen, your attention ple-e-e-ase," cooed a warm, breathless voice with the reassuring tone of a stewardess on a silver starship settling into infinity glide. "*El Teatro en la Selva* presents—*el espectáculo!*"

Out of the darkness appeared a figure in white, not a human figure but a strange cellular shape that bowed and twisted and stretched, ever so slowly, to life. Sheathed in white fiber, it was the ghost of many living things evolving on invisible limbs and wings. Another form crawled in, and the two moved and breathed together, and when they folded around each other, a conch blew, the drums beat, and a light from somewhere above wrapped the figures in rainbow colors. Now the ghosts were swept in a kaleidoscope of changing patterns, fractured geometric shapes, yellow, blue, red, black, breaking up and bursting into flower.

Just as the flower faded, five women emerged from its dark center and began whirling under a sudden halo of light. Across their swirling skirts appeared clouds and rivers, ocean waves and sandy shores dissolving into snow-capped mountains, snowflakes, glittering crystals, which turned into lightning, burning branches, radiant jungle ferns. Images of the sun erupted, real flames spun in wide circles—and Minerva was dancing in the eye of the fire. Air, earth, fire, and water: all creation taking shape, splitting apart, and coming together.

Chapter 41

ALBERTO'S SIDE OF THE STORY

Creation doesn't happen in a single day. The Maya universe came into full flower over time. Years went by before space began to revolve and the three patron deities of Palenque saw the light of day. For the young gods, a millennium unfolded in the blink of an eye. For Panchanecos, a month seemed like an eternity.

It wasn't that time was racing forward or creeping back into the shadows for a languorous nap. The hours were simply standing around in their dirty feet, kicking gravel. Nothing, absolutely nothing, was happening on the darkened stage, not a click or a whisper or the *phsst* of a match. None of the actors were fighting or stealing or falling in and out of love. Even the artisans had slowed their pace, and many a long night passed when the bare-chested, dreadlocked freaks hung out by the bridge, pants drooping, stomachs growling, without a lovesick blond in their tattooed arms. Surely something was brewing besides mint tea, but whatever it was melted in the rain.

Some attributed this curious dampening of the spirit to the tourist lull. Others were afraid that swine flu had reached the south and its symptoms had mutated into another form: total apathy. Alux reminded me that although we had recently celebrated zenith passage and the beginning of Maya creation, we were actually living in the last days of a great cycle and time was winding down before gearing up for the next epoch.

He himself was a superb, semi-ambulatory example of time's contrariness, shuffling around with a tape measure in his hand, looking busy, but whiling away the hours soaking in his sweat bath and watching TV. Podwell, we noted, hadn't come up with a new theory in weeks. Stranger still, instead of pacing the floor and talking to himself, Podwell was sleeping a good twelve hours a night. After poring through the hieroglyphic texts and five oracular books, we found no Maya prophecies remotely related to plagues of dreamy, no-mind, out-of-mind states. When I mentioned the weird noise in my head, Alux suggested I was sympathetically tuned in to the silent electromagnetic hum from Alberto's broken generator.

A henna-haired woman who dreamt she was a cat from the Pleiades tried to convince me that the star people had landed among us and were beaming out waves of tranquility.

"You may be on to something," I said, and began searching for signs.

Apart from the steady electromagnetic pulse in my brain, I discovered that the oppressive peace was releasing a musty aroma stronger than a bucketful of mushroom spores. Everyone was feeding at the trough except for the Morales family, who stuck to their daily diet of leftover bitters.

The old man was getting thinner and more bored with each passing day. His dog pack was shrinking, too, first the big black one that had taken a chunk out of the Hermit and then the nervous brown runt that had attacked three tourists. No one was sad to see them go, so nothing much was said beyond a whisper here and there implying that they had been poisoned. Even Moi was silent about their sudden disappearance. They weren't his dogs, after all, just untamed strays gone back to the wild. But then one night a figure dressed in a black jumpsuit and black mask was seen darting up the path. A shot rang out. The next morning the old shaggy white was dead on Moi's doorstep.

Yes, Moi was growing thinner. Followed by two mangy dogs, he dragged his feet along the path, pausing to say good morning to Petunia, his bristling beauty, before plodding on for coffee at the new café.

"I am ready to die," he told Filipa, the cook, as he lowered himself into his favorite seat.

"Oh, Don Moi, take your vitamin. I'll bring you a bowl of vegetable soup. You'll feel better in an hour."

"I will not feel better," Moi said, clinging stubbornly to the arms of his chair. "I am cursed with miserable children."

The new café was Empress's former soyburger bar, with a fresh coat of paint on the yellow counter and the addition of six mismatched chairs and two heavy worktables holding down the dirt floor. The menu was purely Mexican: sausage, shredded pork, *picadillo*. Every Friday a vat of shrimp, twitching their long antennae, swam in a soupy pool of orange tomatoes. The yucca tortillas were tougher than five-day-old bread. Maybe the rumors about Empress practicing voodoo were true. Without her beautiful jive, the place seemed shabby, and no matter how cheery Filipa's smiles or how many hippies lolled around, playing guitars and pounding on the tables, the atmosphere wreaked of decay with a side of bacon.

The café was Aida's bright idea, dating back to the golden week of reconciliation when she was staying in one of Chato's cabañas and looking for ways to improve her situation. Brimming with confidence, she speeded things up by trying to sell Chato a piece of land that actually belonged to her older sister, Miranda. As soon as Chato discovered Aida's scheme, he tossed her baggage out on the landing. Down she dropped, into her old rut, and she and Chato became sworn enemies again.

The following day, Don Moises gave his homeless daughter permission to occupy Rakshita's abandoned house. Only temporarily, of course, because he had plans to convert the lofty memorial into a literary salon for Gabriel Garcia Marquez and friends. In the meantime, Aida and her prodigal family enjoyed three spacious rooms, one stacked on top of the other, with a panoramic view of the pestilent forest from the upper deck. Mice were sleeping in the stove, Aida complained, the shower was choked with vines, but since she was definitely coming up in the world she took the liberty of painting the three-story tower a pale, fairy-tale mauve. Next, she took over Rakshita's rundown cabañas, and before anyone could stop her, she painted the slumping walls a flaming fire-engine red. The interiors were filthy, but no one seemed to mind. Most of the clientele preferred sleeping in hammocks or directly on the naked earth. Once word spread on the backpacker circuit, whole tribes started pitching rainbow tents on the muddy field and simmering beans over communal fires. The grounds came alive, with hippies singing and dancing to African drums until four in the morning. It was just like the old days, except Moi wasn't collecting any money.

"I don't understand it, Filipa. The place is crowded. There's plenty of noise. Some of them stay for weeks, helping me plant more trees and birds of paradise. They feed Petunia, and they're not afraid to pet her. Some of them even come here to eat your delicious yucca pancakes."

"True, Don Moi, I don't make much money, but what I earn is a help. But I know for a fact that many of them don't pay. They sleep in the woods."

"I will have to tell Pito to stop riding his golf cart and be more vigilant. He behaves like a kid."

"A big bastard with a drug habit, if you don't mind my saying so, Don Moi."

Moi took her words into consideration. The next time he saw Pito mincing around with two of his workers, he pulled the lunkhead aside and asked him where the rent money was going. Pito looked down at Moi and growled, "Mind your own business, old man."

That was too much! The old man sent them all to hell.

And that is exactly where his dutiful daughter and her mister went. In the heat of the day, the outcasts grabbed their belongings and made a beeline for Alberto's. Happy as the devil to see his old allies, Alberto installed the ill-fated family in his finest room, which meant four beds, one fan, no ceiling, and no private bath. It was back to brute survival now, although the first two nights were free.

So there they were again, Aida rocking the baby, Pito reaching across the table to fondle Alberto's army helmet, Aida slapping his knee and shouting, "A-TEN-SHUN," and the three of them howling as the clouds rolled in. It looked mighty suspicious to the witch, who was hiding behind the bar, eavesdropping on the latest wicked scheme. Then again, maybe it was the witch who instigated the plot in the first place. It's hard to say, because that night Medusa and Esmeralda disappeared into the relentless, bone-drenching storm.

Post by post and plank by plank, Alberto tore down the bar faster than most people shake off a bad memory. For a low, low monthly rate, Alberto, the real estate mogul and enterprising owner of the dirt lot, became a silent partner in Aida's Burrito Stand.

There it stood in the hot sun, hand-lettered menu flapping in the evanescent breeze. There it leaned in the nightly storm, rain raking the gravel, chairs afloat, the cardboard menu as wrinkled as crocodile skin. The last of the hustlers sauntered off in his genuine leather cowboy boots, and there wasn't enough money in the rusted till to feed the kids, much less support Pito's habit.

How long can a person endure beans and eggs, beans and cheese, beans and sausage without getting a serious case? One night the grump got so strung out he headed for Don Mucho's. Just as lightning came ripping through the trees, he lumbered across the bridge. Chato was pouring himself a drink behind the bar. The monster shook his fist. Chato lifted his glass. The waiters scrambled, but Pito came no further. Thunder drowned his pitiful rage, and he stumbled away, into the blackness.

It was like a grade-B horror movie or like history repeating itself. But history, even when time is winding down, never repeats itself exactly.

Without shame, embarrassment, or the slightest glimmer of imagination, the devil's trio resurrected their old standby. When all else fails, bring back the rock band and drive everybody crazy.

The rockers were practicing for their eleven o'clock set—a few cymbal crashes, a few supersonic twangs on the guitar—as Moi and I sat in the eerie light suspended over Filipa's best table, when who should appear out of the rancorous night but Alberto wearing his orange baseball cap pulled down over his eyes. Crash went the drums.

"There's no water, Papa," he began. "And where there is no water, there are no guests renting rooms and no one coming to my bar."

"Chato is digging a well. His men are down there at dawn every day. Wait till they go deeper and maybe you can siphon it off. You know, the same way you tap his electricity."

Alberto frowned. "His water is his water. Mine is mine. Pito has already taken a look at Chato's well. He says the water is yellow."

"How does water turn yellow? There's only one way, and that way is a very serious crime." Moi glared at his son with one cold, shriveled eye. "Let Pito drink it. Then we'll know for sure."

Ignoring the comment, Alberto turned to me and smiled. "We are going to move the Panchan," he said in his mild, even voice. "Don't look so surprised. There is no reason why we can't have more than one. Perhaps we will have two, three, or four Panchans. I've already bought the land. It's beautiful. My father loves it."

Moi nodded. "Yes, beautiful. Four hundred acres of green swamp."

"Birds, and plenty of pasture for cattle. There are crocodiles in the pools. We could raise them and sell the hides. They are very popular for boots and purses. And it will provide an income for the local Indians. We can build cabañas and make an eco-resort."

"Why in hell would tourists want to see crocodiles or cows?" I snapped, somewhat startled by the anger in my voice. "Cows destroy the land and poison the water. How can you call it an eco-resort? It would be just the opposite."

Alberto was dumbfounded. "My brother has ruined this place. We have to do something."

"All I'm saying is that no one from France or Italy comes all the way to Palenque to look at scrawny cows."

"My brother is in serious trouble. I've done everything I can to help, but he is not interested in my help. He will destroy this place. All my brothers and sisters are very worried. It's the drugs. Everyone sitting at the tables and everyone standing on the bridge is a dealer. You think those hippies are small time, but they are part of the Mafia, all of them, the pizza man and also my brother."

Alberto waited for his words to take effect, but I just sat there, crushing ants on the table.

"You probably think I came here to work," he said. "But no. I made plenty of money selling real estate in Texas. I don't need my little business here. I came back to take care of my father, protect him from the sinful things that are going on."

Moi turned away and ordered another coffee.

"Chato has guns. They supply him with guns and he sells them. Guns and drugs. Fortunately, I have connections in the government. It's the only thing that saves him."

"And why are you spreading these lies? Do you really expect me to swallow this lame-brained crock of shit?" I couldn't believe the words spilling from my mouth, but Alberto remained remarkably calm.

"I know you're writing a book. I want you to hear my side. It isn't easy seeing your own brother ruin his life and the reputation of my family. I just stay here because of my father. I once dreamed of being a pilot, like him."

"You took two lessons," said Moi.

"Now I will start a new Panchan. My brother is dangerous. He needs to be put away." Alberto hung his head. "It's a terrible thing to have to do to your own brother. Sometimes I don't know if I am doing the right thing."

Chapter 42

SPLIT

Talking to Alberto was like eating a bad walnut. Crack the shell, peel away worthless bits and pieces, and what's left is an excruciatingly foul taste that causes the brain to pucker, the tongue hairs to curl, which also happens when you suck on an umeboshi plum. There was a smell to it, too, the indelible odor of burnt amber, the stink of a polluted well tainted with whatever poison stains water nicotine yellow. One whiff and it left her on the brink of low. She didn't have the blacks and she didn't have the blues. Her mood was like a bruise, red chasing purple across an infested bog. She could hear the crocs sloshing in the slough. She was losing touch with reality, but she had lost touch with reality before and usually enjoyed her spooky little forays on Uranus's third moon. Now there was a vacancy in her tenth lunar house, sinister winds blowing through the crystal palace where she wandered through rooms so vast she couldn't see the walls, but someone had painted the ceiling puce and furnished the conservatory with the kind of velveteen love seats that fill downtown storefronts and abandoned malls. "Maybe jaguars have consumed my soul," she thought, but since her soul was made of dust and metal filings, the notion of clean, clean, clean set her off again. She was running on empty. Maybe it was good to feel empty. Isn't that what the Buddha taught? But it didn't feel good. She had no idea how she got to the disco at three A.M. and ended up with that English swine. She didn't know why she was drinking too much, smoking too much, and keeping a gun in her closet. At least she hadn't lost her mind. What bothered her most, and this goes to show how intuitive she could be sometimes, despite her spiteful nature, was that I was losing my perspective. "Too many characters," she said, and I said I could easily do without hers. That's when she began to question who was writing this book, Mingo or me. Even though I was scribbling one word after another, they weren't adding up to a narrative plot. "Don't be crude," I said. She said I was repeating pages in a book that had already been written, the book that Mingo had seen in his dream and had been remembering at random. Of course, that idea was far too complicated for a non-entity like her. If I were Mingo I'd be dreaming of stone palaces, wouldn't I? Besides, I knew I wasn't Mingo, because I had seen him at zenith passage a few months ago. I looked in the mirror, and instead of Mingo, I saw her staring back at me. She looked like a Goth from Avenue B, with kohl smeared around her eyes and hair dyed tar-ball black. That's when I put two and two together. The shaky identity, the funk, the total disconnect started the day I lost my shadow.

Maybe I had retrieved the wrong one. Maybe she had been there all along and I didn't know it, wasn't sharp enough, wise enough, sensitive enough, pure enough, etc. "Congratulations, girlfriend," she said. "You just won a timeout in northern Chihuahua."

During the peace and quiet allotted to me, I decided to seek Don Moi's advice. Even when he wasn't agitated or self-absorbed, you could never hit him with a problem directly; you had to rummage around his cabinet searching for the right curiosity and then hope for the best. So I began by asking him why Mingo had stopped coming to the Panchan.

He said that he hadn't seen Mingo in years and that for him, Mingo had become a mere shadow.

"Mingo is your best friend. We went to the ruins together last August."

"Oh, that Mingo," he said. "I thought you were talking about that dark fellow who always sticks to the wall as if he were hiding from the cops."

"The wiry one with the glasses?"

"No, the wiry one who is blind."

"I can see we're getting nowhere," I said.

"You must do something about that temper," he said. "It's unbecoming, *chulita*. What has happened to your sunny nature?"

"Tired of smiling, I suppose."

"Yes, you are facing an occupational hazard. Góngora, Lope de Vega, all the great poets have written about the shades long before the age of Freud and Jung."

Strange how Moi's memory slipped in and out of sync while his perceptions grew sharper. The old man could see right through me!

"Am I that transparent?" I asked.

"Years of experience," he said. "Once upon a time, Mingo and I were as close as two peas in a pod. He saved my life, you know, for which I am both grateful and sad."

I heaved a sigh, anticipating one of Moi's long, drawn-out stories.

"Alright, then, to accommodate your impatience, I'll make a long story short. I will set a record for succinctness, even though the story will suffer. But I warn you, this means you will have to listen carefully and not daydream or run off in the middle because you have something important to do. 'Work.' What a terrible word. You would be much happier if you did nothing, like me."

"I swear on a stack of Bibles," I said.

"In no way does this impress me," Moi said.

"A bottle of rum, then."

"Alright, I'll begin at the beginning. One evening Linda and Merle knocked on my door. The door was the door to my house at La Cañada, where I lived for many years. My house at the Panchan has no doors and no windows; it's completely open. I used to live closed in, like an animal in a den. This was long ago. Linda and Merle came to tell me that two boys were lost in the jungle, and they were very worried because night was coming on. And so Mingo and I went into the woods to find them. We knew those woods very well. They lay near the Chacamax River, where we had been many times. We spent several hours climbing up one hill and down the other and hacking through the narrow ravines. All the while we kept calling, 'Cerci, Miguelito.' The trouble was, we ourselves were lost, although we didn't want to admit it.

"Finally we reached the crest of a hill, and looking down, we could see the river, and beyond the bend, the lights from a few scattered houses. We were badly scratched by this time. So we climbed down to the mud bank and thought if we could get across we'd find ourselves close to the dirt road leading to Palenque. 'Cerci, Miguelito,' we called, but no one answered. It seemed hopeless, and our situation was hopeless, too.

"We entered the river, but the current was fast, faster than we had imagined. The rocks were very slippery. There was no way. We both fell in and were caught in the undertow. I was holding on to a tree branch, and I remember thinking—I don't pray very often—'Dear God, don't let me drown.' Even though they say that drowning is a pleasant way to die, I was still afraid. Mingo was clinging to a log, kicking with his feet, but it did no good. The current was too swift. It was dark and I couldn't see. The tree branch I was holding on to cracked, the water was rushing over my head, I couldn't breathe. I don't remember the rest. Mingo says he grabbed me, scooped me up like a fish. I don't know how, because he's not a strong swimmer. Somehow he reached the other side and pulled me up on the bank. I had no pulse. I wasn't breathing. He sat beside me for a long time and then he fell asleep. When I woke up in the night, he was still sleeping, like an angel. I died in the river, and I came back to life."

"That's frigging amazing!" I said.

Moi gave me a nervous look. "Yes, it's as you say, frigging amazing. I was wandering around in a place so black I couldn't see my hands. It smelled like a train station where the damned must wait to go down. I drowned, but I was dry as a bone in the bone-dry vestibule of hell. But this is what makes me sad, and helps me to understand and forgive you. To this day, I think my better half died, and it's the dark one that goes on living."

"And what happened to Mingo?" I asked.

"Haven't you heard, Carola? My *compadre* won the lottery. Twenty thousand pesos. Not twenty million, but it's plenty."

I wanted to hear what happened immediately after the accident, but now it didn't matter. As far as I knew, Mingo had survived at least two near-fatal accidents. "He's truly a lucky man," I said.

"A born fool, you mean. Against my good advice he bought five head of cattle and moved back to the ranch in Salto de Agua. Poor man. Who knows if he'll ever finish his book?"

"You'd have to agree he's an accidental writer," I said.

"Isn't that true for most? Now he's really stuck for good, tending his Jerseys and taking care of Señora Steele's ghost. He has his cows. She has her poetry. It's a perfect match."

Chapter 43

SAGE ADVICE

True to his guiding principles, Moi advised me to do nothing. "Don't worry," he said. "You'll be fine as long as you offend the right people." I told him I lacked the nerve. He suggested that half of me had enough steel for two. As far as he was concerned, my predicament was universal. "People are always expecting storms to raise the roof, quakes to shake the foundations where they live. But pay no attention. Just look innocent, like me, and smile." He glanced at the sky, batted his eyes, and put on his best angelic face. "Practice, practice, practice, but don't make it seem like work. There's nothing in this world that's worse."

"Same old mantra," I said, and reminded him that my very being was being ripped asunder by unknown forces.

"Not as romantic as drowning," he said, "or living with a ghost. I've already told you the story, but since your head is in a black cloud, I'll have to draw you a picture." He reached for a napkin. Apparently my anxiety could be reduced to a simple diagram, which Solange, his French shrink and one of the great loves of his life, had passed on to him years ago.

"Here's a circle, which represents the Self. This line through the middle divides Consciousness from the things we don't see. Jung called this dark part the Shadow."

In my case, the Shadow was a shadow and she and I were well acquainted. Moi considered my *état existentiel* a great advantage.

Easy for him to say. From my point of view, I was the sunny yolk, she was the runny egg white, though I was losing my mind and she, a mixed-up pain in the butt, sometimes got it together. The differences were beginning to ooze and shimmy, like a cheese soufflé. I was a changed person, she kept repeating while huffing and bluffing her way into my air space.

Actually she didn't take up space, per se. She was the hapless creature of time, having vanished and reappeared with the twelve o'clock sun. Yet somewhere in the nanoseconds ticking by, she acquired a solid personality and I, totally cowed, dreamed only of escape. Therein lay the mystery.

What really blows my mind is that the ancients underwent this solar transformation twice a year, at planting and harvest times. To grasp the astronomical and practical significance of zenith passage demanded a high degree of brainpower, but it took first-hand experience to imagine what the Maya made of shadows.

"For argument's sake," said Don Moi, "let's suppose the upper crust—doctors, lawyers, warriors, priests, the oh so wise and corrupt ruling elite—propagated the notion that the flat, black shapes chasing everyone around were supernatural pests, part of the dark armies of death, bent on destruction. There they were, glued to your back all day, aping your every move, making you look like a crippled midget or a monster. It was very frightening if you were a mediocrity and didn't know any better. And that is how the shadows kept the masses in their places."

"Losing your shadow is a completely different thing, Don Moi." I suggested that the average person, who was rooted in the soil and had so little to lose or leave behind, probably thought about it as any observant farmer would. The sun stands still. The body separates from its most intimate companion, like a seed dropped down a hole, and then springs back to life instantaneously. The entire cycle of death and resurrection in under a minute. And every man and woman could do it: bathe in naked noonday light and reactivate in full glory, at the center of the world.

But in these godless times, most people who have been rent and rendered by the sun seemed totally unaware of their condition, lost in a fog they could only describe in vague, abstract terms. "The trouble with you is you don't resonate with Higher Consciousness," they told me. "You need to get in touch with your inner vibe."

So I got in touch with my inner vibe, and a voice said to me, "You think it's too much sun! Well, you are so wrong, kiddo! Don't you know you caught it from Alberto." Hmmm, that shallow blabbermouth had flashes of insight.

I was about to ask her the following questions: Was this creation a complete bust? Were we doomed to repeat the same mistakes over and over again, *ad nauseum*?

I already knew the answer, and it was hopeless. Besides, she was wrong about all this being Alberto's fault, another cruel attempt to mislead me, to alienate me from the ups and downs of the natural world and what Moi called my "existential state." I was sick of the whole shadow business, sick of her voice. Maybe it was just my imagination, maybe I had lost my marbles. What difference did it make? I was going around in circles.

There I was, floundering in the bottomless depths of despair when the most insane thing happened. As the saying goes, there's nothing like a little excitement to take your mind off its chosen misery.

Chapter 44

ROCK BOTTOM

It was the witching season—Day of the Dead or Nadir—the time of year when the sun goes down to the depths of the earth and summons the souls of the damned.

On the morning of nadir passage, the rising sun blazed through the central doorway of the Temple of the Sun, flooding the main chamber and illuminating the holy of holies. Camera in hand, Alux fell to his knees. He crawled on his stomach, then rolled over on his back, literally swimming in light. Now he had dazzling photographic proof of the temple's true orientation.

This was as far as he was willing to go in the interests of science. Later the portals to the Underworld would open and the sun's ominous angle would alter human destiny. In the larger drama of life and death, he wasn't cut out to play the hero who follows the sun through hell and back. No, he protested, the gods had already punished him enough. And so, not one to fool with fate, Alux limped home to savor his discovery in silence. He told me he spent the rest of the day fixing leaks in his roof.

Something stranger happened to me that morning. I was standing in the Temple of the Inscriptions, recording the spectacular sunrise over the Temple of the Cross, when a ball of light swept through the eastern window and landed in the middle of the corridor. I expected it to shatter, like a comet, into a million incandescent sherds, but the ball continued to glow, a stunning white halo utterly distinct from the golden rays that had enveloped Don Moi as he stood in the same place at summer solstice. He was the king then, basking in divine splendor. I was a pale shadow trembling inside a frozen pool of light. It shone directly over Pakal's burial chamber, the monstrous maw, the Mirrored Tree, the Nine Lords of Night. A cold needle ran straight through me, from the sun above to the tomb and moon below.

At midnight, as the moon climbed to the center of the sky, the sun settled in the dark heart of the Underworld, and its oblique light woke the dead. Wearily they left their labors in the burning kitchens, their backbreaking work in the cane fields, and slowly felt their way along the tunnels toward the surface of the earth. Candles lit the stony paths, the pungent scent of marigolds drew them upward. When the dead arrived at the gravesites, their loved ones were waiting with sausages, pork tamales, and sweet breads. There were dolls, toy trucks, and candies for the little angels, cigarettes, rum, and tequila for the men, everything they had longed for on their brief day of rest. Mothers wept, mariachis played, skeletons danced in the streets. The dead got so drunk they had to be carried partway home.

Three days after the spirits returned to their grim chores underground, Chato rushed out of his house, firing his gun and hollering at the top of his lungs, "Gas, gas! I'll shoot whoever did this!"

When I got to the bridge, Aida was screaming, "Papa's been shot!"

Before I had a chance to search for Don Moi, five Humvees pulled into the parking lot, and a dozen armed soldiers dressed in green camouflage and black balaclavas began swarming through the Panchan. They turned Chato's house upside down, marched up the path, and stormed the empty swimming pool. All they found was an old .22 rifle. After an hour of beating the bushes, they jumped into their Humvees and drove away. They took Chato with them.

An hour later, troops roared past the Best Western and the huge plaster statue of Pakal, the one where he's holding a jade cube in his right hand and a jade sphere in the other. He who rules the universe visibly shuddered as the squat, snub-nosed vehicles swung down the only tree-lined street in town. "So this is where the kingpins are hiding out," muttered the gawkers, "the best address in Palenque." It looked like a full-scale operation, though the rumble of the Humvees over the

cobbles gave the gunmen plenty of time. With or without the element of surprise, there was bound to be a shootout. Tourists ran for their hotel rooms, locals fled.

The street was deserted when twenty masked men descended upon Chato's mother's manicured lawn. Waving M16's, they ordered the old woman to open the door. Instead, Doña Paulina went to her room and hid under the covers. Meanwhile, Chato's sister Miranda strolled out to the front porch and, with stunning nonchalance, faced the assembled squadron.

"Where's your search warrant?" she demanded.

"Let us in!" the colonel shouted. "We have reason to believe you have arms in there. We have a right. And we want the keys to your brother's house down the street. We know you're harboring guns and drugs."

"Over my dead body!" said the sister. Aside from her big lip, she probably weighed two hundred pounds. After considering the great girth of her, none of the soldiers made a move.

"Step aside!" shouted the colonel.

Miranda began to laugh. "Hah!" she said. "I'd know that voice anywhere. Come out, Alberto. Come out from under your mask!"

The colonel pulled off his black balaclava, and sure enough, there stood her crazy brother.

"Tell them the truth, Alberto. I know for a fact you've never been a colonel. What are you boys doing, listening to this man? He's never been in the army. He's never been in the air force. He once took a couple of flying lessons, but that's all. Today he's a colonel! He usually calls himself 'El Capitan.'"

The soldiers lowered their rifles, climbed back into the Humvees, and drove off, leaving Alberto standing alone in the dark, cobblestoned street.

Meanwhile, Chato sat in the jailhouse quietly conversing with the general, a portly epicure who dined at Don Mucho's on Sunday nights. After five minutes of polite interrogation, the general realized that Alberto's accusations were completely trumped up and that his squad had acted too hastily.

"Bring this man a good steak!" ordered the general, his pudgy face turning a pugilistic red. Just as suddenly he adopted a soft, conspiratorial voice and resumed his cordial conversation with the prisoner. "Believe it or not, Mexico has laws," he confided. What he didn't say is that according to law the military was here in Chiapas to catch big fish, not to serve the whims of mad civilians. As Chato well knew, the general was in hot water. But all the commander could do on such short notice was to send out for a decent bottle of Chilean wine.

"You've already been charged," he shrugged. "Now, possession of a .22 rifle is a minor offence since anybody who's been in the army has one. Shooting live bullets in the air is considered a more serious crime, because someone could be hurt by random acts that clearly set a bad example. Our informant tells us you were running around in the woods, shooting a pistol. What did you think you were doing?"

"That's bullshit! I wasn't running around in the woods. I was standing at my bathroom window!"

"Which brings me to my main point," said the general. "You, Chato Morales, have been charged with shooting your father."

Chato swallowed hard. "I haven't seen the old man lately," he said, "but I'm sure he's alive. Believe me, it would take more than a .22 to kill the bastard."

"Alive or dead doesn't matter," said the general. "By our Napoleonic code, you are guilty until proven innocent." He raised his hand to his forehead in a cheerful salute. "And furthermore, the judge has set a high bail. Have a good weekend."

Immediately Alfonso called his sisters in the States and reported the whole fantastic story. He summed it up by saying that he hoped there was a good witness protection program, because Alberto was in deep trouble. "Informants are bad enough," he said. "But our own brother! It's a moral crime, beyond the law."

The sisters agreed, but tears were powerless against bad timing. Banks were closed, the wires asleep. Either it was a trick of fate or Alberto was more devious than anyone ever gave him credit for. Chato was stuck in the jailhouse until Monday.

"No point crying about corruption," Alfonso said. "No time for revenge until later." And so, in accord with the time-honored rules laid down by the best of men, Alfonso set about raising money to pay off the judge. "I should have been a lawyer," he said, and called everyone he knew. "Even a thousand pesos will help," he implored.

Friends scraped the jar, the bottoms of their pockets, begged and borrowed from the local loan sharks. One old auntie hobbled out to the garden and dug up the wooden chest where she stashed her silver coins. It was a miracle she could still use a spade. Little by little the money mounted.

"Don't worry," Alfonso assured his brother. "As soon as this is over, we'll have Alberto put away. In a year or so, they'll let him out and he'll be almost normal." Alfonso hadn't lost his brittle sense of humor.

The womenfolk were inconsolable. Three days of cooking and sitting with the dead and now they were staring into the living abyss. Poor Doña Paulina slipped into what doctors described as acute shock, while the brave Miranda, already suffering from high blood pressure, experienced a complete collapse. Stress and worry drove the six sisters and two ex-spouses into alarming states of worry and agitation. Minerva was afraid to leave the house. The female hysteria was justifiable; there was a real possibility that Chato could be sentenced to forty years. "If I go, the Panchan goes," Chato had often said, and his dependents knew that to be true. Fortunately, his thirteen-year-old daughter kept her head. "I'll bake Papi some chocolate brownies," she said.

Oddly enough, during the heat of the crisis, the family completely forgot about the victim. Finally, in a dramatic Saturday morning appearance, Don Moi walked into the courthouse looking quite hale and hearty. Dressed in his finest blue shirt, he stood before the magistrate and flatly denied that his son had shot him.

"Does he look dead to you?" said his lawyer. "Does he look like a ghost? Of course not. Justice will be done."

"I may look like a ghost," said Don Moi, "but believe me I can testify that I am alive and well. You may search me if you like. I have many holes in my body, but not from a tiny .22 bullet. My son is innocent!"

No one said a thing about the gas hose in Chato's house or how it might have gotten there. No one mentioned the water in the well and how it had turned yellow. What truly mattered at a time like this was that family, friends, waiters, and workers tossed their hard-earned cash into the pot and by Saturday night Chato was free.

Before you could say Chato Morales, the two prime suspects vanished. Alberto jumped into his car and drove to Asunción. Pito, according to rumor, was holed up in some cheap dive near the bus station.

Which one, no one knew for sure until Pito punched the hotel manager over the rotten service, the hotel manager called the police, and
Enrique tracked him down. While he was doing his detective work,
Enrique discovered that Pito was wanted for assault in several US states
and three of the toughest cities in Mexico. The bruiser had a record as
long as Enrique's right arm. Enrique showed him that arm and Pito
hightailed it out of town.

As soon as Chato inhaled his first breath of freedom, he went ballistic. He threatened this and threatened that, stomped and banged and
slammed. He was on a rampage, acting wilder than Petunia, but who
could blame him? Two days behind bars and a mile-long list of debts,
all because of his jealous brother.

"We'll have to sell this place," Alfonso stated. "We'd be better off
with money in our pockets and no headaches. A little fixing up and the
Panchan will become part of a resort chain."

"Never!" shouted Chato. "I'd rather kill the bastard."

"Then you'd end up back in jail for good."

"I'll report it the Human Rights Commission. I'll take it to the
highest court."

Moi shook his head. "Son, your brother Alberto is the wrong target," he said. "I am doing what is right. This morning I went to city hall
and filed my complaint. I am suing the Mexican army!"

Alfonso broke into one of his famous giggles. "You of all people,
Papa. You're pleading for justice in a place where justice hasn't been
invented. It's not even a dream. We're better off taking the law into our
own hands, and I suggest the kindest thing."

Having Alberto committed was at the top of his list.

Chapter 45

THE CHASE

The local newspaper called it a Cain and Abel story, and from then on, Alberto would be branded with the mark of Cain, forever guilty and forever immune. Gross hyperbole considering he hadn't murdered anybody, but no one in town bothered to draw that distinction. In these parts, vendettas were fairly common and crimes of passion often defensible. But snitching to military forces sent to harass the general population, including Señora Morales, the bastard's mother, *dios mío*, that was unthinkable. And so, before the article even came out, the most disreputable members of the community condemned Alberto as an unpardonable sinner, and that was putting it mildly. There wasn't a shred of compassion for the childhood scars he bore as the family scapegoat, not a drop of sympathy for the lunatic who ratted on his brother.

"That *cabrón* is plain loco, a rotten devil through and through," concluded the director of the asylum. "Only the Lord can save him now. With a little help from me."

As a former addict, the director had been in and out of a dozen rehabilitation centers. Although he lacked formal training, he was a hardcore veteran of various psychoanalytical schools, prison programs, and AA. Twice he had his blood replaced and three times underwent exorcisms by Jesuit and Tantric priests. Yet the only relief he found from his habitual cravings was going to the movies. One night, while high on crack and hunkered in the dark theater, he discovered the formula for total recovery: Ninja boot camp. He tried it out on himself and his circle of friends and achieved a one hundred percent success rate. Then he began proselytizing. After a grueling three-month schedule of cold showers, sleep deprivation, round-the-clock surveillance, and physical abuse, followed by three more months of the same, no graduate of his program went back on the stuff or uttered a cross word again. Patients came out absolutely tame.

"I know it sounds like torture, but it works," he assured Alfonso. "I will even give you a written guarantee. For me, your brother is a special case."

During his years in the gutter, the director had worked night and day at developing his full criminal potential, and if there was one thing the director despised was a stool pigeon. Here he held up his battered right hand and showed off the stub of his missing middle finger, which he lost in a fight with a heavyweight shill from Coahuila. The blade of resentment was etched on his face. Yet, in an extraordinary gesture of generosity, he offered the Morales family a ten percent discount on professional services and accommodations, which meant a woven mat and a special low-fat meal served once a day. As an added bonus, three hulking staff members, driving a custom-outfitted, unmarked van, would pick up the offender outside the main gate of the Panchan. "Wouldn't want to get caught for kidnapping," the director smiled. In view of the statutes protecting the insane, the brothers would have to unite, form a cadre, as it were, then wheedle, bribe, bully, or otherwise escort Alberto off his property and out to the road.

"Let's go to a movie and get some Kentucky Fried Chicken," Enrique suggested to him. "We'll drive to Villahermosa and stop at Palestrina's on the way home."

"You remember that blond who had the hots for you?" said Alfonso. "Well, she's waiting for you on the road."

It was a wonder Alberto had returned from Asunción in the first place. Now no ordinary enticements could lure him away from the Mono Blanco. For the first time in his life, he was taking a genuine interest in running the business. He could be seen checking the bar, straightening the tablecloths, and hiring the band to play for no one on Saturday nights.

Once in a while he would break his pattern and threaten to kill Miranda or Enrique over some imagined slight. But instead of arguing with him, the victims adopted a new, more sensible strategy; they complained to the judge. And just in case Alberto got carried away with one of his twisted real-estate schemes, the sisters and brothers signed an agreement stating that no sibling could sell Panchan property without majority consent. Seduced by the spirit of the law, Chato sued Alberto for defamation. Alberto responded by cutting off the water supply.

"The dick's got nerve," said the voice, and she was right. He was also pathologically stubborn, chronically oblivious, compulsively fastidious, and, except for his good taste in American Blues, pitifully out-to-lunch.

"Painkillers," she said. "You can see he doesn't give a fuck."

True enough. After throwing away money on lawyers, notaries, restraining orders, and other useless, non-binding powers, the family renounced their faith in blind justice and left the future to blind fate.

One morning a magic band of Rainbows, festooned in swirling colors, swooped out of the jungle on horseback. What an astonishing parade! Forty flamboyant "Riders for Peace" and their sweating chargers, cloaked in banners and eagle feathers, came trotting through the Panchan on their way to Guatemala and Peru. Hungry after an all-night rave, the tripped-out riders dismounted in front of the Mono Blanco and left their steeds to graze on the grass. For no good reason, Alberto flew into a rage, grabbed a stick, and swung at the grays and bays chomping on his greenery.

"We ride for peace," insisted the naked German with the war bonnet and blond dreads, but Alberto's demon refused to listen. How could the Rainbows know he was planning to exchange his parcel of weeds for marshland near the lagoon?

"Horseshit!" he shouted, and the frightened ponies reared. Rainbow braves scrambled for the reins, but it was too late. Like Petunia, the neighing horses stampeded in every direction, galloping through the restaurant and down the dirt road, with bedraggled Rainbows and Alberto chasing after. Even then, Alberto had the presence of mind to stop short of crossing his boundary line.

Most of the horses came back, and for days the nomads danced around their teepees, attracting sizable crowds sympathetic to the cause. But soon the non-stop drumming disturbed the peace and they were forced to move on. None of them made it across the Guatemalan border. An itinerant sandal maker who went along for the ride later told me, "The moon was not ripe for the horses."

Apparently the moon was ripe for devilfish. The streams that meandered through the Panchan became infested with ugly, black bottom feeders. There were thousands of them, wide-finned scavengers migrating upstream to their spawning grounds, which was located, according to Don Moi, in Lake Metzabok, deep in the Lacandon rainforest. This seemed unlikely. Nevertheless, hundreds congregated below the small dam Alberto had built to enclose his swimming pool. Since the devilfish couldn't leap over the dam and no one had heard of constructing ladders, as people do for salmon, the fish started dying en masse. The streams were black and the air reeked.

Then came the flood. The swollen river swept over the banks and through the bar. Tourists sleeping in riverside cabañas woke with a start to discover that their dreams of floating were real. The boiling river swallowed everything: beds, chairs, laptops, forty-kilo backpacks. Wading through pounding rain and waist-deep water, dazed travelers struggled toward higher ground. Two Swedish girls who tried to cross the bridge clung to the submerged railings until the rescue squad carried them to safety. Others crowded, wet and shivering, into second-story rooms where they threw off their sopping clothes and survived the night smoking and drinking whatever they had salvaged. You had to admire the resiliency of the human spirit. All the while, Alberto peered down from his nest above the river, grumbling about the racket. He did nothing to help.

When the water subsided, the woods were full of devilfish, drowning or dead, and the sky thick with crows. Once again there was talk of tying a rope around Alberto's neck and dragging him to the main road.

When it came right down to it, Chato didn't have the heart. Apparently he was following Moi's "do nothing" philosophy to the letter, and given the tragic undercurrents, I could see the wisdom of it, for the family and the whole of nature. Wherever I looked I saw fragile efforts to maintain the precarious balance between life and death, good and evil. Chato offended the right people yet performed countless acts of kindness, compensated for his innate cowardice with moments of true compassion. In his own maverick way, he was the guru of the Panchan.

For example, he was so worried about Aida's children he let them eat unlimited pizzas at his restaurant. The thought of their growing up without a father kept him awake at night. Despite the many times she turned against him, lied, connived, broke his trust, and finally helped to have him jailed, Chato gave Aida bus fare so she could join her skin-headed husband in Purgatory, somewhere in the north.

He also handed a chunk of cash to Minerva and suggested she take a vacation to settle her nerves. She stared at him blankly, then quietly packed her things and took a cab to the bus station. As soon as she was gone, Chato found this note, written on pink paper, lying on top of her empty dresser:

Dear Opal,
I am dancing fire in Cancun and thinking about coming to the Panchan for a visit and also make some money even tho' I'm doing great dancing at a fancy night club with good food and expensive mixed drinks there are stars on the ceiling and palm trees made of shiny paper in between the tables, the guys are pretty cheesy but the pay is good and if you need a vacation you could come here I'm sure the owner would love you and pay you like 2000 pesos a night in dollars which is a lot better than the Panchan tho' not as cool you know it's just as easy to get strung out here and there's a beach, blue water and tasty lobsters also a bunch of sharks that chase you but I had a boyfriend for awhile and that was great because he liked to spend a bundle going places before he had to fly home to his wife and there was a gorgeous guitar player with long blond hair but he was like strung out on crack and I sat around not doing much of anything else and had to sell my gloves and hitchhike here to Cancun still a little dizzy but my knees are ok and I'm saving up to go to Burning Man next summer and you could come too just to see that I'm still alive and going where the wind takes me.
Love and xxx Bliss

Chato called reception and told the boy to drive to town and bring Minerva home. But when Sami got to the station, the bus had already left.

"Follow the bus!" Chato shouted over the cell. It's a good thing Sami was driving Chato's new Peugeot. He stepped on it and roared off.

Fifty miles, a hundred miles down the road and Sami was still pushing the pedal. Those first-class buses don't make a stop until they change drivers and that could be another five hours, he knew. Eighteen-wheelers and doublewides were rolling by, he had to stay alert. No sign of a bus at the Pemex or the all-night restaurant looming ahead on the right. Then there was just black road and a solitary porch light in the distance. He passed sleeping towns, closed cafés, a drunk staggering along the highway. Ink-black rivers running toward the Gulf, clanging bridges, tollbooths empty. The moist night wind was making him drowsy. He'd never been this far from home and neither had she, but he would go back to his home and his job and she, well, what did Minerva have in the end, living with a man as wired up as the rest of the family and, no thanks to his mad brother, in terrible trouble with the law. Minerva was young and pretty and deserved better, Sami would treat her better if given half a chance, and someday Chato would regret it, but it would be too late and he'd be left alone. He probably knows that now though he wouldn't admit it, feels the kind of pain in his heart that drives some people crazy, maybe that's what's wrong with Alberto, but what else is there besides love and longing for love, especially when you're by yourself and there's nothing but a dark road and dark ocean waiting.

Manatees Escape Preserve

Residents of El Paraíso, a small fishing village on Laguna de Catazaja, today held a demonstration outside city hall after filing an official denouncement against the violent invasion of their communal property. "Save Our Land!" protesters shouted, "Down with Developers!" The village, located on the eastern tip of the Pantanos de Centla Biosphere Reserve, had thus far escaped the conflicts plaguing the region. As Corazón de Jésus Entregada, one of the plaintiffs, stated: "The narcos are murdering people in Jonuta. This situation is worse."

Last Wednesday, at 2:34 P.M., Corazón de Jésus Entregada and two other plaintiffs, Juan Bautista Utrillo and Urias Urias Xut, were hauling their launches out of the water when they spied a distant figure hammering posts into the sand. His orange baseball cap aroused suspicion. Cholan Maya in this area wear straw cowboy hats. The plaintiffs, all lifelong members of the *ejido*, approached the stranger to apprise him of the fact that he was trespassing on communal land. The stranger contended that he was standing on the perimeter of his private property and suggested that they remove themselves immediately. Corazón de Jésus Entregada, Juan Bautista Utrillo, and Urias Urias Xut refused. The man in the orange Chicago Cubs baseball cap pulled a .38 caliber pistol from his leather belt and fired four shots over the heads of the plaintiffs. The bullets not only disturbed the old-fashioned harmony of the village, but also knocked a gold iguana out of a nearby cacao tree. The gold iguana had been the pet of La Señora Eustacia Bermudez for the past fifty-seven years. Hearing gunfire, other villagers rushed to the scene, and they too were subjected to the man's aggressions. In addition to firing his pistol, the accused punched Juan Bautista in the face and kicked Urias Xut in the leg when the pair attempted to apprehend him. Before police arrived to tranquilize the subject, he smashed the planks that used to bridge the gray runoff between the *ejido* and the marshland claimed as said assailant's private property.

Twenty fishermen from El Paraíso have filed charges for trespassing, assault and battery, attempted murder, and animal manslaughter, each of which may be punishable by up to five years in prison. "That man went berserk. He killed my beautiful Eulalia," La Señora Bermudez wept. "And noise, it upsets the fish. Fish are our lives."

The accused, Alberto Morales, of Austin, Texas, and Palenque, faces separate charges for his attack on the national preserve, designated as a sanctuary under article #374960238 of the federal wildlife act. During the debacle, Morales purposefully opened the wooden sluice damming Section 5. In the ensuing flood, four manatees were subsequently released from their protective habitat.

"Manatees are a rare breed, distant cousins of the elephant and therefore very smart," explained Dr. Javier Solarzano, Director of the Center for the Preservation of Endangered Tropical Species (CERPENTS). "They are facing extinction due to oil drilling, cattle ranching, and the projected Usumacinta dam. This inexplicable act of vandalism on the part of Sr. Morales presents a clear and present danger to these beautiful animals, and to all species of bird and mammal surviving in the preserve. Without further study we cannot judge the precise impact of the loss on the dwindling manatee population or on the general avian

and marine inhabitants of the lagoon. However, it is safe to assume that the consequences are grave. On their behalf, we are filing this suit. Morales should have known better."

Alberto Morales is the owner of El Mono Blanco, a late-night haunt on the outskirts of the Palenque National Forest. He is the former sub-director of the Palenque Office of Tourism, which makes every effort to work closely with organizations dedicated to preserving the environment as well as with citizens occupying sites of great beauty.

For thousands of years, the Laguna de Catazaja has been free of development. Its scattered human residents wish the ancient waterway to remain pristine.

"That guy wants to bring in tourists and ruin our fisheries and our birds," said Corazón de Jésus. "Before the shooting incident, he approached members of our village, demanding twenty percent of their catch. We don't want any part of that. If he were sincere, he wouldn't have released our manatees into an unprotected part of the lagoon where they have to fend for themselves. How are we going to find them now in this muddy water?"

In recent years, Alberto Morales has had several

well-publicized altercations with his brother, Chato Morales, a successful local businessman. His father, Moises Morales, is a famed expert on the Maya and an honored member of the community. Following the army's search at El Panchan, reported in our 15 November issue, Don Moises officially denounced the Mexican army.

In the performance of their duties, arresting officers discovered three expandable bullets on the person of Alberto Morales, the private possession of which is illegal. Moreover, the pistol he was waving when he tried to resist arrest is registered in the name of General ___, commander of the local military squadron. Sr. Morales was carried off in chains. When questioned by the presiding judge, he said that, if given another chance, he would fire upon the fishermen again. Morales is currently being held without bail at the maximum security prison outside Playas de Catazaja. No trial date has been set.

Chapter 46

PINBALL

With Chato on probation and Alberto in the penitentiary, Christmas was officially stricken from the record. The holidays had always loomed as a feeble hypothesis, a cloying reminder of unhappier days. At the Morales house it was either feast or famine, nothing but beans on the table or *bacalao* and apple pies spoiling in the heat. Not to mention certain relatives who couldn't hold their liquor. Why pretend? The real misery was getting together. In this family, no one knew the difference between a celebration and a fight.

"We are beyond these bourgeois customs," Moi said to me. "And it's too late to keep up appearances. Look at my sons. Look at Tumbala."

"The village of Tumbala?" I said. "Isn't it in the mountains, on a very rough road filled with potholes?"

"The road was worse in the 1950s. There was a large *finca* up there, near the sacred cave of Hol Nel. The German who owned the plantation was incarcerated during World War II. They sent him to a camp in Veracruz. He was a cruel man who kept his workers in virtual slavery, but after he left they mourned his absence, and even though they were free they continued working his land. They maintained their traditional ways, totally isolated from the outside world. That is, until the road came in.

"The road brought many things, and one of them was the Virgin of Guadalupe. You see how crazy the Mexicans are about the Virgin? Carrying torches and running relay races all the way to her shrine in Mexico City every December. Imbeciles! It is a worthless waste of breath and bones, a sacrifice of youthful innocence and whatever else those ignorant high school students lose along the road. And all because the Dominicans made up a story about her having dark skin. Overnight she became the savior of the Indians. It's like the Black Christ in Tumbala, an ordinary image someone found in the rubble. The Indians talked to it, prayed, and offered candles, and in time the smoke turned it black. Anyway, the workers on the *finca* remained loyal to the Franciscan friars and refused to go on pilgrimages to Mexico City. The Church, you see, just encourages people to sin. It took a long time to convince the people of Chiapas to become *Guadalupanas* and to accept Mexico City as their authority.

"But they needed something of their own, I thought, a symbol of who they were. I suggested they make a cross in the shape of a T, the Franciscan cross, and carve some hieroglyphs on it. This was done. The cross was like the T-shaped windows in the Palace and like the trees on the tablets in the Cross Group. Now the cross in Tumbala is a legend, and it was my idea."

"And what is your symbol, Moi?" I asked.

"A broken heart for all my lost loves. And all my lost children."

By New Year's Eve the whole world had succumbed to various forms of heartache. Retired bureaucrats nuzzled their weekend women in forlorn pockets of the woods. Instead of flirting, six-deep at the bar, Dreamers refused to make eye contact. The regulars went to bed early. Don Mucho's was deader than a past-lives convention. On the spur of the moment, Chato borrowed his ex-wife's Datsun and drove off to Cancun, in hopes of finding Minerva.

People were doing some serious cleansing, because this year the layers of memory and desire bristled with foreboding. The rumor crackling on the cold front, needling everyone in the chest and gut, was that the judge would release Alberto on New Year's Day. So far, he had shown no signs of remorse, and the big question was whether he would make a fresh start or go off the deep end and kill somebody.

The gravity of the situation weighed heavily on Don Moi, who sat in a corner, nursing a Noche Buena and gazing steadily across Devilfish Creek. I tapped him on the shoulder and asked if I could join him.

"Only if you've left the other one at home," he muttered.

Determined to cheer him up, I took a seat. "I promise," I said. But when I caught a whiff of the dogs under the table, complaints started rising inside me like a New York freight elevator.

"Moi, sometimes I think the Panchan is a black hole."

He continued gazing across the water. "You're exaggerating again," he said.

"No, this is the beginning of the end."

"What time is it? I have to meet my cousin."

"Emptiness is everywhere. According to a Russian mathematician, it can be calculated."

"What would a Russian know about the jungle? Examine the scenery around you!"

The stones in the streambed looked like cellular tattoos. I took off my glasses.

"Your children suck, Don Moi."

"Haven't I been saying that all along? Tell me something new!"

"It's your fault they're the way they are. They're driving this place into the ground because of you."

"That's impossible. They cannot destroy Mother Nature."

"You're constantly stirring things up, like the devilfish polluting the water. This place could be a paradise, but underneath the surface, it's crawling with termites."

"Termites that can eat a man. But no. The Panchan is the best thing I've ever done. It used to be a cow pasture, and now, you see. This land is so beautiful. There are more species than I can name."

"Maybe a little pruning, Don Moi, a bit of landscaping, a little self control."

"Don't worry, I still have plans. If Alux can hammer all day, I can do something, too. Forget about the purple cabañas. I am going to plant a tree for everyone living here—Santa Claus, Roque, the Hermit included—whether I like them or not. We will be a village of trees."

"A lovely thought, Don Moi. But we need less shade and more sunlight. Sun for flowers, open spaces for wind and breezes."

Moi placed his hand on my knee. "And as soon as I finish straightening my papers, the many thankful letters I have received from the rich and famous, humble scientists and pretentious VIP's—my modest collection of souvenirs from a lifetime of guiding the greats—people

who fell in love with Palenque before it was overrun by ignoramuses—
we will write a book."

He stared into space as his hand groped higher. "You know," he
mused, "it's not such a bad thing that you have turned into your opposite, a different sort of woman."

I brushed his hand away.

Moi shrugged. "Lady's wishes," he said without complaint. "Well,
in any case, a book. A book with short paragraphs and wide margins."

"And what shall we write about, Don Moi?" I asked.

"Whatever happens, I am ready to die. But before I die, let me tell
you a little story. Once I was on my way to the beach, and by the side of
the road, just before Comalcalco, stood the remains of some madman's
dream. He had built a simple cantina, but his dream didn't last long.
All that was left was a little piece of the mud wall, which had survived
by some miracle. These words were written there:

I do not know if it is blood or red wine
That stains the heavenly mantle of the sky.
The sun comes up, wounded or drunk,
And stumbles at dusk into the sea.

Moi dabbed a tear from his eye. "The immortal words of an anonymous poet," he sighed. "The last of his immemorial kind."

An ice queen with a shaved head and silver skin strutted across the
bridge. She was sporting a studded leather bikini and five-inch voodoo
heels.

"The grim reaper, come for me at last," Moi smiled. "Perhaps the
evening is about to pick up."

Sure enough, someone whom Moi was delighted to see, a Doctor
Labro from Colombia, came up to our table.

"Handsome as ever," Moi said, "and still doing good works in the
jungle, I presume."

The good doctor bowed and kissed my hand.

Then she ruined everything. "Quite a hunk!" she said. I almost
died.

"Call me Spunk," I said, my voice climbing a half octave too
high.

Moi raised an eyebrow. "Spunk," he laughed. "It suits you."

The drummers began their intergalactic beat, but as they were approaching warp speed they were totally blasted out by a high-pitched scream that sounded like something in between a cosmic police siren and a dozen crying manatees.

"Must be the reverb from the stage amps," I told Moi. But I could see from the puzzled expressions on the musicians' faces that the supersonic, electromagnetic whine was coming from the parking lot.

"Sounds like the wail of a baby vampire," she said. "Get that kid some blood!"

"Be right back," I said and rushed off to investigate.

A silver disk was circling overhead, sending out a cold white beam of light. Twice it reconnoitered, and then hovered, motionless, the beam illuminating what appeared to be elevated structures that had somehow sprouted across the gravel. There were pyramids and temples, a replica of the Palace and Palace Tower, all built to scale and set in a landscape of trees and streams. A miniature Palenque!

A tiny door opened in the hovering saucer and down a little ramp rolled a shiny steel ball. It dropped on top of the Temple of the Cross, bounced down the stairs, and struck the dance platform, which Podwell called the Compass Rose. From there it headed for the Temple of the Sun but suddenly ricocheted off the cornerstone and catapulted—who knows how—over the stream to the Palace Tower, where it wound down the spiral staircase, rolled across the courtyard, and by means of some sort of spring, shot to the top of the Temple of the Inscriptions. Amazing! It landed on a track that ran around and down the pyramid, circled the stone altar where seven Russian dolls were standing, and crossed the wooden bridge spanning the Otolum River. It sped down the path by the waterfall and raced along the road, past plastic cows and plastic Humvees, and then, turning sharply, glided into the Panchan.

There was Don Mucho's, built out of straw and toothpicks, with little plastic Dreamers and Drainbows sitting at the tables. The ball bumped three drums, tipped over a row of tiny tequila bottles, knocked the head off a toy pit bull, and hit the trigger of a toy rifle. The cork went pop!

The ball sprang to the soyburger bar, tinkled across an African thumb piano, and after striking the last key, bounced to the top of Rakshita's purple tower. A pink mechanical monkey caught the ball and carried it along a sliding cable, safely over the windup dogs and Petunia's wire corral, to Don Moi's ramshackle house. The large numbers on the roof were sprinkled with glitter and read "2012."

A minute later—Kaboom!

2012 was on fire and sparks were flying everywhere. Moi's house, Don Mucho's, and the Mono Blanco burst into flames. The stick trees, the stick cabañas, the popsicle-stick bridges were burning, tumbling, turning to ash. After the last embers died, there was complete silence.

Out of the billowing clouds came a whistle, then skyrockets whizzing in every direction, crisscrossing the sky like shooting comets. Against the background of stars, the planets glowed with an inner light. The Moon flashed, the silver rings of Saturn turned, Mercury flew round and round on its metal track. Earth, Mars, Venus, and Jupiter started spinning faster and faster—pinwheels exploding in the blue night air—and our beautiful universe went up in smoke.

"Bravo, Bravo!" Moi applauded. "And good riddance!"

Alux was standing there now, grinning from ear to ear. Moi gave him a proud hug, then turned and kissed my cheek.

"This is what we will write about, *chula*—Joi de vivre! I'm going to live for another sixteen years."

DON MOI'S TOAST

Salud imploribus
Cesar imperatus
Changus pongus
Abusatus
Mentolatum
Pom est fin.

Made in United States
Orlando, FL
19 March 2022